Toward the Stars

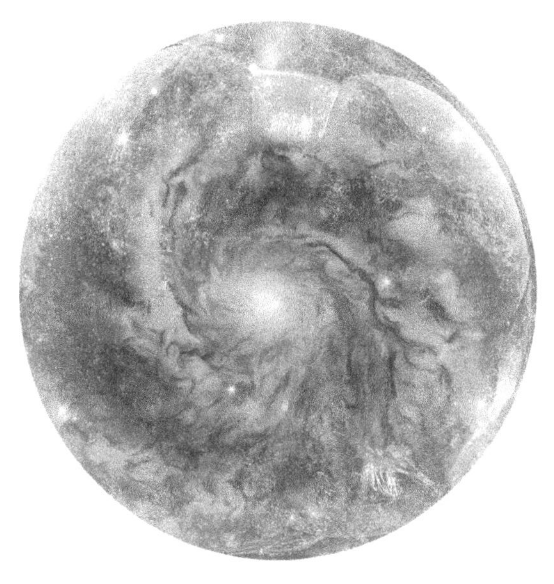

K. M. PARKE

Toward the Stars by K. M. Parke

Published by Parke Publishing

Adelaide, Australia

Cover designed by MiblArt

ISBN: 978-0-6456347-6-1

First Edition

For the readers
who dream of magic

Content Warning

Toward the Stars is a work of fiction which explores the ideas of love and fate and is intended for adult audiences.

Be advised, this book contains explicit swearing, sex scenes and other sexual acts, violence, death, alcohol consumption, as well as themes of abuse and sexual assault in various forms.

Please practice self-care before, during and after reading this book if you are affected.

ENDENCE
ALZIROS
DEMON'S FALL
ELLONA
ARGENSIR MOUNTAINS
WINTER PALACE
CARAULT
NOLDARAL
EMELLE
WINTER KINGDOM
FALLEN COURT
BROCKCREEDLES
OLUSA MOOR
KEVILLA
HUNNESWICK FOREST
LLEISCRAY
LLEIDRID
TECIRAS
THESARI
TORRINE
YORRIL
ORELLA'S TEMPLE
THE ASOTINES
EVANDER'S END
ASTORIA
SUMMER KINGDOM
ROSHEIA'S CAVE
ORROUX
ELDEN WOOD
ELDEN
SUMMER PALACE
KILEAD
CERUL

Pronunciation Guide

People
Alora: uh- lore- uh
Lito: lee- toe
Caldwell: called- well
Eira: ear- uh
Nakir: nah- keer
Orella- or- ella
Farro: f- arrow
Valefor: val- eh- for
Erela: eh- rella
Noteas: no- tae- iss
Argensir: ar- jen- zer
Nephamir: nef- a- meer

Last Names
Lòkith: low- kith
Ìréis: ih- ray- iss

Gods
The Bless- ed Four
Rharuer: rha- ooh- er
Ruasis: roo- ass- iss
Rhoston: ross- ton
Ryuna: rye- ooh- nuh

Places
Evamere: ever- meer
Remberlie: rem- ber- lee
Amesburne: aims- burn
Altenbury: all-ten-bur-ee
Endence: en- dense
Kevilla: keh- vih- luh
Carault: car- oolt
Argensir: ar- jen- zer
Asotines: ass- oh- tie- ns
Hunneswick: huns- wick
Lleiscray: lees- cray
Lleidrid: lee- drid
Alziros: al- zeer- oss

Other
Nulralt: null- rult
Volcac: vol- kak
Sisyn: sis- in

Complete waste of my time.

I already knew what the sealed parchment held by the gangly boy standing on my doorstep was going to say. Dressed in the finest messenger coattails and breeches ensemble of the city of Amesburne, he worked hard to maintain his proud expression as I scowled at the invitation in his proffered hand before I turned my glare on him. It wasn't his fault he worked for the biggest dickhead this side of the forest.

Deciding not to make the poor kid's day more difficult than it needed to be, I kept my face emotionless as I took the parchment from him. "Thank you," I snapped, forcing a speck of politeness into my tone.

His shoulders relaxed and I got a glimpse of his sigh of relief as I smacked the door shut with more force than necessary. Likely thankful a door to the face was all he was getting, rather than the string of verbal insults he copped last time he graced my doorstep.

Resisting the urge to scrunch the small square into an even tinier ball, I stomped through the house to where I knew I'd find my father.

Caldwell Bradford could always be depended upon to be found in his den, sitting behind his solid desk and leaning over his ledgers, or reclined back in his cushioned chair with a steaming mug of milky tea perched on his knee and a book in hand. In fact, he'd only part with his cushions on sunny days, where he'd roamed his lands and get his knees dirty, or put me through a training session.

But at the smallest hint of a temperature drop or even a slight breeze, he'd go right back inside like a spoiled creature of pure comfort.

I'd teased him once over it, but he'd merely pouted and said, *"I've lived long enough dealing with cold weather in my years. I shouldn't have to put up with it if I don't need to."*

I lifted my hand to knock on the entrance to his cosy hideaway, but he called from behind the door before I rapped. "Did you leave him alive?"

I pushed the door aside and smiled sweetly as I leant against the frame. "Whatever do you mean, father?"

His white hair had already been tied back neatly with his maroon ribbon, leaving only a few strands free to frame his ageing face. At first look, it was easy to think *man of leisure* when taking in all that was Caldwell Bradford. Always put together. Neat, tidy and patient.

But upon closer inspection, it was clear that the wrinkles around his blue-grey eyes were at odds with the age of his face. Under his near endless cardigans and coats, one could easily assume he had the soft body of a gentleman, but he was built stronger than any man I'd met.

He could throw a spear further and was a better hunter than any of the men in all of the realm of Evamere who called it their profession.

On top of that, he was the kindest soul I'd ever come across—when he refrained from berating me with sarcastic remarks or rolling his eyes at something I'd said or done.

He levelled a knowing look at me and held it until I dropped all pretence. "You've got a short stature, Alora, but we both know your temper's shorter."

I flopped into the chair across from him. "Yes, but it's too early to yell at teenage boys." I crossed my ankles and reclined my head back. "But if looks could kill, he'd be a pile of ash blowing away in the breeze." I smirked up at my twirling hand, mimicking the imagined remnants of the messenger who'd put a foul start to my day floating away.

"Well, I hope he left feeling grateful for crossing you during one of your good moods." He returned his eyes to his book before taking a noisy sip from his tea. "Is it what I think it is?"

"Unfortunately, yes," I sighed toward the ceiling. Flicking the parchment between my fingers like he'd taught me to do with my dagger, I sent it darting onto the desk between us.

My father put his book down and inspected the invitation. A deep-crimson wax seal immediately signified who'd sent the offending item.

Every six months, Lord Orson Thane hosted the Season Ball at Calchester House to *celebrate* the citizens of Amesburne Province in his care. A farce of a celebration designed to pull more money into his city and give himself an opportunity to assault young women.

He spent the majority of taxes on every finery and magic comfort humans had access to, simply to appease his own vanity rather than help his citizens.

It was a requirement that any and all eligible men and women attend. Mostly so he could prowl the crowds in hopes of forcing a poor girl into letting him sink his cock into her for the night.

I had the significant displeasure of being both a citizen in his care and eligible, which meant that the slimy Lord would *love nothing more than the honour of my presence* at the Ball being held in two weeks.

Dad sliced open the seal with his knife to read over the invitation. Not like he needed to, it always said the same drivel—*I, the high and mighty Lord Thane, invite you and any eligible offspring you happen to have lying around the place, to come and admire all that I have in my gaudy residence. I will offer you the food and beverages which you supplied from your own lands in the first place and pretend to listen to you while lusting after anything with a pulse. Make sure you attend, or I'll send my cronies over to make your life miserable. Sincerely, me.*

Letting out a deep sigh, then muttering a curse under his breath, Dad shook his head in frustration. He and I were roped into this together. Being a woman meant I was required to be escorted by a male family member, despite being twenty-seven and not a fuck-wit. But he had as much distaste for the event as I did. Just as much distaste for the Lord, too.

I watched my father as he rubbed his temples. He and I were so similar in so many ways—and yet there were still unanswered questions I had whenever I looked at him.

I'd always thought the grey hidden in my father's gaze was the same I saw in my left eye. But I noted his colouring so often, looking for answers that might explain me, that I knew it was a different shade. His eyes were grey-blue, whereas mine was just. . . grey. As if something were missing. Like the emerald green of my right eye had forgotten to spread across to its partner.

"I'll be twenty-eight by the end of summer, maybe I should take this one seriously. . ."

"Enough." An odd flash of emotion pulled at his brow.

We'd had this conversation before. The men in our province fell into two clear categories—domineering or dickhead. I had patience for neither, and my father knew I wouldn't suffer from either fate, knowing there was more on offer elsewhere.

But people in our town of Remberlie gossiped. Young brides were uncommon in Amesburne Province, but even still, women who weren't married by the time they hit thirty had suspicions thrown around about why they weren't.

"You need not settle for the mediocre, Alora, if you do not want it," he said softly. Then hesitantly, as though he feared my reaction, "But, I doubt you'll find your match anywhere near here."

I smiled to ease the sudden heaviness of the conversation. "You know I'm not going anywhere. You and Della can't get rid of me that easily."

"Well then," he sighed with animated exasperation, slapping his hands on his thighs as he stood. "You're either stuck being labelled a spiteful old spinster by the masses—a title which suits you well already, my sweet," he said with a wink as he stepped around the desk. "Or you enslave one of the poor bastards on offer here." He slung his arm around my shoulder in comfort, and the ridges of the thick scar on his palm brushed over my arm.

I gasped at the onslaught of insults he'd just dealt as well as the sheer nerve he possessed at delivering them to me when I was already halfway toward a bad mood. I wondered whether to take offence at his jokes or just accept them for the truth they were. Luckily for him I loved his smart mouth as much as he loved mine.

"I'm sure there's a man or two who would put up with you."

A man or two indeed, I thought as I stepped into the back yard.

Our farm was small, but then again, so was Remberlie. The town consisted of a few farms of similar size to our own, surrounding a small town square and a pub, which—thank the Gods—was always open.

If anyone in the town needed anything beyond the basic, Remberlie was forty minutes by horse to the port city of Amesburne. Several other towns belonged to the province, but they were on the opposite side of the city. So, for those who dared to live here, we mostly got the area to ourselves. Not many humans wanted to live in such close proximity to Altenbury Forest, and for good reason.

It was where the fae lived.

Chapter 2
The Love

I took a steadying inhale to shake off any lingering frustrations caused by the messenger and watched my breath leave me with a twirl of fog. The sun had just finished its ascent over the horizon, slowly willing warmth and buttery light into everything in its path. Each day warmed away the claws of winter a little further.

Not that I minded, I'd always run warm enough that the cold never seemed to bother me.

Already illuminated in the morning light and glittering with dew, the Lawns–a pristine stretch of grass fields fifty yards across between our stone fence and the tree line of Altenbury Forest–was the final haven for humans before the expanse of Altenbury Forest rose up to meet it.

Shadows swathed the tall trees. Their inhabitants–both of this realm and the other–were already on the move through the winding limbs and bending roots. But it wasn't any of the forest's usual bounties I could see between the branches as I leant against the damp stones of our farmhouse.

A glittering ball of green floated along a wide tree branch, then took off. Quick as a hare being hunted, the little fae skimmed deeper into the forest and disappeared from view.

For hundreds of years, tiny woodland faeries have dwelled in Altenbury Forest, running wild and carefree within its boundaries. No one knew why the sprites chose to flit between the giant branches. What we did know was that when touched, they would portal you to Endence, the realm of the fae. And it was the fae who dwelled there that we needed to fear.

The hunters said they rarely ever saw sprites. Faeries don't want anything to do with humans or our realm and disappear whenever they're near.

But I never believed their accuracy.

The sprites were always there. Sparkling, coloured clouds of glittering mist darting through the broad limbs like bright, little fireflies.

Several times a year, some brave fool would head into the forest to attempt to catch a sprite and make it to Endence, though I never understood why they'd want to.

We knew the tales of powerful warriors and armies of winged legionnaires ever ready for battle, assassins moving with unparalleled speed. Even ordinary fae could kill without blinking. Then there were the stories of the other creatures that dwelled in the wilderness of Endence, lying in wait to snatch unsuspecting victims or trick the weak-minded.

Thankfully, the fae never came here—despite the rumours humans liked to spread—so crossovers only ever occurred when a human managed to portal to Endence or returned. . . if they were lucky enough to survive there.

That's how we found out what little we knew about the fae and their realm, and how humans obtained the simple, convenient magics we have. Healing potions, spells to heat or cool a space, white lights that shone brighter than candles, spells that kept wind filling the sails of merchant ships.

Personally, I despised magic. Being anywhere near it made my skin itch. Thankfully, we only had a cold spell in our storage room, and Della had a heating spell in her room. Gods bless my father, who preferred good old-fashioned wood fires throughout the rest of the house. So, I barely had to encounter the awful stuff.

I sighed, then collected a stack of baskets at my booted feet. When I stood, I saw the reason for the sprite's quick retreat as the hunting party of Amesburne exited the forest.

They were loud and raucous, their voices carrying across the stretch of grass while they laughed and clapped each other on the shoulder.

It had been a good hunt.

I scanned the group, looking for a particular head of hair, and honey-brown eyes I knew I'd find meeting mine. . . but there was none.

"Pull yourself together, Alora," I chided myself then stepped off to start the day.

My first stop was always to go see Big Charlie and his significantly shorter chestnut companion, Morelli, who were my favourite customers of the day. I liked to think I was theirs too.

"Hello Charlie boy," I cooed at the giant roan workhorse, scratching his muzzle after I slid open the barn door. He nickered back his welcome as I opened his stall. "Let's get you sorted, eh?"

Morelli snorted from the next stall, sounding his irritation that I hadn't gone to him first.

"Be patient, you grump, Charlie has places to be today."

I sighed while I readied Charlie and my thoughts crashed around me–wishing and dreaming he could take me to the place I longed to be. The place I knew was calling me to find it. It wasn't anywhere in particular. I didn't know its name or location–I just knew it wasn't here.

I wanted to be anywhere but here.

Away from the inevitable life I could see before me. Away from the pressures to marry. Away from the balls that pushed me toward that end. Away from my family's responsibilities. Despite the love I felt for my father and sister, even my stepmother, I'd always felt trapped by situation.

I was barely four when my soft and gentle mother died birthing my sister, Della. Even the aid of healing magic wasn't enough to save her. My memories of her were faded and few, but a handful of images appeared when I shut my eyes and thought of her.

I could still remember her pale hair—curling waves that fell below her waist and tumbled over her shoulder when she bent to brush my eyelids closed with her cool fingers. She smelled of camellias, the stunning winter flower that brought colour to the cold and frozen land. Fitting, given how her vivid blue eyes and rosy pink cheeks were so stark against her alabaster skin.

So different from my own complexion and features.

Mostly, I remembered how my father wept as they whispered closely on her birthing bed—soon to be her deathbed. How he wailed when his beautiful wife let out her last breath.

Yes, I remember how he loved her so completely.

He always called her Snow, her pale features so similar to the winter frost. The only cold he'd ever loved. I rarely ever heard her called by her name, and had to think hard to recall it was Eira. She was always Snow. And since she passed, my father had never spoken of her. Not even to Della.

It was for her alone I stayed.

Sometimes though, the thoughts of what waited for me outside the stone walls of our farm bubbled up from where I'd squashed them deep down. That if I left this quiet corner of the realm, I'd find the place where I belonged and would finally feel. . . *complete*. All I'd have to do was mount my horse and leave—throw my hands wide and fly away on the wind toward the stars that beckoned me to find them.

But my responsibilities made me ignore their pull.

So here I stayed. Away from wherever it was my soul longed to be.

Once Charlie was fed, brushed and suitably tacked, I led him along the dirt path and past the pond to the side gate where the cart waited for him. I handed his reins over to our farm hand, Tory, then retreated back to the farm. Only, I didn't get far before someone else decided to ruin my day.

Dale.

Hell incarnate took the form of a black swan that laid claim to the large pond against the farm's fence. A beautiful natural pool, with deep blue water and green lily pads floating in its centre. Dragonflies and butterflies and mayflies all sought refuge in the reeds and flowers that bordered its banks.

The soft quacking of the little family of ducks mixed with the near-constant ribbits of frogs that hid beneath the muddy edges. That's until death's shadow spread his wings and hissed at anything in his path, simply to ruin the mood.

Dale stood squarely in the centre of the road, and the only other way into the farm was to trek around the entire property to the other side. I weighed up which option was more desirable and took my chances with the winged beast. I pulled the small dagger from my boot, my only defence against the angry creature.

His beady eyes never left mine in a blatant challenge.

"Don't you even fucking think it, Dale," I threatened as I edged past him, dagger raised. For a moment, I thought he was feeling considerate, until he slowly raised his wings and hissed his displeasure at my mere presence, as though *I* was the one ruining *his* day, then charged at me. I dodged his attack and ran through the gate, cursing at the evil bird.

"One day, I'll stuff my pillow with your feathers, Dale, and sleep soundly through the night!"

Dale honked at my retreating back, knowing he'd won this round.

I sheathed the dagger back inside my boot with a glower. It wasn't even noon, and I'd already been accosted on the front step by a teenager and attacked in the backyard by a glorified fucking duck.

My father's voice rang out from behind me. "Come pick on someone your own size."

My smile kicked up in full force.

Together, we entered an empty storage shed and came face-to-face with a tall, human-shaped bundle of straw.

"I think Dale was more menacing than this, Dad."

"Dale's more menacing than the lot of us—but for today, we need this invulnerable straw man." He clapped the figure on its back.

Without warning, my father swiped his dagger from his belt, flicked it around in his hand and stabbed the figure through its dirty brown shirt, right where their liver would have been—if it'd had one.

"What did you just do?"

Dad yanked his blade from the target and sheathed it back into place. "Remember to always work alongside your strengths. For you, your speed is your greatest asset, Alora. Wielding your weapon to gain the advantage is critical. Whether it is to incapacitate and flee, or to weaken and fight, mastering this move will help. Always use everything in your arsenal," he said pointedly, making sure I heeded his words.

Standing before me so I could better see, my father performed the same move, grabbing the dagger's hilt, twisting it in his palm, then thrusting it forward, stopping the blow just before it entered my belly.

My heart rate didn't kick up. I was never under any threat here in the safety of his sharp skill-set.

"Okay, do it slower," I told him, and this time, I came around to his side and copied his slow movements.

Over and over, I repeated the motion, forcing my muscles to commit it to memory. Next, I changed where my dagger was kept around my body—pulling it from my boot, my belt, from next to my thigh or behind my back. Making sure that no matter where I'd planted my weapon, I could wield it before anyone ever saw it coming.

My hand ached and the tendons in my wrist felt pulled too tight, but still, I pushed through until I could flip the blade without faltering.

Dad tossed me a dull training blade. "Right, now let's see how you fare against something that moves."

I sheathed my real dagger inside my boot and slipped the training blade inside the top of my pants. Dad and I matched one another step for step as we circled one another, looking for any opening to pounce through.

I used to be terrified of sparring with him. His massive size and incredible strength were too hard to ever win against. Why face an opponent you knew you couldn't win against? But he trained me, not only to ensure my strength or recognise the strengths of the enemy, but to learn how my abilities could be wielded to win, no matter who I was up against.

"When you believe in your strength, there are none stronger than you, Alora," he would tell me every lesson. Every time I showed doubt or anticipation.

When you believe in your strength, there are none stronger than you.

So, over the past seven years, his size and strength simply became obstacles my speed and agility needed to find weaknesses against.

And they did.

"Are we just going to walk around all day, old man?" I teased as we continued to step around one another.

"If you're so worried about my age, then you'd better hurry up and make your move before I keel over."

He mirrored me. Every twist I made he countered, keeping his defences perfect as we stepped.

"You'd like me to make the first move, wouldn't you, Dad?" I murmured and narrowed my eyes on him.

"Oh, I'm counting on it." He almost seemed giddy at the anticipation.

"Are you also counting the seconds you have left before I smack you into the dirt?"

He *tsked.* "I'm disappointed, my dear. I expected better insults from someone with such a sharp tongue."

"It's not my sharp tongue you need to worry about right now."

"Worry? Who said anything about being worried?" he said, letting my words roll off him. "There's only little ol' you in here. Not much to worry about, and no one is going to walk through those doors to save–"

There.

His eyes left mine to look pointedly at the closed doors mid-taunt, and I had my opening. His shoulders tensed the instant he knew he'd made his mistake. But it was too late.

I'd already come for him.

I lunged forward as I grabbed the hilt, and flicked it out, but he was fast enough to flinch his torso out of harm's way.

He continued his trajectory, rolling away and over my left side while he went for his blade, readying to come around and attack from my back.

I spun, beating him there, and brought my wrists down, smacking against his strong arm. The force of the block made the bones in my arm rattle, but I clenched my teeth against the pain and rolled my hand around the back of his, shoving his arm against his body to keep on his outside.

I stayed on the offensive, throwing my hand out to slice and jab at any opening I saw. My body never stopped moving, always stepping and lunging, changing weapon hands, swiping and angling around his attempts to incapacitate or open up a weak spot–his own movements were just as relentless.

Within minutes, my hair stuck to my temples, and sweat beaded between my shoulders.

When I found the opening I needed and jabbed into it, I realised too late it was a trap. Dad blocked my attack, trapped my wrist, and stripped the blade from me in a flash. The dagger slid into the dirt out of reach, leaving me unarmed and on his inside edge.

He held me firm, pausing our match. "What are you going to do about it, Alora?" he asked, giving me time to formulate my response. He didn't want me to answer with words, but with actions. So I did.

I twisted into him, catching his weapon hand to protect myself, and jabbed my elbow into his side, breaking his grip on me.

Like a cat, I dove for my fallen dagger, tucking into a roll after my hand landed on top of the hilt. But my father was right behind me, determined I wouldn't make it in time to defend.

My knees scuffed against the dirt as I exited my roll, dagger angled up to clash against his as he drove onto me. But he pulled up short, inches before his crushing force collided and sent me sprawling. Stopped by the very real, very sharp dagger I'd pulled from my boot and had poised at his exposed left side.

"That's cheating."

I cocked my brow and kicked my lips up into a boastful grin. "Always use everything in your arsenal, right?"

He let out a raucous, panting laugh, still frozen against my blade. "That's my girl," he praised and stepped away, ending the lesson.

He pulled me from the dirt and slung his arm over my shoulder, gripping me in a punishing hug. We stepped toward the heavy door and he pulled it open, letting the bright sunlight spill in.

"Still want roast swan for dinner?" he joked with his face tipped to the warm rays.

I snickered, replacing my dagger in my boot and palming off the training blade back to him. "Nah, Dale can live another day, I guess." I leant against the door beside him. "How about roasted Lord?" I glared at a spot on the ground, anger still simmering under my skin from the invitation.

"Don't be ridiculous," he admonished. "He's far too greasy to eat."

I smiled weakly, but the attempt at humour didn't crack through my irritation and he saw it. “Why don’t you take the rest of the day? Go see Pepper. I’m sure you could both do with the distraction.”

“But what about everything here? I can’t–”

“Ahh, don’t worry. I’ll pick up your slack, lazy arse,” he joked and tapped my thigh. “Go on, get.”

I smiled and rose onto my tiptoes, planting a peck on his cheek. “Love you, Daddy,” I hummed.

He batted me away gently. “Yeah, yeah. I’ll love you again once I’ve gotten over the sting of your cheating back there.”

“Don’t be a sore loser. Sulking doesn’t look good on you,” I teased and strolled toward the house.

“Better a sook than a swindler!” he called at my retreating back.

I turned to face him, walking backwards as I *tsked* in return. “I expected better insults from someone with such a sharp tongue.”

His eyes rolled skyward as I laughed at him, and went inside to clean up before heading to Pepper’s house.

Pepper Woode lived two farms over and was my dearest friend in life. When I thought about the entire Woode family, rabbits came to mind. Not in the twitchy, nibbling sense–but their softness, their gentle nature with just a touch of mischief. All the Woode’s were a bit like that. Even her eldest brother, Acker, who I watched walk with purpose across the yard with his two matching toddlers weaving through his legs.

Creeping ivy covered their stunning cottage, and quaint white windows opened to the warm midday sunshine. I took a deep breath of the sweet-smelling wildflowers and lavender as I strolled up the path.

Pepper opened the door before I reached it and lolled her head to the side as she watched me approach. “The invitation put you in a mood, didn’t it?”

“And Dale.”

Her lilting laugh fluttered to me and she stepped aside to let me in.

We spent the morning together gossiping and helping her mother bake–though the latter was only so we could indulge in our sugary efforts once we were done.

Pep tried to convince me to try on dresses with her for the upcoming ball. I said no at first, but one doesn't resist Pepper for long, and soon after we were surrounded by silks and tulle and heels from her closet—not that I truly minded, she did have the better dress collection after all. I had half a mind to tell her a hessian sack would do, but she wasn't having it.

It wasn't that I disliked dressing up in finery. I actually loved wearing gowns and feeling beautiful. Donning every twinkling accessory, with heeled slippers clicking over stones, hair pinned and curled. It made the night magical without the cloying thickness that came along with the real stuff.

What I didn't like about it, was that as soon as I dressed up like a treasure, it was all men were capable of perceiving me as.

A glittering jewel to possess and place on a mantel—its only use to sit and look pretty. To be on display and looked at, or to be shown off as a possession for others to envy, but ignored all at the same time. And I refused to be subject to that fate.

I knew I wouldn't amount to much more in the eyes of a husband who saw me only as a rare trinket to behold—which was the going opinion of the majority of them.

But nevertheless, dress up and show up to the ball I would, but I'd be damned before I was perceived on anyone else's terms but my own.

Mood suitably lifted, I left Pepper's house in the early afternoon and headed in the direction of Remberlie's market. I ducked down an alley between two buildings to get me there quicker and silence the noise of the horses and carts along the main road.

A third of the way down, I dodged a puddle spanning the width of the walkway with a swift step but reacted too slowly to the splash I heard behind me, which didn't come from my own boots.

A strong arm wrapped around my middle and pulled me into the shadow of the brick building looming above. My back pressed against a firm chest as a second arm snaked over my ribs and held me in place. The sudden pull backwards snuffed out the squeak rising in my throat.

"Have you decided what colour dress you'll wear for me?" the warm voice rumbled low against my ear.

The scent of leather and spice enveloped me, and my heartbeat simultaneously calmed from the lack of danger to my life and quickened at the danger to my heart the man holding me possessed.

"Unless you plan on dressing to match, I think I'll leave it as a surprise," I whispered to my captor.

Fletcher Kingsley-Vidolito was the closest confidant I had in life, next to Pep. The only difference was that Pep and I played with cards at the pub on weekends, and Lito and I played with each other.

Lito released me just enough so I could turn in his arms and face him as he leant against the wall, tipping his head back.

"I didn't see you this morning," I pouted, resting my chin on his chest, staring up into his honey eyes.

"Alora Bradford, are you lusting for me again already?" he crooned, smiling down at my lifted face, his warm eyes heated with mischief. "I thought from the sounds I had you making the night before, I'd satisfied you enough to last more than a day."

I'd say he was full of himself, but the man spoke the truth. My insides went molten.

"Don't flatter yourself too much, Lito. You're simply nice to look at." I winked, trying to remain composed.

He held me tighter, lifting me so my toes just touched the ground. "Well then, I'll try better to be within view of you more often, my lady," he promised against my lips and kissed me softly.

I wrapped my arms around his neck and deepened the kiss. It was so easy to love Lito, but I knew a life with him would tear me in two.

He would only get the half of me that thought staying was the better choice. As though my eyes were the physical embodiment of my deepest thoughts and betrayed me to the world, showing everyone that only half of me was really here, and the other half was missing.

And I wouldn't do that to Lito. He was all that was good in the world and deserved someone content to be in his arms, not dreaming of where else life could take them if they weren't forced to stay.

But he loved me so completely, convinced it wouldn't matter. That we had been wrapped in each other so long, moaning each other's names so often, that they had echoed into destiny. Sometimes he managed to make me believe it.

I pulled back as he set me on my feet, and straightened my white shirt back in place, fixing where it was loosely tucked into the front of my pants.

I toed the ground at the sudden pang of guilt I had at falling under his spell again so easily. "What are you doing here, anyway?" I muttered.

Lito curled his finger under my chin to lift my face back to his. He'd do anything to stop my thoughts from turning sad and always refused to heed my reasoning for why we shouldn't keep colliding.

He'd told me he could bear any torture, except listen to me tell him I wasn't enough.

Lito had an answer to every doubt I issued, every reason I tried to give as to why he should forget me and find happiness with someone else. He would tell me another woman's love was barely worth half of mine, and half my love was double he'd ever need to die a happy man.

His gaze softened as he looked at me then pressed a gentle kiss against my lips. "Same thing as you, I imagine."

My lashes fluttered, and my lips twitched. The love and adoration pouring from him easily pierced my rising guilt.

I smirked and tried to stay in the pull of his light mood. "Oh? And what colour dress did *you* pick for the big event?"

Lito gave me a playful shove and rolled his eyes skyward. "Smartarse." But quicker than I could anticipate, he snapped forward and fisted my shirt, pulling me back to his chest, like he couldn't stand the distance he'd just created.

He flipped, pressing me into the building we'd been leaning against. I was completely trapped between the rough wall at my back and the smooth planes of his body to my front. "Whatever shall I do with it?" he whispered against my ear as he squeezed my backside through my tight pants, his other hand firmly planted next to my head.

Not the only firm thing about him right now.

My eyes rolled back beneath my closed lids as I sank against his thigh pressing in between my own.

Merciful Gods.

We didn't know the names of the Gods who watched over and protected us. They were known only as the Blessed Four, and I wasn't sure which of them would hear my lustful pleas. Perhaps none of them would, and some other minor God was the overseer of them. I just hoped one of them was listening and willing to help a girl out.

My body clenched and I tipped forward, claiming his lips against my own. I felt his smile curve beneath my touch. "There's my girl," he whispered, happy that he'd pulled me from my thoughts. "One day, you'll finally realise that worrying about my heart breaking is a waste of your efforts." He pressed his head against mine and stroked my cheek in soft sweeps with his thumb. "It is already whole with you."

"You know I'll always worry for your heart, Lito. You deserve someone who is whole to love you in return. Not someone divided, like me."

"There could be an endless stream of women, with wealth and riches throwing themselves at my feet, and I would still choose your sharp tongue," he said and started peppering my cheeks with kisses. "Every day, I choose you." *Kiss.* "Every waking minute." *Kiss.* "With every breath I take." *Kiss.* "I choose you. Your mind, and your beauty, and your strength. I choose your faults, and failings and short temper." He kissed my lips one last time before pulling back to look at me. To deliver his final words–and make sure I was paying attention.

His honey eyes zeroed in on my grey, speaking to the emptiness, as though he could see it anyway. "And I will still be choosing you when you remember you're exactly enough as you are, and stop playing martyr for my heart's sake."

I smiled weakly and tried to hold back the tears that prickled behind my eyes at his devoted words. "You're the only one who makes me remember."

"I'll make sure you never forget it, either," he murmured against my lips, then kissed a line across my cheek to my ear, and nipped my earlobe playfully. I batted him and his mischievous mouth away. He took half a step back and his scent went with him. "Because, if you think the way you love me is the flaw I need to worry about, I have some bad news for you, Miss Bradford," he teased, laughing.

I scoffed at his brazenness. "Firstly, I never told you *I* loved you. Only that you deserve someone who does. And second of all, precisely which flaws are you referring to? I don't seem to recall having any."

"Firstly," he said pointedly, "you don't have to say you love me, for me to know it's true. And as for your flaws. . ." He cupped his chin and hummed as he pretended to think.

My eyes lowered to those long fingers playing around his lips.

"You've none you don't make up for when you moan my name."

"Mighty presumptuous of you, Mr. Vidolito," I uttered, lust making my words thick.

"Tell me which part I've gotten wrong, my lady. I shall make it up to you immediately." Lust filled his promise as he paced away to lean against the opposite wall.

He tipped his hips up as he situated himself, drawing my attention to exactly how I affected him. His gaze dripped with heat.

Thank the Gods he distanced himself before I jumped him here and now in the street.

I captured my bottom lip beneath my teeth, pulling on it as my thoughts ran rampant. Lito watched me toy with my mouth and he clenched his fist as it hung beside his hips. I imagined that hand clenching into my hair as he pulled my head back and—

A flock of birds startled and burst from the rooftop high above where we stood. The flinch it sent through me severed that heated thread that was pulling and wrapping around us.

Lito cleared his throat. "I figured you'd be around the market at some point today. And I knew you'd be reeling because of the invitation, so I came to find you."

"Track me down, did you, master hunter?" I laughed. "Yeah, it ruined the mood for sure, I was just on my way to get some things for Della before I was so rudely interrupted."

"Well, you'll forgive me, my lady, but I just had to have you near me."

His tone was joking, but there was a deeper truth behind his words. "I shall detain you no longer." He bowed at the waist with an exaggerated flourish.

I returned a terrible curtsy back with a sarcastic expression plastered on my face. "Until next time I'm wandering the streets alone then," I joked and walked away from him. I had to leave now before we were pulled into each other's orbit again.

"Just tell me one thing before you leave me."

I turned back to face the gorgeous man and waited for him to speak.

"If you won't tell me the colour of your dress, will you at least tell me if your underwear will match it?"

I burst out laughing at the scandalous question he'd asked in broad daylight. "Does it matter if they don't?"

He shook his head. "Only matters if they're easy to take off."

Merciful Gods, indeed.

Chapter 3
The Sister

The dying rays of sun shone through the window at the end of the hallway, bringing all the dust motes floating around into light. The rug that ran up the length of the hall cushioned my footsteps as I made my way to the end where Della lived.

My sweet sister, Delilah, silently entered the world sickly and weak. The doctors said without the healing magics, they would have lost her as well as our mother.

Our hair fell in the same long waves, but mine was a richer shade of champagne. My creamy skin, though still pale from the winter months, didn't come close to her fair complexion, and she had no sign of the smattering of freckles that covered the bridge of my nose that could only been seen if someone were looking hard enough to notice them.

Della was the one who inherited all our mother's looks. But where mother's pale skin had been lit from within, Della's skin tone was muted and grey. Her blue eyes—the same shade as our mothers—were dull and rimmed with purple fatigue.

No amount of magic potions or spells improved her condition, and after more than twenty years of ill-health, there was no end in sight, so she seldom left her bed.

Only the way she would smile sweetly whenever I walked into the room made me almost forget she lived a half-life. She was content in her perfectly magically heated room, left to her books and paintings and thoughts.

Her room at the back of the house had the best view of the farm with the pristine beauty of the Lawns and Altenbury Forest beyond. The closest to outside as she could get.

I took a steadying breath and tapped on her smooth door. It swung slightly at the pressure, and I peeked around, smiling at the thin figure huddled under blankets.

"Hey, Del. You up?" I crept in, bracing myself for the magic to hit. The spell put on her room to heat it in a never-ending thoroughness made the air thick and clammy. In a few minutes, the itching sensation would creep over. Della never suffered the same reaction I had to the magic, so I never commented on how it affected me. "I brought presents," I sang at her little form, wriggling the flowers and box of eclairs I'd bought for her at the market.

Her eyes opened slowly, adjusting to the low afternoon light, and she smiled weakly when she saw me. She spied the wrapped box in my hand, knowing full well it contained her favourite dessert. "You spoil me."

I walked over to her side table and arranged the flowers I'd bought into the terracotta vase kept there. I couldn't remember the last time she'd made it into the gardens outside, so I liked to bring the outside to her whenever possible. Their sweet smell quickly filled her room.

Decorated with soft watercolours, fluffy round rugs and cushioned seats, the whole room demanded you relax wherever you chose to place yourself.

"I spent the afternoon with Pepper. She made me try on dresses for the Season Ball, and afterwards I stopped by the markets." There was no point in small talk or asking Della how she was.

She was always the same.

I scooched under her plush covers after I'd finished fussing over the flowers, then rested the chocolates on her lap. "I couldn't *not* get you something while I was there."

She exhaled a soft laugh and started opening the box, tilting her head to rest on my arm. I returned the gesture and propped my head lightly on hers.

"Did you find a dress?"

"I found something that'll do."

"You could wear a sack and still look incredible, Lor."

I laughed, and my heart warmed at the affectionate name only she used. "That's what I told Pepper."

"Of course you did," she said through her giggles.

Our laughter ended, and the silence that followed was sad.

Her fingers toyed with the ribbons on the box between us. "I wish I could go."

My heart cracked.

Della barely had the strength to stay out of her room for more than an hour, so of course she didn't attend the Season Balls. Lord Thane granted his pardon that she be exempt due to her health. It was about the only gracious act he'd ever bestowed.

I always played the event down, just to spare Della's feelings.

I planted a kiss on top of her head. "I wish you could, too. You'd be the only reasonable company I'd have. Plus, you'd be an excellent dance partner."

"I'm sure you'll find plenty of excellent dance partners," she muttered, finally untying the ribbon holding the box closed. "Besides, if I go, I'll just be a distraction to you finally relaxing around Lito."

Oh, I'd relaxed with Lito alright.

"Not like that," she chided as though she could read my thoughts.

"Delilah Bradford!" I squeaked, and she laughed again.

The thought that Della may have seen precisely how *relaxed* Lito could make me from her window was mortifying.

I shifted my head a fraction to peer out into the yards below and judge whether Della could see down to the stable at this angle, tallying the number of times Lito had taken me against its walls. I resisted the urge to run my hands up and down my arms at the shiver it caused—no, not a shiver—an itch, caused by the magic pressing in.

"Will you tell me all about it when you get home?" Her words killed my train of thought.

"Every minute, Del." I smiled back down at her. "Get some rest now." I left the stifling warmth of her comforters, but it didn't do anything to ease my temperature—not with the spell spreading magic across the room. "I'm sure dinner will be ready soon. I'll bring your plate up." I kissed her once more and left before I started clawing at my skin.

When I came back an hour later with her dinner, she was sound asleep, chocolates still untouched.

Chapter 4
The Ball

The day of the Season Ball came around all too quickly. I stoked a raging fire in my room so Della could spend the afternoon with me while our stepmother Margaret—whom we affectionately called Maggie—helped me get ready.

Standing at the foot of my bed a few hours later, I gave a twirl, asking if the final product standing before them was suitable.

"You look beautiful, Lor," whispered Della from under the covers of my bed, awe lacing her voice—or fatigue.

"Radiant, my dear," Maggie hummed.

I dipped my chin at the compliments and couldn't help the blush that heated my cheeks.

A floorboard creaked behind me and I turned at the sound of footsteps, which halted on the threshold.

My father breathed in a soft gasp. "Alora, you're—" He squared his shoulders and smiled, grey-blue eyes glittering. "Even the fae would be envious of your beauty, my darling."

"You scrub up alright as well," I said lightly, complimenting his grey vest and dark suit ensemble.

The gown I'd chosen with Pepper was stunning. I'd chosen a deep plum dress with enough volume in its puffy skirts to feel full and luxurious. The tiered layers flared out from my hips and swished around my feet as I walked. The intricate lace on the stiff bodice had tiny crystals dotted amongst the swirling designs which caught and reflected the lights with every movement. Even my chest rising and falling with each breath set them glittering. The whole ensemble accentuated the pleasant curves of my chest and hips. One of the few things my gentle mother had passed on to me.

Maggie had done a magnificent job of readying me as well. Though my hair was loose and gently curled in waves down my back, my eyes lined with kohl and lips darkened with colour, Maggie ensured the look was gentle enough that the dress did all the talking.

"Ready?"

I couldn't help but feel as though my father's question implied two meanings.

My response answered them both. "I'm ready."

The light wooden floors in the grand ballroom of Calchester House were waxed with such a glossy sheen that I could see my reflection peering back up at me. I had the good fortune of being sure-footed, so I didn't need to worry about going arse-up while I danced. Though, I did hope that the smooth surface claimed at least one dignitary during the night.

Hopefully Thane.

The ceiling was decorated with intricate moulding and three enormous chandeliers glowing with bright faelight. Wide columns of white marble bordered the space, providing a small semblance of privacy within the open room.

A wall of windows and arched doors led to the outdoor terrace, and the sprawling gardens and topiaries beyond were sculpted into perfectly swirling formations that not a single leaf was out of place.

At the front of the room a small orchestra played their strings gently in a welcoming song.

I spied Pepper standing near one of the pillars with her little sister, Daisy, and her eldest brother, Acker, their chaperone for the night, and steered my father over to them.

Daisy had just turned eighteen during the winter and this was her first time at the Season Ball. She could barely stand still in her puffy, teal ball gown. Her eyes flitted around the room, taking in all the sights and sounds on offer, already trying to lock eyes with her prince charming—wherever and whoever he might be.

Poor girl. If only she knew how slim the pickings were.

She was half a foot shorter than her older sister but had the same thick mass of curling tawny ringlets atop her head, as well as the matching round, chocolate-hued eyes and deep olive skin all the Woode's possessed.

Pepper looked resplendent in a beautifully simple, grey gown. The silky material flowed over her gentle curves like a glossy waterfall, pooling at her feet, and the deep *V* on the back showed off her flawless skin.

It was customary that all the guests stay with their chaperone until the Ball officially began, always marked with Lord Thane giving a speech and waffling on too long about the realm.

After the speech came the first dance, which was the part I despised most about the evening. Eligible ladies were chaperoned by a male family member, but eligible men didn't require one. Which made the first dance a pure spectacle for the single men to stand back and watch the women be paraded in front of them, so they could get a quick assessment of who might interest them—likely for the night.

Most of the girls loved the attention and didn't see it for the scrutinization it was. Only my father's mutual hatred for the display helped me through it. He'd even confronted Lord Thane at the first Season Ball we attended. "*My daughter will not be showcased as an offering to be drooled over by common rabble*," he'd growled in the new Lord's face. Thane had looked ready to shit himself at the fury in my father's eyes, but he held his authority over my father's head. Some part of me was sure that if my father had been carrying a weapon, Lord Thane would no longer be reigning over us.

The ballroom filled as the five of us stood against the pillar and spoke. Pepper's other older brother, Reed, would be somewhere close by, though he wasn't a chaperone and also eligible, so he was allowed to mingle wherever he desired and was most likely off causing trouble with Lito in tow.

I found myself standing on the tips of my toes, trying to spot him around the room, but the musicians in the corner stopped playing—a sure sign that Lord Thane was stepping up to make his speech.

My father watched me with his eyebrows raised, a smirk plastered across his face with a playfully judgemental look in his eyes that told me he knew exactly who I was searching for.

Caught red-handed.

I never thought I'd feel lucky to hear Lord Orson Thane's drawling voice ring through a space, but it spared me any smart remarks my father was about to make at my expense, so I was thankful nonetheless.

"Welcome, ladies and gentlemen."

I immediately wanted to roll my eyes at the figure poised at the front of the room, drenched in opulence. He wore a shirt with a collar that was far too open in my opinion, and his black hair was slicked back.

"Welcome to my home, honoured guests." Applause sounded.

My humble home, I'm sure he wanted to say.

"We are all so fortunate in Amesburne Province to have such strength, such prosperity and such camaraderie to survive another winter season together."

Applause.

What rubbish.

"I am delighted to host this Season Ball so that we can enjoy our offerings and celebrate our success for another year. And of course, to join those around us, as we grow stronger together."

I rolled my eyes skyward.

"Are you paying attention?" a low voice whispered in my ear.

I startled, again surprised with the silence the man was capable of—I suppose that's what made him an efficient hunter.

A singular finger traced from my neck along the back edge of my shoulder. My skin tingled in its wake.

"I could hear your snarky remarks from the opposite side of the room," Lito teased as his finger continued down my arm.

I kept my eyes forward and cleared my throat of the squeak that threatened to escape. "You might need to see a physician about that,

Lito. Hearing voices is not a good sign," I whispered over my shoulder. "I didn't make a sound."

"No, you didn't. . ." he said with equal quiet, still against my ear. "But I'll have you making all sorts of sounds later."

My core tightened at the exact moment my jaw dropped. I twisted further to see him more fully. Lito always looked good, but tonight there was something different. He wore tight black pants and a forest green tunic over his shirt, with black boots up to his knees. If he'd had his sword attached to him, I might have fainted.

His expression was one of pure satisfaction at the reaction he'd caused. His honey gaze never broke from mine as he stared into my eyes.

He winked, lifted his gaze to the man we were supposed to be paying attention to, and kept a warm presence at my back.

I turned as well and looked around to check that no one around noticed what Lito had said. Luckily, my father was standing on the opposite side to where Lito was. There was no way he could have heard, though his expression was strained.

Probably just sick of the waffling happening from the cock—I mean peacock—at the front of the room.

I tuned back into the speech, praying to the Gods he was nearly finished.

"And finally," Lord Thane called, "it brings me immense pleasure to announce that by the graces of the Gods, a great event will occur." The crowd awed. "I've been sent word by the astronomers of Wickley that in five days, the sun and moon will align, causing a full solar eclipse." The crowd gasped and cheered as Thane continued speaking. "Myself, along with the other heads of Evamere have decided to host a gathering on the Lawns of Remberlie, to celebrate and watch this momentous event."

Fucking hell.

I looked to my father, who kept his attention to the front, but it was clear by his clenched fist he didn't like this either.

Not only did we have to be here in his residence, but in a few days, Thane would be camped out at ours.

Gods spare us.

"But for now, let us focus on the night at hand and enjoy the celebration!" He threw his hands in the air as the crowd applauded, and the orchestra started up for the first dance.

My father and I turned to each other. His face was grave as he reached for me, stroking his thumb along the back of my hand. But he swallowed whatever feelings were bubbling inside and smiled softly.

"Let's not worry, my dear," he reassured when he noticed the look of concern written on my face. "Right now, I want to dance with my beautiful daughter."

A stream of escorts and eligible ladies floated into the centre of the room ready to put their best foot forward.

Acker escorted Pepper onto the floor. As the elder of the two sisters, she had the right to her chaperone. Even though Reed wasn't expected to dance with Daisy, he came out from the crowd and led her through the twirling steps. A good pair, given his level of mischief equally met Daisy's level of excitement. Daisy beamed the whole time Reed held her, muttering things in her ear and making her giggle.

My father was just as graceful and sure-footed as I was, never missing a step. He held me close, making me feel as though it were just him and I twirling around like he used to do when I was little.

That is—it would have felt just like him and I, if it weren't for a pair of honey eyes I saw locked on mine each time I looked toward the pillar.

The music ended on a long note, and the chaperones bowed deeply to their partners as polite applause rose from the onlookers, then the room became a flurry of movement. The men relegated to the sidelines were finally allowed to sweep in on the ladies they were eyeing off, while the chaperones were now free of their duties to spend the evening as they wished.

My father kissed my cheek, gave me a wink and turned to search for a server holding whiskey.

I'd been attending the Season Ball for long enough that my position on being approached at this event was well known, so I was left in peace as the men came to make their introductions.

Unfortunately, there was one man in particular who knew he was an exception to my ire, and was no doubt striding toward me, regardless.

Chickening out before he arrived, I made a split-second decision and darted to where Pepper was saying her goodbyes to Acker. "Let's go outside," I interrupted and grabbed her hand, leading the way to the terrace doors and plucking two glasses of champagne as we passed.

Pepper and I perched on a stone wall surrounding the pale terrace and were soon joined by some of the other women at the ball. We'd gotten to know many over the years, seeing them every six months.

There was Emma, a twenty-two-year-old blonde from Wickley who was besotted with one of the hunters from Amesburne and spent each Season Ball hunting him. Sofie, a stunning redhead from Amesburne, had as much interest in the ball as I did. Three of the girls came from Mekroy, a fishing village in the southern region, and Hazel, a shy nineteen-year-old who was only just finding her feet at these balls came from Schrie.

The final member to finally join our group—after having her fill of the men inside—was Avery, a curvy brunette the same age as Pep and me. Flawlessly stunning, with full sensual lips and deep-brown eyes, her husky voice dripped with lust. Her tight glittering gown did nothing to hide her assets, which there were plenty of in all the right ways. Each of the girls was as beautiful as the next, dressed immaculately in their finery with floral scents lingering in their wake. We'd been standing in the same spot long enough that the area smelled like a bouquet.

Together we gossiped about the girls who no longer came because they'd gone and married *what's-his-face,* then swapped recommendations of the men from their towns who they thought were worth the effort.

Avery noted every name, adding it to her list of men she wanted to seduce. It was refreshing having a woman in the group as bold as the men were. To use them for their assets as they did to us. It wasn't surprising she hadn't married yet—too much fun to be had with the masses.

Once judgement had been passed on the men at the party, Emma leant in close, her eyes looking left and right to check no one was nearby before speaking. A sure sign that hot gossip was about to spill from her lips. "I overheard Tadd speaking with some of the other hunters. Apparently, one of their men who went missing in Altenbury Forest a while back recently returned from Endence! They say he's been speaking of an evil in the realm and that humans need to worry, because they're coming for us."

Sofie rolled her eyes. "Emma, for your sake, I hope your beloved hunter has a dick half as big as the truths he inflates."

I snorted my champagne in a laugh, while Pepper looked appalled.

Emma stomped her foot. "It's true!" she squeaked.

"I must admit, even stories of unrest in Endence have reached us all the way down in Mekroy," whispered Grace, one of the girls who hailed from the town.

They were both right, of course. The accounts that somehow spread from unknown sources throughout Evamere never changed too much. The latest rumour currently circulating was that the fae had assembled their legions and were preparing for a war.

Lito had told me months ago when his fellow hunter disappeared. They assumed him dead, taken down during a particularly nasty hunt that day, but weeks later he showed up again, rambling about a mysterious enemy needing something to *finish what they started.*

I just hoped that the fae, their war, the plan their enemy wants to finish, and whatever they needed to accomplish it, had nothing to do with us in Evamere.

"You don't need to whisper, Grace," I said while laughing. "The fae aren't here."

Victoria, another girl from Mekroy lowered her brows in scepticism. "So everyone claims."

Pepper pulled a wry face. "Truly you don't believe they walk among us?"

"Of course they do!" Victoria shouted.

I shook my head then rolled my eyes at her and the others nodding in agreeance. "You southerners are so suspicious," I teased.

"And *you're* not wary enough," Grace quipped back. "You're telling me you wouldn't be shivering in your boots if a fae warrior emerged from those woods at your back door?"

"Nope," I said letting my lips pop, being wholly sarcastic with a touch of cockiness. "I'd tell him to fuck off." I slid my eyes to Pepper and we laughed together.

Sofie saluted her drink at me. "He'd flee at the sight, too." The girls from the southern towns looked horrified. "Emma, if your plan is still to win over Tadd, you'll need to live closer to the forest. You'll need to be made of tougher stuff."

Emma pouted.

"What about you, Avery?" Hazel timidly asked. "Do you think there are fae already here?"

Avery took a slow sip of her champagne as she considered. Her dulcet voice hummed as she spoke. "Not a chance. I've certainly not slept with anyone I'd describe as *otherworldly.*" We all laughed. "And I've been with enough to have surely encountered at least one."

Pepper widened her eyes and looked at the floor. Her propriety making her bashful.

"Well, if they're supposed to be *otherworldly* in bed, then perhaps I won't tell that fae warrior to *fuck off,* but to fuck something else instead." I winked and we all clinked our glasses together as we burst out laughing, then went back to enjoying the evening.

After a few hours, Daisy bounded over to us, red-faced and sweaty with Reed in tow. He looked happy to finally be off the dance floor and in the company of other women. He made short work of peeling away three of the girls into a secluded section of the terrace, no doubt to charm their skirts off—literally.

Unfortunately, that was when Lord Thane chose to poke his greasy head out of the doors and spy the little group of women standing together—without a man in sight.

My eyes caught the shadow of his form and flicked to him before I could stop myself, and our gazes clashed. He looked at me, and his decision to approach set into his features as he strut across the stones.

I cleared my throat to warn the girls, then curtseyed low at the approaching Lord. The others followed suit.

"Lord Thane," we all said in sweet welcome.

"Ladies," he drawled and gave a shallow head bob back to us in greeting. "A pleasure to see you all again, looking so well." His eyes roved over the bountiful sight before him, yet he didn't look a single one of us in the eye.

Disgusting lech.

His attention landed on Daisy, unmissable in her ballgown. "And who do we have here?" he crooned, raising her hand to his thin lips. I swallowed the bile that rose up my throat.

"Lord Thane, allow me to introduce my sister, Daisy," said Pepper politely, though her voice shook. "This is her first Season Ball."

"Daisy," he smiled at her. "Beautiful."

I widened my eyes at Pepper. With the Lord's attention fixed on them, she could only meet my gaze and smile. Daisy was unaware of our exchange as she giggled at Thane and did a girly curtsy at him. Heart probably exploding from the attention of the most important man here, despite knowing full-well he was a creep.

But the vile Lord quickly turned his gaze to me and held me in place with his stare.

Fuck.

"Alora," he said plainly. "You'll do me the honour of the next dance." Not a question.

Fuck.

"My pleasure," I said through my teeth. He gripped my hand and took me through the ballroom doors.

Fuck.

As I entered, I searched for my father's gaze. As though he was already tuned in to my whereabouts, he saw me immediately, and as soon as he realised whose arm I was on, he lifted his hand to the man he was speaking to, abruptly halting their conversation.

I shot him an urgent look as Thane led me to the dance floor, the crowd parting to let us through.

My father dodged party-goers standing along the wall and aimed for the orchestra. There was no point in him coming for me, there was nothing he could do to stop this directly. He whispered something to the conductor when he got there, who curtly nodded his head in response to whatever he'd said.

Thane stopped us in the centre of the dance floor and a shiver went down my spine—so at odds with the shiver Lito had caused hours earlier during the welcome speech. Orson Thane was as dangerous a man as he was despicable. I wasn't sure my shaking was out of fear of his power, or disgust of his presence, or rage that I couldn't say no to his attentions. He met my gaze, locking onto my grey eye.

Like I'm not here.

I always marked the way another person looked at me. Their eyes flitting between my two vastly different coloured ones, trying to make sense of them. Or they would lock onto just one in particular because it was easier.

Drawn in by the beauty of one, or the emptiness of the other.

Thane didn't need a woman properly present to take what he wanted.

I blinked away the foul thoughts and kept my expression blank. But relief flooded me when the music started.

Caldwell Bradford, you genius.

My face lit into genuine happiness as Lord Thane's fell. The dance that started was called *The Turn*, a quick and lively dance that had the participants swapping partners with the others on the floor. I'd hardly have to dance with him.

Disappointment laced his words. "It seems I've picked a poor dance for us to have proper time together." His accusatory gaze slid to where my father was standing, watching the events unfold like a sentinel.

I didn't dare follow his gaze. "How unfortunate," I chirped as the fiddle finished its introduction, then we moved to the music.

He spoke above the instruments. "I find you to be an intriguing woman, Alora."

"I'm not sure which part of me you're familiar with enough to intrigue you, Lord Thane."

"Well, your eyes, of course," he said bluntly as if I were the idiot in the room.

"If my appearance is my only intriguing quality, I'm afraid that most people in this room also hold your same opinion."

"I don't presume to know your other qualities. Is there *more* to you I should find intriguing?"

In other words, *you look interesting, and I don't care if you have a personality.*

Cunt.

"I don't think these balls allow anyone quite enough time to form adequate opinions on others, other than what lies on the surface," I replied flatly.

"Then I guess I should thank the Gods you and I will be seeing one another when I come to Remberlie in a few short days," he said with a repulsive leer, showing all his teeth. "You and I have so much to discuss."

My eyes widened at what he was implying, but our time together was over. He pushed me away, and we spun in opposite directions to our next partner.

A hunter a few years younger than me, whose name I think was Hayes, caught my spin. Thankfully he didn't speak much during our time together, his eyes longing for the beautiful blonde he'd twirled away from.

It gave me time to unscramble my thoughts, only I didn't succeed—I just worked myself into a state of panic. Families had to have a legitimate reason to turn down a Lord's offer of marriage—and in the eyes of the province, I had none to give.

I was well and truly old enough to be married by now, as well as completely unspoken for. If Orson Thane was setting his sights on me, then I needed to have one hell of a reason to get out of it.

Was now the time I made the leap and left Remberlie? Left the entire province? Or should I ignore that pull to a distant life and settle for a simple existence here so I'd be unavailable for him?

Panic set in at the thoughts of my limited options, and I was spun again to my next partner. It felt like I was tossed into a spiral, unable to get my balance. My body reeling along with my train of thoughts.

But strong hands caught me. "Breathe."

Lito.

I let out a sob and dropped my head onto his chest.

"What did he say to you?" he rumbled darkly. Lito's glare slid to where Thane danced with another helpless soul.

I took a steadying breath, fighting to break free of the whirling anxiety dragging me down as we danced. "I think he means to. . . pursue me," I worried, unsure how to finish that sentence any differently. "He said he had a lot to talk to me about at the Eclipse."

"Oh, well that doesn't mean anything," Lito said quickly. An air of indifference laced his voice.

My temper instantly flared. "What the fuck do you mean? Don't you realise how big of a deal—"

"He can see you at the eclipse, we'll smile and wave at him together." A slow grin spread across his face, lighting his golden eyes.

"I don't think he was implying–"

"He cannot have you, Alora."

I could only watch him as he turned us together in time with the rising music.

"You're mine."

Mine.

I was stunned. At the confidence, as well as the arrogance he said it with.

His.

I huffed a quick laugh. He was surely joking, but I was about to be passed on to the next dancer, and there was no time to finish the conversation.

Alright then, two can play at this game.

I pulled a sly smile of my own and whispered in his ear as we came together for the last time. "I don't see your ring on my finger," I purred, then twirled away to my new partner.

But swift as an adder, Lito struck out and caught my wrist, pulling me back to him. He gripped my hand between us, his eyes gleamed like he'd just won a prize. We stood staring at one another, our chests rising and falling.

"Ahh. . . excuse me. . ." my would-be dance partner chimed in, tapping Lito on the shoulder, wondering why he hadn't received a new woman as the dance demanded.

Lito shot the man a venomous glare. Message received, he stepped around and grabbed onto the girl who was destined for Lito and carried on away from us. We stood in the middle of the dance like a rock amongst the waves. He took a step forward, closing the gap between our bodies and lowered his head, our foreheads touching. His scent wrapped around me. His familiar leather and spice was there, this time muted by a heady smell of roses.

He'd dressed up for the occasion.

His voice was low and thick like honey against my lips. "Shall I put one there for you, Alora?"

His question short-circuited my thoughts, and I reeled back, eyes wide.

Clearly, he was *not* joking for my sake.

"Lito, I was only teasing. I—"

"No," he cut me off, hand still wrapped around my wrist. "Not this time. Not about this," he growled and pulled me outside into the night.

He didn't speak the entire time we walked, leading me past the faelights in the terrace and through the twists and turns of hedges surrounding the massive residence. He took long determined strides, while I had to nearly break into a jog to keep up without being dragged behind him. His shoulders were set with tension that hadn't been there moments ago.

As I was led to our destination, the only thought ringing through my head was that I'd royally fucked up.

Lito stormed to the opposite side of the manor, away from other guests. Away from any chance of a distraction.

Satisfied with a small secluded garden, surrounded by walls of climbing jasmine, he finally let go of my hand, but took three extra steps away from me and ran his hands roughly through his hair.

"Lito, I'm so sorry. I shouldn't have joked—"

He spun. Closed the distance in two long strides and crashed into me, pushing my back against the trellis. The sweet smell of the jasmine perfumed around us.

Lito's mouth pressed firmly to mine in a punishing kiss, his hands raised to either side of my face to cup my cheeks. Then, as quickly as he found me, he left—ending the kiss abruptly—though his body remained pressed to mine. I gasped in a deep breath, recovering from the shock.

Lito was taking in heaving breaths, his eyes frantically searching both of mine. "How could I—" he began, speaking more to himself than me.

He opened his mouth to speak a few times but never succeeded. When it became clear the words he wanted to find weren't coming to him, I tried my apology again.

"I shouldn't have joked about it, Lito. I'm sorry," I blurted and dropped my head in shame. I knew now what I said would have been devastating for him. "I thought you were joking, trying to make me smile—not actually offering a solution to Thane's suggestion." Tears sprang to my eyes. "Lito, I would *never—"*

"Do you not think you would have had a ring there years ago, if only I thought you would've ever fucking said yes?" he roared, hand hitting the trellis next to me in frustration.

I sobbed, and silence stretched between us as evidence of my guilt left wet tracks down my face.

It was his turn to hang his head, the irritation in him immediately subsiding. He wiped away my falling tears with his thumb and kissed my cheeks.

"Forgive me," he whispered.

"Forgive *me*," I sobbed back.

"There is nothing to forgive," he said against my skin, his kisses trailing across to the shell of my ear. "Alora," he sighed as I continued to weep, and he ran his hand gently through my curls. "Spare us both the agony," he pleaded and lifted his head to look me in my eyes again. "You try to keep yourself at arms distance to spare my heart, but you don't realise that's exactly what is breaking it. And it's breaking you."

"You deserve more than I could give you, Lito," I said, shaking my head. "I will never stop dreaming of what else could be waiting for me—a life I'll never get to have." I raised my head, determination lacing my next words. "I will not deny you every happiness in this realm for my own sake. I love you too much to do that to you."

I nearly missed the twitch his lips gave. "Say it again," he urged.

"Say what?" I said, frustrated that after all his stomping through the gardens to get here that he now wasn't taking this seriously.

"Say you love me again." His fingers still toyed with my hair.

"I—That's not—I didn't mean. . ." I growled in frustration, but Lito only laughed at my fumbling words.

"I know what you meant, but it was the only important thing you said in that entire ramble." He drew his face next to mine. "I already told you, my heart is whole with you, Alora," he whispered against my neck and planted a soft kiss there. My eyes shuttered. "You say you'll not deny me every happiness, but fail to realise that you *are* my every happiness, and keeping yourself away is doing exactly that."

I swallowed, unable to respond to his declaration. Lito merely kissed my throat as it bobbed.

"Now say it again," he repeated, lips staying where they were at my neck.

I kept my eyes closed in an attempt to mentally block his pursuit. My heart pounded in my chest.

"No." My quiet determination still laced my voice, but it was quickly fading.

He huffed a laugh as he planted another kiss, slightly higher this time. I could feel his smile on my skin. His hand that had been playing in my hair reached the ends, but instead of returning to stroke down once again, he slowly brought it up my front.

Starting from my waist, his fingertips trailed toward my chest, playing with the lace on my bodice.

His voice was thick like honey. "Alora, you have two options before you right now." His hand came up and lightly palmed my breast as it passed. Wetness slicked between my thighs.

"Option one," he said, kissing higher. "You can leave this garden, right here and now, and take my broken heart with you. Leave me behind, crying out your name and be done with this."

Kiss.

"But know, that even when it's broken, my heart will forever be yours to keep, and will love you all the same."

Kiss.

"Or. . . you can go with option two."

Kiss.

"You can say those three little words I want to hear again and finally give in to me, which will still leave me crying out your name. . . but you'll be moaning mine as well."

Kiss.

Merciful. Fucking. Gods.

My eyes rolled back. His hand reached my neck on the opposite side and he pressed his thumb along my jaw, holding me in place.

His kisses reached my ear and he drew my lobe between his teeth. I let out a whimper and my knees nearly gave out. Lito stepped toward me, breaching the gap between us, and I could feel him rock hard against my stomach.

"So, what way will you end me, Alora?" he rumbled. "For no matter which option you choose, either decision will surely destroy me."

"Lito," I moaned.

Decision made.

He kissed me with more ferocity than he'd ever done before, sealing our path with passionate finality. His hands fisted my hair as he angled my head toward him, deepening our kiss as his tongue swept against mine.

My breathing turned ragged as I grasped him back, trying to keep up with him and his burning needs. I breathed his incredible scent, the rose of before had faded, giving way to his familiar leather and spice. All that was Lito.

His hands dropped from my face and went to palm my breasts again.

"Tell me you love me, Alora. I will give you all that I am, all that I have. We'll build a life that you choose for yourself, if you'll only choose me, too. Stop worrying about whether it is enough, whether you would be enough. To be yours, even for a moment would be more than I deserve. I would happily go to my grave if I'd known you loved me, even if it was by half."

This was it. The point of no return.

If I rejected him now, there would be no coming back from it. It would break him after he'd just bared his deepest feelings to me.

But if I accepted him. . .

"I love you, Lito," I whispered.

It took a moment for the words to register for him, as though he couldn't believe they'd passed my lips. His smile lifted at the corners further and further until his whole face lit with pure happiness.

His voice dropped to a serious tone. "You and I have done more than court for years now, can we skip the bullshit? Let it be forever and just Gods damn marry me."

He felt me flinch at the heaviness of his words and cut me off before I could form my protest.

"Just say yes, Alora. I know you want to say no, but I'm asking now anyway, because I cannot bear to have you apart from me. Knowing there might be a chance you'll say. . ."

Tears sprang to his eyes, but he shook his head, clearing them. He leant his forehead reverently against my own and squinted his eyes shut, his words a whispered prayer in the fog. "Just say yes."

My heartbeat slowed as time stood still, and my head raced with reasons why I shouldn't.

But none came.

All the excuses I'd made suddenly didn't make sense anymore with him in front of me. Lito loved me, and I loved him back. It was a foolish thought that my love would be a disservice. I knew he cherished every part I had to give. And if we wanted to leave, we would.

We *could.*

So, I whispered the only word that made sense. "Yes."

The word had barely left my tongue before Lito had it swept up with his. He smiled against my mouth, which made my lips curl as well.

His kisses turned frantic again, like he had to get them out before he burst from their pressure. He laughed freely as he pressed them over my cheeks.

I broke apart from him, my chest rising and falling with excitement and fear. But as I looked at Lito, only happiness pushed through.

"If we're going to do this, then you'll need to do it right, otherwise my father will kill—"

"Shhh," he hushed. "You let me deal with Caldwell. Before you know it, there will be a sparkling jewel on your finger, and then there will be no excuses from you when I say you're mine." His voice turned dark as he kissed along my jaw. "But I don't want to talk about your father right now." His fingers ran down my sides. "I never told you how fucking incredible you look tonight. I even had to stop myself from touching you back in that ballroom."

"You *did* touch me back in that ballroom," I quipped back at him, smirking at the memory of him stroking my shoulder.

"No, Alora. . . I wanted to touch you like *this."* He lifted my thigh over his hip and ground his own against my centre.

My breath whooshed out of me at the change of position. I leant my shoulders back against the flowered trellis to keep steady and angled my head to watch his gaze rove over me.

He lowered his hand to my ankle and started an agonisingly slow trek up my calf. His fingertips tickled as they roamed, prepared to take their time.

"Is this where I find out if your underwear matches?"

I curved my lips and winked. "I'm not wearing any."

"Fucking. . . Gods," he groaned and abandoned his slow perusal and shot his hand straight up to cup my bare ass. He leant in close again, driving his hips forward into me and kissed me roughly.

Lito took my breath away further as his hand came over my hip, thumb pressing to my clit. He swallowed my moan as he kissed me once more.

"Fuck, Alora," he growled as he felt how slick I was, thumb swirling on the sensitive spot.

"Please," I whimpered. The only word I could manage amongst his continuous kisses and touches.

Lito let go of my leg and stepped back to undo his pants. He never broke eye contact as he made quick work of the strings. My gaze flicked between his skilled fingers arching around his front, and his eyes that were laced with desire.

But it was back at his fingers I stayed watching as he pulled his cock free and stroked his hand along the length. I bit my lip, mouth watering at the sight.

"Give me that lip." Lito claimed my mouth as his hands bunched my layers up to get back to the warmth underneath, holding my leg over his hip again.

He let out a groan at the wetness that coated his finger.

"I went home that afternoon in the alley, and have spent every night, and every morning since, thinking of you and that wall, and all the different ways I could have taken you against it."

I couldn't help the cry that escaped my throat at the picture he painted–at imagining him pleasuring himself to the same fantasy. He spoke so slowly, toying with my clit, his words were their own form of torture as he played.

"You enjoyed every finger," he groaned as he slid one into me, soaked from the first instant. I let out a groan of my own as he pushed into me. "Every thrust," he breathed as he added another.

I gasped at the pressure and rocked my hips into him. He cursed as he watched me slide on his hand. "Fucking Gods, Alora."

"Stop beseeching the fucking Gods, Lito, and start fucking me."

He didn't need to be told twice. The moment his finger left me, *he* was there.

He pressed the tip of his cock at my entrance, moved his hand to my hip then pulled me onto him. I let out a cry, my breath curling into fog.

That first push inside was the only slow thing about our collision. Once he was seated, he withdrew then drove into me, again, and again, and again. Setting a pace that attested to his burning need.

I couldn't stifle my moans, but luckily Lito had chosen a spot so far away from the party that I didn't need to.

He parted my lips with his tongue, swallowing each scream of pleasure he wrought from me.

My climax roared through my body as Lito swirled his fingers around my clit again. His name moaned on my lips as I came was his own undoing, where he cried out mine—exactly like he'd promised.

With a final thrust, he withdrew and spilled his release onto the shrubs beside us. The only sounds left were our heavy panting.

Maybe I won't tell Della about every *minute.*

Lito and I spent the next few moments slowing our breaths with gentle kisses and whispered words—and also fixing our appearance so everyone wouldn't know we'd just spent the last half an hour fucking each other in the bushes.

We decided to return to the party taking opposite routes. It was best to keep things quiet, at least for now. We'd work on how to officially tell my father about us later.

Lito insisted I go along the path we'd taken through the garden back to the party, and he would go the opposite way. The hour was more early than late now, and the route was better lit.

I strode quickly and quietly through the hedges, past a trickling fountain and flowered bushes sculpted into perfect balls, past tall topiaries of deep green and teal.

No.

Not a topiary. A dress.

A teal dress, almost hidden amongst the surrounding green and shadows. Pressed in by a looming figure who had one hand cupped on her cheek to hold her in place, the other cupped on her breast.

I would have kept walking, given my own recent need for privacy in these very gardens just minutes ago, had I not noticed the look on Daisy's face. Not noticed who exactly was pressed against her.

Thane.

Rage surged and I ran as quickly as my heels allowed on the loose stones, my swift feet keeping me steady. A startled expression flashed across Thane's face at being found before he reset his composed expression. That alone told me enough about what was happening—what had been about to happen.

"Get your fucking hands off her," I seethed, and shot forward, grasping Daisy's wrist and pulling her behind me.

"Miss Bradford," he crooned, showing too many teeth. "Miss Woode and I were only talking, no need for your hot temper here." He fixed a steely gaze on me. "But I would be careful with it, nonetheless. I could have your tongue cut out for speaking to me that way."

I scoffed at how quickly he jumped to meting out punishments.

"I know the penalty for speaking rudely to a Lord, but tell me, *Thane,* what's the judgement given to those who assault young ladies?"

Anger contorted his features. "How *dare you.*" He stepped toward us, the cracks in his demeanour wide open for us to see.

"Daisy, go back to the party," I ordered, shoving her toward the terrace. Thank the Gods she obeyed straight away. As I turned back to face Thane, he was right in front of me.

My father's training kicked in and I raised my hands to my face in sheer response to his proximity, but I reacted wrong.

His fist slammed into my stomach and I doubled over then dropped to the ground. The stones bit into my knees as I fell, but it was secondary to the pain ricocheting through my middle. Angry, pulsing heat bloomed where he punched me, but it was the burning ache of my lungs failing to draw a new breath that hurt the most.

"You fucking bitch."

I could do nothing else but cough and try to catch my breath as he loomed over me. I prayed to the Gods he didn't strike me again, and that Daisy had the good sense to send someone.

"First the little trick you pulled with the dance, now this," he said, voice levelling as he straightened. "I'll see you at the eclipse, Miss Bradford, perhaps you'll have learnt some respect by then." He didn't need to waste any more energy here.

He stepped around me like I was a pile of waste, his boots crunching on the stones as he strolled away.

I curled tighter around myself, tears spilling from my eyes onto the ground.

A minute later, a set of boots crunched the stones as someone ran up the path toward me and I turned my head, hoping it was Lito—probably wondering why I hadn't appeared back at the same time he had.

But it was my father who dropped down and pulled me onto his lap without saying a word. His broad hand cradled my head as I leant into him and cried.

He held me tight and waited until my tears subsided then raised my head to meet his eyes, which were full of heartache and worry. He scrunched his face tight against whatever feelings raced through him at seeing me this way, then cupped my cheek, his rough palm coarse against my skin.

"Let's get you home."

Chapter 5
The Horse

The journey back home was silent. A quiet rage simmered under my father's skin, along with a deep well of pain. I didn't tell him what had happened—but he knew. Knew when he saw Thane emerging from the shadows, satisfaction lacing his expression. Knew from my crumpled body and tears.

But there were two things that *I* didn't know.

First was how he knew where to find me so quickly. I'd hoped Daisy had told him, though I wasn't so sure she'd freely fess up. She didn't know anything had happened to me after all, and she wouldn't tell anyone she'd been alone in the bushes with the Lord.

The second thing I didn't know was what my father planned to do.

He'd helped me stand and walked me to the safety of the terrace, then told me not to move while he organised our departure. Pepper had long gone home, so I sat alone for ten minutes while the cold air tried to steal the remnants of my strength.

My head ached from the alcohol and my body ached from the impact Lord Thane had dealt, but not even Lito came looking for me, and that was a different kind of pain altogether.

As I sat next to my father in the cart, I couldn't remember a time I'd ever seen him so angry. Nothing good would come from his fury if it didn't dissipate.

One thing I did know, was that this night—this morning—could fuck off. I wanted to crawl in between my sheets and sleep for a week. But as Big Charlie clopped around the last bend, and our house came into view, it was apparent I wouldn't get what I wanted just yet.

Shouts from a group of men standing inside our yard rang out. Lanterns and torches lit up the centre of the farm along with the lights within our house itself. But it was what the men were shouting at that drew our attention.

Standing in the middle of the yard, tall and looking wild, with its ears back, rearing up and braying noisily, was a horse.

"What the—" I looked across to my father, but his face was white with shock. I slid tenderly from the cart as it pulled up to the gate and rubbed Charlie's neck to calm him, while dad leapt down and ran into the yard.

"It came out of nowhere, Caldwell!" Tory shouted over his shoulder as my father ran toward the men trying to contain the wild beast.

"Everybody step back," he commanded as he joined the others circling the mare. His voice dropped low to calm the chaos of the scene and the mare responded in turn.

I stood by the cart and admired how my father controlled the situation—how adept he was with the creature.

"There girl," he soothed, taking a slow step toward her. "It's only little ol' me here, no need to panic."

The horse let out a snort that I could have sworn sounded like a laugh. My father had never been described as little.

But the words he hushed to her were working. No longer surrounded by shouting men, the mare quickly calmed. She let out a last stomp of her silver hoof, displaying she meant business if yelled at again.

My father reached the beautiful creature and ran his hand along her coat, still whispering words to her too low for me to hear. She turned her head to him as though she were listening.

"Tory, would you get Charlie back in his stall? I'll take this one into the stables and get her sorted in a box for the night." He nodded at the other men in the yard. "Thanks for helping, boys," he said gruffly. "I'll get word out in the morning, saying we've found a mare."

The men turned toward their homes and Tory reached me to take over handling Charlie, who hadn't batted an eyelid at his home being invaded upon by the feisty intruder.

"Come through, Alora," my father called. "Get yourself up to bed. You need rest."

The mare and I kept our gaze on one another as I edged past, her bright blue eyes watched me intently as I entered the house.

I made my way straight up to bed, peeled my gown away and dropped between my covers, letting oblivion take me swiftly.

I remember waking sometime later, but the moon still hung in the inky sky. Stomach aching from hunger and the assault, I hobbled to the bathroom, not caring I was stark naked, then crawled back beneath my sheets.

My sleep was riddled with blurred turmoil. Angry heat from my injury engulfed my entire body, and darkness swept me into an infinite void. Endless and dangerous, I knew violence thrummed in the hollow cavern I'd dreamed of. My thoughts had plagued my dreams and turned them destructive.

I coiled around myself, willing the hurt to stop. Finally, the heat in my stomach ebbed and soothed, and that familiar pull I always ignored replaced it. A determined tug wanted me to grab hold of it so it could lead me away from this place where I didn't belong.

For the first time, I was tempted to follow.

I was greeted immediately by Big Charlie when I slid open the barn door late the next morning. His huge head came over his stall to sniff my hair.

"Hello, my boy," I cooed to him like I always did and scratched his muzzle. "Sorry I've been away. Did your guest behave?"

He bobbed his head and chuffed.

Further down at the far stall, my father stood in with the mare, talking to her softly and stroking her side.

Now drenched in morning light, it was easy to make out her markings—or lack of them. She was flawless. Her silky creamy-brown coat shimmered in the pale rays of sunshine, second only to her long silver-white mane and tail. This horse was clearly cared for.

Where in hell had she come from?

As I stood gaping at the mare, she lifted her head and locked her stunning blue eyes onto mine, drawing me in. I stepped toward the stall, scratching Morelli as I passed and stopped at the door.

Dad smiled at me. "It's good to see you up, my dear."

I returned the gesture and rested my chin on top of the stall door.

"Made a new friend, have you?" I joked, nodding to the mare.

"Isn't she incredible?" he awed, staring up at her. "You know. . . we can't keep her locked up in a box all day. She could do with getting out in the yard. . ." He looked pointedly at me.

"Me?"

"You're capable, are you not?"

"Yeah, but. . ."

"Only until we get her back to where she belongs," he said, attention back on the horse. "And she clearly isn't a wild beast." The horse stomped her hoof as though she was offended. "Just lead her around the yard for now. If she isn't claimed beforehand, we'll wait until the eclipse to decide what to do. Maybe someone coming into town will recognise her."

"Yeah, okay," I agreed, then bristled, a sour thought running through my mind when I skimmed my hand to my stomach where a certain disgusting excuse of a man had purpled my skin. The sight of it when I'd awoken had made my blood boil.

But the bruise wasn't the only cause of my anger.

I was annoyed at myself for not being quick enough—not strong enough—to prevent it from happening. And since I'd been overpowered by him, an enraged creature of sorts clawed in my chest, demanding to be appeased with violence.

Soon, I would plan out all the different ways I'd skin Thane alive—I just had to be stronger. "I'll exercise her after I've done some training."

"Actually, I want you to take a few days off to rest."

I cast my eyes down, the anger at what had happened rising in me further.

"I'm so sorry I didn't protect you, Alora."

Shock raced through me—surely he didn't blame himself.

"Dad, no, you don't need to apol—"

"I do, Alora," he said bluntly. "It is my job as your—" He huffed and shook his head, frustration burning across his expression. "I was there to ensure you were cared for that night. Every night. And I didn't." His face fell, guilt creeping into his eyes.

"There is only one person responsible for what happened, Dad, and you aren't it."

His scarred palm scratched my fingers as they curled around his hand.

He studied me, gaze serious. "He will pay for laying his hands on you. He deserves his titles stripped and a prison sentence for what he did to Daisy. But for harming you, he deserves a death sentence."

I sneered back at him. "Only if I get to do it."

He winked. "That's my girl."

A companionable silence fell as we watched the mare move about her stall before she wandered over to my father for another scratch.

"Pepper dropped by while you were sleeping. She was very concerned."

"I'll go see her later, let her know. . . everything."

He made a noise of agreement, attention still fixed on the mare.

"Mr. Vidolito also called by," he said, scratching the horse's cheeks, not looking at me. "I told him you were resting and that you'd see him at the eclipse."

I paled slightly at the mention of Lito but didn't miss the implied rule my father had placed on him. Not to come back until the eclipse.

I needed to tell my father about our engagement, but I needed to talk to Lito first and tell him everything that happened. It would have to wait until the eclipse then.

"You've known him long enough, Dad, you can call him Lito."

He let out a gruff scoff in response. I wasn't a fool and neither was my father—he already knew something was up.

"Okay, well I'd better go find Tory and—"

"I meant it, Alora," he interrupted. "You're on rest until further notice. No chores, no training."

"I'm fine, really."

"Sorry, my dear, decision made." He exited the stall. "Your duties extend to the mare and no further until I say otherwise. I'd hate to be accused of mistreating her when she leaves this place." He kissed my hair then left the barn—his watch over the horse apparently ended.

I reached to scratch her ears. "Right, you and me then, old girl."

She threw her head and stomped a hoof in reply.

Touchy about her age then, I guess.

I tracked down Tory right after leaving the stable to offer my services, but my father had beaten me to it. "Nice try," he laughed and turned me away.

Fighting my father's directives was futile, so I stomped back inside and decided that if resting was now mandated, then I would take full advantage. I ran a bath and soaked for an hour in the scented water. Muscles I didn't know were tense, relaxed in the searing heat and soothed my stomach.

Once I was dried and dressed, hair finally washed and detangled, I made two cups of hot chocolate then padded to Della's room and found her reading. I spent the time it took to drain our mugs, telling her a version of what happened during the Season Ball, mostly repeating the gossip I'd gleaned from the other girls while we'd sat sipping champagne on the terrace. Though, I left out the major events regarding Lito and Thane.

I left Della to her book, my skin itching from staying in her room too long, then walked down the road to Pepper's.

It turned out that Pepper had also had a rather exciting night, just not in the same way as mine. Shortly after Lord Thane had taken me inside to dance, Dawson Calloway, a respectable merchant from Amesburne came and declared his affections for her publicly and the two spent the rest of the evening ogling at one another.

As expected, Daisy hadn't fessed up about her run-in with Thane, but nothing got past Pepper. "I had to force the information from her.

I knew something was wrong—guilt written all over her face. She said Thane charmed her with sweet words and once he had her alone. . . You got there just as he started to—well, you know."

"I'm glad I was there to stop it, though I'm sad it started in the first place."

"She's a foolish girl who should have known better, his high standing or not," she reprimanded harshly. "I saw Hazel this morning, she told me she saw you leaving with your father and said you were hurt. Maggie told me when I got to your house that you were resting. . ." Her unasked question hung in the air.

I kept my eyes down. "He didn't like that I had. . . implied he was assaulting Daisy. I told her to run, and he struck me."

Pepper's gasp was audible. "He should be thrown in a ditch!" she whisper-yelled. I giggled at her despite the seriousness. Angry Pepper just never quite hit the mark.

"If my father gets his hands on him, he might just end up in one if I don't get to him first."

"Good," she snapped.

Pepper and I spent the rest of the afternoon eating sandwiches and filling one another in on the other gossip of the night. Apparently other than who was courting who through the night, the rumours concerning the fae and their impending war was whispered more and more.

"Acker was told the hunter was taken to a different part of the realm by the sprite. He saw and heard things no one else has."

I scoffed around my mouthful of cake. "I think these whisperings have gone on long enough that they're no longer the hunter's words, but everyone else's."

Pepper shrugged. "Perhaps, but Acker said even your father went pale when Lilah Hudson's father told him the fae's enemies were looking for something."

I quirked an eyebrow.

Now that is strange.

Even still, there was no reason to be worried. "The fae don't come here, Pep, you know that. Don't get sucked in by this nonsense. Not once has even a sprite emerged from the forest boundary, let alone some great and powerful warrior strolled our streets, or a war in a different realm come to harm us."

Pepper hummed in agreeance. "I know, but something about the rumours feel different this time. . ."

"Well, if it's juicy details you're looking for, I have some news. . ."

She leaned in and I told her what Lito and I had discussed and that he planned to make his proposal official after we'd spoken to my father. My ears rang with the squeal she let out, but I made her promise to keep her lips sealed until then.

Once I was sufficiently full of both desserts and gossip, I returned home, and to the new resident waiting for me.

The mare eyed me closely as I entered her stall with a halter and rope in hand. "We're just going to go for a walk," I reassured. I worried she was going to be difficult, but the mare simply dipped her head and let me clip the halter in place.

We walked to the middle of the farm, where I led her around as we got to know one another, and let her take in the space.

When the sun was setting, I led her toward the gate to show her where Big Charlie was hitched up to the cart–his duties nearly finished for the day.

The mare clopped with a steady rhythm as we neared the fence, but there was one farm member who hadn't gotten the memo that my days were supposed to be relaxing.

Spawn of hell itself, Dale ran hissing toward us with his wings spread wide. I didn't have time to form a reaction to the charging swan before the mare reared into the air. I let go of the lead as she lifted, scared I'd get caught in her outburst.

Her silver hooves slammed onto the path, the impact so strong the ground rumbled, and she stomped forward twice more toward the oncoming swan.

Shiny black feathers exploded as Dale quickly realised his error and retreated to the safety of the pond.

The mare let out a ferocious scream, ears flat to her head, and stomped once more for good measure. I expected she'd suddenly take off into the distance now that she was unrestrained, but the glossy horse simply turned back to face me and let out one of those snorts that sounded like a laugh.

We stared at each other for a moment and I closed the gap to her, grabbing hold of the rope once more. I rubbed my hand on her cheek and smiled. "I think you and I are going to get along just fine."

Chapter 6
The Eclipse

As ordered, I spent the next few days milling about the farm and taking time to recover. But still spent each night slicing the air and flicking my daggers in hand at the foot of my bed, trying to appease the urge that demanded I better my skills.

The mark Lord Thane bestowed upon me didn't bruise as badly as I'd feared and faded quickly. I probably had the stiff bodice of my gown to thank for that.

By sunset the day before the eclipse, a few dozen tents and merchant stalls dotted the Lawns, and it was inevitable someone camping out there would come looking for the mare.

The day of the eclipse was one of perfect spring. The sunshine had just enough strength to warm my face, and the gentle breeze through my window ensured nothing got too hot. Thick, fluffy clouds dotted the sky, but they were so few and far between that the main event of the day was sure to be in full view.

I stuffed my dagger into my shin-high boots, pulled my waves into a braid that draped over my shoulder, then swept a line of kohl across my eyes—the grey and green twinkling back at me. I headed straight to the stable and found my father beside the mare's stall, his head once again lowered, whispering to her gently.

"I think you're going to miss her," I said as a way of greeting and walked over, scratching Charlie and Morelli as I passed.

"More than you know," he said sadly.

Hope snuck into my voice. "What are the odds no one comes forward and we get to keep her?" I'd become rather attached to the creature over the past few days.

My father took a moment to consider. "I don't think she belongs here, my dear." He raised his hand to rub my shoulder in comfort.

"I'm sad to agree with you."

"When you're on your way out, I need you to hitch her up to the post by the back fence. Tory's going to muck out the stables while everyone is out. By the end of the day, she'll either be gone back to her home and the space will need cleaning anyway, or on the off chance she's not, she'll be here to stay and would appreciate a pristine residence."

"Sure thing. You don't need me to do it, to spare Tory?"

"No, no," he replied gruffly. "I think you have bigger things to focus on today."

Thane.

"Yeah, I suppose I do."

"Alora, I want you to know that, wherever—" He paused, and cleared his throat, tears welling in the corner of his eyes. "Whatever happens today, know that everything will be fine. *You* will be fine."

"I know, Dad," I reassured. "Thane won't know what hit him when we're done with him."

He smiled weakly, as though he was trying to believe the words himself. "No, I don't suppose he will." Dad raised his hand to cup my cheek, his scarred palm gently scratching. He pulled me into a tight hug. "I love you, Alora."

"I love you too, Dad," I said, squeezing him back as best as I could.

We pulled apart after a beat, and he cleared his throat. "Right, best get this girl outside and go enjoy yourself." He scratched the mare one last time before exiting the stable.

I walked the mare out of the barn shortly after, sliding the door back into place as we left, and led her to the back gate, ensuring she was secured just inside the stone wall.

She and I had the perfect view of the Lawns, and we surveyed the now busy area. Altenbury Forest loomed beyond the stretch of grass like a watchful sentinel—its trees were lit by the mid-morning sun. In the distance, a group of teenage boys skirted the edges of the forest, most likely daring one another to try their luck with a sprite.

Idiots.

As I watched the young group, a strange shiver ran down my arms and made my stomach squirm, but I brushed away the nonsense thoughts about the forest and what lurked beyond their branches. Those trees were no more or less dangerous than they were before these rumours kicked up.

Sucking in a grounding breath, I patted the mare on her side. "Right, sit tight, girl. We'll see if we can't get you home today." She nickered in response as I left her and walked onto the Lawns.

It didn't take long before I spotted Avery at a florist stall, the heady perfume of roses surrounding her. Apparently, plans had been made that our group of girls from the ball were watching the event together, so we wandered the market stalls looking for everyone else.

The brilliant-blue spring sky was already muting into a dull tone at the impending darkness, so we didn't have much longer.

Avery and I stopped to browse a stall selling jewelled trinkets when someone tapped my shoulder. I turned, expecting to see another member of our group, but instead found the snivelling face of Lord Thane's messenger.

Gods spare me.

"Lord Thane summons you to join him at his tent, Miss Bradford," he proclaimed, hand gesturing in the direction he intended I go.

I stepped sideways into Avery's space and hooked my arm through hers. "Tell Lord Thane I'll be there as soon as I've finished—"

"He means now, Miss Bradford," the boy cut me off in a monotone.

I glared at him, wondering whether the trouble I was already in would worsen much more if I did indeed tell him to *fuck off,* like I wanted to a few weeks ago.

He must have read something in my expression because he added, "He's not asking, Miss Bradford. You are to come with me."

No excuses allowed then.

I looked at Avery, trying to keep my expression plain. "Tell the girls I'll be back soon." I smiled as warmly as I could, but the look Avery had as she flicked her eyes between me and the messenger said she saw through the bullshit. I followed the messenger past the stalls on shaking legs.

Lord Thane's gazebo was in the open, which was a small blessing, but the massive structure's aesthetic screamed *don't approach.* Thane sat in a high-back armchair, his legs perched on a table laden with food, ankles crossed. His whole demeanour screamed *misogynistic prick.*

The messenger led me to the table, bowed without a word and strolled off to go be useless somewhere else. The Lord stared into the distant sky and didn't acknowledge me, so I didn't acknowledge him with the curtsy I was supposed to.

"Thank you for coming, Alora," he said with a bored tone, still not looking at me.

"I was under the impression I didn't have a choice," I replied curtly. We were in the public eye right now, his proverbial hands tied with social etiquette, so I wouldn't go down without a fight, consequences be damned.

He turned his head to look at me, my fiery tone drawing his attention. I raised a single eyebrow at him, daring him to make a scene.

He stood and stepped toward me. "I do hope you've recovered from the Ball, and that you've forgiven my monstrous behaviour."

What a cunt.

I remained silent and still, lest I speak the words out loud.

Thane turned to the table to pick at the offerings. The sky darkened another shade, and the temperature dropped with it.

"I called you here, not only to check on you but to inform you that this evening, I'm meeting with your father to discuss an arrangement between you and me."

I couldn't help the laugh that rose up my throat.

"Something funny, Miss Bradford?"

"Several things, yeah," I said, still giggling.

He gestured with his hand that I elaborate.

"Not that I wouldn't thoroughly enjoy watching that particular meeting, I'm afraid you've waited too long, Lord Thane. I am already spoken for."

His expression remained unaffected. "Is that so? Because my sources have told me that as of this morning, you remain entirely *un*-spoken for," he said, putting extra emphasis on the *un*. "And I should think that an upstanding gentleman such as Caldwell Bradford would want what is best for his daughter, so your father will hear my proposal. Be thankful I am still willing to consider you, given your atrocious behaviour and lack of respect at the ball."

I'm going to fucking kill him.

My hand twitched, but common sense prevailed while my temper soared. "My father does want what is best for his daughter. Which is exactly why I know he will turn down your proposal before you have even uttered it. That is, if he doesn't strike you where you stand as you did so to me."

My chest puffed with rising anger just as strongly as my legs shook with fear at the words I'd just yelled. I could get Dad and I both killed for suggesting such a thing.

But Thane just smiled at me, gauging my threat.

He stepped into my proximity and raised a clammy hand to my cheek. I jerked away as he came to touch me, but he struck out and squeezed my chin so it hurt. Anyone walking past would be too far away to tell it wasn't an affectionate touch.

His cool expression turned into a vile sneer as he leaned closer. "Such spirit," he praised. "I am very much going to enjoy breaking you, Alora." He closed the gap and kissed my lips. He still held my jaw so tightly that I couldn't move, and the rest of my body froze. My skin burned like fire, bile rising in my throat at the assault.

I glared at him as he pulled away slowly then finally let go. The urge to give in to my violent desires only seconds away from taking over. Without permission, my lip quivered and tears welled in my eyes, but I refused to let them fall.

"I'll see you soon, Alora," he promised with an evil smile then walked away.

Dismissed.

My fist clenched and unclenched–the rational part of my brain fighting against what my instincts wanted me to do. I had to be smart, not savage. I turned, stomping toward the safety of the crowd. The messenger appeared beside me, meant to escort me away, but I whirled on him and grabbed his shirt, yanking his tall frame down to my level.

"Fuck off," I roared and shoved him backwards, sending him stumbling, then stormed away.

The sky had turned an eerie sort of sunset haze, which was a strange sight to behold considering it was barely noon. I looked up at the darkening sky and saw the sun and moon were now next to one another. I hurried through the crowds, my mind reeling. I didn't know whether I wanted to find the girls to distract myself, find Lito to cry on, or find my father to warn him. But when I rounded the outskirts of the market area, my decision was made for me.

Pepper sat with our little group on a patchwork picnic blanket, baked goods lined the centre. I schooled my expression into neutrality and walked over, my skin prickling with adrenaline.

One look from Pepper told me she could see right through my facade, and she silently asked if I was okay. '*Later,'* I mouthed to her, and she dipped her head. The girls all rang out their welcomes as I sat and started on a chocolate muffin, needing the sweetness to give me strength.

"Glad you finally made it," Hazel chirped happily.

"What did I miss?"

"Hazel was just about to tell us how she spent the Season Ball with Sofie and Avery drinking Lord Thane dry," one of the girls teased.

Sofie raised her wineglass in a salute and Hazel blushed. "I did not! It was Sofie drinking everything in sight, and Avery joined in later, cursing off all men after she was led on. I was just an innocent bystander!"

We all giggled. "Where is Avery? She and I were together just before," I asked.

"I met up with her just after you left, but she saw a man from the Ball and tracked him down over that way," Hazel said, pointing to the farms behind her, as the other girls started their own conversations. "Everyone else showed up right after that."

"Oh, well she'd better hurry up or she'll miss it," I mused when suddenly the crowd hushed as the pale sphere crept further in front of the sun.

The temperature dropped again, and the sky turned the colour of dusk and dawn all at once. Only the slightest sliver of sun remained and the Lawns turned silent as everyone took in the incredible sight.

Then it happened.

The moon slid perfectly in the sun's path and stars blinked to life in the sky while the sun's rays tried to illuminate around its shield.

The gathered crowd let out shouts and cheers as they watched it unfold. But just as the moon cast its perfect shadow down on us, the sun flared with blinding light around its edges. The cheering turned into screams of shock at the burning light.

A wicked wind lashed out, toppling over some of the market tents and scattering the picnics laid out.

I turned my head down and closed my eyes at the explosion of light and harsh wind.

As the two celestial bodies continued on their paths, and the sun peeked out once more, the burning light drew back, the wind died down and the whole space returned to the picture-perfect, peaceful setting– just with a few cakes and pies thrown about.

People looked up as the moon and sun drifted apart, and after a silent pause of trepidation, everyone cheered loudly. The exhilaration of the event struck the conversations back up and noise returned to the Lawns.

"*Merciful Gods,"* Pepper gasped. "What *was* that?"

Emma spoke as she pulled bits of muffin out of her hair. "I didn't know that was supposed to happen."

Some unexplained part of me didn't think it was supposed to either.

With the shock subsiding, along with the darkness, the conversation turned back to how incredible the sight had been.

"I can't believe Avery missed it!" one of the girls whined.

"I'm sure she saw it from wherever she is," replied another.

"Where did you say she went again, Hazel?" I asked.

Hazel swallowed the mouthful of pastry she'd managed to hold onto. "She saw the man from the Ball who led her on and went with him to one of the farms over there." She pointed to the houses near us.

I pulled my brows together. I knew those houses—one of them was mine. There was no eligible man Avery could've been talking to who lived over there. Reed was the only eligible man in the area, but he'd been off with Grace and Victoria at the ball.

Pepper seemed to be on the same train of thought as well. "What's his name?"

"Flynn, maybe? Avery said he's a hunter from Amesburne."

"There's no hunter from Amesburne called Flynn," Pepper mused, looking to Sofie for help. She was from Amesburne, so had a better chance of knowing for sure.

Sofie merely shrugged and tipped her wine back.

"Umm. . . maybe it wasn't Flynn," continued Hazel, trying to be helpful. "It was something like Fenrich or Florian or—"

"Fletcher?" I interrupted.

"Oh, Gods," exclaimed Pepper, her hand covering her gasp.

Hazel squeaked. "Yes!"

No.

"That's it! Fletcher," she chirped, happy someone had figured it out. "I saw them going—Alora?"

"Alora!" Pep shouted.

But I was gone.

Already sprinting toward the houses Hazel had pointed to. I knew which one they were in. Knew why the man she'd seen had been wandering the markets.

He'd been there for me.

Fletcher. Fletcher fucking Kingsley-Vidolito.

I tore along the stone walls that bordered the farms—a stream of memories flared through my head. I tried not to spiral, but the evidence was all there.

'Avery joined in later, cursing off all men after she was led on.'

Led on.

I sobbed as I tore down the path, the farm gate coming into view.

In my head, I remembered Lito from the ball. His familiar leather and spice scent, muted by a heady smell of roses. His heaving breaths as his eyes frantically searched mine.

'*How could I–*'

Realisation dawned, and tears ran freely down my cheeks.

Avery smelled of roses. It wasn't the flower stall, but her.

Her scent on him.

Lito hadn't been waiting at the Ball after Thane assaulted me. Had he gone from my arms back into Avery's? I swung around the corner into the farm and flew past the mare still tied to her post who gave me an indignant snort as I careened through the gate.

I skidded to a halt in the centre of the yard, looking for signs of movement. It was like a bright faelight had been turned on, and I saw it all so clearly. My sadness dissipated and burning hot anger flooded my veins.

Lito had been so persistent at making me admit my love, had even wrung a proposal acceptance from me. Had he simply tired of waiting for me? Or had it all been some sick game?

Either way, I'd made my stance on being with him clear from when we first started fooling around and then falling for one another. I knew he would regret choosing me–but to persevere, finally get me to say yes then toss me aside–

I swiped the tears from my face, and blinding hatred seared my vision. I bent down and pulled out the dagger from my boot, and rage fuelled my every thought and action.

I'd been itching for a fight since Thane, and I'd scratch it with their blood.

I'll fucking gut the both of them.

I looked left toward the stable and noticed the door was ajar. I knew I'd shut it on my way out with the mare earlier, so it was as good a place as any to start.

On light feet, I tiptoed over and tilted my ear toward the opening. Sure enough, Avery's tell-tale voice whispered out from somewhere behind the door.

Thankful for my natural stealth and skill at sneaking around with nimble silence, I stepped around the door and slipped unseen into the dim space, determined to spit hellfire on them. But the sight I came upon stopped me dead in my tracks and sputtered my fire out.

Lito stood with his back pressed to the wall of the mare's stable a few yards past the door, with Avery pressed against him. There was no space between their bodies–she'd have felt every taught muscle and firm aspect Lito had on offer. They were locked into one another's gaze like they were under some spell, with Avery casting her huge round eyes at Lito's warm ones. His gold hair fell over his brow as he looked down at her.

Lito's hand rested on her neck, and her palm laid on top, stroking her thumb along his fingers. Her full, ruby lips were a hair's breadth away from his.

This would have been what he and I looked like down in that alley.

It was not them under a spell, but they who had cast one on me. I couldn't look away as they stood together. All fight left me in a singular, thumping, broken heartbeat. All that remained was emptiness. Cold and infinite.

My life was now split between two choices. A vile abuser, or a cheating lover. Denying one pushed me toward the other.

It felt as though the world tilted off its axis. My arms slackened at my side and the dagger slipped from my fingertips, clattering to the stone floor with a scrape.

The noise of my falling blade slashed through their intimate bubble and they flinched apart, startled by the interruption.

Caught.

Avery cocked her head at me. Her expression gave away nothing. She didn't even have the decency to look innocent. Lito's face on the other hand, fell into shock. His eyes widened like a rabbit spotted by a fox.

"Alora–" he breathed and took a step forward.

No.

I knew what he'd do. Knew he would grab me and whisper honeyed words in my ear. Tell me there was a simple explanation. That it was me–had always been me he loved. Loved completely and no one else. That it was all a misunderstanding.

But I'd seen enough. There was no explanation that could make this okay. I couldn't give him the opportunity to get beyond my defences.

There was one other choice I could make.

Leave.

As Lito breathed my name and took that first step toward me, I turned and bolted.

"Alora, NO!" he roared. The sound of his boots giving chase echoed. Despite our love for one another, our relationship was fragile. He knew. Knew this would be my breaking point and our end.

He had to catch me to keep me. And I wouldn't let him.

I was quick and had a head start, but I knew Lito was faster. Knew he'd wrap his arms around me and hold me until I listened, and I couldn't let that happen.

If I ran inside the house I'd fall into a dead end, plus, Lito knew his way around and would find me in seconds. So I turned right as I blew past the stable door, back the way I came.

I pumped my arms and legs as quickly as they'd go, my braid flying out behind me as I ran. I frantically searched for a place to go, but hiding here wasn't an option either for the same reason as the house. Lito knew this place intimately, and again I'd fall into a dead end, or he'd catch me as I leapt over a fence—so I ignored the pens on either side as I aimed for the back gate and the Lawns beyond. Maybe salvation could be found amongst the crowd.

But as I sprinted across the yard, dirt flying from my footsteps, I heard Lito behind me again, closer than he was in the barn.

"ALORA!" he bellowed. "ALORA, STOP!"

He was close. Too close. I wouldn't make it ten steps past the gate before he caught me.

But then I saw the only thing that could get me out of here quicker than Lito could run. And she stood stomping her hoof at the gate I was sprinting for.

I reached the mare without slowing then skidded underneath her neck to the side that was clipped to her lead rope, and prayed to the Gods that I was skilled enough to pull off the move that would get me away fast enough.

Still with the full momentum of my sprint, I kicked my legs up and swung onto her back. As my hand slid up her cheek on my ascent, I flicked the catch on her halter, untethering her from the rope keeping her tied to the post.

The moment I'd kicked up onto the mare, Lito was already there and his fingertips brushed my leg from atop the horse. But as though she knew she was suddenly free, the mare reared and kicked out, forcing Lito back. I clung to the horse's neck for dear life as her legs lifted into the air.

Lito cursed and threw his arm over his face. His sudden halt from the breakneck speed he'd been travelling at to catch me, caused him to slip on the loose dirt and fall backwards.

"ALORA!" he roared again, as the mare continued to rear in a rage.

She slammed her hooves back onto the ground with a threatening blow and snorted her fury at the man on the ground inches in front of her.

I looked from the panting man before me, up toward the house, where my father was standing by the door, his face grave.

He gave a single, sad nod.

"Get me out of here," I whispered to the mare.

Before I'd kicked her into motion, she coiled power into her legs and charged forward with unprecedented power. She twisted her body around the gate and took off like a shot across the Lawns.

I heard Lito scream my name one more time before I was out of earshot. Devastation rang through the sound.

People squealed and dodged as the mare blew past. Her silver mane flew as she galloped along the green expanse. My plan was to just get away from Lito, find a place to coalesce, and go from there.

Under any other circumstance, I would have revelled in the feeling of this moment, so close to what I'd dreamt of when I thought of leaving my life behind. But my heart was racing with the panic the chase with Lito had caused.

I looked over my shoulder as the mare charged, checking Lito hadn't somehow found a mount of his own, intending to hunt me down. But she had taken off so quickly that the yard wasn't in view anymore, only the blur of tents as we flew past.

Looking over my shoulder at the flat-out speed the horse was travelling at made me disorientated. I expected as I faced front on again, that I'd see the continuous stretch of green in front of me as we ran alongside the tents. But it wasn't the bright green of the Lawns I saw–it was the looming deep green of Altenbury Forest.

I screamed. Not entirely sure if I'd done it aloud or not.

The mare broke through the tree line and forged ahead, racing in between the branches, her breath coming fast and heavy.

I pulled on the strap behind her ears, trying to gain control, but despite my efforts and shrieking at her to stop, she did not relent.

We burst ahead, deeper into the forest. Her thundering steps were unfaltering as she leapt over roots and wove between trees—I had to lay flat against her back to avoid being taken out by a branch. With my head bent down against her neck, eyes scrunched tight, I gripped clumps of her mane, hanging on for dear life, wondering if it would be better to fall from her and make my way back to safety on foot rather than be taken further amongst the trees.

I opened my eyes and lifted my body, prepared to make a last-ditch effort to regain control of the creature. But as I raised my head, a glittering, clouded sprite appeared, and we charged head-on into it.

Chapter 7
The Fae

Light.

There was nothing but bright, brilliant light.

I felt weightless, as if I was submerged in a deep sea.

No. Floating on air.

Beneath me, figures moved in graceful twirls, their silhouettes clouded as if veiled in fog. I drifted from where I floated—down, down, down, until I was level with them.

I knew it wasn't men and women beyond the haze. Their movements were too exquisite, their appearance too ethereal.

Fae.

Then there were the other details that gave them away—their pointed ears could be made out even through the fog. But it was another feature that drew my attention.

Wings.

Great leathery wings held high and proud. Some fae draped their wings behind them with relaxed ease, several held them in tight, while some flared them around their bodies as they danced in twirling steps with their partners.

Slowly, the white light faded, and more of my surroundings came into focus. Colours filtered through the cloud, which had dissipated to a fine mist. Females dressed in diaphanous flowing gowns, and males dressed in high collared jackets stood strong and tall, talking and drinking in groups amongst the stunning setting.

It seemed to be the ruins of a temple. Incredible mosaic tiles dotted the floor in spaces, worn away by aeons, and white stone encompassed the rest.

Music filtered through to me. An incredible melody plucked on a harp accompanied by cellos and flutes, rising and falling as gracefully as the fae who moved to it. Music I'd never heard the likes of.

That thick feeling of magic pressed in on me from all sides like a vise, making my heart race and my body tremble. I wanted to throw up, but somehow managed the strength to slide down from the damned creature who had gotten me into this mess.

I stood in the centre of the huge foundation, the mist of the room clearing further. That was when I realised there was no fog clouding the space at all—but rather a veil, slowly being pulled back over *me* as the magic brought me into the realm.

The fae dancing and standing around the ruins didn't notice the human girl in the centre of the temple floor—and her horse.

Until they did.

A glass shattered somewhere behind me, and the liquid it contained spilled onto the floor. Gasps rang out and the music fell away one instrument at a time, filling the garden with bated silence. Followed by the unmistakable sound of swords being drawn from their sheaths, though I couldn't tell from where—no one seemed to move.

Now in perfect clarity, I took in all that was around me.

Crumbled stone pillars stood with ivy climbing up their remains, shadowed by giant redwoods that I could hardly see the tops of. The brilliant blue sky was a patchwork, hidden behind vines that stretched between the trees.

A stone wall and glass doors twenty feet high lead to a patio between a home and the wide outdoors. But more fae congregated inside those doors to look at the commotion.

Eyes and faces of nearly every shade stared at me, shocked at the sight that appeared from nowhere in the middle of their event.

A few fae moved around me to get a better view. A tall head of tousled auburn hair slid across my peripheral as a male moved to the front corner of the foundation.

I wanted to close my eyes and pray to all the Gods that this was a dream, or that I at least make it out of here alive.

But I couldn't close my eyes to say that prayer, because they were fixed on the two forms standing at the front of the space.

A female stood proud at the steps of a dais, canopied in flowing amber curtains. She squared her thin shoulders perfectly and held her black wings high. Her skin shone from within, and the glass flute she held in her hand looked dangerously close to slipping from her pale fingers. She fixed her golden eyes on me, her expression drifting somewhere between ferocity and shock. She had sharp cheekbones and her raven hair curled around a twinkling, black diadem.

Royalty.

The handsome male beside her was tall, with rich brown skin, and the perfectly groomed stubble over his strong jaw highlighted the angles of his face. He was resplendent in his black and red regalia with a gold crown on top of his short hair, his mahogany wings spread wide as he considered me with brilliant blue eyes.

I expected someone to start shouting—to be grabbed or questioned. What I didn't expect was for the two—clearly royal fae—to dip their heads and bow.

What the fuck?

The movement of the leaders was repeated by the several hundred other fae in the temple ruins. One by one they lowered themselves, dipping and curtseying reverently.

WHAT THE FUCK?

I slowly turned, looking around at the scene. I reached for the mare's halter, simply to touch something familiar and ground myself, but my fingers found only air.

I twisted fully to where the horse should have been, only to find a delicate female standing quietly in its place.

Fae—but not.

She had the same pointed ears as the fae around the room but had no wings I could see. I blinked at her and she smiled gently in return.

She clasped her hands in front of her charcoal dress that touched her bare toes. Her buttery brown skin shimmered under the glowing sunshine, and her silver hair hung loosely down to her waist. She raised her gaze over my shoulder to the two fae at the front of the room, who lifted out of their bow.

Her voice rang out through the garden, both loud and soft, unyielding and kind, commanding and gentle. "Look for deception, prepare for betrayal, train the weapon, and ready for war."

Then she vanished entirely.

WHAT THE FUCK!

Gasps rang out in the crowd as I stared at the empty space in front of me where the female had just been standing—where my horse was supposed to be—and almost forgot how to breathe.

"Who are you?" a stern voice asked from the dais.

I turned and met the stare of the female, but I'd apparently forgotten how to speak.

"Who are you?" she demanded again when I didn't answer.

More fae crept around to the front of the temple, closing in on the dais. An impossibly tall and muscular male stood to the side of the gauzy structure—sword held low in front of him.

"I—where's my horse?" I asked, my mind entirely sure that was the most important question right now.

The male with auburn hair lifted the corner of his lips in an amused smirk.

"That was no horse," came the deep voice of the other royal at the front. "That was Orella, Oracle of Endence."

"Oracle?" I whispered to myself, my pitiful human brain reeling. "My horse was an oracle?"

No, I was right. . . this has to be a dream.

"Why did the Oracle bring you here? Who are you?" came the steely voice of the female once again.

"A—Alora." I hated that I looked so pathetic standing here trembling like a mouse, so I straightened a little higher and tried again. "My name is Alora."

She looked down her nose at me. "And why was the Oracle with you, Alora?"

"I don't know! Until ten seconds ago I thought she was a horse!" I yelled back. The uncomfortable pressure of magic building against my skin made my temper rise along with it.

I immediately regretted my outburst as the female's wings flared, and a sweep of hot power blew through the air.

I was standing amongst fae, and the rumours that drifted through Evamere never altered when it came to noting how dangerous they could be, how powerful they were.

Don't yell at them, Alora. They'll cut you in two with half a thought.

But that red-headed male smiled again. His green eyes glittered as he leant casually against a crumbling pillar, midnight wings hanging around his sides.

"I'm just a human from Remberlie," I said, much calmer.

"You might be from the human realm. . ." rumbled the enormous, dark-haired male with the sword. He crossed the distance to me, sheathing his weapon on the way.

Like he even needs it. He looks like he could kick a house down simply by tapping mud from his boots.

His black hair brushed his shoulders as he marched over, his pointed ears poking out from underneath the thick waves. He planted his feet in front of me, just close enough to feel invasive and stood wide, tucking in his charcoal wings tight, then leant toward me and sniffed. "But you are no human."

Not human?

I jerked back and grabbed onto my braid as if that was where the scent came from and glared. "Well neither are any of the others standing around by the look of it, so go sniff one of them."

Someone giggled.

The male's eyes flashed and a growl resonated from his chest.

Doesn't like to be spoken back to it seems.

"I think it's best we continue this conversation in private," announced the royal male at the front, cutting off any retort the fae in front of me was about to make—verbal or otherwise. "And so we don't take up any more attention from your evening," he continued, speaking to the fae standing around the ruins.

He looked toward the musicians who played again at his silent command, and the crowd immediately huddled in their groups to whisper.

"Killian, bring her forward," he said to the male in front of me, "and someone bring me Farro," he commanded to no one in particular.

Killian stepped to the side and gestured forward with his arm to start walking. On shaking feet, I stepped up to the dais, hoping their fae hearing couldn't pick up my trembling.

I wasn't confident though, as that auburn-haired male watched me from his pillar like a hunter. Something in the way his bright-green eyes followed my every movement screamed *predatory.* I dropped my head and continued walking, trying to ignore his and all the other sets of eyes on me.

I couldn't waste my efforts processing their reactions, I could only focus on the moment in front of me.

The two fae from the dais led the way down the back of the temple foundation and through an unremarkable opening away from the giant glass patio doors, then down a short corridor. The enormous fae named Killian stomped behind me.

They led the way into a plush space clearly reserved for private conversations. The female perched herself elegantly on one of the sofas, the male, who I could only assume was her husband, stood behind her, and Killian loomed by the door. They each looked at me, waiting for me to move.

"You may sit," said the female, her voice stern but not unkind.

Definitely royal.

"Do you know where you are?" she asked as I lowered, her eyes flitting between my own, searching for something there.

I willed my voice not to tremble. "Endence."

"Correct. To be more specific, you are at the Summer Palace, in the city of Elden," she said coolly. "I am Fleur Lòkith, Queen of the Summer Kingdom, and this," she gestured to the male behind her, "is my moiety, King Nakir."

I scrunched my face in confusion. "Your what?"

"My moiety," she repeated. "He is my other half." She smiled up at the male and grasped his hand.

Surely she doesn't mean that literally.

"Is that the same as a husband?"

Queen Fleur's eyes flashed with annoyance, and I immediately felt stupid. I had the good sense to sink lower into the lounge.

"It is not the same as husband and wife," King Nakir answered kindly. "Although Fleur and I are also married. A moiety is akin to a soulmate, a connection that transcends love. Two halves of the same soul. It is uncommonly rare for a cleaved fae to find their moiety and unite their souls, and so they are revered beyond measure. The bond between the two is unbreakable and possesses deep power."

"And. . . what is Farro?" I asked nervously, referring to the command Nakir had called out before we left the temple, terrified it was some sort of poison or torture device.

"A spoilt bastard," muttered Killian from where he stood to my left.

Fleur levelled him with a scathing glare only a mother could bestow. Now that I looked, the resemblance between Killian and the other two fae was easy to see.

Clearly related. He had Fleur's black hair and Nakir's blue eyes—his skin tone was a mix between the two. "Farro is the Crown Prince to the Summer Kingdom and should be here soon. But we are not here to discuss the gaps in your fae knowledge, girl," said Fleur. "Who are you?"

"I already told you—"

"Not your name." She lifted her hand to interrupt me. "To have the Oracle bring you directly to us is unheard of. Orella does not even speak to those who have not gone through her trials, yet she would escort a would-be human straight to my palace and deliver a warning?"

What in hell does that mean?

"That's been said twice now. What do you mean I'm not human?"

"It's clear you are undoubtedly fae. You haven't been around magic, have you?"

"No, I. . . I avoid it whenever I can. It irritates my skin." I ran my hands up and down my arms. Sweat had gathered at the nape of my neck and my skin tingled.

Time was almost up before the itching began. Fear lanced through me at what might become of me being surrounded by all this magic, particularly if what they were all claiming was true. "I have to go home, leave before—"

Fleur lifted her hand once again.

"You won't be leaving," she stated, brooking no argument. "But I presume you're referring to your reaction to magic?" I nodded. "Fae who aren't born in this realm grow without the features that define us until they find enough magic to transition. I've only come across one fae who transitioned, and I'm afraid you're in for an uncomfortable night, but we will provide a healer to help you through it."

"Transition? No, you don't understand, I have to go home. I don't belong here! It was a mistake. I was just running—and my horse—"

I hugged my arms around myself in an attempt to block my emotions. Block the magic from reaching me.

My efforts were futile, of course.

Everything was not as it seemed. Not an out-of-control horse, but an Oracle. Not a mistake, but intentional. I dropped my face in my hands.

Nakir rounded the sofa to sit beside his moiety. "I understand it must be quite a shock, Alora. But you are fae. . . you do belong here. Your parents would have undoubtedly known of their heritage, and with the Oracle's involvement, we need to understand what's happening—need you to tell us what you know."

I nodded—refusing to cooperate wasn't an option. "I don't know anything."

"Well, let's start with what you *do* know. What's your family name?"

"Bradford."

Nakir looked to Killian, who folded his arms across his chest and shrugged, his muscles straining against his dark tunic with the movement. "Likely an alias," he said in a deep voice. "What's your father's name?"

"Caldwell. But he's human. . . I mean—he doesn't have. . ."

"There are ways fae can mask their power and features if they wish. If your family name is indeed an alias, your father may have been in hiding and was likely taking precautions. Caldwell is also a name I don't recognise."

"What about your mother?" asked Nakir.

I dropped my gaze. "She died when I was young, after giving birth to my sister. I don't really remember her."

"I'm sorry you suffered her loss," said Fleur. "What was her name?"

I was taken aback by her sincerity. The queen seemed like she didn't show a softer side too often.

"My father called her Snow. . . but her name was Eira."

If they hadn't blinked, I might have thought they'd turned to stone. Fleur and Nakir sat with a preternatural stillness, while Killian's arms went slack at his sides and he took a step forward—his blue eyes burning into me as he assessed whatever he saw looking back at him.

I glanced between him and the two royals, who still hadn't stopped staring.

My discomfort reached new heights, and not just from the magic, though it now felt as if there were tiny creatures under my skin trying to burrow out.

It was clear my mother's name meant something to them. "You knew her."

"Where is Farro?" the queen whispered in a shaking breath.

"If he hasn't come yet, he won't be coming at all," Killian replied tightly.

King Nakir rose silently and walked to a liquor cabinet in the corner. He poured himself a tall glass and tossed it back, then a second. Killian ran his hand through his loose hair and turned on the spot like he was trying to find something to do with his body.

"Tell me how you knew her," I demanded.

Queen Fleur shifted uncomfortably and looked to the males in the room before she finally answered me. "Eira Ìréis is—was—the Queen of the Winter Kingdom."

Her words echoed through me, my brain struggling to accept what she said.

It was the last thing I remembered before my skin erupted with a burning irritation, and I was consumed by imagined flames.

I was screaming. That I knew for certain.

Screaming out air and failing to gasp any back in.

When I wasn't shrieking in pain, I wasn't there. My mind drifted somewhere unknown. Somewhere distant and peaceful and warm.

I slipped in and out of consciousness for what could have been a lifetime.

Strong hands had held me against a broad chest as I exploded with pain in the sitting room. The only soft thing about the male was the way he'd laid me down in my bed.

No, not my bed. But it was soft against my burning back, so I didn't fight it.

I remembered flashes of conversations at a door and faces next to mine. The memories were hazy, as though they had been dreams I couldn't quite hold on to. As quickly as each image appeared, it faded before I could see it clearly.

I saw Nakir at the foot of the bed, speaking to someone in the room. I'd seen Fleur on a separate occasion, standing in the doorway with a dark-haired male I didn't recognise. His black wings reflected a fire from somewhere, his lean body clearly tense as he whispered words at her I couldn't hear.

Most often there was a female with a round face and hazel eyes who spoke gently to me, though I never heard what she said above my screams.

Each time she appeared, the thick feeling of oil sliding down my throat was the last thing I'd remember before I slipped into oblivion.

Then.

The air thinned.

The magic lost its cloying effect. The feeling of drowning faded as I sucked in a breath, and the burning sensation eased to warm licks of flame that heated and soothed.

My brain fizzed to life, and my thoughts became clearer while time slowed to normal. My consciousness settled into place—lucidity returning to my crazed thoughts and a voice that I'd never heard but recognised called me further into the room.

'Open your eyes, Alora.'

I cracked my lids open, blinking back the gentle light. I looked down to find my body hidden beneath a woven blanket. I didn't notice anything amiss, but I did notice. . . something.

Noticed *more.*

Nakir's words echoed through me.

'You are *fae.'*

And now I was.

I looked around the small, empty room, its painted green walls and dark brown floorboards gave no hint at where I might be located, though I was sure I hadn't been moved far from the sitting room I'd been in.

I pressed my hands on the mattress to sit up and noticed the strength in my hands—the strength in my legs as I swung them and planted my feet on the floor. I even *heard* the faint press of my toes as they curled onto the smooth floorboards.

I'd been changed into a linen nightdress, its length halted at my knees as I stood and padded to a mirror leaning in the corner. Starting at my feet, I focused my attention and worked my way up, assessing as I went.

'Your parents undoubtedly knew. . .'

Of course.

If it were true my parents were both fae, then it was no surprise my body was already fae-like. Though where the fae were carved with utmost perfection, it was obvious I'd been cut from human cloth.

But not anymore.

The reflection looking back was without question, fae. Unchanged, yet still different. The strength I'd gained from my life on the farm and my father's diligent training was next to nothing compared to the strength coiling in my muscles now.

Definitely fae.

I wanted to vomit. Or cry. How could my father have kept this from me? Why had he kept it from me? Killian hadn't recognised his name—did that mean he'd been using a false one?

And then there was my mother. *A queen?* Was I the reason she deserted her throne?

More and more questions roared through my mind and made my head spin.

It already felt like a lifetime ago my life had been peaceful, my biggest worry being whether I stayed in Remberlie.

But in the space of a day, I'd been faced with an unwanted proposal, seen my fiancé in the arms of another woman, careened through the forest on a not-horse, told I wasn't human, told my mother had been a queen and finally my blood feel as though it boiled in my veins as I turned fae.

Even one of those things happening could tip a girl over the edge, let alone every single one at once. It was too much.

On second thought, I don't want to cry or throw up.

I want a drink.

I looked at my face and took note. Again, the same—yet changed. Gently pointed ears poked through my blonde strands. My freckles were harder to spot, my cheekbones a little higher and my black lashes a little longer. Though my emerald green and grey eyes sparkled back at me all the same.

But it was with those eyes that I noticed the biggest change of all. I twisted my torso around and looked at my back, my jaw dropping at what I saw.

All fae possessed leathery wings of some form. The fae in that temple all had differing shapes and shades—some large and strong, some small and insignificant, some were even elegant, but they were all similar in composition.

But the ones on my back, shining in my reflection, were not comparable in any way. They weren't even really there. White smoke curled around my back in twisting shapes and swirls, glowing with their own soft light as they drifted.

The wispy tendrils formed the arches and curling shapes of wings, their form flowing with every movement my body made, trailing in the air around me. As though the magic had thought to form my wings, but gave up halfway.

I didn't know how to process the sight, or even whether or not their appearance should alarm me.

"Oh, you're up," chimed a voice from the door, breaking my chain of thoughts.

I looked at the female who walked in with fresh linen and a tray of food. "We were beginning to wonder when you'd wake."

I recognised her. Recognised her brown hair and hazel eyes.

"You're the one who took care of me." My voice rasped as I spoke, a testament that the screaming had been real.

"I wondered if you'd remember. I'm Olette, one of the healers." She placed the items on the table. "We began to worry you wouldn't overcome it."

"You mean I did? I'm fae now?"

She planted her hands on her hips. "From what I heard, you always were, but yes, you're fae now. Fully transitioned."

"How long have I been out?"

"General Killian brought you here five days ago."

FIVE DAYS.

"Yes, five days," she repeated, and I realised I'd yelled it out loud. "I've never seen a transition happen, but one of the other healers said the last one she helped with had taken little more than a day. But, I believe your circumstances are greatly different."

"So, this is normal then?" I gestured to my wings. . . or lack of them.

"Ah, yes. . . um, they are definitely unusual–but that's not to say there is anything wrong with them," she assured. "Some strong fae are blessed with other abilities, and if what the king and queen said about. . . about who you are is true, then you having other abilities wouldn't be a surprise. A fae's wings are a source of their power, they are very important to each of us for it."

"Right. Okay, well that's. . . something I guess." I returned to look at them in my reflection as Olette bustled around with bottles and jars in a tall cabinet. A heavy scrape of clinking metal sounded against the shelf, and a strange sensation pulled at the base of my neck.

I spied the offending black mass high above. "What is that?

Olette edged away from the cabinet and contorted her face in a grimace. "It's Nulralt."

I looked at her blankly, conveying I'd need more of an explanation than that.

"It's a dark metal that nullifies magic. Vile stuff, but sometimes necessary. I'm sorry to say we had to lay it over you at times during your transition. Your magic was flaring, and we didn't know how devastating it would become."

I flinched and watched her with newfound weariness.

"We didn't want to, but it got extreme a few times," she placated. "I assure you, you're in no danger here, Alora."

I watched her carefully, but couldn't see any reason for her to be dishonest. If these fae wanted to kill me, they'd just passed up five days to do it in.

"Who's *we*?"

"Hm?"

"You said, '*we were beginning to wonder*', and '*we began to worry*', and '*we didn't want to*'. Who's we?"

"Why, the Lòkith family, of course. They all came to see you. King Nakir sat with you several times, and Queen Fleur was rife with concern. Even Prince Farro left his duties with the Summer Legion in Astorla and came to check on you."

That's awfully. . . considerate.

"I'll go tell them you're awake. Make sure you have something to eat," she said and motioned to the tray of food, then left me to my thoughts—and wings.

Less than an hour later, I was escorted through the hallways. Olette had provided me with loose cream clothes suitable to fit over my wings, though my smoky tendrils just seeped through in a wispy cloud that hung around my shoulders.

The fae leading me was dressed in the same flowy material as my own, and her small wings draped low. I kept several steps behind as we moved through the palace.

She led me along the halls and out through a grand marble archway that opened into what had to be the palace foyer. White and gold veins wove across the floor's black marble, punctuated by two great pillars and a sweeping staircase that curled around the circular room to a floor upstairs. The glass domed ceiling looked as though it touched the sky.

Fae moved about the foyer and along the balcony on the second floor. Everyone we passed turned their heads to look at me as I walked by, only this time, I heard their whispers. Even if I didn't catch their words, their questioning eyes on my form gave away who they gossiped about.

We walked around the back of the staircase and through an archway hidden behind, which led through to a much wider and quieter passage. The black marble fell away to large glossy white tiles, and together we walked uninterrupted along the hall. The only sound was the pad of my escort's slippered feet.

As I followed and peeked around her slim shoulder, I noticed the hallway opened up to reveal a stunning, rectangular arboretum. Glowing light filtered in through the windowed ceiling to the lush garden below.

Even looking with human eyesight the garden would've been beautiful. The magic of Endence turned colours bolder and brighter, so the verdant garden popped with dazzling shades of green and vibrant hues of pink and orange. But with my new fae eyesight, the result was astonishing.

The female I followed turned right at the garden and I was so encapsulated at the sight that I hadn't noticed the figures speaking together in the hallway that continued straight.

An older male stood just beyond the corner of the arboretum, holding a stack of tomes. His deep brown wings curled around his short frame as he leant forward, muttering to another male, too quietly even for my new fae hearing to pick up.

The male he was speaking to stood with his back to me, but even that sight itself was devastating.

He was tall and lean—his strong muscles easy to pick out even underneath his black shirt. From what I could see behind his wings, he had short, silky, raven hair. But it was those wings blocking his face I couldn't take my eyes off.

They were the same black wings I'd seen on the king and queen, held high and stretched wide, likely to give him and the male he was speaking with privacy.

But this male's wings weren't just black.

Warm, molten light moved along his membranes, like living veins of flame and embers. If what Olette said was true of a fae's wings, then this male was unimaginably powerful.

As my escort turned the corner to take us right, the males halted their hushed conversation suddenly, as they, too, noticed me.

The male with his back to me stilled—though my improved eyesight noticed the tiny flinch his impressive wings made. How he pulled his shoulders down and stood firm to accommodate the movement. He tilted his head just the barest fraction to look my way, but his wings blocked me from seeing his profile.

The other male holding the books snapped his eyes to mine and widened at what he saw, but recovered quickly and dipped his shoulders in a respectful bow as I walked.

Neither spoke to me as I continued down the path leading away from them, and I didn't look back, but I couldn't help but feel watched as I kept up with the female ahead.

A small antechamber came into view with a single carved gold door on the other side. My escort knocked and a warm voice answered from the other side.

King Nakir's office was luxurious. The enormous space was set up in three distinct areas. First, to the left sat two armchairs facing an unlit fireplace carved from the same black marble as the walls, and a small liquor cabinet to the side with crystal tumblers, polished and ready.

Above the mantle hung a huge map, with four sections of land marked out in ink, which I presumed was Endence.

A second sitting area to the right housed two large leather lounges positioned around a low glass table, clearly designed to accommodate larger groups.

The entire far wall was made from a single pane of glass, letting in light and giving an uninterrupted view of the arboretum I'd just walked past.

In front of the window was the Summer King's desk, cushioned by a large rug and framed on either side by bookshelves, neatly stacked with volumes that looked as though they were only pulled out for necessity rather than enjoyment.

The king stepped out from behind his desk and strode toward me as I crossed the threshold into his office. "Alora, how are you?" he greeted me warmly and bowed as he finished his approach.

"Oh, um. . ." I panicked and dropped into a poorly formed curtsy back at him, not knowing the protocols. He barked a laugh as he gestured toward the lounges.

More guests were expected then.

"I mean, I'm alive," I said, sinking into the cushions, my white tendrils sweeping around my shoulders. Somehow, I didn't think saying, *good thanks,* summed up the whirlwind brewing inside me.

"I'm sure you have questions."

You fucking bet I do.

"Firstly, I want to assure you of your safety here, Alora. I'm not sure what the human realm knows of ours, but humans who venture into Endence are always fearful, leading me to believe the stories of fae aren't kind."

"But I'm no human, am I."

He assessed me. "No. You certainly are not."

The door burst open and I whirled around to see who'd entered.

Killian stepped into the office and turned immediately to the liquor cabinet then poured himself a drink without uttering a word to either of us. The top half of his black, mid-length hair was tied at the back of his head, and his charcoal wings were tucked in.

The sword he'd drawn on me days ago was sheathed at his hip atop some kind of armour, made of tight, black leather–though it looked manoeuvrable enough to move at speed and not be restraining.

He drained the glass then turned in place to look at where the king and I sat.

"Alora, I don't believe the two of you have been properly introduced. This is my son, Killian Lòkith, General of the Summer Legion and Commander of the Winter Legion."

Why is he commanding the Winter Legion?

"Princess," he rumbled, not giving a shit, and wandered to the window at the back of the room.

I glared at his back as he went.

Asshole.

Nakir gave me an apologetic look and turned to face his son. "I saw Farro by the garden just now, did you pass him on your way?"

The male with the molten wings.

Killian made a rumbling noise that resembled a yes.

"Is he coming to join us?"

"No." He turned to face his father and palmed his glass. "The Almighty didn't deem the meeting important enough to schedule into his busy day, and has returned to Astorla."

Not important enough? So they're both assholes then.

Nakir kept his face from revealing anything further as he turned back to me with a weak smile, attempting to ease the awkwardness.

I looked down at my lap and kept my eyes locked on my fingers which I wrung together.

"Fleur will be here soon," Nakir continued. "But in the meantime, I was hoping you'd be able to answer a few questions, and we will help answer any of yours of course. How does that sound?"

I nodded silently, apprehensive of how much further life as I knew it was about to be changed forever.

"The other night, you mentioned a sister?" He gestured for me to start talking.

He probably hoped an easy topic would help break the ice.

"Yes, her name is Delilah—Della."

"And does she know you were brought here?"

"No. She is. . . unwell." A question pulled at the edges of my mind, just out of reach. "Only my father would have seen me enter the forest."

"Your father being Caldwell, that is?"

"Yes. You really don't know who he is?"

"I don't recognise his name, no," Nakir said. "But as Killian said, it's likely an alias. Gods, he could be a human for all we know, though I doubt it, given who your mother was."

I thought of my father and moments from our past surfaced. Almost every conversation took on a whole new meaning, and I became dizzy from the realisation.

"He's fae," I whispered. "I'm sure of it. But why would my father use an alias and not my mother? It doesn't make sense. Is he even my father?"

Nakir sighed. "There are many possibilities. It would be best to wait for Fleur to discuss your family any further, though."

Silence stretched between us as I cast my eyes back down to my lap, wondering what the truth was.

"I want to go see him. I want to leave." I looked back to the king and tried to let my expression be one of determination. "I want to go home."

Killian raised a brow and flicked his gaze between his father and me.

Nakir just looked apologetic once again. "I'm sorry, Alora. But that's just not possible."

Stabbing pain and the feeling of utter helplessness flooded me and I didn't know whether I wanted to cry or get mad. I squeezed my eyes closed, willing either emotion to leave. I was here for information, and blowing up at these fae wouldn't help my case, nor would it persuade them to let me have my own way, either. So I decided to make the most of the situation and find out what was happening to me. "I had a question. . . about my wings," I said nervously, breaking the quiet.

It was then that the office door clicked open and Fleur swept in. Her deep-orange dress floated behind her as she walked, and she kept her black wings angled down in a gentle drape along her back.

I went to stand and greet her formally, but she waved her hand at me to stay put. "Alora, I'm glad to see you've made it through the transition finally. Your fae heritage suits you," she said then sat next to her moiety.

I nodded, not sure how to respond without sounding vain.

Nakir draped his arm over her shoulders. "Alora was just asking about her wings."

"Yes, of course you have questions. What do you want to know?"

"The healer said she's never seen wings like them, but that nothing is wrong. That wings are a source of power. I—I don't know anything about being fae. . ." I dropped my head, feeling foolish. "What does this all mean?"

To my surprise, it was Killian who answered.

"Olette was right." He stepped forward and stood amongst the lounges. "Endence is a realm of magic—it's in the land, in the air, the soil. The fae and all creatures of Endence are born from it. Fae use their wings to draw the magic of the realm into them like a plant draws energy from the sun. We use it for any manner of power we might possess. The greater our wings, the greater our power."

I couldn't help but look at his own incredible wings showing over his shoulders. He smirked at me as he saw my eyes assess them. A smug sneer if ever I saw one.

This male is powerful, and he knows it.

Farro's wings also came to mind, how his had that living flame within them. I guess his tremendous power earned him the right to command their legion.

"As well as wings being their own key to power, breeding is also a factor. Royal bloodlines are exceptionally strong," Fleur interjected with pride. "The final way a fae may possess great strength is from being the offspring of a united couple, which you also are."

"My mother and father were moieties?"

"Queen Eira ruled by her husband and moiety, Valefor, for over two centuries, though. . . he is not the same male you know as Caldwell. I sent my spy to confirm it while you transitioned. I am certain you are Valefor's daughter. We all knew your father, but he has not been seen in years. I am sorry."

My heart fell. Just another shattering revelation to add to the list. Caldwell wasn't my father, and I didn't know the male who was. Tears sprang in my eyes.

"Is he still alive?" My voice cracked as the words left my mouth.

"Yes, we know he lives because of the Oracle's Amulet," she answered. "It's a stone that Orella gave our ancestors when our Kingdoms were founded. Each amulet glows with the power of their sworn monarchs and will stop shining when they Fade, only to shine again when the heir takes the throne. The Winter amulet has not stopped glowing. It's one of the reasons the fae of the Winter Kingdom have remained strong, waiting for their leaders to return. News of their queen's death will devastate them." She winced as the grief brushed over her.

"You have made no vow to your Kingdom," she continued, "and therefore it will not shine for you. To hear that your mother passed decades ago means the amulet continues to shine for Valefor. He is out there somewhere."

I tried to make sense of my feelings—a strange mix of grief for Caldwell, as well as happiness that I had a father out there somewhere, and a little pissed off he'd never been part of my life.

Did he even know I existed? Was he safe?

"What happened to them? To my mother and Valefor? Why did they leave?"

"That, I don't know the answer to," the queen answered sadly. "Given your age and the timing of it all, I would presume they left when Eira fell pregnant with you. That Valefor was not with you is distressing. They were moieties after all, and the soul will not split so easily apart without great cause. Eira never disclosed any reasons with us."

Nakir shook his head in agreement.

Fleur continued. "Alora, you are a royal fae, the child of a united pair—undoubtedly powerful with abilities you cannot control, nor know the full extent of, *and* you had a personal escort into Endence from the Oracle. Make no mistake, you are here for a reason."

I swallowed audibly at the weight of her statement.

"Nakir and I knew your parents well, Alora, and we were close allies. The boundaries of the Kingdoms were not drawn to divide us, but to divide and conquer against our enemy."

I glanced at the map above the fireplace and the rumours from Evamere about the fae and an impending war circulated in my memories.

Fleur followed my gaze to the framed parchment. It wasn't detailed—black lines outlined four territories and highlighted features like mountain ranges and lakes.

"Who *is* our enemy?"

The queen paled and drew in a long, steadying breath. "All you need to know right now is that demons once walked this realm, Alora. Demons who, along with their followers, sought to destroy everything we hold dear. The fae did what was necessary to stop them, and we paid dearly for the reprehensible acts they executed."

A chill swept across the back of my neck.

"For our Kingdoms to continue their success—for the realm to prosper—we must maintain all that is already in place." She paused, then swallowed before she went on. "You are the future queen of the Winter Kingdom, and we would like to continue our alliance through you as you take your throne."

My tears dried up as the heavy words pressed on me. "My *throne*? No. I don't—you can't mean—I'm not—"

Speak a full sentence, Alora!

Nakir merely gave that warm smile again, sending reassurance to me. "It's okay Alora, we don't mean immediately. We realise it's a lot to take in. The Winter Kingdom has been led by others these past few decades, they will continue to manage just fine while you learn to understand and control your power. I do, however, think it would be wise to keep your lineage between us for now, just until we find out why you've been brought here. We never know when our enemy is looking for ways to gain an advantage."

Fleur and I nodded in agreement. Killian rolled his eyes.

"Can't we just go ask the Oracle ourselves?" I asked.

Killian let out a bitter laugh. "The Oracle lives in her own territory. To get to her temple and survive her trial in order to speak with her is a near death sentence, even for a trained warrior. You wouldn't last three minutes."

What's the bet you can't last three minutes, either?

Fleur smiled knowingly at her son. "Which is exactly why *you* are going to train her."

Chapter 9
The Start

"What!" Killian and I shouted at the same time.

"Might I remind you I have duties to perform?" Killian growled at his mother.

"Consider this your duty now, Killian," Fleur levelled.

"Are my skills worth so little to you, mother, that you would have me babysit some faeling princess?"

"It is for your skills that I choose you to train this princess." Annoyance flickered in her sharp tone.

I sank into the cushions at the awkwardness of the brewing argument—of being spoken about like I wasn't three feet away.

"I have no interest in playing chaperone and tutor," he fumed. "Find a master of arms if you wish for her to know how to swing a sword."

"No, Killian, I choose *you* to teach her how to wield more than a piece of steel."

"I am the Commander of her Legion!" he roared.

Fleur's power thrummed through the room as her temper boiled over. "And I am your Queen!" she snarled back with the same vehemence and stood to meet his level.

Killian clenched his hands. There was no argument he could give to get around that one. He puffed out a breath in anger and stomped back over to the liquor cabinet to refill his glass. Twice.

Nakir stood and rested his hand on Fleur's shoulder, urging her to sit and calm down.

Killian shot a glare at his mother but wisely kept his mouth shut.

"Killian, it is precisely your position as commander that we would ask this of you," Nakir said, trying a calmer approach. "You are in a perfect position to guide her through what you already know, and your skill—not only with a weapon, but with wielding your own power—will help teach her to develop her own. Your acceptance amongst her people, amongst the Legion as their Commander and as a royal yourself in her court, will ease her passage onto her throne. She was brought here by the Oracle, Killian. We are not asking you to watch over a fae of no importance. We are entrusting a royal into your care, who is here for reasons only Orella knows, and until we do, we are entrusting her to you so that she might be ready for whatever is to come."

The rumours of the looming war ran through my mind again.

What is coming?

Killian scoffed and disdain dripped from him in waves, then he glared at a spot on the floor with his arms crossed. Nobody spoke while they waited for him. I thought about breaking the silence, but I was terrified one wrong word would stoke the flames of the argument again.

Despite being fae, despite being told I was a royal, despite being told I was safe amongst allies, the truth was I was a stranger here. I knew nothing of the fae, save for their power. Knew nothing of their protocols. I had no allies here, nor any standing or authority.

So I kept silent.

Killian finally lifted his glare and slid his blue eyes to mine.

"Pack your bags, *Princess,*" he growled as he stomped toward the door. "We fly at dawn."

"Well that'll be a quick task, I have neither bags nor wings to fly with," I retorted at his departing back.

His rumbling, "*fucking hell*" reached us as he stormed away.

✧ ✧ ✧

After Killian left, the king and queen assured me that despite his demeanour, Killian took his duties seriously and that the only danger I should fear from him was his brooding.

However, I couldn't help but think I'd just agreed to be ushered off with one of their most powerful leaders who made no attempt to hide his contempt toward me. Then they'd summoned my escort, who brought me to a guest suite in a different part of the palace.

Apartment was a more appropriate word for the space. If a suite had an entrance hall, it was more than just a room.

Decorated in warm tones and sleek tiles, the space exuded the decadence. This place was pure luxury.

My eyes watered when I stepped into the bathroom and saw the size of the tub. My first thought was it could have easily fit four people in it, but I had to remind myself there weren't *people* here–but winged fae. So I adjusted my estimate to two.

My second thought was that it was going to take forever to fill such a large bathtub, but when I twisted the taps on, I could've cried at the high pressure, making quick work of filling it to the brim.

I sunk into the steaming water up to my shoulders and my swirling wings twisted around me in unison with the steam from the bath.

The last time I'd bathed had been the morning of the eclipse, which was now nearly six days ago.

Gross.

I soaked until my skin wrinkled, and lost count how many times I scrubbed my hair and body with the sweet soaps and oils left for me, then changed into a set of clothes an attendant brought.

As I sat alone at a small dining table and ate my dinner in silence, my mind flooded with all the events that had happened. Even though it had been about a week, no thanks to my transition, to me it felt like everything since the eclipse had occurred within twenty-four hours.

Reeling with too many life-altering circumstances, I abandoned my food and crept into the massive waiting bed and curled on my side to avoid flattening my wings, which were a strange, soft presence at my back.

I couldn't keep carrying the pain I'd brought with me into Endence. With so many hurts and revelations wanting to batter me in this new life,

I couldn't be concentrating on the ones from the life I now couldn't return to.

So I let it hurt, and let it go.

I pulled my knees to my chest, buried my face in the pillows, and let the tears I'd been holding back finally fall. Every piece of information threatening to blow apart life as I knew it cycled through my mind. I let misery take me to sleep with the same words looping through my mind.

Lito. Oracle. Fae. Queen. Caldwell. Valefor. Throne. Killian.

I wouldn't say I woke the next morning. Waking implied sleep. I'd laid in that bed on the verge of oblivion, but every time sleep tried to pull me under, a face of someone I loved flashed in my mind's eye along with their secrets.

Lito and his deceit, my mother and her title, Orella and her warning, Caldwell and his identity, my own face—now permanently altered and frozen in time.

I crawled out of bed and saw to my needs. An attendant brought a bag with another set of clothes and breakfast, which I ate in silence once more. With every bite, my tiredness ebbed, but my anxiety rose.

I had no idea where I was headed, no idea how long it would take, no idea how Killian planned on getting me there. I was putting my very life in the hands of a powerful fae I'd only just met, who had a clear dislike for me.

And then there were those enemies that neither the king nor queen had elaborated on yesterday.

I dressed in the black tights and a cream sweater I'd been provided then donned a forest green cloak to block the early morning chill.

My dutiful escort was waiting as I stepped into the hall and led me toward the entrance to the palace. As we neared the top of the grand staircase, a looming shadow came into view.

No, not a shadow. Killian.

He stood in that black-on-black-on-black battle armour, in what I now assumed was his usual stance. His feet planted apart, arms crossed in front of his chest, ridiculous muscles bulging, pectorals puffed, wings tucked in, eyes narrowed and impatient.

He looked me over as I approached, his expression fixed in an unwelcome scowl. I made sure I planted the sweetest smile on my face as I came to a stop in front of him.

Despite looking like he could crush my skull with one broad hand, and the clear disposition that he'd like nothing more than to do it, I didn't need to let his petulance affect me. I wasn't going to add *tiptoeing around a pissed-off commander* to my growing list of worries.

If what was discussed yesterday was true, then he and I were equals in terms of rank. Me even more so if I was to inherit a throne and he wasn't. Despite not having a singular clue how to be a royal, I wasn't going to take shit from him.

"So good of you to finally grace me with your presence, *Princess.*"

"You're welcome," I chirped and beamed faux cheerfulness at him, coming off far too strong to be anything but sarcastic.

He growled his annoyance, rolled his eyes then turned on his heel, leaving me to chase after him down the curved staircase. As we reached the marble floor and strode toward the entrance, I spied a gleaming figure out of the corner of my eye.

Something about it demanded attention, and I couldn't resist locking my eyes on the dark shadow.

Leaning on a pillar with an air of indifference, was the auburn-haired fae from the temple, holding a wickedly sharp dagger lightly in his long fingers and picking at his nails.

Killian pulled up short as he noticed the male as well, causing me to do the same before I smacked into his wings. He made that noise of annoyance again as the mysterious fae flipped the dagger in his hand and sheathed it with practised ease.

He strode toward us with elegant steps and his midnight wings spread slightly.

He was lean, and even without my improved fae eyesight, I would have seen his tight muscles beneath his fitted black jacket.

Do these males not know any other colours?

He strolled toward us with lazy intent, but his eyes rooted me to the spot like prey caught in a predator's stare. When he stopped in front of us, I noticed he was about as tall as Killian. The ridiculous flick to the front of his hair gave him an extra inch or two.

"Took you long enough," he purred with a voice like smoke and a sinful smile.

I bristled at yet another male time-keeping me.

"What are you doing here?" Killian growled before I could respond.

"Nothing to worry your pretty little head over, General. I was just on my way out," he said to Killian, though his gaze was still fixed on mine.

Killian huffed and went to step away, but the fae spoke again, halting him. "Where are you going?" he asked with polite curiosity, cocking his head and finally looking at Killian.

A shiver ran down my spine at how he moved. Lethal and fluid—unmistakably fae.

"You already know the answer to that."

"And who is your lovely companion, General?" He slid his sparkling, emerald-green eyes back to my grey one, smiling.

"You already know the answer to that, too," Killian said impatiently.

I wanted to glare at Killian for speaking in my stead, but something about this mysterious fae screamed danger, so I kept my mouth shut.

Either the male had the same thought, or my face had given me away, because he smiled broadly and his pointed canines flashed. "I do hope you'll let her speak at some point, General."

Killian flexed his hand like he had to reach out and grab some of the patience that just left him.

"Though be careful when you do, she looks capable of undoing a male with more than just her words."

My brows pulled together in confusion before I understood the depraved double meaning of his words. The white tendrils of my wings flared in annoyance.

I did indeed open my mouth then, in preparation to spit *fuck you* at the stranger, but before I could, he bowed deeply—his great wings stretched out. "Princess Alora," he purred darkly before I could fire my retort, then raised his head to smile at me one last time, finishing with a wink.

I startled. I could count on one hand the amount of people who were supposed to know who I was—and he wasn't any of the royals from the king's office, the healer, or Killian's brother, Farro, with the living fire flowing through his wings.

The male's wicked grin spread further as he noted my shock. As though he could read my thoughts and see me trying to process how he knew who I was.

Merciful Gods, can fae read minds?

Without another word, he straightened and strode past us and out the door before the beat of his leathery wings sounded as the male flew away.

Killian clenched his fists and rolled his neck, like he was brushing off his annoyance. I'd prepared myself to not allow Killian's bad temper affect me, but this unknown male had easily managed to grate my mood.

"Who the fuck was that?" I shot at Killian, entirely pissed off.

He rubbed his temple and groaned. "He's the Fox. The royal spy."

I looked back out the open entrance the fae had just strolled through as though I'd see him there.

The spy the queen sent to confirm Caldwell's identity.

"Is that how he knows who I am? He works for your mother?"

"Even if he didn't do the queen's bidding, he would still know who you were." He turned to me. "Rules don't apply to the Fox, so I'd stay clear if I were you. Especially if you want to live."

I was taken aback by his warning. The impression I'd gotten yesterday was that all fae were on the same side despite which Kingdom they belonged to.

"Surely someone who does the queen's bidding is someone safe?" I pried, wondering why my ally's spy was someone her own son was telling me to stay away from.

Killian walked toward the door and said over his shoulder, "None of us are safe, Princess."

Well, that's just fucking great.

I followed Killian outside into the morning air and took in the palace grounds. The redwood forest I'd glimpsed at the temple upon my entrance into this realm surrounded the entire estate. There were no curling hedges or manicured gardens to be seen, only the stunning natural beauty of an ancient woodland.

The soft forest floor arced in front of us in a large open space and to the right, it was as though the world fell away as soil met a stone ledge and disappeared at a sheer cliff. I wandered over and gazed out.

The rising sun set the spreading landscape alight in a stunning glow. The continuing forest was nearly all I could see stretching to the horizon where it met tips of mountains that cut across the skyline, stretching across from the east and blocking what lay beyond from sight.

I closed my eyes, letting the morning breeze blow away the tension that had just built. Not only at what the Fox had said, but this whole situation I found myself in. From Thane, to Lito, to every life-altering development I'd been told, to finding myself now on an unavoidable trip with a brooding male for Gods knew how long.

It was that particular brooding male who I sensed at my back, and his caramel and wood-smoke scent wrapped around me.

Ironic that such a cold bastard could have a scent so warm.

"The Winter Kingdom," he uttered over my shoulder, "lies directly north over the Asotines, that mountain ridge on the horizon."

I opened my eyes and followed the direction of where he pointed. "It'll take four days to reach the legion campgrounds over the border, it's time to get moving." He strode to where two horses waited.

"Wouldn't it be quicker to fly?" I wondered why he wouldn't want to get rid of me as fast as possible.

Killian faced me. "Yes, Princess, it would be quicker. But as you may have noticed, you don't have wings. Not useful ones, anyway." My misting wings flared as if personally offended, and I scowled. "And I don't feel like carting your arse for hundreds and hundreds of miles for the better part of an entire day."

Stubbornness set up my spine, and I folded my arms across my chest. "You can't just *click* your fingers or something and appear wherever you'd like?"

"That would be called *sifting,* Princess, and to do that requires an incredible amount of power."

"Fall short, do you?" I sassed under my breath, seeing the easy jab.

A growl ripped from his chest. The irritable male clearly didn't appreciate being seen as anything less than high and mighty. In the time it took to blink, Killian went from standing before the horses to standing right in front of me with his boots butted up against mine.

A yelp escaped me before I could control myself and I stumbled back a step.

"No, as a matter of fact, I don't," he rumbled as he leant over me.

I pressed my hand over my thumping heart. Thankfully, Killian backed off straight away and returned to the horses.

"But if I sifted with you, I'd run the risk of splitting you in half in the process—and I'm sure the Summer Queen, as well as the entirety of the Winter Kingdom, would be rather displeased with me if I were to arrive with only part of you." My face twisted in disgust at the image he created. "So mount up, Princess."

I walked over to the two brown horses saddled and waiting against a giant redwood.

"Is this one going to turn into an oracle, too?" I asked sarcastically at Killian's back, scratching my mount's nose while he adjusted the straps on his own.

"Hopefully one that will take you back to Evamere."

"Fuck you," I spat, releasing the words I wanted to fire at the Fox moments before.

Killian twisted at his hips, facing me slowly, his gaze laced with venom.

I wanted to shrink into my skin, realising I'd once again mouthed off at a powerful fae prince in the front gardens of his damn palace. I made my spine go rigid, remembering I, too, was a royal and supposedly powerful.

But Killian ran his gaze over my body, and a cruel sneer curled his lips. "No thanks," he scoffed and grabbed the reins of his horse to lead it down the path. My mouth popped open at his sheer nerve.

"Egotistical prick," I muttered.

I followed reluctantly, leading my mount a few paces behind. After several minutes of winding through the trees, stone buildings came into view, and the soft forest floor gave way to the cobbled streets of the city.

Elden melded effortlessly with its natural landscape. A little creek that flowed through the trees wended between the houses that popped up, before falling over a small waterfall and widening to cross under an arched bridge.

Houses that lined the roads behind were flush with plants and bordered with wooden fences. I was taken aback as I watched the fae going about their day, noticing they seemed as ordinary as humans completing their tasks. . . if it weren't for their wings and pointed ears and stunning, youthful faces.

As we went further into the city and walked on the main thoroughfare, the street became crowded and a few sets of eyes landed on us.

Landed on me.

As fae lent into one another to whisper, I hoped the rumour mill in Endence wasn't as brutal as Evamere.

I followed Killian through the crowds, but my attention was fixed on the tops of the buildings—at the fae flying above. Their wings gliding across the rooftops or taking higher into the clouds away from the city altogether.

I smiled to myself at how beautiful they were to watch.

How long had I dreamed of that feeling of freedom? To take off on a horse and leave my town behind? The thought warmed me for only a moment before my heart ached. How long had I dreamed of leaving my town behind, and now, all of a sudden, I *was* gone? I winced at the pain that shot through me.

Caldwell. Della. Lito.

Not now, Alora.

When I raised my eyes, Killian had stopped ahead and was watching me intently. A strange expression swept across his face but was gone before I could get a read on it.

"Wait here," he instructed and went over to greet a fae working at a produce shop. She handed him a wrapped bundle which he stored in his saddlebag. He left again to speak to a male at a different shop on the other side of the street and was again handed a package before he returned to his horse.

Provisions stored away, he continued on without speaking to me, clearly assuming I was following diligently. I hoped he could feel the daggers I was glaring at his back.

He led us wordlessly through the main city street, and it was only when we passed through a set of gates and the cobbled stones fell away to soft forest floor again that he mounted his horse and looked over his shoulder, seeing that I did the same.

Again, without deigning to speak to me, he nudged his horse forward with a kick and set out through the forest, expecting me to follow.

Four days is going to feel like four lifetimes.

Chapter 10
The General

Killian led the way at a slow pace and didn't once turn to speak to me. Not that I minded. For one, I was too busy taking in the spectacular beauty of the forest, and secondly, I didn't have much to say to the irritable prince.

Instead, I listened to the creatures of the forest chirp and call to one another amongst the branches and roots. The peaceful sounds helped my mind become empty and calm, but I soon filled the blank space with all the worries I had. All the unknowns I now faced.

We spent the majority of the day travelling on a main road, passing fae with carts laden with supplies. Somewhere around midday, when the sun's heat reached us through the trees, and I stripped off my cloak, Killian turned off onto a smaller path that led amongst a quieter, denser part of the forest. We didn't pass another traveller after that.

After several more hours travelling in silence, Killian gestured to a small clearing just off the path. "Here will do."

He dismounted and unstrapped the saddlebags from his horse as I pulled up beside him. I hopped down from my mount and winced at the searing pain shooting through my thighs from riding for hours. As I came around the front to scratch between my horse's ears, Killian came around his own horse and pulled up short before he collided with me.

"Gods, what good are your fae senses if you don't use them?" I snapped. Despite not having much to say to the male, being ignored all day hadn't been fun either, and my temper was on a short leash because of it.

Killian cocked his head to the side and a flash of confusion swept across his face before his familiar brooding scowl returned. He opened his mouth to no doubt shoot a retort back but stopped himself. "There's a stream just beyond those trees," he settled on instead, motioning a little further into the forest. "Take the horses to drink while I set up the camp."

I furrowed my brow at the lack of fight the moody general put up, but just nodded my okay and took the reins of his horse.

I didn't think to worry about my safety since Killian had been at ease the entire day, and I hadn't heard any dangerous noises from the creatures amongst the trees.

Hopefully, that struck true through the night as well.

I took the opportunity to rinse at the edge of the cool water as the horses drank and refilled the water pouches. I contemplated throwing Killian's into the rushing stream, but his temper was nearly unbearable as it was without being provoked. It wouldn't be worth the foul mood I'd be condemned to suffer through afterwards.

When I came back to where I'd left him and secured the horses to a tree amongst a patch of growth, he'd already set up a small shelter with a decent fire going. The sun was dropping quickly beyond the trees and the temperature along with it. I laid out my bedroll between the fire and shelter then sat down, stretching my legs and easing the tension from riding as I massaged my aching muscles.

Killian wordlessly passed me a plate of food and walked off between the trees out of view. He hadn't returned by the time I'd finished eating, but I refused to be concerned for him. He stomped around like a big, tough fae, so I'd treat him as such. And if he ran into something he couldn't handle, I wouldn't be any help anyway, so there was no use worrying about that either. Instead, I turned on my side, closed my eyes and let my troubles find me once again.

I woke with a gasp and bolted upright. The fuzzy images of the dream that woke me faded too fast for me to grab onto.

The sky was midnight black above—the trees too thick to see the stars that peppered it. I looked across and saw Killian sitting on his bedroll, his huge forearms resting on his bent knees, dark wings curled around his broad shoulders and blue eyes fixed on me.

I was immediately fatigued. Whether from the turmoil of my life, the lack of sleep or the riding, I wasn't sure. But I certainly didn't want to deal with his mood right now, so I dropped my gaze and turned to lie back down.

"You talk in your sleep."

I almost didn't hear him above the crackle of the fire between us.

My cheeks heated with embarrassment, but I was at a loss as to what to say.

I focused on a particular curled leaf on the ground in front of me, trying to remember what I'd dreamt about.

"Who's Pepper?"

A sad smile tugged at my lips. "My best friend," I muttered as a tear crept along my lashes. "She's the kindest person you'd ever meet, and could give your spy a run for his money with how well she could figure out everyone's secrets." I chuckled softly.

Killian scoffed at the mention of the Fox.

"I miss her," I said more to myself, though I know he heard me.

"And Della is your sister, right?"

I made a small noise of agreement and nodded.

"You said she's sick?"

I made that same noise again then creased my brows. There was something I was supposed to remember about Della. Something that didn't make sense.

"And who's Dale?" he asked after a beat of silence when I didn't elaborate any further on Della.

I let out a stronger laugh at that one and shook my head smiling, despite the thoughts of that wretched bird. "You don't need to waste any effort learning who Dale is."

"What about Lito?"

The question was asked with the same levelled curiosity as the others, but that name cut through the air like a knife, severing any happiness that had momentarily built inside and silenced the night.

My smile faded as I kept my eyes firmly locked on that curled leaf, my body racing to shut itself down and build walls around my mind before the hurt could creep its way in through the cracks. I was afraid if I so much as blinked, it would set my tears loose, or if I let out the breath I was holding, I would release a sob along with it.

I didn't trust myself to let the pain out and be able to stop. I didn't want Killian to see me so vulnerable.

It felt like a lifetime passed before I was confident enough to move after hearing that name out loud. The only thing I could manage to do was turn away from Killian and lay back down, shutting my eyes against the pain.

Yeah, what about Lito?

The morning sun shining through my closed lids pulled me from sleep. As I squinted through the light and focused on the trees standing above, I noticed the little birds flitting through the branches. A rustle across from me drew my attention to the dark shadow that was Killian, sitting on a fallen log and drinking what smelled like tea. He didn't look at me, but I knew he realised I was awake. I turned my head to look above me once more.

"Are there sprites in this forest?"

"There are," he replied, his deep voice hoarse with sleepy disuse.

"Why haven't we seen any? I've only seen birds and animals that I'd find in the human realm, nothing magical."

"Trust me, Princess, it's a good thing we haven't seen anything else."

I glanced at him. "Do we not want to see other magical creatures?"

"Typically not. But there's nothing in these woods that we need to be concerned about. . . in case you were fretting."

I caught the condescension laced in his words and rolled my eyes.

He didn't elaborate any further and took a long sip of his tea. Then, "But to answer the question you're really asking–you don't see sprites because they don't want to be seen."

"I saw sprites in the forest by my house all the time."

He looked at me like I was missing the obvious. "Considering who you are, that's not surprising."

Wait.

"What are you saying? They showed themselves to me so I'd come here?"

Killian continued giving me that pointed look and drained his tea with an obnoxiously loud sip.

They showed themselves to me so I'd come here.

I stared into the middle distance, my brain trying to come to terms with what that meant. Killian stood and poured another mug of tea then handed it to me while refilling his own.

"Sprites are as mischievous as they come, but they're not stupid. They react to the power in Endence on a level that us higher fae can't feel. Any humans who came here and back would have served a purpose. You saw sprites for a reason."

What purpose did that hunter serve?

"So, what? They showed themselves in the hope I'd go out to the forest so they could portal me here for whatever reason I'm needed? And because I never did, they tired of waiting and Orella came and got me herself?"

"Oh, I wouldn't dare assume to know Orella's motives," he said, gesturing to himself. "But your guess makes sense, Princess."

I glowered at him, but he ignored it.

Fucking hell.

"So, if I found a sprite, would it portal me home?"

"Don't get your hopes up, you're not going anywhere." I noticed a vein throb at his temple. "But yes, if a sprite wanted to, it could. Though none would go against Orella."

"She can control sprites? Is the Oracle really that powerful?"

"Not specifically, but she's incredibly powerful. . . in her own way."

"Care to elaborate?" My patience with the male wearing thin.

He rolled his eyes. "I don't know if she can swing a sword or fire a bow, though I still wouldn't bet against it. Her powers are that of the mind. She can see parts of the future, glean what is to come–give prophecies. She can also tear a mind apart, will a being into doing whatever she desires, plant visions or nightmares."

My eyes widened. That kind of power was terrifying. The ability to interfere with someone's mind like that was truly frightening.

And I'd kept her in a barn.

Killian pulled a smirk at whatever he saw in my expression. "I wouldn't worry too much, Princess. Orella doesn't interfere with fate. She's only stepped in once, and that was a long time ago."

I was almost too scared to ask, but did anyway. "What did she do?"

"She cast an evil from our realm. Some claim she ripped their minds apart, but it's all exaggerated nonsense."

I blanched at the idea of such a sickening punishment. "Exactly how long ago is, *a long time ago*, to fae?"

Killian scratched the back of his head like he was thinking. "Depends on the fae I guess, but the business with Orella was thousands of years ago."

"She's thousands of years old?" I yelled. That amount of time to be alive was unfathomable. "But what even is she? She's not fae." I'd come to that conclusion when I saw her in that temple.

"No, she's not fae," he said, agreeing with my assessment. "We fae don't possess prophetic magic, being just one clue."

"Do prophecies always come true?"

He pulled an expression too briefly to track.

"Yes. Prophecies can always be interpreted in different ways, of course. What one *believes* it means may not be what it *actually* means. But yes, Orella is always right. But. . . I couldn't tell you exactly what she is. It's possible she's from another realm entirely."

Another realm?

Humans only knew of Endence, how many other realms were there? I let the thoughts sink in as I looked around the forest surrounding our little clearing, but Killian's voice interrupted the peace once again. "Now get your royal arse up. It's time to go."

We packed the camp quickly and stopped by the stream before we continued down the path. Killian resumed his brooding and barely spoke another word to me other than saying we'd be out of the forest by midmorning and would reach the mountains at nightfall.

Apparently, he'd reached his word quota for the day after being so forthcoming at breakfast.

I followed silently as we kept a steady pace. Just before we reached the edge of the forest, Killian stopped us to rest the horses before we took a straight shot to the mountains.

When we were ready to get going and I kicked my leg over my horse, Killian finally broke whatever vow of silence he'd made against me.

"Once we leave the forest, we also leave behind any safety it afforded us," he said with total seriousness as he came to stand by my horse.

The General was so tall I barely had to look down at him. He pulled out a dagger and held it out for me to take. It was longer than the one I'd kept in my boot on the farm.

I took the weapon from him and admired it. Plain and certainly not a weapon writers would tell adventurous tales about, but the black leather hilt was comfortable to hold, and the silver blade would gut a pig with ease.

Or a general if he got too mouthy.

"Do you know how to use it, Princess?" His words were laced with condescension.

"If you're worried my pitiful, female brain can't figure out which end to use, Killian, save your sympathies."

"Can't be too cautious, Princess. Wouldn't want you hurting yourself now, would we?" He winked before turning on his heel.

Gods, he's a dick.

I glared at his back and secured the dagger under the saddle bag strap.

Killian swung onto his horse and kicked it into motion. His brown mare took off down the path at a gallop, and I nudged mine to keep up. After a minute, the redwood trees thinned out and the land beyond peeked through. Then, all too quickly, we broke the tree line and the uninterrupted view before me took my breath away.

Stretches of wild grass and gently rolling hills covered the expanse between the forest and the sprawling mountain range known as the Asotines. The meadow was dotted with white and purple wildflowers and spent dandelions that burst apart, sending their tiny little tufts to float on the breeze as our horses pressed ahead.

Where the Lawns outside of my farm had been green and manicured, this meadow was untamed and free, but just as breathtaking.

I couldn't help the smile that stretched across my face as the wind rushed through my hair.

Nor could I help the freeing laugh that left me.

I dropped my shoulders down and threw my hands out wide as I tilted my head back to the brilliant sky, revelling in the warmth on my skin and the pull of my twirling wings as we charged ahead.

This is what I wanted to feel.

When I grabbed the reins and refocused, Killian turned his head over his shoulder to look back at me, and his lips curled into a smile.

I closed the gap between our horses and rode alongside him. He kept his vivid blue eyes fixed on me while he stood in his stirrups and raised his leg, planting his thick boot on the top of his saddle.

I looked at him questioningly, but he merely returned my expression with a wicked gleam before he spread his wings out and shot into the sky several feet above his galloping horse.

He soared overhead, keeping the same speed as the horses for a moment before he looked down at me still galloping below and gave me that smile again.

I couldn't tell if it held any cruelty, or if he was simply showing off—or perhaps he was genuinely happy to be in the air. With another beat of his leathery wings, he took off in front, spinning in the air as he flew.

I knew immediately I wanted to be up there. But the white, curling smoke of my wings remained as they were, unable to take me where I wanted to go.

I could only assume that Killian was still leading the way from high above, so aimed my horse in the direction he was flying.

Luckily for him, his mount followed along, though I didn't think it would bother him entirely if the mare went off on her own. It's not like he needed a horse when he had those wings to carry him.

When my own horse tired, I slowed our pace back to the gentle walk we'd taken through the forest, and secured Killian's horse to mine when I remembered all the provisions were in his saddlebags. I didn't care if he walked, but I certainly wasn't going to go hungry at his expense.

After the sun had peaked, Killian finally came back to solid ground, landing gracefully for a male his size.

He was out of breath like he'd completed a thorough workout, and sweat beaded across his forehead, making his bronzed skin glow. The top half of his hair was pulled back with a leather strap and tied in a knot behind his head. If he wasn't such a sullen bastard, I might have enjoyed the image he cut.

He walked alongside his horse and stretched his wings and arms out as he went.

Call me a glutton for punishment, but I couldn't help but ask the burning questions I had.

"Something occurred to me. . ."

"Oh, please, do tell," Killian drawled.

I ignored his tone. "My sister spent her life surrounded by magic. Her room was heated with a spell—so why didn't she transition?"

"Perhaps she's not your sister," he taunted.

I sent a glare that promised violence his way and clenched my fist.

Killian must have sensed my anger because he peeked at me. "It's only heating magic, it's nothing strong."

"It was enough to affect me."

"You said she was weak and sick. . . perhaps her body isn't strong enough to react."

I twisted my lips as I contemplated. There'd be no answers on the matter from Killian—he wasn't the right fae to ask. So I decided to question him on something he wouldn't have to guess about.

"Would you tell me about a fae's wings? You said they held power?"

Killian just kept striding and flexing his arms across his chest.

Deciding I no longer wanted to talk down at him, I swung my leg over and jumped onto the ground beside him. I caught Killian watching me from the corner of his eye, but he quickly looked ahead.

"So many questions today, Princess," he sneered.

"Can you blame me? I don't know anything about what I am. It's not as if I have anyone else I can ask," I said, gesturing to the empty meadow around us.

"It's not my doing you're no better educated than a faeling, Princess," he scoffed. "Wait until you get to the lofty towers of your castle and ask the scholars to teach you."

"Gods, give me strength!" I cried skyward. "What have I done to offend you, Killian? I've done nothing to deserve your patronising treatment, yet I'm constantly on the receiving end of it!" I was tired of holding my tongue against his biting remarks. "You're all well and good to rub my face in my lack of knowledge, but you keep sneering at my title as though I've held it all along and am nothing more than it!"

He turned and raised a brow in a silent challenge. "I'm sure you are more than your title, but I don't give a shit, *Princess.* You get to walk into your title nonetheless, with exactly as you said—no knowledge."

"Enlighten me, Killian. How is that so different from you? You're a general of a whole fucking legion and a descendant from a royal family and all the other bullshit. You're telling me you had to work hard for those titles?"

His gaze turned murderous as he set his jaw and crunched his teeth together. He turned from me and stormed ahead.

"You don't know the first thing about me, *Princess,*" the cocky bastard said, unable to stop himself from trying to get the last word in.

Pity he didn't realise who he was up against.

"And you don't know the first thing about me, *Prince.*"

I wasn't ready.

No amount of training or power could have made me ready—could have helped.

Killian whirled on me. He lifted me by my shirt so my toes just touched the ground as he held his dagger against my throat. I hadn't even seen him draw it. I paled at the rage burning in his eyes.

"I am no prince!" he snarled. His charcoal wings cast a dark shadow where we stood, and the air pulsed around me with the power he threw out.

I flinched. Anyone could see this male was powerful. But to be on the receiving end of his aggression was terrifying. A small spark in me hated that he'd made me afraid—that he'd intimidated me. I wanted to set my shoulders and call his bluff.

Shut the fuck up before he kills you, Alora. This is no bluff.

Killian's chest rose and fell as he drew in heavy breaths. He still held me high by my shirt and glared into my grey eye. Neither of us blinked or moved beyond breathing, but his power still pulsed around us, like it was seeking its target to crush under its heavy pressure. After far too long, he pulled the dagger away and dropped me onto my feet with a shove before beating his wings and shooting into the sky.

It took everything in me not to fall to my knees. To not cry at his threat, or simply at how he'd held me so roughly. But the fear Killian just shoved down my throat quickly turned to a wave of fiery anger, burning my insides like acid. Boiling me from the inside out.

How fucking dare he!

My mind flashed back to the last person who had handled me. Images of Lord Thane standing over me after punching my stomach, grabbing my jaw and kissing me against my will while I couldn't do anything to stop it.

Only, my father had trained me to ensure no male could ever make me feel that way.

And I'd make sure it wouldn't happen again.

My rage had nowhere to go. . . no one to aim at because Killian had flown away and was now a shadow in the distance.

No, I didn't want to cry. I wanted to flay him alive.

How fucking dare he!

I clenched my fists and screamed. The wind rose and whipped around me. And as I closed my eyes while I roared, I could have sworn a black shadow twirled behind my shoulders.

Chapter 11
The Climb

The only regret I had at unleashing my anger was that I scared off the horses. I didn't want to think too much about what happened when I'd screamed. The wind had died down and my wings were their usual white tendrils after I'd taken several deep breaths and opened my eyes.

Luckily, I could see the path the horses had taken through the meadow, so I followed their tracks up to the foot of the mountain.

It was dusk by the time the horses came into view, along with Killian and the camp he'd already set up.

He watched me as I approached–no doubt had been watching for a while to ensure I arrived safely. He still had a duty to fulfil to his mother after all. Though he'd evidently made no promises of his treatment of me while he fulfilled it, given that display earlier and that he sat high up on a boulder above the camp where I couldn't reach him.

He had the good sense to have a plate of food waiting by a stoked fire and was still glaring at me from his perch when I arrived.

I was tempted to fling my plate at him but decided he wasn't worth the wasted food.

I ate in silence for the third day in a row, then pulled out the dagger Killian had given me that morning and took it over to my bedroll. I dropped it down where I'd lay my head, but instead of dropping myself onto the bed along with it, I took a few steps away from the camp and sat on the edge of the grassy meadow and watched the stars blink to life above me.

As their soft light dotted the inky sky, I wondered whether these were the stars that had always called to me. Begging me to find them.

Was this it?

Surely destiny wouldn't have called me to a fate so cruel and lonely.

Both Killian's and my own mood hadn't improved much by morning. We stepped around one another as we packed up the camp with ruthless efficiency and started our trek up the Asotines.

Unfortunately, the intimidation I silently threw at Killian failed to hit its mark as we began our incline. It's hard to be seen as an irate, take-no-shit female when you can't fucking breathe.

Killian, however, walked ahead like he was strolling through the fields on a sunny afternoon, rather than hiking up a mountain. I could almost feel his smug sense of satisfaction rolling off him along with his unlaboured breaths.

Fuck him.

We made several stops along the way, each time not speaking a word to one another.

There was something about being in a bad mood and not wanting to show weakness, despite how my legs burned and my chest ached. I knew Killian stopped only for my own sake—he was a Legion General and in peak physical form. I wouldn't be surprised if his muscles had muscles. So every time he stopped and leant on a rock to pause our incline, that stubborn part of me wanted to just keep stomping past him like I didn't need to rest.

You're not kidding anyone, sit down before you pass out.

Despite walking behind him, I knew he was paying attention to every move I made. It was always when I was panting heavily and my lungs were near bursting point that he'd stop our climb. I'd even seen him flinch when I'd slipped on loose stones during the steepest part of the climb, like he was prepared to pounce on me if I slid too far.

He had been watching me with all but his eyes. I suppose I had been watching him right back.

By late afternoon, as the sun began losing its fight against the darkening sky, we approached the summit. Killian stopped our advances up the mountain at the entrance of a narrow canyon. The jagged, grey peaks rose high above us on both sides, and fallen boulders from the cliffs above littered the trail ahead. Mercifully, though, the path before us was flat. A short reprieve from the constant, steep angle we'd travelled at the entire day.

I sat down on a fallen rock and took great inhales to calm my breathing and was relieved to see Killian had finally broken a sweat. We each pulled the water skeins from our horses and sat across from one another on opposite sides of the path. We still hadn't spoken a word since his outburst yesterday.

I was still furious at him, and would happily have continued on without speaking to him until we reached our destination, but my treacherous eyes flicked to the imposing general as he leant back on the rocky wall behind him. I couldn't look away as his bicep curled to bring his water to his lips, and noticed his throat bob as he swallowed—his hair, damp with sweat as it brushed his shoulders.

But once again, I was too slow. After taking a gulp, his blue eyes landed straight on mine, like he knew he'd find them there.

Shit.

There was no point looking away, he'd already seen me watching. So I did my best to level him with a look that expressed he could still go to hell.

Either he had a tick, or the corner of his lip flicked up in the tiniest hint of a smirk. That enough told me he was indifferent to how he'd behaved yesterday and stoked the flames of my anger even higher.

I jolted upright, incensed by his indifference, and went to stomp away, but that moment of eye contact was enough to break his silence.

"I—" Killian cleared his throat and tried again. "I'm sorry."

I turned back to him and folded my arms across my chest, as though I was blocking the words from breaching my defences, then raised my brow at him. The message clear. *Try harder.*

"My behaviour yesterday was—is—unforgivable. I should never have lost my temper the way I did, nor should I have handled you so roughly. I apologise, Princess," he said solemnly and dipped his chest in a bow.

He stood up tall and rested his hand on the hilt of his sword, watching me closely with those blue eyes, clearly waiting for my response.

His chest rose and fell gently. A trained warrior waiting patiently for his enemy to make the first move. I made sure I didn't move a muscle.

I was taken aback by how sincere he delivered the apology—I almost believed it. I also think it was the first time he'd used *Princess* as a title and not as a name.

Too fucking late though.

"You're right, Killian," I said, and curled a gentle smile. "It is unforgivable." I let my hatred burn through before I spun on my heel and stalked ahead on the path through the canyon. I didn't want to look at him anymore.

"Stop!" he yelled. But his call fell on deaf, pointed ears. I wasn't going to indulge him, so I kept walking.

His boots crunched as he shot forward before he grabbed me by the back of my neck like some wayward kitten, then swung me around so my front collided into his chest.

"I said, stop," he rumbled above my head.

I tried to jerk my neck free of his grasp, but he held me in a punishing grip. His thumb dug in against my racing pulse, making it all too noticeable how it skipped a beat and kicked up to a rapid rate under his hold. The words that were about to spill from my mouth in a rage died on my tongue and turned into a scream as he drew his sword and thrust the blade up.

I thought being stabbed would have hurt more, but I didn't feel the blade pass through my stomach. My eyes widened in fear as I looked up at the rage burning through the ruthless general. But he wasn't looking back at me, couldn't look me in the eye as he ran me through.

That's when I felt it.

The raspy breath at my neck. I turned my head in Killian's palm and the high-pitched shriek that left me this time was a mix of fear and disgust.

A gaping grey mouth was just above my shoulder. Black blood dripped between its pointed teeth. I looked just in time to see its beady eyes roll into the back of its head as it dropped to the ground in a crumpled heap.

"What the f–"

"Goblins," he growled above me and released his hold on my neck. "Get to the horses."

Killian stepped past me and faced two more of the bony, grey creatures that were crawling over a boulder on all fours toward us.

No sooner had he twirled his sword in his hand, one goblin leapt into the air to attack with a piercing screech and its arms out–wicked claws arched and poised to tear his skin apart.

Its attack was short-lived as Killian drove his sword through its centre, but it wasn't the one he should have focused on. It was the second goblin that charged straight at him, aiming low to grapple around Killian's waist. But that one also didn't stand a chance against the powerful general. As Killian dodged to the side and swept his sword down in a brutal swipe, black blood sprayed as it was split in half.

Two more goblins crested over a cliff edge a few feet above us and crawled across the rock face, eyeing us greedily.

He turned to me then and saw I was still rooted to the spot. "Get to the fucking horses!"

I spun and bolted, hearing another one of those shrieks and the sound of swinging steel behind me. But the straight shot between me and the mares a few yards away was interrupted by yet another goblin that launched itself down from the cliffs above.

I skidded to a halt and flung my arms out to keep from falling on my arse. The creepy figure in front of me hunched itself over and drew in a ragged breath. Sullen and thin grey skin hung over the goblin's ribcage as it gathered air, then screamed that ear-splitting cry. Its mouth was a gaping pit of pointed, rotted teeth.

Fuck, fuck, fuck.

By the sound of the steel swinging and flesh tearing, Killian was still dealing with more goblins at my back. I didn't like the idea of running to the horses in case they became targets themselves, but I needed a weapon. My dagger was strapped under the saddlebag, but this goblin looked determined to block my path.

It only took a split second to think through what I needed to do. But a second was all I had before the goblin leapt at me—its hands stretched out to make use of its black claws.

I'd always been light on my feet and quick. But as a fae, my reactions were even more remarkable. So, as the goblin launched itself, I sprung forward.

Right before the creature collided with me, I ducked under its arm and skid across the ground, then sprinted to the horses and my awaiting dagger.

Killian roared my name as I pumped my arms faster than I ever had. But that goblin was right on my heels—there was no time to second guess my plan.

"Alora!" Killian bellowed. The sounds of his fighting had stopped—it was just this goblin's clawed footsteps behind my own that remained.

I reached my mare without slowing and skid underneath her neck to the opposite side where I kept my dagger strapped. The goblin ran straight at my horse from the other side. I couldn't let it reach her.

I kicked my legs up, mimicking the near exact move I'd performed when I ran from Lito, only this time, I planted my hand on top of the saddle, and leapt clear over the horse's back.

I saw the shock in the goblin's depthless eyes as I came down on top of it and slammed my dagger through its chest. The white tendrils of my wings flowed along the ground as I landed, crouched above its sickly body, so I didn't get its gore over my clothes.

The goblin's life ended in a wet gurgle.

I squeezed my eyes shut and paused to gather my racing nerves. When the rancid, rank smell of blood cleared my senses and I no longer wanted to vomit, I looked up to find Killian right in front of me.

He stood as though someone had frozen him in place—his breathing heavy, with black blood sprayed across his face.

It was how he looked at me though, that sent a chill down my arms.

He dragged in a few more breaths of air, his lungs spent from the scrap with the goblins he'd gone up against.

"How—how did you do that?"

"How did I do what?" I puffed as I stood.

Killian kept trying to catch his breath. He looked to where I'd run from and back to where we stood now.

"You're quick."

"I always have been."

"Yeah. . ." he said, drawing out the word, but something in the way he looked me up and down told me there was something he wasn't saying. "You thought I stabbed you," he said flatly, not a question.

I bit my lip, a flush of embarrassment swept over me and I looked at my feet. "Can you blame me? You've made your feelings pretty clear."

"Killing you is a big jump from disliking you."

I didn't have a response for that, so I kept my eyes focused on my boots. Killian curled a finger under my chin and lifted my gaze to his and leant in close—his blue eyes flicked between my green and grey like they were searching for something.

"I won't let you come to any harm, Princess." His deep voice fluttered through me and sent a shiver down my spine.

"Don't make promises you can't keep."

"I don't intend to." His finger stayed under my chin for an extra beat before he let go and withdrew from my space.

I only realised after his touch faded that I'd been holding my breath.

He bent to wipe his blade clean on the dead goblin by our feet and took my dagger to do the same.

"Thanks for dealing with the rest of those things," I said, gesturing to the dead creature next to us.

He huffed a laugh. "No problem, Princess. I'll let you off the life debt this time, considering you also saved yourself."

My eyes widened. "The what?"

"I was only joking."

I let out an audible sigh and took my dagger from him. "Thank Gods, I thought you were suggesting it was a real thing."

"Oh, it is a real thing," he said plainly as he stood.

I paled. "What is it exactly?"

"When a fae protects another and saves them from death, they are owed a life debt. To be repaid in any manner and at whatever point in time the one who did the saving decides."

I didn't think I wanted to be owing anyone one of those any time soon.

"But *I* owe *you* an explanation on another matter." He watched me closely. "About what you asked yesterday."

"Wings," I said, filling in the blank.

He nodded. "A fae's wings draw in power from the magic around us. It happens as easily and as seamlessly as breathing. In the same way, a fae can also draw in more power if they concentrate, but it can't be held for long. It needs to be released. Our wings often determine how we can best use magic—what we can best use it for. How we will be strongest."

He took a moment and sat down on a small ledge, wiping the blood from his face. I was worried that if I moved, he'd stop talking, so I stayed where I was.

"There are other factors, of course, like breeding and everything else my mother mentioned. . . but most commonly it is a fae's wings that determine their strengths *and* their strength. Almost as if they are predestined for their skill set. Does that make sense?"

I nodded. "So, for you. . .?"

"I am suited for battle. Strong and infallible. I won't give out in the middle of a war, I can cover great distances and draw in huge amounts of power to decimate an enemy."

I'd call him cocky, but it was plain to see he wasn't bragging. Killian was the biggest male I'd seen, well over a foot taller than me, and a pure warrior from head to toe. The corner of his lip kicked up in that infuriating smile again as he watched me watching him.

"Your power," I said, breaking the growing awkward silence, "it felt like pressure." He gave a small nod of agreement. "But your mother's felt like heat back at the palace."

"My mother's line carries the power of fire, but that doesn't mean her offspring or other blood relatives always inherit that same power. Nor does it stop any other fae from any other bloodline having an affinity for wielding fire magic."

"So that's why you're a general?" I asked, connecting the dots. "Your power is strength itself, so you were predestined to lead?"

He nodded again. "I believe it's my duty to protect. Not just the Summer Kingdom. . . but all of it. All of Endence. The entire realm needs to be protected from those who would seek to harm us. Being a general puts me in the best position to do that. Being powerful makes it easy."

Protecting the entire realm. How admirable of him.

"But your brother, he inherited the flame of your mother's line, right? I saw his wings." The image of Farro's midnight wings came to mind. The lines of embers flowing across them as they curved around his frame.

"Yes," Killian's tone deepened, edging on dangerous. "Among other things."

"So, because he was the first born, he was predestined to inherit your mother's power along with her throne? Is that how it works?"

"Farro inherits the throne because he possesses a nearly unchecked level of power. His magic and place of birth weren't a factor." That vein throbbed in his temple again.

I'd felt Killian's magic during our argument. It was immense. To consider what Farro possessed–it must be staggering. Was he jealous that his brother had inherited all that power just because he was born first?

Feeling brave, I decided to just ask.

"Despite your own strength, do you wish you'd been born first so you had his power?"

A muscle in his jaw ticked. "I already told you, Princess, his place of birth wasn't a factor."

I scrunched my brows in confusion.

"Farro isn't the first born. I am."

It was as though the clouds parted and I could see the reason for his anger at my questions yesterday, and despite how unfair it was, his contempt toward me.

Here stood an incredibly powerful warrior. The first born in a royal family. But he didn't get to inherit–what would, under normal circumstances be–his birthright, simply because his little brother was stronger.

And then here I came.

An outsider, human-raised-fae who knew nothing about the realm. And I just waltzed in and got to be the heir to a throne without lifting a finger. The throne that oversaw the legion he was currently commanding.

Whoops.

I definitely didn't deserve his ire, but I wasn't above being able to understand where it stemmed from.

Killian watched me as everything he'd said settled over me. I drew in a deep breath. "It's not my fault, Killian."

He drew in his own. "I was wrong to treat you so unfairly. It's hard given our circumstances, and especially that you—" He twisted his lips, catching himself before he finished that last part.

"Especially that I what?"

He contorted his face in a growl, annoyed by his slip-up.

"You remind me of someone, that's all."

His dangerous tone was enough of a warning to stop me from asking who. I'd clearly reached another quota from him.

"Come on, Alora," he said, standing and grabbing hold of our horses. "There's a place that's safe to rest just up ahead. We'll reach your legion tomorrow."

I followed silently, but the only thing I could think was that, just now, was only the second time he'd called me by my name. And I didn't know what to make of it.

Dawn broke before me over the realm in golden, buttery light. The first glimpses of the day revealed pinks and oranges that washed over the clouds, giving way to pristine, fluffy, white pillows as the landscape below soaked in the sun's rays and lit up a brilliant green as the minutes ticked by.

It was breathtaking.

I was so enraptured by the world below that I didn't pay attention to anything Killian was doing.

The peaks of the mountain range we stood on divided the Summer and Winter Kingdoms, which meant everything in view was–

"Your Kingdom, Princess."

Killian sidled up behind me, his chest was a warm wall just out of reach at my back. His sleep-addled words sent tingles down my spine as he gestured in a wide sweep.

Despite the loud swallow I took, there was a knot in my throat that didn't quite go away.

To the northwest was a lake of the most stunning deep blue, which stretched as far as I could see. Farther west were more open plains that almost mirrored the ones Killian and I rode through two days ago, only more beautiful–if that was even possible.

East of where we stood rose an incredible evergreen forest. The height of the trees rivalled the redwoods surrounding Elden.

"Our destination," he paused, passing me a steaming mug, "is just down there."

Killian had told me about the Winter Legion last night and painted a picture in my mind. The Kingdom held a significant force to protect our land—a company of over fifteen thousand warriors, half of which lived and trained together at a site called Kevilla.

Images of a muddy war camp came to mind. Rows upon rows of tents, soldiers huddled around campfires, rationing food to keep from starving.

What was lying at the edge of the lake in that open plain was anything but.

As Killian and I descended the mountain and crossed the meadow before us, the state of the legion camp became clearer.

Kevilla wasn't brown or muddy or starving, but green and lush and beautiful. I don't know why I was confused by the lack of dirt or stench or harsh lines. I needed to remember this was no human army. Fae might be brutal in their power and ferocity, but they were also ethereal and beautiful. It made sense they lived that way, even in their training camps.

Kevilla was more like a town, built in a circular configuration in a glen that stretched between the south-eastern edge of the lake and the forest. On the outer rings of Kevilla were small houses—little wooden cabins, only big enough to house one or two fae.

Killian and I walked together along the paths between the cabins and further into the circle. The closer to the centre we travelled, the busier the paths became and any hopes I had of going about my time here unrecognised died swiftly at the first trio we passed.

The female and males stood to attention, their wings tucked in tight as they smacked their closed fists to their chests at the sight of their commander. Their expressions were serious and respectful. But I definitely didn't miss their eyes widening as I walked behind their imposing leader. Nor their hushed whispers after we passed when they were let out of their salute.

It was clear that word of the mysterious female brought into the realm by the Oracle had spread amongst them. I decided that watching my feet as I walked was easier than pretending I didn't notice how they reacted when they saw me.

After several lanes of cabins, we stepped into the next ring, clearly reserved for businesses and services to keep the legion operating.

Bells above shop doors rang as fae passed in and out. The tell-tale smells of butchers and bakers reached us from several yards beyond. Hammers of blacksmiths and armourers and weaponsmiths striking metal sounded as we walked through the bustling area.

All the way along our walk, warriors of all shapes and sizes stepped to the side and saluted as Killian passed, and then looked at the nearest fae they could find to whisper together as I followed behind.

At the centre of the camp was an open area reserved for training. Sparring rings, training dummies, archery targets and obstacle courses littered the huge open space. I watched as groups of fae honed their relevant skills in the marked areas, their bodies blurring as they ran and leapt and flew in the air, moving as quickly as the arrows fired from bows at the targets beneath them.

Killian strode ahead toward a wide building at the top of the circle, which was clearly a communal gathering area for the legion. The hall was a behemoth, and could easily house hundreds of fae inside.

On either side of the massive structure were a handful of larger stone houses, obviously reserved for the higher-ranking warriors.

I looked back to the hall and took in its beauty. The swirls and intricate, decorative architecture around the roof and pointed archways looked as though it belonged in a palace rather than in a legion camp.

Before Killian and I reached the open archway, a stunning blonde male stepped out of the shadowed portico and walked straight toward us, his perfect white teeth and sharp little canines glinting as he smiled broadly at the hulking figure walking toward him.

"Commander," he said in a welcoming voice, giving the same salute as the other warriors had. After his formal greeting, he wrapped Killian in an embrace which Killian returned, hugging like long-lost friends, smacking each other on their backs.

The handsome newcomer turned his attention to me, so I didn't have time to be shocked that the stoic fae I'd been stuck with the past four days melted away before my eyes into an emotionally regulated, likeable, grown-ass male.

He was shorter than Killian, but still a strong, tall presence, and his eyes were as blue as a summer sky. He looked as though he were my age, with cream wings and soft, straw-blonde hair that brushed over his ears and at the nape of his neck. A longer lock draped over his forehead when he stooped into a quick bow before he brushed it back into place as he stood.

"You must be Alora," he said warmly and smiled. "I was very excited to receive word you'd be joining us here in Kevilla. News of your. . . unprecedented arrival into Endence reached us several days ago. I do hope I'll hear the full story soon."

I liked him instantly and couldn't help smiling right back. It was refreshing to be around someone cheerful after spending days with the gloomy general next to me.

"Alora, this is Veric," Killian introduced, as the blonde male bowed again at his introduction. "The General of the Winter Legion."

"Nice to meet you, Veric."

Killian secured the horses to a nearby fence and led the way inside.

The massive hall was decorated in cool tones and lit with bright orbs of light and warm blue rugs decorated the wood floors. A small set of steps ran along a low platform where several enormous chairs sat and beyond the platform, doors led off to other rooms, though I couldn't see what was back there.

A dozen or so fae walked between the doors and around us. Most were dressed in the same tight, leathery armour Killian wore, but in a shade of pale grey.

We sat at a table already topped with food and drink. I hadn't noticed until that moment how hungry I was and plucked a handful of berries from the plate before my stomach started growling.

"Killian, why are you referred to as a general when you're commanding this legion?"

"I'm the General of the Summer Legion, which is where my title comes from. It's only while I'm here that I'm called commander." He took a long drink and continued. "As I belong to Summer, I cannot truly command this legion, though my expertise as a general gives me exceptional skills to do so. Veric here is the General of the Winter Legion; however, he's a little fresh, and needed guidance. . . so here I am," he said with teasing sarcasm and clapped Veric on his shoulder.

A flash of embarrassment crossed Veric's face before he laughed and put his own hand on Killian's shoulder. "I'd be lost without you, brother," he said in that comforting, warm voice.

My jaw dropped.

People actually like Killian?

I came to my senses quick enough at something he'd said. "Wait, brother?"

"Don't fret, Princess," Killian levelled at me with a mocking glare. "I'm only cursed with the one sibling."

I widened my eyes in alarm, shooting Killian a warning look about the sarcastic name he referred to me by. He mimicked the glare back at me.

Veric looked between us and cocked his head at Killian.

"You'll agree with the name once you see how entitled she thinks she is. Her audacity matches the lofty heights of even Farro's sense of self-importance."

Veric didn't press any further, he just shook his head, laughing softly as though his friend was equally as exasperating as the description he'd given about Farro, and continued.

"I only mean brother in arms," Veric reassured, and smiled. "Killian has been an incredible resource for our legion these past few decades, though I've known him nearly all my life."

"Which is how long, exactly?" I asked, eyeing both of them.

Veric huffed a loud laugh. "I'm two-hundred and twenty-five, just this past winter."

Two-hundred!

He laughed again at my shocked expression. "Quite young amongst us fae, but especially compared to this one." He elbowed Killian in the side. "Who is–"

"Much older," Killian interjected, and shot him a glare. The irritated rumble Killian reserved for me returned to his tone.

"If Killian isn't allowed to command the legion, then why aren't you the commander, Veric?"

"Alas, only the reigning royal of our Kingdom can appoint a commander to their legion. It's been nearly thirty years since we have had either a king or queen, and the last commander, Warven, Faded into the Evers shortly after they disappeared."

I dared not look at Killian out of fear Veric would catch our exchange.

Little did Veric know the next supposed reigning royal was sitting right in front of him. My lashes fluttered as I tried to think of a response.

"Faded into the Evers?" I asked, though part of me had grasped the meaning already. I vaguely recalled Fleur using the term in Nakir's office.

"When fae die, their soul does not die with them. They Fade from their mortal body and leave this realm, returning to live for eternity in the Evers–the realm where magic is born and interminable," Killian responded. "For fae lucky enough to join their soul with their moiety, it means they get to spend eternity together, united as one."

"That's. . . really beautiful." I smiled softly and squeezed my eyes closed for a moment thinking of my mother.

Had she reached the Evers all the way from the mortal realm when she died? Would she be waiting there for my father's soul to join her?

Killian fidgeted and knocked my boot under the table, bringing me out of my train of thought.

"So about commanding," I continued after I'd gathered myself. "The only reason you're not in charge is because a royal hasn't granted their approval?"

Veric nodded with a small smile but didn't appear disheartened. "They would have to deem me worthy of the position as well, but. . . yes."

"Despite his young age, and that he still has *some* things to learn," Killian said, eyeing Veric sideways, "he's an excellent warrior and is deserving of his rank."

Veric's cheeks flushed slightly at the compliment. It clearly meant a lot to him to have Killian's approval.

"I'm sure whenever Valefor returns, or we sort out who the next downright irritating Winter fae is to take the throne, the first thing we'll do is sort out who will lead this legion." Killian's tone was dripping with derision, aimed silently at me.

Gods, he really is a dick.

Veric at least had the gall to look offended at his words. Loyalty to his royal counterpart keeping him faithful.

Before Veric could give whatever retort was building, Killian said pointedly at me, "Veric would be an excellent choice to promote. He is, after all, the king's nephew."

If I hadn't been sitting, I would've fallen over.

He's my cousin.

I studied the male across from me again. Despite not knowing what my father looked like, as I studied Veric, I could see familial features between him and I.

Veric's blonde hair wasn't the colour of straw as I'd first thought—but of champagne. The exact same shade as mine. He had the same creamy skin and the same smattering of freckles across his cheeks, though he had slightly more than I did. The main difference between our features was still in the eyes. Veric's blue was so brilliant and clear, unlike my mismatched green and grey.

I looked to Killian, almost to check he'd been serious. That he hadn't made some cruel joke. He dipped his chin in an imperceptible nod, confirming my unasked question.

"I—" I swallowed and took a steadying breath, then tried again. "That's a very exciting uncle to have." It was all I could manage.

Killian shook his head like he was embarrassed for me.

"I suppose it is. He's a great male." His smile turned more thoughtful.

Then something occurred to me. "If you're the king's nephew, then wouldn't that make *you* next in line for the throne?"

He laughed and gave me that warm, reassuring smile. "King Valefor wasn't from the royal line. Queen Eira was. His title as king comes from her, not his own birthright. My mother was his sister and therefore of no royal title, either. So no, not a royal."

"You must miss him a great deal."

"Very much. We hope he returns to us one day."

I wanted to ask so much more about my father, but Veric's warmth had all but faded from his smile.

Another time.

Instead, I tried for more neutral territory regarding my family.

"Did Valefor have any other siblings?"

Any other cousins I should know about?

"No, just my mother, Elvenia."

I leant back and took all the new information. How was I going to learn everything I could about my father without drawing attention?

Killian must have realised my train of thought. "If you'd like to get to know more about the King of Winter, Princess, then perhaps Veric could arrange for you to visit the Palace."

I tried my hardest to remain calm. "That would be amazing."

"Consider it done," Veric said, his warm smile pushing through once more. "I'll arrange it with Erela, the Steward of the Palace."

Killian smirked again as he raised his drink to his lips and paused. "It might be a good opportunity for us to seek some answers on why Alora had such an important usher into our gentle realm while we're there. I'm sure your *sister* would enjoy the company, too," he said to Veric as he smiled over the rim of his glass at me.

"Your sister?" I couldn't help but blurt the words. I took a breath and tried again. "Your sister manages the Palace?"

Two cousins.

"Mmm, indeed she does," Veric said, not catching the hidden conversation that'd just happened between Killian and I.

Killian dusted his fingers off and stood. "It will all have to wait, though." His seriousness returned as though he couldn't manage to be cheerful for more than ten minutes at a time. "Alora needs to train, and I need to focus on the upcoming Treaty, so I'll need you to take care of her instruction. Veric, set her up in a cabin then meet me back here so you can give me a full report and tell me where we're at with the volcacs."

He spoke to Veric like I was no longer in the room, then walked away, as though that were enough dismissal.

We both protested, but I got my words out quicker.

"I thought *you* were going to train me?"

"I am the commander of this entire legion, Princess," he said, turning back to look down at me. "Although I was made to be your guide here, I will not be your mentor as well."

Veric and I called out again as we rose from the table, but he continued striding purposefully to the doors across the platform.

I stood shoulder to shoulder with my cousin—as close as we could with our wings in the way—and watched the storm cloud that was Killian stride off without so much as a farewell.

He'd endured me for not a moment longer than he needed to, and rid himself of me the first chance he got.

Gods, he really is awful.

As we walked to our destination, Veric brought my attention to all the points of interest throughout Kevilla and told me little pieces of information about the legion. I really should've been paying attention considering it would one day be *my* legion, but my head was spinning from the *big* pieces of information I'd just learned, and I couldn't concentrate.

I glanced around as Veric led his tour, looking toward the various buildings and businesses he pointed out. Just beyond the centre of the camp, a shadowed garden caught my attention down a wide lane, and I lingered, unable to keep myself from moving–like I was being beckoned toward whatever was at the other end.

I walked along the cobbled lane. A tall trellis covered the expanse separating the buildings I walked between, and over the wide courtyard it led into.

Set amongst a solid wall was an incredible fountain carved into its white stone. The crawling plants from the trellis had grown from the sides of the wide arc, surrounding the statues standing amongst the shallow water.

A small altar sat at the low wall bordering the scene, with food offerings in little baskets and incense burning. Four strong figures were carved in exquisite detail. Warriors, each with their own pointed crowns across their brows. Brilliant, clear-blue water drizzled from the sides, as though weeping from the rock itself.

Veric's scent of vanilla and citrus ebbed at the edge of my senses, as he came to stand behind me. It was already so familiar.

"Is this the Blessed Four?"

"Yes. Do humans not have statues of the Gods?" He seemed amazed that I didn't recognise the figures carved in the stone.

"They know of the Gods, but there are no statues or shrines built in their honour. Their names and stories have all been lost to time."

Veric's eyes widened in my peripheral.

I was saddened by the form of a Goddess carried in another's arms, with her head nestled against their chest. "What happened?"

"Rharuer, King of the Gods, loved his children," Veric said thoughtfully as he came to stand beside me. "This carving depicts the story of the fall of his daughter, Ryuna and the loss of her Immortal Weapon, Hush. It is one of the few times the Blessed Four came together. It is here to remind us to lead and not take, and that even if one shall fall, together we will prevail over those who seek us harm."

The one Veric pointed out as Rharuer stood impossibly tall and strong, cradling his daughter to his chest. Her immortal bow hung from her limp fingers, broken in two. Two Gods guarded either side of them, their own weapons drawn.

"Rharuer's daughter, Ryuna, grew restless and was curious of what lay beyond the Immortal Lands and sought to test her strength with Hush. She found a realm of dark creatures she thought would serve her will and desired to rule over them as high authority, but they refused and struck her down. When Rharuer learned his daughter had left their world and fallen to the evils of the one she found herself in, he summoned his sons and laid waste to it. He saved his daughter, but her bow, Hush, which was blessed with True Sight, was destroyed. Ryuna was weakened and has never strayed from the Immortal Lands since her father brought her back."

"Why would Ryuna want to rule when she was already a Goddess?"

"There are many Gods and Goddesses, each prevailing over one thing or another. Strength, courage, wealth, love. . . sex. But the Blessed Four are different. They are divine beings of creation, protection and giving–encompassing all that life brings and offers us. Not destruction and rule. Ryuna sought more and paid her toll. To prevent history repeating, Rharuer discarded his Immortal Weapon and commanded his sons to do the same so that they might never be tempted by the same desires."

That's one hell of a cautionary tale.

"The God on the right is Ruasis, the youngest. His javelin, Strike, is the only Immortal Weapon to have been found. It was last seen over nine hundred years ago, wielded by one of our greatest warriors, Evander, during the Uprising of Orias. The weapon is imbued with Recall, once thrown it will return to the wielder. It made Evander unstoppable during that battle, and we likely wouldn't have succeeded without it."

I ran my gaze up and down the tall weapon clutched in the young God's fist.

"The weapon of his eldest brother, Rhoston, is a sort of twin to his javelin," Veric continued, and nodded at the tall figure on the left. "Where Ruasis' javelin would return to his hand, Rhoston's dagger, Kiss, would allow him to *blink* to whichever target found the blade buried in their skin. An ability similar to *sifting*, but it was as though Rhoston and the blade were attached by some invisible thread, making it impossible for blade and wielder to be parted."

"As well as this, Kiss is also blessed with Concealment. Rhoston was able to change its form however he desired, making the God more dangerous to those who underestimated him when they thought he was unarmed. It's likely the reason it's never been found. It's probably disguised as a fork or a stick right now."

I laughed at the joke, but Veric was completely serious. Another little laugh escaped me at the thought of an incredibly powerful Immortal Weapon lost in someone's cutlery draw.

"And what about Rharuer? What was his weapon?"

Veric reached forward and reverently touched the carved hand of the King of Gods as he held his daughter. "Rharuer had a sword, called Hum." My eyes dipped to Rharuer's hip—the sheath of the sword he spoke of was only just visible behind the form of his daughter. "It could syphon magic from the world around him and was a conduit to focus and increase his might. Hum's chaotic power could be unleashed however he wished. It was how he destroyed the realm that harmed his daughter. But when he discarded Hum, Rharuer knew it was too strong for any one being to wield and not be tempted by its power, so he drained it of its magic."

"It's just an ordinary sword now?"

"Hum is an Immortal Weapon, so would still be very powerful, but without the full might of its magic, the sword wouldn't be capable of the great and terrible things it once was."

I blew out the heaviness of the story in a breath and took one last look at the trickling fountain.

"Maybe it's good humans don't know of the Gods and their weapons," I mused, looking up at them. "I don't think they would have considered the tale to be a reminder, but rather one of opportunity."

We stayed for a moment longer and a deep sense of melancholy overcame me as I looked at the carved figures. The immense loss that Ryuna must have felt when Hush was cleaved in two, then the loss of the other weapons–the sacrifice the males gave to protect their family.

And here I was, thinking that staying with my family was some kind of sacrifice.

We left the shrine and continued through the town, all the way over to the easternmost edge of Kevilla that bordered the forest where my lodgings were.

Veric opened the door to the little wood-panelled cabin and led the way into the open living area, only big enough to suit the most basic of needs.

"I'll speak with Killian in more detail when I go back to Kevilla Hall and discuss what your training regime will look like then arrange to get you fitted with proper battle leathers, too."

"Thank you, Veric," I murmured, embarrassed by how Killian had dismissed me so thoughtlessly, especially compared to how warm and welcoming he clearly was with others.

"I'll also arrange for someone to bring you food, though many choose to eat at the hall together. Or there are several pubs around, just follow your nose and you'll find one, I'm sure." He smiled.

I couldn't help but feel like he was trying to cheer me up.

"But for now, rest, and I'll look for you tonight back at the hall."

I didn't miss the polite invitation behind his words.

Veric dipped in another little bow, and I thanked him again as I followed him to the door.

He stepped outside and swept his wings out, flying over the rooftops, back in the direction we'd come from.

It occurred to me that Veric had escorted me on foot purely for my own sake because I couldn't fly.

I snicked the front door closed and leant against it. My wings twirled in the space around my shoulders and pooled around my feet as they hung low. But I barely noticed their presence, as I beamed a ridiculous smile at the ceiling. Happiness buzzed inside me like flickering lightning.

I had found family, and there was more waiting for me out in this Kingdom.

A tear formed of pure joy snuck out the corner of my eye and trailed down my face as thoughts raced through my mind at everything else I'd learned.

Then a second tear, formed of heartache, rolled down my opposite cheek as thoughts of the family I'd been ripped away from consumed me. I wanted to be held by Caldwell and have him tell me I was going to be okay—that this training I was about to go through would be easy compared to what he'd taught me. For him to tell me that it would all be worth it so I could get stronger like I needed to be.

I wanted to lay with Della and tell her of our cousins. Tell her our mother was a queen and that our father loved her with a depth that this entire realm revered beyond measure.

Worst of all, and shamefully, I wanted Lito. I wanted him to tell me everything had been a bad dream. Have him whisper that I was his then moan my name as he took the hurt away with his body through the night.

I wanted to go home. But there was no use pining for the impossible. I had to force myself to look ahead.

A sob burst from me and I covered my mouth with the back of my hand, biting down hard on my skin to focus on a different kind of pain. Finally, when the ache in me settled, I swept my thumbs across my lashes to free the tears still clinging there, then inhaled a deep breath. I held it, letting it clear my mind, and released it only after I was successful.

Then I went in search of my bath.

Killian's brash dismissal earlier that morning made me feel completely unwanted and was a key contributor to my desire to stay in my cabin on my own all night. This was, after all, *his* domain—his legion to control. He was the commander here, and could out me as someone not worth anyone's time, and they'd all believe it, no doubt. Everyone knew and respected him.

But I'd had enough of not speaking to others. Had enough of only my own or Killian's company to endure. Had my cousin here who wanted to see me.

And I'd had enough of eating in silence.

Decision made, I stood, pulled my boots on over my black pants, and fastened the green cloak across my chest. I ran my fingers through my blonde tresses, leaving them down for the first time since waking as a fae.

Confidence prevailing, I sucked in a steadying breath ready for whatever socialising with fae would throw at me, and let a different thought take up residence in my mind—this time, one to lend me strength.

Fuck it. I'm the future queen. This isn't Killian's legion.

It's mine.

Kevilla Hall buzzed with life by the time I reached its grand archway. I kept my shoulders back and my gaze fixed ahead as I wandered through the crowd, pretending I couldn't see everyone staring and whispering.

It was strange how the magic heating the space was so ordinary to me now, after how stifling and clammy it felt before I'd transitioned. Now, it was no different than the radiant heat of a fire warming the space perfectly.

The long tables I'd sat at earlier were now crowded and laden with food and drinks. Males and females sat together in large groups and laughed and cheered with one another, tapping their glasses of wine and ale together as they enjoyed their night. I smiled to myself at the camaraderie they so easily shared.

As I stepped further into the hall, the confidence I'd mustered dwindled, and I looked to catch someone's eye—anyone's eye—just so I didn't feel so lost and alone.

A waving hand caught my attention, but I didn't recognise their smiling face, so I ignored them and moved on.

"Alora!"

Definitely meant for me, then.

I turned and found a male beckoning me over.

I wove my way around a small group, dodging their wings, then over to the table the male sat at with a group of others—that happy smile plastered across his face as I approached.

He was short—only my height. His brown eyes were so dark they looked black, but they lit up from within as he smiled before wrapping me in a fierce hug. The smell of citrus and sandalwood closed in around us. His wavy, jet-black mane of hair puffed around his petite face and swept past his shoulders—I almost couldn't see his wings poking out from behind his back. They were the most astonishing deep red I'd yet to see on any other fae, the colour of a rich wine or deep garnet.

"I hoped you'd arrive soon! Here, you must be starving." He piled every food within reach onto a plate, then passed it to me along with a glass of wine.

I could kiss him.

"Oh, thank you, ahh—"

"Oh Gods, sorry. Jude! I'm Jude. I've heard so much about you that I feel like we already know each other, so I forgot to introduce myself. Though I am rather offended no one has mentioned me!"

Jude spoke so fast and energetically, he reminded me of one of the fizzing sparklers children waved around to welcome in each new year, full of spark and enthusiasm. His explanations turned into near unintelligible rants as he carried on introducing everyone else sitting nearby, who all belonged within his unit. They all gave polite little waves as they were introduced, but turned to talk amongst themselves, leaving Jude and I to speak together. Which was a small blessing, because I barely retained any of the names Jude rattled off in his haste.

"I hope whoever told you all about me said only good things." I smiled at him. "Though there's only one person who could give a description, and I'm not sure he says anything nice."

"Ha! Oh, please, like I'd listen to Killian anyway." He laughed around his drink. "No, it was Veric who had only good things to say. He was rather impressed after meeting you and made it his mission all afternoon to make sure everything you needed was organised. It was like he was organising us for battle rather than making sure you were properly accommodated."

"Well, I hope you'll switch to preparing for battle soon to ease your workload."

He laughed again, clinked his drink against my own then threw his head back, finishing it off. It clearly wasn't his first—or even his second—one of the night.

It was impossible not to be infected by his happy energy, so much so, that I tossed my head back and skulled the rest of my drink as well.

Jude hollered and cheered as I drank, then clapped me on the shoulder as I tilted upright once more, coming up for breath.

"I knew I'd like you, Alora!" he cackled and reached over the table to grab us more drinks.

I took the time to glance around the room. I looked over my shoulder toward the top of the room, and as fast as a lightning strike, my good mood zapped out of me as my gaze landed on Killian.

He sat slouched in one of those giant chairs, all too reminiscent of a throne. His charcoal wings low for a change swept to his sides. He palmed a glass of amber liquor as he cast his dark glare at me. It was only for a split second before he looked away, but it was enough to know he was watching me—and was wholly unimpressed.

What's new?

I turned back to see Jude holding out a second drink for me.

"Actually, I think I might head back," I muttered, defeated again.

"Already? No, c'mon, stay Lor."

I flicked my gaze to him, and a small smile touched my lips. "My sister was the only one who called me Lor."

"Well, now there's two of us," he chirped and pressed the drink further toward me. "Now stay and tell me all about her and everything else I need to know about you."

So I did.

I woke to thudding.

Both inside my head and at my front door.

I peeked one eye open and promptly closed it again against the blaring sun coming through my window. But my pillows were calling me back into sleep's embrace, so I rolled away from the rays pouring into my room, determined to return to the darkness.

Until that fucking thudding started again.

I groaned and stood–then leant and doubled over. Hands on my knees, still dressed in last night's clothes, I breathed through the nausea before moving, using the wall to balance as I went.

Still, whoever was at my door kept up their incessant thumping.

"If you bang on my door one more fucking time, I'll beat the ever-living shit out of you!" I yelled, as I shuffled toward the door and yanked it open.

Standing tall as ever with his arms folded over his chest, with an extra sprinkle of cocky arrogance was Killian.

If I'd blinked, I would've missed his gaze dip to my lips and his own twitch like he was going to bite back at the uncivil greeting I'd thrown at him.

He smirked. "Careful, Princess. Keep talking to me like that, and I might start thinking you actually like me."

"Well, in that case, I'll make sure I simply tell you to *fuck off* next time so there's no confusion," I said with bleary sweet sarcasm and leant my shoulder against the frame.

Killian bent at the waist, holding eye contact as he slowly moved to my level. I pulled my head back as he drew over my shoulder.

"You smell like a bar," he whispered against my ear.

"Oh, fuck off," I spat and tried to slam the door in his face.

Killian merely shoved his hand against the closing wood, stopping it from smacking shut and followed me inside. "I gladly will, Princess, but only after you get your arse into the training ring. You were supposed to be there an hour ago." His gravelly voice rumbled through my little house and made my temples throb.

"And when were you going to relay that message, Killian? You had plenty of opportunities while you were glaring daggers at my back last night."

A muscle in Killian's jaw ticked as he set his mouth in a firm line.

Yeah, no come back for that one, huh?

I went to the kitchen to pour a glass of water to cease the internal thumping I was enduring, and downed the drink as swiftly as I had the alcohol the night before, then immediately refilled the glass.

Killian wordlessly tossed a small velvet pouch onto the counter next to me.

I untied the two little gold strings that cinched the top, and the smell of perfectly balanced sweet and spicy herbs wafted through the little kitchen. I looked down at the red-brown powder inside then turned to see Killian bracing his arms on the countertop behind me. "What's this?"

"Figured you'd need all the help you could get after your display last night."

"My display!" I reared, anger rising, much to my pounding head's dismay.

"I didn't think females conducted themselves so inappropriately in the human realm. . . or did you just make a special exemption to keep up with all us fae?"

I glared. "Careful Killian, you sound almost jealous."

He scoffed, and I thought that would be his only response before he pulled his wings back and set his focus on me. "Not that you make the cut for me in the first place, Princess, but it would take more than giggling with Jude to make me jealous."

My wings flared with a white flash as I let the insult wash over me. "You certainly kept a close watch to judge whether it affected you. It seems like giggling with Jude was plenty enough, *Commander,* given your reaction to it."

That muscle ticked again and I knew my remark had gotten under his skin. He didn't like that I'd caught him watching.

"By all means, Princess, do as you wish." He gave a mocking bow. "For all the good it'll do you," he muttered under his breath but loud enough he meant for me to hear it.

"Then it's a good thing that Jude has fast become my new best friend. You'll have plenty of time to watch him be the object of all my *giggles* for the foreseeable future." I smiled with mocking sweetness.

The pressure in the room grew as Killian lowered his brow and glared at me with an anger I hadn't seen on him since our fight in the meadow. His muscles bunched in his arms as he clenched his fists.

I stood up straight, no longer leaning against the cupboard. My body responding to the magic he poured into the room, ready to fight or flee.

Or fucking duck for cover.

After a few moments the air thinned and returned to normal. Killian's eyes turned expressionless as he looked at me, but the anger in his voice remained.

"You're late for your training," he said with disdain. He jabbed his finger at the pouch next to me and continued, hatred dripping from his every word. "Drink your tea, wash off the alcohol clinging to you, and get into that fucking ring within twenty minutes. Or Gods help you, I'll kick your fucking door down and drag you there myself in whatever state of readiness–or undress–I find you in."

I opened my mouth to spit my vitriol straight back at him–to tell him where he could stick his orders–but before I'd sucked in the air I needed, quicker than I could track, Killian was in front of me. He cleared the counter and pressed his body against my chest, giving me no space of my own. My back smacked against the cabinets and his fingers squeezed my cheeks with a pressure just short of causing pain, but enough to stop my venom from pouring out.

"Don't," he threatened in a low rumble, "test me, Princess." Just like before, his gaze dipped to my lips again, caught between his fingers.

As quick as he came, Killian stepped away and strode toward the door. My breath came fast and heavy as I reeled from his thinly veiled threat.

"You're a fucking brute, Killian Lòkith," I yelled at his retreating back.

"I dare you to take longer than twenty minutes and find out how true that statement is, Alora *Ìréis.*"

He was already out the door when his response came to me before his wings swept him into the air and away.

I flinched at the sound of my true name but didn't have the luxury of time to process it. I put my hands on my knees and doubled over again, feeling like I could finally breathe easily since opening that door, while simultaneously feeling weak from the whole interaction.

And from the alcohol roiling in my empty stomach.

The urge to be sick all over the kitchen floor climbed up my throat, but I wasn't sure whether it was the hangover or Killian that was the cause.

I stood, sucking in slow breaths to ease the bile that rose in my throat. I took just one minute to compose myself, three to ready the tea to help my aching head, and made sure I left the house ten later.

Mercifully whatever was in those herbs made fast work of helping my poor head, and my hangover cleared on the cool walk to the centre of Kevilla.

Veric greeted me as I entered a training circle. He looked handsome in his pale-grey battle leathers, with his cream wings flared and his short hair lightly mussed.

"Sorry I kept you waiting," I said sheepishly as my own greeting. Killian could go to hell, but I didn't want to be a burden on Veric.

"No matter," he said warmly, putting me immediately at ease. "I hope you weren't made to feel. . . guilty." His gaze flicked over my shoulder to where a brooding Killian stood in the distance.

Veric turned toward a weapon rack and pulled off a sword and two daggers. "How trained are you with weapons?"

"I kept a small dagger on me, back, before. . . well *before,"* I said and he nodded his understanding. "My father taught me how to use it, but never a sword."

I wanted to give a better account of how Caldwell had trained me to wield a dagger to not only defend myself, but to gut a man of any stature in both the most discreet *and* the most brutal ways with confidence. But this was a fae Legion General I was talking to. Trying to tell him I knew what I was doing would've just sounded pathetic compared to his skill.

Besides, any adversary I'd been prepped to go up against was human, not fae. I'd never fought or practised against anything that came close to their speed or strength. I was way out of my depth here.

Something in my chest stirred, eager to come out and strengthen under the guidance of these fae.

"Right, good. We'll start with daggers then, as you're already familiar, then move onto swords later once you've gained some strength. And with any luck, that'll make wielding your magic easier down the track." He passed me two short blades along with their thigh sheaths which I strapped on. "I'll come by and do some meditation to help you recognise and control your magic whenever I can, but there's a situation that needs my attention for the time being."

As I stood, Veric gestured to someone behind me. "I believe you've met Jude."

I turned to see the happy face of the lithe fae already standing right behind me. A chill ran down my spine as I wondered how he'd approached without me noticing.

"How's your head, Lor?" He grinned.

"Better now." I smiled with a little extra strength, knowing that Killian was pretending not to pay attention in the distance.

He chuckled, then stood with his hands behind his back, looking to Veric to continue and he almost morphed before my eyes. His happy features and welcoming stature melted away, and a hard, sculpted seriousness fell into place.

I was taken aback by how different he looked compared to last night.

His ripped muscles stood out from underneath his battle leathers—there wasn't an ounce of fat on the male. Lean and strong, I could already tell he was built for speed and stealth. Jude's mane of black hair was tied in an intricate braid that ran down the back of his head and he had a small weapons stash sheathed all around his body, including a sword peeking out from behind his back. He was wearing the same grey battle leathers as Veric, clearly the uniform of the Winter Legion. The colour stood out starkly against his black hair and deep-red wings—I couldn't help thinking that Killian's black Summer Kingdom leathers would've suited him better.

"Jude will be in charge of your training for the time being. There is no one better suited to weapons fighting than he is," Veric assured, praising the small male standing before me. "I'll leave you in his charge for now, but I'll see you tonight, yes?"

"Yes." I smiled. Veric nodded his farewell at us both and walked toward Killian. They spoke together briefly, then with a small unit, he flew toward the forest and out of sight.

I looked back at Jude and held out my daggers. "Teach me, oh wise one."

Jude gave a small laugh and bent down in front of me to adjust my dagger's sheaths. I looked at Killian standing by Kevilla Hall, and pulled a look of superiority as Jude knelt in front of me, running his hands around the tops of my thighs. I could see Killian simmer from where I stood and a smug sense of satisfaction rolled over me.

Jude stood and began instructing how to grab and flick out my dagger with quick efficiency and had me practise the action over and over. I didn't tell him I already knew how to perform it—that it had been the last thing Caldwell taught me. But it was good to feel the cold press of steel in my hands once more and practise with my improved fae agility.

We skipped over where to aim in a close quarter conflict—Jude was impressed by my knowledge in that department, courtesy of Caldwell's teachings—but he did take time to note where to aim on wings to disable an enemy from flying, and how to cause major damage.

"Ready to put that all in action, Lor?"

"Let's do this," I said, feeling confident. Jude gave me a tight smile.

I wasn't silly. He was a legion fighter, skilled well enough to be charged with manning his own unit. Jude would absolutely kick my ass, but I thought I'd at least be able to not make a complete fool of myself.

Or so I thought.

I sheathed my daggers and let my hands hang loosely by my sides. Jude stood tall and straight, his hands clasped behind his back and his garnet wings tucked in tight, waiting for me to move. He didn't prepare his stance or even look like he was ready to start. His face went blank, and his dark eyes dull–devoid of any emotion as he stood across from me. I almost didn't recognise him as his focus settled.

I fixed my eyes on his and let a calm wash over me. Let my mind take me back to all the times I'd gone against my father and listened to his commanding instructions to duck, swing, kick, slice, stab. He'd made it feel all so natural–so easy. Despite his size and his skill with weapons, I could easily go toe to toe with him.

My father was the strongest man I knew. And if I could go against him as a human, I could go against a legionnaire as a fae.

I willed my mind to clear the images of my father, but I let his voice remain, as clear and commanding as though he was standing beside me.

'Believe in your strength, and none are stronger than you.'

My fingers tingled with awareness as they brushed the hilt of a dagger. Jude merely stood at attention, like a statue waiting to be brought to life.

I waited an extra beat before I twitched my fingers and grasped the hilt. The rough leather hadn't even pressed into my hand before Jude moved, flaring his wings out to give him lift and jumping feet first at me, kicking me squarely in the chest.

I went flying and landed on my back nearly ten feet from where I'd been standing.

Coughing and gasping for breath, I closed my eyes against the sky as I tried to drag air into my lungs.

Jude's shadow hovered above and I squinted up at the silhouetted figure. He reached down to help me stand, but I swatted him away and sat up.

"What the fuck, Jude?" I cursed at him, my chest aching and throbbing. I was surprised he hadn't cracked my sternum in two at the force of his kick.

He had the gall to look shocked. "What?"

"What do you mean, *what?* I thought we were sparring. You didn't say you were going to use your wings and fly kick me in the chest!" I shrieked, finally standing. I was grateful he was only my height, so I didn't feel so pitiful yelling at him.

"You always need to use everything in your arsenal."

I froze and eyed him suspiciously. "So I've been told. . ."

"Besides, an enemy isn't going to tell you how they'll attack."

"I didn't think you were my enemy," I grumbled, rubbing the sore spot.

"I am in here, Alora. I'd be doing you a disservice otherwise." He was full of sincerity which was his only saving grace from any further verbal lashings. He truly thought he'd done the right thing.

It annoyed me to agree he had a point. All anyone knew, was I'd been brought to Endence by the Oracle. Not even *I* knew why. I didn't even know anything about this big, bad *enemy* Queen Fleur had mentioned. Only the way her skin paled as she called them *demons* told me I probably didn't want to know much else. I knew better than to have asked Killian about it, so it was important I was prepared for anything—and Jude knew it, too.

I sequestered my annoyance and rubbed the last ache from my chest.

"Alright, let's try again. Just—fucking hell Jude, give a girl some warning." I looked over his shoulder to where Killian stood. He'd stopped what he was doing to watch my arse-kicking, with a shit-eating grin on his face.

I held my middle finger up at him and watched that smile fade and a scowl fill its place.

Much better.

Jude walked back to our starting positions and moved to stand in that same relaxed-statue way that tricked me into thinking he wasn't prepared the first time.

But *I* was.

Before Jude had fully turned to me, I grabbed my dagger and launched myself to the right, then stepped into his space. A flash of surprise lit his eyes before he swept his leg out and kicked my feet out from underneath me.

I went down like a heavy sack, the air whooshed out of my lungs once more as my back collided into the ground. I looked up to see Jude with his dagger out and pointed at me from where he stood. His breath came a little quicker than it had seconds before.

"I didn't see you." Surprise laced his words.

"Yeah," I grunted as I sat up. "That was what I was going for. Arsenal and all, you know?"

This time I took his hand as he helped me stand. I glanced at him when I was on my feet and caught him looking at Killian with an expression that seemed to be silently asking whether he'd seen what just happened.

I turned to study the commander, who was watching me with the same surprised expression Jude had.

Jude looked at me seriously, his dark eyes flitting over my face in question, before he nodded like he'd decided something important.

"Again."

We stood in the centre of the ring, and this time both stood in a stance with our daggers drawn. I came at him, this time stepping left and Jude came toward me to match.

I tracked his movement better as he threw his arm out. I slashed my own arm against his outstretched limb, sliding my blade along the top of his hand and hitting the guard of his dagger, knocking it from his grasp.

Jude reached across his body to grab me, but I spun behind him out of reach. He followed me around and raised his hand to block as I threw my fist out to jab at him.

He swept his wings wide and drifted back, creating distance between us, but I ran and closed the gap as quickly as he created it, my misting wings trailing behind me like smoke. I wanted to call foul play—that he got to fly while I couldn't—but it was a wasted effort.

As Jude landed, I came at him, dropping to my knees in a slide to bypass his defence. He used his wings to jump high into the air and came down from behind, so I twisted as he reached me and my blades clashed against his as we blocked each other's attack.

We stood there, breathing heavily before Jude took a single step away, silently resetting our spar.

"You said your father trained you?" I nodded. He led the way to a jug of water and poured us each a glass. "Who was he?"

"His name was Caldwell, but no one seems to know who he is beyond that."

Jude nodded as he drank. "Whoever he was," he said as he finished his drink, "he was fae."

It wasn't a surprise to me, given what I'd already pieced together. But to hear someone else say it was jarring.

"I already figured as much. Can I ask why you think so?" I asked, purely curious of his opinions.

"I'm a good teacher, Lor, but no one is *that* good when they start, even if they have had prior training. If you can already defend yourself against me, you've had some serious training only a fae could deliver."

I considered his words as I finished my drink, a smile touched my lips as I thought about Caldwell and our training sessions.

From then on, Jude and I played fair. He would pause our sparring to adjust me the slightest fraction, or play out a scenario—show me how to get the upper hand, correct my stance or change my position to cause the most damage.

After another hour my body was completely spent. The bones in my arm vibrated like jelly after blocking blow after blow Jude dealt. He told me to go home and wash up, then meet him at the armourer later in the afternoon. Veric had arranged a time for me to be fitted for my own set of battle leathers, which would support me better than the tights I currently wore and keep my temperature even when I trained.

I'd been so immersed in Jude's training that Killian had faded into the background. When I had the strength to sit up from where I'd dropped in exhaustion, he was nowhere to be found.

I told myself I was relieved he'd taken himself and his sullen mood elsewhere.

After everything had been taken care of, I spent the rest of the afternoon walking through Kevilla, orienting myself with its layout and businesses—mostly noting where all the pubs were.

It was such a beautiful place, it was strange calling it a camp. Town wasn't right either since the place was the designated operations hub for the Legion.

All the buildings were made with light wood and pale stone, decorated with greys and blues and accented with silver metal. The same tones as Kevilla Hall and the grey battle leathers. I registered they were the colours of my Kingdom as I found the tones repeated everywhere I looked.

Narrow paths of compact stone wended through the buildings and covered the walkways between the cabins, but the rest of the area was edged in lush grass.

As the late afternoon temperature dropped, I headed toward Kevilla Hall to spend the rest of the evening. Though I vowed to be more considerate of my poor head—and liver—this time around.

Jude commandeered me the moment I entered and ushered me to the same nearby table we'd sat at the night before. His bubbly personality was back in full force—gone was the warrior of the training ring.

We sat and talked lightly about the day and he praised my skill to the fae around us. As evening slipped into night, the conversation turned to their favourite stories of their own battles as we ate and drank together.

I sat back to listen to one of the females from Jude's unit, Lyra, tell her favourite story of the warrior, Evander. She fawned over the male known as the Untouchable Warrior, and how he threw Strike, the star-shaped javelin, and recalled it again and again to decimate the enemies on the battlefield against the leader of the Fallen, Orias.

She'd been so enamoured with the warrior, famed for his skill with the weapon, that she had his mark tattooed above her heart as though she'd been struck by the javelin herself.

I averted my eyes when she suddenly yanked her top down over her breast to show the tattoo, but at that exact moment, a looming shadow came overhead and all the warm buzz I'd revelled in, seeped out of me before I even looked up at who'd caused it.

I didn't need to.

"You're blocking the light," I quipped as Lyra's words died on her lips seeing her commander while she nearly bulged out of her leathers.

The entire unit all gave a murmuring salute and wandered away to a different table.

"And now you've spoiled the story. I wanted to know more about your famed warriors of old." I rolled my head back to look above me at Killian, standing with his arms across his chest as usual.

"Apologies, Princess. I do so hate to spoil your fun." His voice was laced with sarcasm.

"No matter." I smiled sweetly, knowing just how to piss the male off. "I'm sure Jude can. . . *fill me in* later." I leant forward and placed my hand on Jude's knee. It was a little forward of me, but I kept the touch light enough to play off as casual and I loved seeing Killian simmer. Jude angled his head, and a strange smile played on his lips.

But when I turned around to wink at Killian, the commander simply arched an eyebrow and smirked.

"I don't want to speak on behalf of Jude here," he said and smacked his own hand on Jude's shoulder, "but. . . I'm not so sure he'll be willing to, as you say, *fill you in.*"

Jude looked between us and slid low in his chair, taking a long drink of his wine, clearly not willing to get in the middle of our spat.

"Why not, Killian? Jude and I are becoming great friends." I smiled sweetly at my new trainer. I was being wholly honest with what I said. Jude was exceptionally easy to like. . . when he wasn't trying to kick the shit out of me.

"Who are we filling in?" asked a warm voice from over my shoulder.

Veric passed our little group and sat on the other side of Jude, immediately reaching for the wine and pouring himself a glass.

"Alora," Killian said, a smug grin still on his face.

"Oh, we'd love to," Veric said politely as he looked across at the three of us. Jude snorted his wine, clearly clued in to the innuendo. "About what, though? I may not be an expert."

Jude leant forward. "Oh, you're an expert, Veric, no question. But ignore them. Killian and Alora are just being vile. . . I'll fill you in later." He planted a kiss on Veric's lips and winked at me.

Oh.

Heat flared in my cheeks, telling me I'd turned a shade of crimson, and Jude exploded with laughter, patting my leg in consolation. I tossed my drink back in a single hit.

Killian just shook his head and reached over to grab the wine but remained standing.

"Did you deal with the volcacs today?" Jude asked Veric.

Veric's expression soured. "No. We found a nest deep in the forest and destroyed it but didn't find any of them. I'll send another team tomorrow to see if we can pick up their tracks."

"What are volcacs?" I asked, looking at Veric.

"Revolting creatures. They belong to the Fallen Court, but every so often they creep out and try their luck elsewhere. They're annoyingly hard to get rid of."

Veric paused and took a drink but Jude continued for him. "They can turn invisible, you see. Camouflage themselves perfectly to the land around them and so are difficult to track. The only way to find them is to wait them out, unfortunately. Their worst asset is their undoing, which is their desire for torture and cruelty. They kill for sport and make such a mess as they go about it, that there's usually a trail of bodies after a while."

I shuddered.

"Once they've been in an area long enough, their kills will lead us right to them," Veric finished. "This group are only somewhat new to the area but because they are so close within Hunneswick Forest, we want them taken out as soon as possible."

"Maybe after a few training sessions, you could join the party, Alora. Put those daggers to *real* use," Jude said, wiggling his brows.

"No," Killian growled from above.

Jude sank back in his chair, defeated by Killian's authority, but I wasn't so quickly silenced. Killian knew it too, because he looked at me before I'd even begun speaking.

"And why can't I–"

"No," he repeated and levelled me with a stare, which I returned. He must have sensed I wasn't going to let it drop, so gave a better answer. "Volcacs are too dangerous, even if you are good with a dagger. Unlike the goblins we met in the Asotines, along with a wicked set of claws at their disposal, volcacs have magic in their arsenal, and you, Princess, do not."

"Yet," I simmered.

"Yet. But until you do, you'll stay put where I tell you to."

I leant back in my chair and schooled every ounce of confidence I had into my expression. I didn't *want* to go and fight these creatures, but the way Killian deemed himself to be an authority over me rubbed me the wrong way—and I damn well wasn't going to back down to him.

"I'm not in your legion, Killian. You can't tell me what to do." I cocked my brow, passing the silent message to him that only he and I knew—the exact reason he couldn't order me around.

Technically, I rank higher than you.

Killian swished his glass of wine as he sucked on his bottom lip, I couldn't help my gaze dip to his mouth as he chewed it in thought. After a beat, he pulled that same infuriating move to get into my personal space—bending at the hips to put his face in front of mine. This time I didn't draw back. No retreating.

"But you'll be a good girl and listen to me anyway, won't you, Princess," he rumbled quietly, a hair's breadth away while staring into my grey eye.

Not quietly enough, though, given the way Jude gave a low whistle and pulled a face at Veric, which didn't escape my notice.

"Or what?" I challenged, refusing to blink.

"Or you'll find out how much of a *fucking brute* I truly am."

He straightened and finished the last sip of his wine, leant over me to plant the glass on the table, causing his smoky caramel scent to wash over my senses, before striding away wordlessly through the crowd.

Yet again, Killian had dominated the space. Had taken up all the air in the room.

"Gods, I hate him," I seethed, speaking mostly to myself but loud enough that the males easily heard.

"Is that what they're calling it these days?" Jude mumbled under his breath. Veric smacked his arm with the back of his hand.

"I know your allegiance is to him as your Commander, but I honestly don't know how you stand him," I grumbled, finally turning to the table and topping up my wine. With Killian gone, Veric's warm disposition eased my annoyance.

"Don't pay his dull mood any mind, Alora. It isn't your doing," Veric said, trying to ease my feelings. "But he does mean well, and he is right. . . you really shouldn't be involved with the volcacs."

"I wasn't arguing for that sake. I just don't like that he has a say in my life," I sulked, folding my arms over my chest.

Jude gave me a small comforting smile and kicked his legs up on top of the table. "Until we know why you're here, Alora, I hate to say it. . . but he kinda does."

I groaned and lolled my head to the side. "What's the Fallen Court?"

"It's an area to the west of the realm. Ruled by a race of angels called the Fallen," Veric explained.

"They already sound like bad news."

He nodded. "They are. Millennia ago, fae and angels lived together in peace. That is, until a pair of them tried to conquer the realm, and destroy everything in their path. But they were stopped by one of our greatest warriors. The fae let the angels who survived continue to live amongst us as a gesture of goodwill—we understood they were led by demons and we trusted those who remained were not of the same ilk."

"Let me guess, peace didn't last?"

"Mostly, it did for a while, but no. A few centuries ago, their leader tried to start an uprising, but they were decimated on the battlefield once more. Afterwards, Orella carved out a corner of our realm, redrew the borders of the Kingdoms and the angels were sentenced to stay in their region, banished from living amongst us as punishment for their transgressions. There's more to the story of course, but that's about the gist of it."

"I've never heard of angels."

"I'm not surprised," Jude said. "It's a dark past and happened centuries ago. The fae don't speak of it, and the angels aren't wandering around to tell their story."

I nodded slowly, considering it all. I would have to study their history books if I was to have any hope of being a leader worth my weight.

"Thank you for organising everything for me yesterday, Veric. You've been an incredible help," I said, ready to leave the heavy conversation behind and enjoy what was left of the night—head and liver be damned.

Veric lifted his glass in a distant salute. "I am always at your service, Alora." He hit me with one of his sincere smiles again. "But it's not me you need to thank." I cocked my head in question. "Killian's the one who threatened to pin me to the archery targets by my wings if you hadn't had everything taken care of by the end of the day." He gestured with his head in the direction Killian had walked off earlier.

I turned and looked through the crowd to where Killian stood. He was such a tall and intimidating presence he could be found even through the packed hall. He stood with his back to me, but I watched him all the same for a moment as he spoke and laughed so casually with a group at the top of the room.

Well, Gods damn.

"I need to apologise for earlier," I admitted, turning back to them. "Jude, I should never have made such an offensive joke to appease my own fight against Killian. You were right. I *was* being vile, in the truest sense of the word." I hung my head, guilt ripping through me.

"Oh Gods, Alora. Don't think twice," he laughed. "He's a sullen bastard. Has been for far too long now. . ." he mumbled, though I heard it. "I welcome any and all attempts to mess with his sour moods. Whenever you want to get under his skin, just let me know. Or you know. . . if you want him under yours." He winked.

"Jude!" Veric and I screamed at him in shock.

"Hate to disappoint but that won't be happening. He hates me with a passion."

"Mmhmm, it's a passion, alright," Jude muttered. I glared, but it didn't bother him in the slightest. Besides, he was too tipsy to argue with, so I clinked my glass with his and together the three of us finished off the wine.

In the early hours of the morning, I danced my way back to my cabin, feeling the buzzing effects of good conversation and alcohol spark in my body. The cold night air was a comforting silent as I walked to my door at the edge of the camp.

Despite saying my goodbyes to everyone at the hall, I couldn't help but sense someone was watching from the shadows, perhaps making sure I got inside safe.

Chapter 14
The Fight

Over the next several weeks, Jude would start my day by demonstrating how much he hated me, by making me run laps of Kevilla over and over until the morning fog cleared. I'd always been quick over short distances but had never managed to maintain endurance. The long runs each morning were utter torment and a terrible way to start the day. I questioned the sanity of the other warriors I saw running each morning. How they did it with the extra weight of their wings I didn't know.

Then until lunch, Jude and I would spar together, which was my favourite part of the day. My muscles strengthened under the daily practice, and soon my speed easily matched his.

I could track him as he shifted around the ring and learned to anticipate his moves, noticing every muscle tick, or flinch of his fingers. Every now and then I'd get past his defences and pin him beneath my blade, then I'd catch him throw a look at Killian.

The only time he truly got the upper hand was when he used his wings, which I still complained about and considered it cheating.

Always use everything in your arsenal.

My own wings still hadn't changed and continued to whisp around my shoulders and down my back like white ghosts.

Veric only had time to lend his expertise to train my magic once or twice—the volcacs still evaded his searches. We'd sit in a quiet area beside Kevilla Hall to meditate, but I just spent the time trying not to fall asleep while I plucked blades of grass absentmindedly. My magic was determined to stay far away.

If only the same could be said of Killian.

He mercifully kept his distance physically, but I kept feeling his eyes on me when I had my back turned, and he constantly watched from the shadows as I trained. I'd almost have preferred it if he'd just come closer, but then I remembered he was an arrogant dick and changed my mind.

After three weeks, the effects of my physical efforts were paying off. I could go farther faster and last longer in the ring. The fighting combinations came naturally as I went up against Jude, and I bested him more often. I liked how the power made me feel—how noticing my strength made me feel strong in other ways.

But it wasn't enough. Something in me demanded more.

My battle leathers arrived unexpectedly one morning at my cabin. The thick, ash-grey leather was lined with the most incredibly soft, pale-blue fabric, which was silky smooth as it slid over my body, fitting perfectly to my shape.

The leather was ribbed and overlapped like scales from the shoulders and down my arms. The cuff came to a stiff point across the back of my hand and was edged in soft blue. There were clasps at the back to open and accommodate wings, but my coiling tendrils continued to seep through without needing to be fitted.

I strapped the matching sheaths around my thighs at the exact right height to brush my hand against the daggers that belonged there.

A set of darker grey boots with silver straps rose up my shins and completed the look.

I braided my hair across my head from one side to the other and let it drape down my arm. As I looked back at the reflection meeting my eyes, I wondered if my mother had ever donned armour like this. Had Valefor? Had Caldwell? I pictured my mother and Caldwell in the same uniform and tried to picture a man with Veric's face alongside them.

A solemn tear escaped my eye and trailed down my cheek. I left it there as the vision I'd conjured of my family standing beside me, dressed in colours of our Kingdom faded away. Several more fell across my cheeks as I let the emotional walls I'd constructed break down—as I gave in, and the hollow feeling of loneliness spread from my heart.

My breath caught as I let the deep pain consume me. Part of me still wanted nothing more than to go home. The home I'd known all my life. To read books with Caldwell in his study, or go toe to toe with him in the yard. To bake in the kitchen with Maggie, and spend the day curled up in bed with Della. Gossip with Pepper. . . even see Lito—

The ache turned into a sharp pain, and I decided that was enough torment. There was no use hoping for home. It was unreachable. I threw up my walls again, blocking out all the hurt, dashed the tears from my eyes, sucked in a grounding breath to centre myself then left for the day.

I threw open my front door and nearly crashed into Killian, who had his hand raised ready to knock.

He startled and his expression went from shock, to surprise, to concern as he looked at me.

I clutched my hand over my heart as I squealed.

He took a step back to put space between us but kept his eyes fixed on my face. They lingered on my red-rimmed eyes before he drew his brows together.

"What are you doing here?" I asked after he didn't speak.

"Jude has gone with Veric for the day." His deep voice was low and wary. "I'll be in charge of your training."

Great.

I rolled my eyes, somehow resisting the urge to mutter under my breath. If we had to get through today without setting the other off into a rage, then I had to at least attempt civility. "Okay," I said simply then pulled the door closed before walking toward the training ring.

Killian fell into step beside me.

I peeked at him out of the corner of my eye. He seemed to be contemplating something—at war with himself. "You don't have to walk with me," I said, giving him an out. "You can just fly and meet me there."

"It's fine," he replied tightly.

Oh good, he's already pissed off.

Civility be damned.

"Gods, Killian, what the fuck have I done already?" I shrieked. "It's been thirty seconds and you're already grouching about like you've been dealt the worst kind of torture! Or am I just such a thorn in—"

"Fucking Gods! Alora, stop." He held his hands out and raised his voice to speak over me, cutting off my tirade. "Gods, you—" He ran a hand roughly through his hair in frustration.

I folded my arms underneath my chest and tapped my foot impatiently, waiting for him to deliver the verbal blow he was undoubtedly about to throw at me.

"You're so difficult, you know that, right?" he yelled, throwing his hands out.

I glared in response to his rhetorical question.

"You immediately think the worst of me just because I don't flounce all over you like everyone else. Or am *I* such a thorn in *your* side that you can't stand to be near me for longer than thirty seconds without causing a fight?"

"You're going to lay the blame on me?" I scoffed back. "You're the one who can't stand to be near me! I just gave you the opportunity to leave, Killian, but you didn't take it. Instead, choosing to loom overhead whilst simultaneously looking like it causes you unending pain!"

"The only thing causing me pain right now is seeing you're clearly upset, and knowing if I asked about your wellbeing, you'd tell me fuck off!"

I stilled. Not at his temper, but at his words.

Surely I'd misunderstood him.

His shoulders rose and fell with the anger he was straining to keep in check, his brows lowered in a scowl.

I straightened and the fight in me settled. "You're mad that I'm upset?"

"No, Alora," he said, the anger in him also dissipating. "I was concerned that you were upset. It's obvious you've been crying, but it's pointless asking whether you're okay, because I know you'd prefer to suffer on your own than have me be someone who you'd be willing to confide in."

I stared at a spot near my boots, unable to look at him. Guilt ripped through me.

"I can't win either way," he continued. "I chose to stay with you, not only because it would be a dick move for me to leave you to walk alone, but also in case you wanted to talk about whatever made you upset."

His tone had dropped all hints of anger, but I winced as his final words still managed to cut. "But for the life of me, I couldn't figure out how to start a simple conversation with you, without spiking your hot temper. Seems I don't even need to speak to succeed at pissing you off. How silly of me to consider you could think of me any differently than this hateful villain you've made me out to be."

With that, he continued down the path, creating distance between us.

Rooted to the spot, I watched his retreating form go down the lane between the cabins. I hit my palm against my forehead in frustration at myself.

It's not like he'd given me much else to go on that he doesn't hold me in high regard, either.

Gods, Alora, the sun has barely risen. You couldn't have stayed calm until noon?

I jogged to catch up and fell silently into step beside him, keeping my head lowered.

"Truce?" I asked after a beat and peeked up at him through my lashes.

He stopped short and looked me over, taking his time to come to his decision. "Truce."

"I'm—" I swallowed. The words were heavy on my tongue, but they were wholly necessary. "Sorry."

He arched a brow, and the corner of his lips twitched in that infuriating way.

"Those words a little hard to get out, were they?" he chuckled.

"Alright, alright. Don't ruin it, asshole."

His laughter faded as he considered me again, full of sincerity. "Are you okay?"

"Yeah," I mused. "Just missing home. It got to me, that's all."

He nodded. "We'll figure this out soon, Alora. I promise."

His words stunned me—the seriousness he said them with.

"Thank you, Killian. For. . . everything." I realised as I went to thank him for wanting to check on me that there was considerably more he'd done that I was yet to acknowledge.

He nodded again as his gaze roved over my leathers. "They suit you," he said simply. Nicely.

I smiled a ridiculous, girly smile as I accepted the compliment. Proud to be wearing the colours of my Kingdom.

"Too bad you're about to get grass stains all over them when I kick your arse today."

I scoffed at his sudden and unprovoked jab. His lips lifted in that cocky grin of his and his blue eyes glistened with mischief.

"Fuck you," I retorted, though the words didn't carry any of the anger I usually put behind them.

Killian squared his shoulders and his black wings twitched as he shifted closer to me, staring into my mismatched eyes. "You know, you say that phrase so often, Princess, I'm starting to think you might want to."

Muscles deep inside my belly pulled at his dark words, and tingles ran down my neck through to my fingertips as he looked at my lips before turning on his heel.

I cursed my needy body for reacting to him so easily.

It took me so long to recover from his insinuation, that he reached the training circle before I'd taken another step.

If I'd ever thought Killian would go easy on me for any particular reason, I would have been sorely mistaken. Luckily, no such silly notions crossed my mind, but I was wholly unprepared for his training, nonetheless.

It was the first time I practised with a sword, albeit it was only a training sword. Killian suggested it was time I give it a go—besides, he was highly skilled with the weapon, so who better to lead the lesson?

After spending most of the morning moving my arms, widening my stance and changing my grip as he took me through a few simple steps, he finally decided I was ready to spar with.

My arm rattled with each clash of our dull blades. Sweat poured down my face and sat between my shoulders after only a few minutes. He pushed me beyond my limits as he swung his sword, forcing me to dig into the steps he'd drilled into me. He outsmarted me at every turn and put me on my back a dozen times before lunch.

Still, my body sang with the effort it demanded of me, knowing it was another step closer to being as strong as these fae.

He definitely didn't go easy on me as we danced around one another in the ring, but I knew without a doubt he was still pulling his punches. I'd hate to be on the receiving end of his full strength.

Our swords clashed in a series of combinations, and I pushed through to a new level of endurance, wanting to get the better of him just once.

Killian swung down heavily in a punishing strike, and my arm gave out as I blocked.

I let out a cry as my knees buckled under the force of his hit. My sword dropped from my hands as I threw them out to catch myself before I fell face-first into the grass. The white smoke of my wings drifted around underneath me.

The cool sting of steel bit against the back of my neck. The flat blade was heavy as he let it press against my skin.

"Yield."

My breath was ragged and my arms wobbled as they struggled to hold my weight. My muscles were utterly spent from swinging the heavy sword, and they were about to give in. I curled my fingers into the soft ground beneath me, my ego demanding I get back up. Frustration raced up my spine and made my shoulders tense.

Killian swept his boot under my chest, taking my arms out. I'd been relying on their support so much that the action set me smacking into the ground. I groaned and rolled onto my side. Killian took a single step in to my space and pointed his sword at my chest.

"Yield," he said darkly.

An order.

Words were still beyond me, but I managed a single nod before I rolled onto my back and gave up, squinting my eyes shut against the bright sun.

Another day, I promised myself.

His mocking chuckle reverberated through me, and I peeked an eye open to watch him gloat.

"For a second there I thought you were going to get up again," he said, bending down to offer me his hand.

"You didn't think—you knew I was going to get up again. Otherwise, I wouldn't be down here on my back." I placed my hand in his and his calloused palm scratched against mine as he lifted me effortlessly.

"Maybe I just wanted to get you on your back, Princess."

He whispered the words so softly against the shell of my ear and walked away, I almost thought I'd imagined it.

Heat that had nothing to do with the morning's exertion burned my cheeks and pooled lower.

Don't fall for it, Alora, he's just trying to get under your skin.

Absolutely fucking right he is.

I watched as he strolled casually to the drinks station, perfectly unfazed at the suggestion he'd made. I was about to follow, when Lyra dove in from the sky and landed beside Killian. She leaned in close, muttered something in his ear, waited for him to nod his response then fled into the air again.

Killian looked to me, his face serious. Whatever the message was, it hadn't been good.

"Training is done for the day." He placed his drink on the table. "I'll see you at the hall tonight," he said, before launching into the sky after her.

As he disappeared amongst the treetops, I had this strange feeling, as though something had just been taken away.

I had no food in my house, so the only hope of being fed lay within Kevilla Hall. But getting off the couch was almost too hard a task to complete with how weak my limbs were. By the time I managed the strength to move, the sun had long set. I was unsure if Jude or Veric would be back by now, but I desperately hoped so. Partly because I enjoyed their company, but mostly so there was a buffer between Killian and I.

The night air was frosty as I closed my door behind me. The mild breeze made the leaves in the woods behind me rustle and shake. I pulled my green cloak around me tighter as I hurried toward the centre of the camp.

I crossed my fingers as I wandered into Kevilla Hall, but it was to no avail. There was no sign of Jude or Veric anywhere as I wove between the crowd. There was, however, no escaping the presence of Killian, who stood in his usual position on the platform.

As though he was keyed into my whereabouts, Killian's blue eyes found mine and held them as I walked around the edges of the room, looking for someone to talk to. But luck wasn't on my side—none of the fae I knew by name were to be seen.

There was only the one fae I knew well enough to talk to, and I wasn't sure it was a good idea that we did. From the heated turn his words and body took this morning, it more seemed like instead of taking one positive step in calling a truce, we'd ran a sprint to a finish line. I mean, it had been over a month. . . and a girl had needs, but—I couldn't buckle to Killian.

I went to an empty table and helped myself to dinner, piling on a few extra helpings—I'm sure my eyes were bigger than my stomach, but the training with Killian had taken everything out of me. I was amazed I was still standing at this point.

Food suitably taken care of, I scanned the tabletop to locate the wine, but it was nowhere to be found.

"Great," I muttered, and turned in place to search the surrounding tables.

I found the wine immediately. Unfortunately, it was held loosely in the fingertips of one Commander Killian, who leant back with smug satisfaction on the table behind him, wiggling the bottle in the air from side to side.

"I think I have what you're looking for," he said, the effects of the aforementioned wine shining through his glassy eyes.

"Only if you're referring to the alcohol." I stepped into his space and snatched it from his hand, then took a swig straight from the bottle.

He let out a dark chuckle and inclined his head. "Whatever else would I be referring to, Princess?" he asked with mock ignorance then swiped the bottle right back and took his own drink.

He followed me to the bench I aimed for and sat with me as I ate. The meat slid down my throat and warmed my belly.

Fae food really was divine.

I let out a soft moan as I took another bite—the meal doing wonders of its own to ease my suffering body. I opened my eyes as I took another gulp of wine from the bottle, then looked beside me to Killian, who was watching my neck as I drank. A muscle ticked in his jaw.

Slowly, I set the bottle down and cleared my throat.

"Will Jude and Veric be here tonight?" I asked, trying to change the strange mood between us.

"Unlikely," he said. "There was a development with the volcacs. They're growing brazen, and efforts need to be increased to deal with them."

"Is it dangerous? Will they be okay?"

He smiled and assessed me. "It's nothing they can't handle, Princess."

I looked down at my plate and nodded.

"Would you worry so for me, I wonder?" he said, a deep whisper between us.

I shot my gaze at him. His eyes softened and his breath hitched as he looked at my lips. His fingers twitched on top of the table as though they wanted to reach out.

"Don't fret, Princess," he said, his eyes clearing of the soft affection that had just shone through. He grabbed the bottle and leant back. "I know better than to think you would."

The words were cutting and he meant them that way.

My temper flared immediately at the insult. "What the fuck does that mean?"

He turned so his wings pressed against the table and leant his elbows back on the smooth surface, shrugging his non-answer.

Drunk fucking fool.

I grunted my frustration and stood abruptly. No point staying here if the only company I'd find was an intoxicated asshole.

I stormed off through the crowd. The vicious look I had must have been telling enough for others to get out of my way, because within a few steps the crowd parted in front of me, giving me a straight shot to the exit.

It was only when I stepped outside, and the warmth from the hall fell away, that I realised they hadn't parted for me, but for Killian.

His hand wrapped around my wrist and pulled me around to face him sharply, stopping my escape.

I yanked my hand free and shot him a scathing glare, willing it to burn him from the inside out.

"Alora, I–"

"Don't, Killian," I yelled, far too loudly.

The fae who stood by the door pretended not to listen, but I turned my angry look on them and they wandered further away, giving us at least the illusion of privacy.

"You're such a fucking hypocrite," I seethed, dropping my voice. "Or is this just payback for this morning?"

"It's not payback," he growled, clenching his fists. His body simmered with anger. "But please, correct what I said that was untrue."

"It was all untrue," I spat. "I *would* worry for you, Killian, despite how much of a dick you are. But to quote *you,*" I snapped, jabbing my finger into his chest, "you immediately think the worst of me just because I don't flounce all over you like everyone else."

He dropped his gaze and at least had the good sense to look like the words affected him. His shoulders rose and fell as he breathed heavily. Slowly.

No response.

So I stabbed further with my verbal assault, repeating more of his words from this morning.

"How silly of me to consider you could think of me any differently than this hateful villain you've made me out to be."

I watched as his own words cut deep. As he winced. Yet still, that rage simmered beneath.

I turned on my heel and strode further into the darkness. The breeze blew my cloak around before I pulled it tightly over my hips.

His footsteps sounded as he came after me, but I had no interest in listening to any apologies he might make, or insults he'd likely give.

"No, stop." My voice rang out in a command as I faced him and slashed my hand through the air.

He halted immediately. His dark wings cast an impenetrable shadow around his body.

"At least let me walk you back." A defeated sort of anger rumbled in his tone.

"No," I growled, keeping the steel in my voice. Unwavering. "I'm giving you another out, Killian. Why don't you take it this time."

I didn't hear him follow as I walked through the rings of the camp toward my cabin. I thought he'd taken my dismissal seriously and stayed away, but that same sense of being watched from the shadows I'd had walking home drunk that second night kept with me as I silently stormed down the little lanes.

Following from the air, then.

My anger ebbed off me in waves as I ignored him from wherever he was. Killian got under my skin and grated my nerves so easily, but it was all second to the hurt he'd dealt at his assumption that I simply didn't give a shit about him.

As I approached my little cabin, Killian's resolve cracked as his footsteps crumbled the rustling leaves covering the path behind me.

"Fucking hell, Killian," I sighed and turned to look at him. "I told you—"

Only he wasn't there.

No one was.

Weird. I could have sworn I heard—

A clammy, clawed hand wrapped around my mouth from behind, silencing the scream rising in my throat. I threw my head back into my assailant, the crunch of tissue breaking as my skull collided with their face sounded, but they held tight over my mouth. A second rasping shriek came from in front of me and I felt another clawed hand wrap around my throat, choking the air from my body.

Felt—not saw. The moon cast enough light that I could see clearly, but there was nothing *to* see. My enemy was invisible.

Fuck.

Volcacs.

My vision blurred at the edges as the one in front continued choking me. Luckily, they'd only thought to silence me and not disarm me, so with the last dregs of strength my fuzzy brain could muster, I let instinct kick in and the moves come naturally as my fingers brushed the dagger I kept at my side.

I grabbed and flicked out my blade, exactly as I'd perfected, and sliced it across the volcac standing in front—though I didn't know where exactly I'd slashed.

But it had done enough. The creature released my neck and I drew in a rasping breath, then in the same instant, I twisted my hand to plunge my dagger into the one who still covered my mouth from behind.

The volcac behind me let out a screech as the blade sank into its skin, but my joy at succeeding was quickly snuffed out. The second volcac grabbed around my throat again and squeezed with such ferocity I thought it'd pull my head off.

Blind panic set in and all clear thoughts vanished along with the remnants of breath I had left to spare. I squirmed and writhed between the two invisible creatures, and screamed against the hand covering my mouth, trying in vain to get free. But my body was spent. Limp and battered from the heavy training I'd done with Killian, I had no strength to put up a real fight, and darkness crept further across my vision.

The wind ripped around in a squall, much more violent than the breeze of before. A heavy pulse ripped through the air, adding to the wild tempest, tearing at the world around us. I felt a heavy pull against my shoulders and had the sensation I was falling backwards.

But then my knees buckled, and I felt so infinitely heavy.

And then I felt. . .

Nothing.

Chapter 15
The Blue

The room I awoke in was. . . dusty. Empty. It was a square, open space. Small. Run down. Abandoned. Rancid.

Then I noticed my body. Gagged. My hands were bound behind my back, my legs folded underneath me and tied at my ankles as I slumped against a wall, brushing up against a tarp.

Then came the pain. Agonising. My throat burned up its entire length, the back of my head ached, and when I leant back, the wet and sticky sensation that pooled in my hair told me I was bleeding. My legs were beaten and bruised, probably from being dragged to wherever *here* was. The state of my braid and dirt covering my clothes suggested it'd been through the forest.

I'm so totally fucked.

No one knew where I was.

Jude and Veric weren't in the camp. Killian was drunk and probably grateful to be rid of me whenever he realised I was gone.

I blinked through the pain lashing across my body as I looked further into the dim room. It was only lit by a single lantern by the door, but the two repugnant creatures in the corner were unmissable.

Their skin was the same deep purple as a mottled bruise, their round yellow eyes the colour of poison. They had slits for a nose and black horns poked from their temples. Sickly, blue blood ran down the upper arm of one, and from the side of the other. I would've had a sense of satisfaction had I not been too preoccupied with thoughts of how fucked I was.

They hadn't noticed I was conscious yet—they were too busy clicking and communicating with one another, so I took the opportunity to look around the room for something to help me.

Nothing.

A broken chair lay in the corner, but it was too far away for me to reach, and I was tied up anyway.

The lantern? Setting fire to the place would only endanger me further, plus they'd get away before they came to any harm.

There were iron hooks nailed to the wall in front of me, but again, I was tied up. Perhaps whatever was underneath this tarp—

Before I had the chance to look, the door creaked open and all three of us looked to see what entered.

Fuuuuccckkkk.

Four more volcacs crept into the hut, blood dripping down their pointed chins and sharp claws. The disturbing eyes of the first one to enter locked on me, and I was too slow to feign being unconscious. It let out gasps and shrieks, and then all six sets of eyes fixed on me as they loomed closer.

One of the creatures who had taken me—the one with the wound on its arm—came to the front, my dagger in its clawed hand. It twirled the weapon around in its palm while clicking and rasping to the others. They made noises disgustingly similar to laughs.

Blood drained from my face and I became dizzy. I wracked my brain at what I'd been told about them.

'They desire torture and cruelty. They kill for sport and make such a mess as they go about it—'

What was the bet this creature just said something about what it planned on doing with me?

It crouched and took its time looking me over. Tied and beaten. Weak and defenceless.

It made those clicking noises as it considered me, communicating something. I couldn't understand what they were saying, but the tone was telling enough.

Time was up.

I'd always considered old age to be the preferred cause of my death. If not, then at least something quick. But I did know that I definitely didn't want to die a coward. I really wanted to keep up my struggle against these creatures, but something about being bound and wholly outnumbered ceased all heroic ambitions, leaving only sheer panic in its wake.

All my training these past weeks had amounted to nothing.

My growing hysteria made me hyperventilate, and my gaze flicked between the creature and my dagger held in its grip. I nearly passed out from fear as it reached its disgusting hand toward me, and stroked a single claw along my jawline. My skin sliced open in the wake of its dirty, black claw digging into my flesh. I gagged at the smell of the creature and the notion of it touching me. The sting of the cut barely registered, but I knew that'd be thanks to the adrenaline coursing through my system.

I jerked my head back to escape it, if only for a moment longer. But the pain that lashed through my neck cut through my body's defence mechanism. I cried out and my eyes welled with tears as I looked back at the creature, its gruesome smile stretched across its entire face at seeing me in such torment.

I knew it would only grow wider as they killed me slowly.

Tears fell from my eyes in a rush, and I sobbed and choked around the oily cloth in my mouth. Breathing became nearly impossible as mucus dripped from my nose while I cried.

The creature took my dagger in its hand again, and this time leant forward—the tip aimed at my grey eye. My body convulsed and I screamed around the gag as I realised it meant to either pierce it or pry it from its socket.

I kicked and thrashed as best I could against my bound hands and feet, but another pain lanced across my back as I pressed into the wall.

I let out another garbled shriek, but the muffled sound didn't travel.

Two other volcacs came on either side of me and pinned me down roughly against the wall, immobilising my pathetic efforts to escape them. Their claws dug through my sweater, impaling my arms several times over and drawing blood. The one with the dagger pressed his free hand on top of my leg, piercing my thighs with its claws and crushing the limb under its weight as it leant over me. It's claws sank deep through muscle and scraped against bone, and I almost blacked out. The action ceased any movement, and my entire body erupted as hot pain lashed every part of my skin.

Every nerve was firing, my bones were surely going to crack under their pressure, and my skin peel open under their claws. Oblivion crept in at the edges of my vision again under their slow, cutting torture, but the adrenaline coursing through me ensured I stayed conscious.

Suitably restrained, the volcac leaned in again, renewing its attempt to carve my eye from my head. There was nothing I could do. I couldn't budge an inch, and any attempt I managed just ripped and pulled against the claws they had driven into my body.

As the volcac held the dagger level with my eye, the last speck of mettle I had left burnt out, as I saw no escape from what was about to happen.

I wailed and sobbed around the gag, and gasped for breath as I came undone. Lost to panic, I squeezed my eyes shut and turned my head away, then drew in a ragged breath and screamed until my lungs burned.

The veins in my neck went taught, the pain nearly ripping me apart at the strain. My nails dug into my palms and drew blood as my shrill cry rent the air as far as the cloth allowed.

And then the room exploded.

The held dagger whizzed past my ear and imbedded into the wall next to my head. The two volcacs on either side of me were thrown out in the detonation, their claws ripping my skin apart further as they were torn away, while the one in front of me was blasted onto my chest, knocking the last drop of air from my lungs.

The other three creatures were thrown around the room. One was impaled on the set of iron hooks on the wall and shrieked in agony.

My lungs burned like they'd been rubbed with sandpaper from the inside, and my vision blurred at the lack of oxygen. But as I drew in a rasping breath and lifted my head from my shoulder, my vision cleared enough that I saw the cause of the blast.

Killian stood in the doorway, his face a mask of raging fury. Sword drawn and wings flared, he stepped over the door he'd blown from its hinges.

One volcac got to its feet and threw its arms back as it screeched. A roar ripped from Killian's throat in return as he raised his hand and released a blast of power that turned the creature into blue mist, crumbling before my eyes.

Without pausing—or so much as looking—he pulled a knife from his thigh and cocked his wrist. The blade flew and lodged itself between the eyes of the volcac impaled on the hooks, silencing its wails.

Killian stepped further into the room and thrust his sword through the belly of a third before it had lifted itself off the ground.

That left the three who had pinned me down. They were the furthest in the room and had the most time to recover. As though they were operating as one, the three creatures turned invisible, blending seamlessly within the room.

A foul ripple of magic pulsed through the room, but it was cut short as Killian let his own power blast through the space once again. The pressure of his magic rose and crushed in on me, making my ears ring and my lungs strain. But as soon as it came, it left. As though Killian created a pocket around me.

The warrior shot his piercing gaze around the empty room, and quicker than I could track, he sliced his sword in two slashes across the air. Dual thumps followed, and blue blood pooled on either side of him as two volcacs met their end.

He focused one last time, his power thrumming as he hunted the last target. I watched him so intently that I didn't notice at first how the dagger next to my head shifted in the wood.

When the remaining volcac peeled back its magical layer next to me, I screamed against the cloth still in my mouth. Time slowed as its yellow eyes, filled with hatred, glared at me as it freed the dagger from the wall and arced its arm to slice across my throat.

But before it could deal its final blow, it jolted and froze—its eyes turning lifeless before it slumped to the floor beside me.

Killian stood behind the creature, his shoulders rising and falling as he breathed through his rage and threw a blue clump onto the floor. It landed with a wet smack and I shuddered as I realised what it was.

I counted the dead bodies littered around the room and knew I was safe. Relief flooded through me as I looked at Killian, but it was far away—so far away that I couldn't grasp onto it.

The emotions barrelling through me made my body shake uncontrollably, while I howled and gasped around the gag still in my mouth.

Killian wasted no time. He sheathed his sword and waved his wrist. The blue blood staining his hand from the heart he'd just pulled from the volcac disappeared as though it had never stained his skin.

Another wave and the bonds disappear from my wrists and ankles, as though they never existed. The cloth between my teeth disappeared and my wails went further into the air as I continued to come undone.

Killian stooped and picked me up, his caramel and wood-smoke scent enveloped me and I breathed it in as he curled me against his chest. Each intake of the smell of his skin tried to crack its way through to my subconscious. Killian whispered soothing words, but they were muffled and distant. I couldn't hear them past the ringing in my ears.

His strong arms held me tight as he walked outside, his thumb rubbing in long strokes at the top of my shoulder. Cold wind rushed over my body, and I realised in the back of my mind that we were flying.

I was in shock, and shivers travelled up my body as blood dribbled out. A subtle warmth that blocked the wind spread across my exposed body, and I realised Killian must have picked up that tarp at my back to cover me as we flew to keep me warm.

Only a few minutes later, we landed, and Killian's soothing words turned into barking orders. It only lasted a moment before the sound of boots around us left, and then it was just he and I again. His words turned soft and calming once more.

Warmth coated me as we stepped into a room. I thought I recognised the space, but then it changed and nothing looked familiar.

Killian gently laid me onto a mattress on my side and kept his hand pressed on my shoulder, continuing to massage his thumb into my skin—kept repeating those same, gentle words I still couldn't hear.

A door burst open close by and I jolted. Killian pressed his hand firmer on my arm to keep me still. Behind me, two voices called out and spoke with Killian who kept his eyes locked on mine.

The smell of citrus and sandalwood floated to me before a bubbling voice called gently from behind, and the fae it belonged to touched my shoulder. I couldn't help the jerk my body made at the unfamiliar touch. I screamed as fear raced through me again at the panic of the unknown.

Killian shot a glare at whoever had touched me, and his words turned sharp and loud again. But then his blue eyes were back on me and I calmed again.

A second, warm voice floated to me from behind as well, but no one else reached out to touch me.

Only Killian.

My instincts were in control, urging me to stay alive. All I knew was that only Killian was safe.

My loud sobs ebbed away into silent tears that dripped freely, and I gained control over my lungs, taking long, shaky intakes through my mouth.

Killian leant toward me, resting his chin on top of his outstretched arm. He nodded his encouragement as I slowly settled.

An ache spread across my head—repercussions of the tears and screams that had left me.

Footsteps shuffled in the room, still muted and unclear and Killian looked up as a brown-haired male I'd never seen, came into view near my feet. I tried to rear up, and another scream raced up my throat, but Killian came back into full view. His hand left my shoulder and rested lightly on my face, stroking my cheek as he continued to talk.

His voice broke through, but I only caught part of his words.

". . . okay, Alora. . . here to help." He lifted his lips in a pained smile, nodding at me. He held my hand and squeezed gently before he lifted it to his mouth and pressed a strangely tender kiss to its back.

I peeled my gaze away from Killian and looked warily at the new male who stood at the foot of the bed.

He lowered into a half bow, then took a small step closer. He held his hands out as though warming them by a fire and closed his eyes. A solemn and relaxed expression fell over him.

Indeed, there must have been a fire somewhere, because warmth radiated all over me. At first, it felt like a heavy mist floated above my body, forming to my dips and curves before it settled over me like a weighted blanket—releasing tension from between my shoulders and easing the sting from my legs.

A deadened thud sounded from across the room, and Killian tensed as he looked over my body at whatever made the noise. I flinched again, but Killian was right there, soothing me with his touch.

A voice muffled into the room from behind me. ". . . is here, demanding. . . we told. . . wants to know. . . said if we don't. . ."

Killian's expression tightened, and his lips moved—but still, his voice struggled to break through the ringing in my ears.

I wanted to ask what was happening, but the sensation of pins and needles tingled down my jaw, coated my neck, then prickled in my arms and legs.

The heavy warmth that seeped into my limbs crept and settled into my torso, lulling me into a strange feeling of complete serenity, and I found myself unable to remember why I'd been so upset. The answer to what had caused my pain drifted further and further from my fingertips, and my eyelids grew heavy, as though I hadn't known sleep for an age.

Killian kept his blue gaze fixed on me, unblinking and worried. I looked back at him, focusing on his smoky caramel scent, fighting the urge to close my eyes.

My subconscious wanted nothing else than to make sure I was near the male keeping me safe.

Staring into his eyes, I noticed the blue of Killian's irises were unlike any others I'd known. Not the summer-sky blue of Veric's, or Caldwell's deep grey-blue, or even my mother's vivid icy-blue from my memories. Killian's eyes were the colour of blue fire. Lit from within with light and flame—intense and burning.

All consuming.

They were the last thing I knew before I was pulled toward the peace that the heat promised.

Chapter 16
The Question

I still had an ache behind my eyes and my throat was raw and chafed when I woke. The dark storm clouds visible through the wide window made it impossible to tell what time of day—or night—it was.

I thought the spacious bedroom I occupied was empty—until a black shadow shifted in the corner.

Killian sat hunched in an armchair—his elbows on his knees, head dropped in his hands, with his fingers scrunched in his hair and his mighty wings curled at his sides.

I drew in a shaking breath, and Killian whipped his head up before I'd even made to move.

It took him two strides to make it to me, his eyes worried and assessing as he knelt beside the bed.

"Hey," he whispered and stroked his hand across my hair. It was almost affectionate.

I shifted to lift onto my elbows, but sucked in a sharp breath as pain lashed through my back, and then my neck throbbed from the breath.

"Fuck," I rasped, and settled back amongst the fluffy sheets.

Killian flashed a look of concern but relaxed and let out a deep chuckle. "Of course, the first word out of your mouth is foul profanity."

I glared at him with all the venom I could muster. It wasn't much.

He kept weaving his fingers through my strands, following their gold lengths down over my shoulder. His gaze lowered as he followed their path.

"You'll need another few days before you're fully recovered," he said, not meeting my eyes. "I'll call the healer back to look you over again and give you something for the pain."

A strange silence fell between us, and I could tell something laid heavily on his shoulders.

My muscles were weak as I cupped my hand under his chin and lifted his head to look at me.

His expression was of complete anguish. A hint of tears shone in his eyes, but he set resolve into his features so they didn't fall.

"I'm so fucking sorry, Alora." His voice cracked as the tears threatened again and he grasped my hand closest to him, holding it tight. "You were right. I was an absolute dick to you. My behaviour was shameful and disrespectful, especially to someone of your rank, within your own Kingdom, and I wholly apologise for my behaviour." He lowered his head in a bow. "I was hypocritical and accusatory, and a drunk fucking bastard, and. . . and jealous."

My stomach had a silly, strange reaction to that last part.

"But my worst crime was not ensuring your safety. For being immature and letting what you said stop me from making sure you were safe. I promised on the peaks of the Asotines that I wouldn't let you come to any harm, and I've failed in the first month to uphold it. I will do whatever I can to earn your forgiveness for being an arrogant asshole for a start. . . but mostly for putting you at risk."

He paused, and his eyes flicked between mine, waiting for me to speak. To accept his apology or cut him down again.

Drunk or not, his scornful words were inexcusable. He *had* been an arrogant asshole.

"You won't earn my forgiveness, Killian," I rasped in the hoarse whisper my voice would allow. Killian winced as the words cut. He tried to pull his hand from mine, but I grabbed onto him. "Because there is nothing to forgive."

"But–"

"But nothing, Killian. Yes, you've been an asshole. Yes, you shouldn't have said what you said, accused me of not caring. But I've said plenty I shouldn't have as well. Bitten back just as hard."

He kept watching me, wary of what I'd say next.

"You came for me, Killian. You're not the reason I was attacked. . . but you are the only reason I'm alive."

Killian's battle with his tears was lost.

One hand was still intertwined in my hair, his other clutching mine, so he wiped the wet tracks against his shoulder to cease their falling.

"I owe you a life debt." A shiver passed down my back as I made the declaration.

Killian knew the weight of the words, too. He looked at me with a seriousness I'd yet seen on him, then nodded gently and squeezed my hand, acknowledging what I'd said.

I squeezed back.

He cleared his throat before he spoke again.

"I wouldn't thank me just yet, Princess. Once you've recovered, I'm going to train you harder than ever, so that the next time your pretty little arse needs rescuing, you can damn well do it yourself."

I laughed at the obscenity and took a second to file that piece of information of his thoughts on my arse away for another time.

"What about Jude?"

He gave a smug smile. "Jude can move over. He's done well, but it's time to move on with bigger and better things."

It was clear the *bigger and better* in question was himself and not anything to do with weapons. But there was no denying Killian was the stronger male, and I was suddenly looking forward to seeing how far he could push my limits and what that could mean for my strength—for the power I could wield.

He drew in closer, leaning over the bed. I don't think he noticed his hand holding mine had shifted so his fingers could move in circles against my wrist.

I certainly did.

"You called for a truce yesterday morning," he whispered deeply as he continued searching my eyes—continued circling my wrist. His breath coasted along my jaw as he spoke. "Might we. . . continue that?"

The way his gaze locked onto mine had me wondering if he meant more than what he was asking.

Heavy. Too heavy. I had to change the mood and how he was looking at me, shift how close his lips were to my own.

I arched a brow, letting my sarcasm shine through. "I'm not sure, Kilian. I still need someone to yell *fuck you* at."

A dangerous smile spread and his blue eyes ignited with heat.

"Oh, you still can, Princess. As long as it starts with *can I* and ends with *please*."

I gasped. I expected him to laugh, having seen he'd gotten a reaction out of me, but that knowing smile stayed—his eyes still hot and wild and pinned on me.

He's completely fucking serious.

My stomach squirmed and my core clenched.

The bed shifted as he leant in closer again, but at the sound of a door opening and boots treading across floorboards somewhere in the house, he pulled back sharply—breaking the spell he was under.

A blonde head peeked around the door seconds later, trying to be considerate if I wasn't yet awake.

Killian was already reclined back in the chair in the corner, looking completely at ease with his leg crossed over his knee, as though he'd always been there.

Veric immediately broke into a huge smile as he stepped into the room, seeing I was awake. Completely unaware of what'd just passed between Killian and I—though Veric shot a curious glance at Killian as he walked over to me.

Surely it was nothing.

He perched on the side of the bed and swept a curl away from my face. The act was affectionate but didn't carry the same weight as when Killian had just done it. "How are you feeling?"

"Like I got attacked by a bunch of shitty pincushions."

"Well at least it's on par with what happened then," he chuckled, but his smile didn't meet his eyes. "But you look fantastic." Nervously he gestured at me. "I mean at least your—"

"Veric," Killian warned.

I looked between the two males, confused at Killian's tone.

"At least my what?"

Veric glanced between us. When he didn't answer, I repeated the question harder. "Tell me now, before I find the strength to gut you both," I demanded, not liking how the two of them exchanged looks.

This time, Veric kept his eyes on Killian, waiting for him to speak.

The commander planted both boots on the floor and leant forward in his chair, clasping his hands together between his legs.

His wicked blue eyes held me in place.

"You haven't asked, Princess."

"Haven't asked what?"

"How I found you."

"I figured you heard me scream or–I don't know, could smell me or some weird fae tracking skill or something. . . I don't know," I rambled.

"Oh, I tracked you alright," he said seriously. "I think the whole damn realm could have tracked you–in fact, some did. . ."

"What do you mean? Tracked me how?"

"When you were grabbed, you let out a blast of magic so fucking powerful it damn well nearly knocked me over."

I what?

"Jude and I felt it too," Veric said quietly in agreement.

"The entire legion panicked, thinking we were under attack, but I knew it was you. It's probably why the volcacs knocked you out. When you went down, your magic stopped blaring, and we couldn't feel you anymore." Killian's eyes went dark as he remembered what happened next. "I had to fight past the damn wine to come to my senses, to concentrate and gather my power before I took off to find you."

The way he'd exploded into that room. . . turned that creature into mist.

"We all suspected it was the volcacs who were responsible. But by the time I made it to the forest, they'd used their magic to mask you. Then a while later, your magic pushed out again, and that's how I sensed where you were."

"What does this have to do with me looking fantastic, Killian? Don't try to bullshit me either, I know I look like shit."

Veric met my eyes. "Your magic, it. . ."

"Look down," Killian offered with a reverent expression on his face.

I peered at my toes hiding beneath the blankets.

Killian rubbed a hand over his face in exasperation.

"No, Alora. Look *down.*" He gestured with his eyes to the bed I was lying on.

A swell of disbelief rushed through me as I looked at my body. At what was underneath my body. Not a tarp—

Wings.

Not flowing, misty tendrils. Not fog swirling around my back. Actual wings. The milky white forms lay limp at my sides, half buried underneath me. They shimmered with the shining iridescence of a freshwater pearl, smooth and beautiful.

Like morning sun glittering over fallen snow.

"Holy fucking Gods!"

Killian's laugh rang through the room as I gawked.

"I—how—"

"It seems your magic needed a bit of a push to make an appearance," Veric said.

"It will take some time, and a shit load of training, strengthening, and practice before they're of any use to you," Killian said then flashed me a wink. "But I guess it's a good thing I'm your new trainer."

"Jude will be devastated," Veric said, smiling.

"This is incredible," I breathed, taking in the opalescent wings.

"Well, I come bringing more incredible news," Veric chimed, shifting my attention to him. "Other than wanting to check on you, of course, I received word from my sister, Erela."

I perked but winced again at the pain that pierced my back, which I now recognised as coming from my wings. Killian shifted in his chair uncomfortably as he watched me settle back down.

Veric continued. "She's able to host you at the Winter Palace in Carault. I know you wanted to learn more about the king and do your own research."

My skin prickled with nervous energy. If only Veric knew exactly how much I wanted to know more about Valefor.

"That would be. . ." I searched for the right word, "amazing, Veric, truly. Thank you."

"I knew it would make you happy."

Killian stood. "We'll leave as soon as you've recovered. I'll send for the healer and bring you something to eat. But for now, you'll stay here on bedrest."

"I'll get the healer." Veric patted my shoulder then quietly left the room.

"Where is *here* exactly, Killian?"

His smile turned wicked. "My house."

I tried to school my features and contain the shock that rippled through me, but Killian still saw it. Read me perfectly.

"That's right, Princess. Not only am I your new trainer, but I'm also your new roommate." He paused his exit at the doorway and drummed his fingers on the wood. "I've got you all to myself."

The healer had come soon after Veric summoned him. His magic took away most of the aches and pains in my body from the attack, and he left me with a pouch of herbs to drink to continue healing the damage to my throat. Only the pain in my neck remained, as well as a heavy strain on my shoulders—but that was due to an entirely different reason. My wings had shifted my centre of gravity, and I hadn't regained the strength I'd lost from the attack to hobble around alone.

Killian helped me stand after the healer left so I could look at them in a mirror. They were breathtaking. The leathery forms were as smooth as polished stone and held a glow within them. Not sparkling like glitter—but fair and frosted, shimmering against the lights above.

They dragged behind me and the strangest scratching sensation prickled my senses as I moved. I only took my eyes off them to watch Killian's feet, afraid he'd stomp on them carelessly as he held onto me.

I warned him and his brutish boots to be careful. He chuckled and muttered under his breath something about *faelings* and *being pedantic*—but he was diligent as he guided me to the bathroom and then promptly back to bed.

Killian's house was one of the larger homes next to Kevilla Hall, decorated in darker, warmer tones than the rest of the decor around the legion. I recognised it as the richer styles of the Summer Kingdom.

I hurt for him being so far away from his home—away from his duty as the General of the Summer Legion.

Moving on my own was a hopeless endeavour, so for the next two days, Killian and I sat around in mostly comfortable silence. I read the books he had lying around his living area, and he conducted his duties from home so he could stay with me, never leaving my side.

Occasionally, as we sat around the house, we would catch the other sneaking glances across the room and the silence would stretch with. . . *tension.* I was yet to bring up the comment he'd made about my *pretty little arse*—I wanted to be capable of a quick escape when we aired out that particular remark. But mostly the conversation between the two of us lightened to an easy companionship.

For a few minutes each day, Killian had me perform sets of exercises to strengthen my wings so I could eventually lift them off the ground. The pulling and flexing motions made my entire back hurt and caused a headache at the base of my neck.

Jude and Veric dropped in at separate times to see me. Jude was devastated when Killian told him his training duties were finished, but took it in his stride, saying I didn't know all the good I'd be missing out on—especially because he was far nicer to look at than Killian.

Veric kept me company whenever he had time, and told me stories from his two-hundred-year past. He talked about his mother and father and his time spent in Lleiscray, a coastal village to the east where he and his sister Erela were born.

My heart ached with longing when he told a story from his childhood of his Uncle Valefor sneaking him from his room at night to go flying over the sandy beaches of Lleidrid. And how his mother chased Valefor through the skies in a rage when she'd discovered them.

I wanted nothing more than to tell Veric we were family. That the story was about my father, and that I wanted to listen to every memory he had of him.

The words were on my tongue, but I swallowed them and instead sat silently and clutched onto every word my secret cousin said.

When dawn rose on the third day, the swelling and tenderness were gone from my neck, and I was able to lift my wings high enough that they only just brushed the floor. Walking short distances was also manageable, but the weight of the wings made the muscles in my back pull and ache.

Veric came up to my room in the morning holding a wrapped package under his arm. He opened the parcel and pulled out an ivory cloak the colour of hyacinths and held it out for me.

The thick velvety material was as soft as clouds and instantly warmed me as he hung it over my shoulders—fastening the three shining, silver chains across my collarbones.

"It's spelled, in case you hadn't noticed," he said as his fingers linked the clasp.

"The heat. . ." I mused, trailing my fingers along the fluffy edges.

He made a deep noise in his throat that told me I'd guessed right. "Despite it being mid-spring, Carault rarely gets warm enough for snow to melt. I wanted to make sure you were comfortable while you were there."

"You had this made for me?" I asked, astonished.

The cost must have been—

But he shook his head, looking thoughtful. "No, nothing but a dodgy hand-me-down, I'm afraid." He laughed and looked at me playfully. "It's mine, actually. It used to belong to my aunt."

My mind whirled thinking of his family tree. "Your aunt?"

"Yeah, Eira."

Shock hit me hard enough I nearly fell over. Veric steadied me by my shoulders and we sat together on the bed. His cream wings draped elegantly next to my limp pearl ones.

"Even though she was the queen, to Erela and I, she was simply, Eira. She always doted on us."

There was no hope of stopping the tears that fell at hearing how much my mother meant to Veric.

"Sorry," I croaked, wiping my eyes with my fingers. "I ahhh. . . I didn't have any family like that. . . any aunts or anything, and my. . ." My voice broke, so I cleared my throat and tried again. "My mother died when I was little. So hearing you speak about how much you loved her—loved Eira, I mean—it's really touching. You giving me this is. . ."

Veric wrapped his arm around me, his vanilla and citrus scent coming with him. "I'm sorry if I—"

"No, please don't apologise. These are happy tears, I promise."

He nodded. "Eira had an affinity for ice magic, and wasn't troubled by cold weather, so she never wore her cloaks—she said they made her too hot. So when Erela and I were around fifty, she gave one to Erela, and one for me to give to my bride. But of course, things didn't turn out that way for me—and I don't think it's Jude's colour." He smirked at me sideways.

Cold weather had never affected me much either, so it was comforting to learn it was a quality I shared with her.

"I'm not just giving this to you because you're going to the palace and could use it," he continued and smiled warmly. "Something feels right about you having it. I don't want it to sit wrapped up and forgotten."

I flung my arms around him and buried my head in the crook of his shoulder.

"I'll treasure it, Veric," I said, muffled against his clothes. His hand wrapped behind my head as he hugged me back.

We broke apart after a while, then he stood and held out his hand to help me stand. "Let's get you to my sister."

He led me downstairs into the living area where we found Killian already waiting. He turned, and whatever he was about to say died on his lips as he looked at me. His eyes went to Veric, then back to me—on my mother's cloak.

"That is an incredible offering, Veric."

"One that's deserving."

Killian just gave a deep nod. "We leave in five minutes, Princess."

Precisely five minutes later, I stood in the open air outside Kevilla Hall, fed and ready to leave. Jude wrapped me in a tight hug before handing me two new daggers to replace the ones lost in the attack. I strapped them against my thighs before leaning into him a second time.

Veric said his goodbyes then propped his arm on top of Jude's shoulder as they stood together.

"Where are the horses?" I asked Killian, looking around.

"We aren't riding, Princess." He stretched his wings pointedly then hooked his arm around my waist.

Absolutely not.

I squealed. "You're not serious."

I didn't trust this bastard not to drop me even if we'd been the best of friends for years. Let alone that we could barely stand one another up until a few days ago.

"I'm always serious," he rumbled with a grin that implied the opposite.

Killian picked up a pack of belongings and flicked his wrist, making the entire bag disappear.

Mounting questions wanted to tumble from my lips, but before I could utter any, he folded my wings together and pressed his arm around my back, then lifted me under my knees so I curled into his chest.

A flashback to the last time I was against him like this whipped through my head, so I turned my face into his shoulder and breathed deeply to calm myself—his warm scent set me at ease.

"Ready to go home, Princess?" he muttered so only I could hear.

A shiver ran through my body and my lips curled against his neck.

My response was a whispered breath. "Yes."

The view stretching before us was astonishing. The forest continued its claim on the land to the east, the tops of the trees turning white the further we flew. As we went, Killian pointed out in which direction I would find *this* town or *that* city.

We travelled for hours, only stopping twice to rest and stretch, and I was increasingly grateful for the cloak Veric had gifted me, keeping my body cocooned in perfect warmth against the dropping temperature. Killian was content to let me marvel at the beauty of the landscape in silence for a time.

On the horizon, the idyllic green wilderness disappeared beneath a blanket of snow. It took a few moments for my eyes to adjust to the blinding coat that threw the world into fluffy white when we breached the snowfield. My breath curled as I blew out my shock at the raw beauty.

After another hour, Killian murmured next to my cheek, bringing my attention back to him. "If you look closely, you'll see Carault at the base of that cliff."

Just as he said, the city came into view. The rooftops of the buildings and homes were nearly hidden amongst the landscape.

"And up there," he gestured with a tilt of his head, "is your palace."

As though plucked from a fairytale I used to read to Della when we were little, the stunning castle rose toward the sky, its silver peaks hidden beneath the low clouds.

I closed my eyes and pictured my mother striding the halls within.

"And beyond," Killian said above the whirling wind as we flew lazily, bringing me back to the present, "are the Argensir Mountains."

I looked beyond the sparkling palace to the imposing, black peaks rising in the distance. Swallowed in a thick fog, the mountains were a dark and jagged shadow in the beyond. Far away enough that they didn't loom over the beautiful landscape, but were unmissable nonetheless.

"Let me guess, they're dangerous?" I asked in a monotone.

Killian rumbled a low chuckle. "Yeah, you could say that. They're named after one of our most famed warriors. Argensir lived thousands of years ago and saved our people from a terrible fate. It's an honour to have the mountains named after him in your Kingdom. The winds are too dangerous to fly in—any who wish to conquer the mountain and reach the peak must do so on foot. A task which is just as dangerous."

"What's up there?"

"You mean, other than creatures that can rip you in half, weather so cruel it can kill you while you sleep and old magic that messes with your head and can drive you crazy? Argensir was a brutal warrior. . . those are brutal mountains, named after him for a reason."

"So why would anyone bother with the effort of trying to climb them?"

"Orella gave a prophecy hundreds of years ago. *You find what you seek at Argensir's peak.* Many fae seeking riches, or answers. . . or fae who have lost their way, try to reach the summit to find whatever it is to fulfil their desire. Though if you ask me, I think Orella was just messing with us."

I tilted my head to look at him. His brow was lowered in thought.

"You've climbed them?"

He dipped his head once in a shallow nod, but his brows drew together as something dark flashed across his expression.

I knew better, but I couldn't help the question that tumbled out of my lips, even though I had next to no hope of him answering it. "What did you seek?"

He twisted his lips as though deciding whether to answer me and remained silent for so long that I stopped thinking he would. But then his low voice coasted over the rush of the wind. "Nothing that was possible."

I dropped the matter and looked back ahead, squinting my eyes against the chill air.

Killian descended as we approached the city in the early afternoon. He soared above the rooftops and up the incline leading to the palace, coming to land gently on a cobbled courtyard in front of the palace doors.

The pillowed snow didn't cover the pale stones—magic undoubtedly keeping the walkways free from the powder. The pretty yard was bordered by a low hedge where a garden filled with shrubs of stunning winter jasmine and camellia bloomed. Snowdrops, winter aconite and tufts of primrose covered the ground—their sweet fragrance floated through the crisp spring air.

It was a different kind of magical place altogether. Idyllic and serene. No hint of howling winter winds or blowing tempest storms.

Just quiet, cool and peaceful.

Killian lowered my legs so I could stand, and my knees wobbled as I found my uneasy balance. He held me steady by my elbows until he was convinced I could manage, but his hands didn't drift far from my sides as he took half a step back.

"Welcome home, Princess."

Tears stung my eyes, but I wouldn't let them fall. I straightened, and we both looked at the palace in front of us. Now that we were closer, the intricate details could be clearly seen.

Made of ivory stone and adorned with intricate, curling silverwork, the immaculate palace was exactly as I'd imagined. The same silver swirls that donned Kevilla Hall wrapped their way around the rooftops, and pointed archways and frosted windows dotted the silver-tipped towers that touched the clouds.

As I stood with my neck bent, taking in the view high above, the grand doors opened with a heavy clink, which brought my attention back to ground level.

An attendant, dressed in grey and soft blue, stood in the open doorway and welcomed us inside. Killian extended his arm to allow me to take the lead, and I focused my effort on lifting my wings and balancing as I walked. Killian's hand brushed my elbow twice as I went, his warmth radiating as he drifted close just in case.

We stepped into the entrance foyer and a rush of warmth spread over us. The interior was heated gently with magic, though not so much as Kevilla Hall. The male who brought us in gave a little bow and left to announce our arrival to the Steward, Erela.

I took the opportunity to look at the immaculate space. White marble coated the floor, and the panelled walls were painted in pale grey. Curved pillars reached high to the levels above where swirls and scenes had been carved into their tops where they met the intricately moulded ceiling. Bright lights from three stunning chandeliers reflected on all the gleaming surfaces.

Two huge rooms branched off from either side of the foyer, hidden partially behind tall cornflower-blue doors that stood ajar. In front of us, a grand staircase led to a mezzanine with two shorter sets of stairs branching off on either side to the upper levels.

My eyes swept around the stunning space, taking in the carved details and vases filled with winter blooms in the grand entrance while we waited.

But within moments, our wait was over.

I sensed her before I saw her. The petite female drifted toward us as though she floated rather than walked. She held her ivory wings at the edge of her thin frame and wore a simple, rose-pink gown with sleeves that reached her fingertips.

Erela was the spitting image of her twin. The same warm skin, the same smattering of freckles across her nose, the same summer blue eyes and champagne-blonde hair. The smooth and glossy strands brushed past her shoulders and wisped as she moved. Her pretty pink lips appeared as soft and full as strawberries, and her long, dark lashes curled up to her strong brow. She looked much younger than Veric, despite being the same age, though she certainly looked like she could run a Kingdom efficiently.

"Killian," Erela crooned and pressed a kiss to either side of his cheeks.

"Erela," he smiled back at her.

She cast her blue eyes on me and the genuine smile she had for Killian faded into one of required pleasantry.

"Alora." She did a double take on the cloak I wore and set her lips in a thin line. "A pleasure to have you here. Veric speaks so highly of you. Welcome to the Winter Palace."

Well, that was fake.

"Thank you, Erela. It's lovely to finally meet you."

She made a small noise that said she *agreed but not really* and turned back to Killian. "Veric said the two of you wish to learn more about King Valefor, though didn't say why." She directed a slightly annoyed gaze to me.

"We discovered that Alora's family came from the Winter Kingdom. She wanted to learn more about the royal family and I agreed it was a good place to start—to see if we could find any connections as to why Orella brought her to Endence."

She looked at Killian before nodding. "I took the liberty of placing everything we had on our king and queen in the guest study for you both. You're also free to use the library as you wish. If you find you're in need of anything else, please speak to our head librarian, Sylvie. She'll be able to help you."

Killian planted a swift kiss on her cheek. "You're the best, Rells."

"Mmm, I know," she muttered, unmoved by his flattery. "How long will the two of you stay?"

"At least the week, though we don't want to outstay our welcome."

"You're welcome to stay as long as you need, though I'm afraid I won't have much time to see you. Too many meetings that can't be rescheduled."

"We wouldn't want to distract you from your work. I appreciate you letting us stay," I said, trying to be helpful.

She eyed me again, looking me up and down with heavy scrutiny, half hidden beneath her perfect courtly manner. Her gaze raked over the cloak again with annoyance.

“Of course not,” she said politely. “You’re free to enjoy the palace as you need—our resources are at your service. We’ll do dinner sometime throughout the week when I can manage it. Until then, enjoy your reading.” She dipped her head the tiniest fraction and drifted back up the stairs from the direction she came.

I blew out a breath when she was safely out of earshot.

“She fucking hates me.”

Killian coughed to cover his laugh. “Nah, you’re fine. You actually got lucky in the cousin department, Princess. Rells is amazing, I nearly prefer her to her twin.”

I pulled a face that told him I thought he was talking shit.

“But she knows you’re hiding something.”

My jaw popped open. “How would she know that? I barely said a complete sentence to her.”

He shrugged. “She just knows. Erela’s always been a bit like that. Can always sniff out the bullshit. And she’s hard as nails, too. Besides, you’re the high and mighty chosen one of the Oracle, and just showed up on Erela’s doorstep wearing a family heirloom once belonging to her deceased aunt and queen—of course she’s got her back up.”

“A deceased aunt and queen who happens to be my mother,” I muttered back with warning in my tone.

“Yes, Alora, but Erela doesn’t know that.” He looked up to where she’d disappeared. “You’ve got the best damn fae running your Kingdom, and don’t you ever forget it.”

“So, I have the best fae running my Kingdom and the other best fae—who happens to be her brother—running my Legion. What the fuck is the point of me, then?” Frustration ripped through me as I threw my hands out.

Killian faced me, his smug smile returning in full force. “That’s what we’re here to find out, Princess.”

Chapter 17
The Past

Over the next three days, I spent hours upon hours holed up in the study, reading every drop of ink I could. Devouring every etched line of text, drinking the words like they were the source of life—trying to conjure up who my mother and father were until my eyes blurred or I fell asleep in my chair, barely leaving to eat or sleep.

The only benefit to the extra days spent sitting around reading was that it offered more time to regain my strength after the attack and gave my body more time to accommodate my wings.

Killian sat with me every so often or moved me to different parts of the palace to enjoy so I could see more of it. But mostly he left me to read in solitude.

When he was with me, he read in the chair alongside mine in comfortable silence, or every so often pestered me about exercising my wings—which I could now hold off the floor without tiring.

He'd distanced himself from the familiarity we'd developed back in Kevilla after the volcac attack. I wasn't sure what that meant, but while I was focused on learning about my family, I appreciated the space to concentrate.

By mid-morning on the fourth day, I'd exhausted nearly all the tomes Erela had sourced on our behalf. I closed the journal I'd been reading and tossed it on top of the pile. It hit the table with a thud, and a puff of dust wafted into the air. I took another book from the stack that remained, then, feeling somewhat defeated, slumped back in the cream armchair without opening it.

I kicked my feet onto the desk and leant back to look up at the intricate details of the ceiling, trying to sort through the mess of thoughts and emotions running through me.

For over three days I'd read everything I could get my hands on about my parents—but I couldn't help but feel it was all rather. . . superficial.

I'd learned they were kind and gentle leaders who'd ruled together in a time of peace. They made all the right decisions to help their citizens and loved one another fiercely.

Yet, I couldn't help but feel a sense of disappointment coating my tongue, and undoing all the happiness I'd conjured.

The door swung open on silent, silver hinges and snicked gently shut. I didn't need to look to know who'd entered.

Killian strolled in, wearing soft pants and a woollen sweater, looking far more relaxed than he usually did in his usual battle leathers. Still black on black though—no surprises. He lifted the book from my lap as he passed, and his fingers grazed my waist. I flinched at his accidental touch.

Mercifully, Killian didn't comment. He just flicked through the pages as he rounded the desk and took a seat on the other side, putting his own feet on the edge of the desk, mirroring me.

"I was reading that," I said flatly, still looking at the ceiling.

"Whoops," he said, not caring.

I didn't have the energy to argue, so I let silence fall between us.

"What's wrong?"

I scrunched my face up as I tried to bring the right words to the surface. "I just. . . sort of feel like I'm wasting time."

"You feel like you've learned everything and nothing."

I blinked. "Yeah." He'd summed it up rather easily. "I've loved sitting here and reading about them, but a lot of it has been a waste. I mean, that one there. . ." I said pointing at a blue and gold book on the table, "is just the inventory of weapons stashed away in the vault."

Killian made a noise of interest and snatched up the tome, no longer listening to me.

Typical brutish warrior, only interested in his play things.

"Killian," I said, trying to get his attention back.

He continued to flick through the pages. "Mm?"

"Killian," I hissed, raising my voice.

He snapped the book shut, finally concentrating on me. I shook my head at the fool.

"What? I bet you've got some good stuff back there." Mischief laced his words.

"Gods spare me. Did you even listen to what I said?"

"Yes, Alora. . . I heard you. All of these," he said, gesturing to the table of books, "didn't give you everything you wanted."

I pouted. "I at least expected to find *something.* Some entry that told me why they left, or a hint of where my father is—perhaps an explanation why I'm fucking here," I said, irritation rising. "But there's just. . . *nothing."* I dropped my head in my hands.

"Did you really think it would be that easy, Princess?"

"No," I replied into my palms. After a beat, I let my hands fall into my lap and looked back at him. "But it doesn't make it any less shitty."

"Come on," he said as he stood and crossed around the desk to stand before me. "I know something that'll cheer you up."

Killian held out his hand to help me stand. I took it warily, and he led the way without letting go.

Together we walked down the carpeted hallway of the guest wing, down two flights of stairs and through the marbled central foyer where fae with official titles and business to conduct went about their day.

Killian took a sharp right past the grand staircase to a door half hidden from view, then strode ahead, clearly knowing where to go. The hallway was decidedly empty, and I had the sudden sense that we were sneaking around.

"Killian," I hissed, "are we allowed to be here?"

He smirked without looking down at me. "Relax, Princess, we won't get in trouble."

That wasn't an answer.

"Where is everyone?" I whispered, looking around.

"No one needs to be down here," he replied, which still explained nothing.

A few more paces and one final turn later, we stopped before a set of silver doors. Intricate swirls patterned the surface and words in a different language were etched between the lines.

"These doors will only open for royals," he explained as he held his hand out. Not to open them—but gesturing that *I* go toward them.

"Me?" I said in disbelief, looking between him and the stunning doors.

"You."

My heart kicked up into a gallop. It was as though I'd been presented with a test I was probably going to fail.

What the fuck do I do if they don't open?

I shut down the silly intrusive thought then raised my hand outward, but my fingers shook so violently that I dropped it back to my side in embarrassment.

Killian's gaze locked onto my face, observing every expression. I closed my eyes and sucked in a steadying breath, willing composure to take over.

I stepped forward and tried again. This time I didn't shake. Palm out, I approached the silver doors and a warm, tingling barrier met my outstretched hand an inch before my skin made contact with the cold metal—like warm dough beneath my hand, only softer. Lighter.

And then it was gone.

A shimmer sounded as the magic seal faded under my touch and my hand fell through to the double doors, which swung open silently.

Killian pressed his hand against my shoulder. "Princess," he said with complete reverence in acknowledgement then signalled me to go ahead.

Warm air drifted past as I stepped into the room beyond, but my limbs resumed their shaking as I rounded the door.

What I saw in front of me wasn't sad, but the heartache it caused was more than I could bear.

The floor of the small room was divided in half by a small dais. On the little platform were low tables and pedestals with collections of shining trinkets—glittering jewels, tiaras and rings. Diamonds the size of blueberries and glistening sapphires set in precious metals twinkled from their cushioned beds. There were intricately decorated daggers laid reverently on silks and a line of books on a shelf.

The wealth in the room was unfathomable—but it was a treasure of a different sort I couldn't look away from.

Hanging on the wall, bordered in a gold frame, was an enormous portrait of my mother and father. The only one I'd ever seen painted of my mother, and the first time I'd laid eyes on my father.

The sob that left me tore my heart out along with it as it escaped my throat. My knees buckled, unable to keep me upright under the weight of what I saw. The tears that spilled landed on my thighs and the polished floor beneath me like raindrops during a summer storm.

Killian crouched beside me and grasped my hand in comfort, bringing it up to his heart as though he could take away my suffering with its steady beats.

My parents stood as though they were trying their best to be regal but couldn't resist clinging to one another. Her slender, pale fingers curled and wrapped perfectly into his golden hands held against his chest.

Moieties.

Two halves of the same soul.

I looked at my mother and drank her in, and let her features—which had been so perfectly captured—fill the haze of my memories, letting her become clearer in my mind's eye.

Snow. The name Caldwell had always called her—and she did look like snow. Soft and glistening. Flawless. She had a round face and full lips with a perfect cupid's bow. Her white blonde hair hung in the same loose waves as mine—as Della's—and was adorned with a spectacular glowing crown. Her tendrils swept gently along her deep-grey gown. Her wings glistened with the same pearlescence my own did, only hers were the colour of blue ice—the most breathtaking shade which I hadn't seen a single fae possess in all my weeks in Endence. Yet somehow it was exactly as I'd imagined them. As though, if I'd seen a different colour, I knew it would've been wrong.

Then I looked at the figure standing to her left.

Valefor.

My father.

Tears welled in my eyes with a renewed surge. My father was painted with such perfect clarity that if he stood before me in the flesh next to his image, I wouldn't be able to pick which one was real.

His jacket was detailed with green and silver brocade, and he wore a gold crown that was the subtle twin to his moiety's. His grey boots rose to his knees where the tip of a sword touched from where it was hung at his hip. The stunning gold guard seemed to glow as it wrapped around the handle like tendrils of smoke, the gold coiling and rising from around the deep black stone housed in the centre of the block.

I looked into his green eyes. Green the exact shade as my right.

I was his.

My mother's figure, painted with his details.

He was strong and golden and *warm.* I'd been right to use Veric as a reference–I could see their similarities. *Our* similarities. He was tall and broad and had the same cream wings as his nephew. The same champagne hair that brushed against his pointed ears and the same freckles smattered across his nose, too.

But it was eyes I couldn't stop staring at.

It was a missing piece of my puzzle that slotted into place. A part of me I'd been searching for my whole life, finally found.

I ceased my sobbing as best as I could and wiped my tears on the back of my sleeve. Killian was there though, holding out a handkerchief to spare my clothes.

I took it wordlessly and blotted my face. A mostly futile effort because more tears still fell, replacing the ones I wiped away.

Killian took hold of my hand and pressed a kiss to the back of it, his soft lips bringing me back to the present.

My breathing slowed as I regained control over my body, and the initial shock of the room abated.

I looked up to my father's kind face with one question burning through me. "Where is he, Killian?"

"We'll find him, Alora." A promise. "Now that we know about your mother, that they weren't together. . . I know it might not be much, but it's more than we've had to go on in decades."

"What if he's. . ." A sob left me as the thought took up space in my mind. The words were too hard to speak. "What if someone. . ."

"There are a lot of explanations–"

"They were moieties, Killian," I cried, cutting him off. My eyes searched his for lies to spare my pain. "They were moieties and weren't together. If he isn't being held captive, then why would he not have been with her?" I looked at how tightly my parents held onto one another.

Two halves of the same soul, desperate to be together.

It was an impossibility they'd left one another willingly.

"Exactly, Alora—they were moieties," Killian said, urging me to listen to him. "Think of it another way. Do you really think if your father were in danger, that your mother simply would've relaxed in the human realm? That she wouldn't have—" Something broke in his voice. His wings twitched and a flash of emotion swept across his face, too quick for me to pinpoint. "That she wouldn't have torn the world apart to get to him?" Killian lent further toward me. "Your mother knew where he was, Alora. Where he likely still is, considering he hasn't returned." He squeezed my hand, sending reassurance through the touch. "We will find him."

Heat radiated from him, not just from his hand on mine, but from his body—from his face that was so close to me. I sensed a change in his demeanour, as if he noticed our proximity at the same time I did.

Our breath mingled, and my gaze dipped to his lips.

His dipped to mine.

Killian and I had gone up against one another so often, sometimes pushing too far, but when I thought back, he'd always been willing to tell me what I wanted to know—unless it was about himself.

But for me—for my needs—he'd always been forthcoming. Helped me. Led me. Supported me. Made sure I was cared for.

Not hungover.

There was no denying Killian was a good male under all his brooding.

And smouldering hot.

Killian's hand left mine and cupped my cheek. His thumb swept across in a light touch before pressing onto my lower lip. All the while I watched his mouth. Watched his breath suck in when I didn't turn him away.

We each couldn't tear our gaze from the other's lips. I watched, rooted to the spot as he lent closer, his thumb still resting at the corner of my mouth when his gaze flicked up to mine and then back down.

I swallowed when Killian dropped his gaze to my throat and stilled, his blue eyes burning. His huge wings arched above, balancing him and creating a dark wall at his back, blocking the world out.

His heart raced as fast as my own, and his lips parted with a shaky breath. He brushed his hand down the side of my neck and wove his fingers into the back of my hair—his thumb pressed on my pulse, which kicked up to new heights.

He remained exactly where he was, not breaching that final gap, while his breath skittered along my jaw.

All I'd have to do was lean forward and we would collide. But his fingers held my head gently enough it sent the message clearly—he didn't want me to move.

"Killian?" I didn't want to think how much it sounded like a plea.

His body trembled as I whispered his name, but he leant back on his heels, creating just enough distance that the tension eased. He kept his hand curved around my neck and absentmindedly played with the strands of my hair that looped between his fingers. "Do you know why moieties are so rare?"

I trembled as I shook my *no* as far as his grasp would allow.

"Only offspring of a united pair are born with a cleaved soul. Only they have moieties."

I tried to concentrate on his words, but his damn fingers kept stroking my neck and took all my attention away.

"I don't—" I swallowed and tried again. "What does that mean?"

"It means exactly that, Princess." His words were slow and purposeful. "Your mother and father were moieties, which meant their parents were also moieties, and so on up your family tree. And as such, any children your parents had together are destined to have their own moiety. It could be hundreds of years before you meet them, but they will be out there somewhere. At some time. The same is for me and my family."

Why was he telling me this?

"It's part of the reason why finding your moiety is so treasured. Powerful. But it does not mean you cannot love another. Deeply. Truly."

"So, you and I—"

"Have moieties, yes."

My heart fluttered and those tears I'd managed to cease tried to break free of their hold again.

I had always considered my eyes to be my greatest betrayers to the world. Showing everyone that only half of me was really here, and the other half was missing.

And now Killian laid the truth at my feet.

It was because it was true.

My soul was cleaved.

Half of me *was* missing.

Was this the pull I had felt? The reason why I'd always wanted to leave my home and family? Nothing to do with Orella's plan or a purpose here. . . but my soul longing to complete itself?

I took a shaking breath before I spoke. "How would anyone know if they found their moiety?"

"Usually it's an innate feeling." His deep voice moved over my skin as he watched me. "They'd just know—or the feeling will be stronger for one of them. Sometimes it's like a pull, like they're the air you need to breathe." He flicked his eyes to the portrait hanging on the wall, to my parents clasping onto one another. "Sometimes, it's a push of sorts—like opposites attracting. Fiery and passionate. . . loud." His gaze landed back on me.

That sounded familiar.

"What are you saying, Killian?"

The tip of his tongue parted his lips before he spoke, leaning in. "That you feel like—"

Footsteps brushing toward the room sounded, cutting Killian's words short. He loosened his fingers from my hair and stood sharply without making a sound then pulled me to my feet.

He took a subtle step back, creating distance between us so we didn't look so. . . cosy. But I don't think it fooled the keen-eyed Erela as she rounded the door and looked back and forth between us, her gaze sceptically assessing Killian.

She clasped her hands in front of her blue gown and tilted her head to the side, wordlessly asking her question.

What in the fuck are you two doing in here?

"Sorry Rells, I couldn't resist the opportunity to show off."

Only royals could open the door. Killian had to take the blame for opening the room, otherwise, my ruse was over. Erela wasn't royal—not even she was able to get in here on her own.

She ran her blue eyes over me with the same scepticism, but to my surprise, she pulled a perfect smile at both of us.

"It's been years since I've been in here," she said with reverent wonder as she drifted past us toward the dais. "I'd almost forgotten what it looked like."

I followed her path as she walked between the pedestals laden with their treasures. It was only then I realised what they truly were.

The glittering diamonds and sapphires, ornate jewellery boxes and combs, sparkling gowns, strings of pearls and books—they were my mother's things. Not just the abundant collection of jewels any rich or titled person could possess, not the accumulation of the vast Winter Kingdom's treasures—these were hers. Theirs.

"I should be cross with you for coming in here, Killian." Erela looked over her shoulder to the tall male who pulled an innocent expression. "But I must admit, I'm grateful." She stared up at the painting. "This is my favourite portrait."

I looked over the items sitting amongst the tables and caught Erela watching me. I gave a swift, polite smile at her. She gave a slow, curved one back.

"These are all her things, aren't they?" I asked, trying to get her eyes off me.

"Yes. This room is different from the treasury, it holds more... intimate items. As I'm sure Killian explained, only a royal can open the door, no matter which Kingdom they're from. After Queen Eira and King Valefor left, Queen Fleur opened the door and ensured any personal items not stored already, made their way safely here. Mainly the jewellery and gowns had to be moved."

She pointed to a blue diamond the size of my thumbnail and my eyes nearly popped out of my head. "This was her wedding ring," she said, gesturing to the priceless piece. She pointed to a silver blade resting against the pedestal. "King Valefor's sword. The crown was already in here, of course." She pointed with graceful fingers to the glowing tiara. "It's always here unless needed for ceremonial events. This journal was here too," she finished, picking up a small, maroon book, separate from the others on the shelf. She flipped the pages gently.

My eyes couldn't look away from the crown cushioned on cerulean silk in the centre of the dais. Physically, the piece was petite. Made of rose gold that swirled in the shapes of laurel leaves—each leaf a diamond. On either side of the centre stone, a blue diamond, as big as a quail's egg, was set and surrounded by a halo of small, shimmering, white gems.

In the centre was a larger oval stone that *glowed*. The inside of the jewel moved and flowed, as though a river of bright citrine, blue topaz and deep amethyst bubbled and ran through its facets.

"It is called Orallite. The Oracle's Amulet." I looked at Ercla as she spoke but was quickly drawn back to the beauty of the glowing gem. "When Orella divided our realm, she created the gem and split it in two. Half was given to who she chose to lead Summer, and the other half to who she chose to lead Winter. It glows as long as the fae who vowed to serve their Kingdom lives."

"Veric told me Orella divided the realm because of an uprising?"

She nodded. "Ten thousand years ago, two angels called Noteas and Lilla sought to tear our realm apart and destroy us all with a great evil. A lot of the facts are lost or exaggerated through stories—but what we do know is a powerful warrior named Argensir sacrificed himself and brought them down. Orella was dissatisfied with their surrender, and so used her magic to cast them out."

"Their defeat was known as the Fall, hence why the race of angels are also referred to as the Fallen," Killian added.

Made sense.

"Despite her power and her thorough sentencing of the pair, Orella later prophesied that Noteas would one day return, and so the vile little cretins have tried every so often to be the ones who bring him back."

Surely not—

"Orella chose two fae who would become the ancestors of the royal lines and each Kingdom was formed as a force against Noteas and Lilla, in the event she, too, returned. The Summer Kingdom against Noteas, and Winter against Lilla."

Killian took over the story. "One attempt in particular got out of hand and a great war started. Nearly a millennia ago, the leader of the

Fallen, Orias, started making trouble, so the fae rose against them. Led by Evander, we decimated their army. Orella carved out a piece of land from the Kingdoms, banishing the Fallen to live in their court rather than amongst the fae as punishment for rising up."

"So, she prophesied he'd return but didn't say how?"

"Orella cannot predict specifics like that, Alora. To do so would turn her into a weapon that could be wielded against any enemy. Imagine the power she would have if she knew which decision to make to win a war, or which target would prevent it altogether."

I stared at the glowing jewel in the tiara as I thought it over, a shudder ran through me at the thought of that possibility.

"What does the prophecy say?"

"When Endence gathers winter's might, Sun will shine its dawning blight."

I looked between them, back and forth, confusion pulling at my brow then said my thoughts out loud. "That could mean anything!" I threw my hands in the air.

"Noteas was the first blight on the realm. The records state, one winter, however soon or distant, he will return."

"Don't you think we should be looking at those records, then?"

"You think it hasn't already been done? This happened ten thousand years ago—why would you think you'd find anything new?"

"You're telling me, there's a big bad enemy who will return and unleash his evil on the realm. . . and the Oracle who was responsible for his downfall brought me here, then gave an obscure warning to you all about being prepared—and you don't think those things are connected?"

Killian and Erela exchanged a look like they *hadn't* thought of that.

"The prophecy states he will come in winter. Despite Orella's warning, we have a year *at least,*" he stressed, "before we need to worry. Hundreds of years, even, to be prepared."

His words fell dull against my ears and I opened my mouth to argue, but Erela cut me off.

"I think tonight is a good time to have dinner together, yes?"

Killian and I glanced at one another.

"Good, it's settled then," she decreed before we'd spoken. "Alora, I'll see you at dinner. Killian," she said, rounding on the commander with an intimidating force stronger than I thought possible for a female of her size. "I'll see you *before* dinner."

Killian nodded and looked almost sheepish like he'd just been told off. Erela gave a small nod in farewell then drifted out of the room.

Killian and I stared at each other—the weight of everything that had just transpired crushing down on us in heavy silence.

I spent the rest of the day in my room trying to concentrate on what I'd learned, but was failing miserably. I'd paced from one side to the other so thoroughly, I was surprised I hadn't worn a track through the plush carpet. I opted to run a bath instead—hoping that a long soak would keep me in one spot at the bare minimum. Calming me might be asking too much, but at least I might sit still.

As I let the sweet, scented water soothe my jittering limbs, it was only my mind that was left racing. Image after image flashed in my mind. From the clear eyes of my mother, to the encapsulating ones of my father. Faceless monsters that sought to end this magical world, mighty warriors ending everything on imagined battlefields, Orella delivering prophecies.

Were we right? Was I here because of some ancient angel who was prophesied to return and release their evil to end the world? Or had we jumped to conclusions?

We.

Killian and I.

What had we been about to do?

The image of us kneeling in that room entered my mind. Even the sight of it in my head made warmth pool in my cheeks. . . and in my belly. My fingers twitched.

Fucking Gods. Alora, no! Think about something else.

Like, why bring up moieties as he leant over me? Or, what had he been about to say? What did I feel like? Because he felt like. . . like warmth and strength and rich chocolate and. . .

I blew out a breath as I realised where my thoughts had drifted. . . and my hand. I looked down and saw my peaked nipples under the surface of the water.

I looked around the bathroom as if someone was going to be standing there, hearing my thoughts and catching me out for letting them loose in my mind. But only steam hovered in the tiled space, drifting up from the water and fogging the wide window that looked into a snowy courtyard.

My hand lingered between my legs. Something had sparked between Killian and I. Did I want to fight the attraction toward him? Did I want him to have kissed me back in that room, or was it all the other emotions leading my choices? Or had it just been too long since I had. . .

Lito.

Nope! It wasn't that.

Killian was more than an urge. There had been a shift, and he knew it too, otherwise, he wouldn't be pressing in on me as well.

The answers all came to me then.

No, I didn't want to resist the attraction toward him. Yes, I did want him to have kissed me. Also, yes. . . it had been too long.

Decision made, and with a final thought, ending in *fuck it,* I let my hand reach its destination, and my mind finish the scene playing in my mind. The one where Killian hadn't drawn back, but instead he'd tightened his fist in my hair and kissed me so thoroughly I gasped for breath when he released me. Where he kept leaning into me so I was flat on my back.

'Maybe I just wanted to get you on your back, Princess.'

He whispered against my ear as he pressed his massive weight into me, along with his massive. . .

I sank beneath the surface and let the shudders of my climax rip through me. The warm water ate up my moan as I came around my fingers.

I came up for breath once the shocks of my orgasm subsided. Finally, I found peace watching the snow drift into the courtyard below my window, my thoughts and worries ebbing for a moment. The orgasm served better than any magical remedy this realm could have conjured for my muddled mind.

I summoned the willpower to exit the bath, to get ready for dinner with Erela and the male who had just done unspeakable imaginary things to me. Imagining Killian finishing what he started in the most delicious way would either satisfy me well enough to get through dinner with a clear head, or it'd be the only thing I thought about when I looked at him.

Either way, one thing was for certain.

I need to have colder baths.

Chapter 18
The Middle

I was the first to reach the private dining room. I wandered around, aimlessly touching things as I passed, then stopped at an ice bucket with a bottle of wine chilling inside and didn't hesitate to pour a glass. I told myself I needed all the help I could get now that a strange nervousness had kicked in.

I managed to throw back an entire glass of the sweet bubbles in the time it took Killian and Erela to arrive with their arms linked.

Despite it being just the three of us, Erela was still dressed immaculately, this time in a lavender gown, with her long hair coiled in a knot at the back of her head. I immediately felt underdressed in my black tights and sage sweater.

Killian had his same relaxed clothes on as before, which made me feel slightly better–until I locked eyes with him and my face heated. I was sure I was blushing the brightest shade of crimson, worried he somehow knew what I'd done in that bath.

Any hopes of my orgasm giving me a clear head vanished under the heat of his burning eyes. Erela unlinked their arms and gave Killian a passing look as Killian's nostrils flared ever so slightly when he saw me.

"You look calmer, Alora," Erela said sweetly as Killian poured her and then himself a drink.

I nearly snorted my wine.

"I, ahh. . . yeah, I'm feeling more relaxed, thank you."

Killian did snort his wine.

"Excuse me," he said, thumping his chest, and turned his back on us.

Kill me.

"How was your afternoon together?"

"Oh, it was good, wasn't it Killian?" Erela answered, inviting him to join the conversation. Killian just made a sound of polite agreement over his shoulder. "Mostly business, unfortunately, but at least that means we have all the pleasure waiting for us tonight" She smiled almost wickedly, then clinked her glass against mine.

Fuck me, was it written on my forehead?

I laughed uncomfortably.

This is your own doing, Alora.

"Should we eat?" Killian said abruptly, beelining for the table. He swished his hand in the air as we all sat, and the table filled with serving plates of steaming roast, golden baked potatoes and buttery winter vegetables. Mouth-watering scents filled the room, and the three of us piled what we wanted onto our plates.

"Killian was telling me about your training, Alora." I looked up at Erela's poised expression and flicked my eyes to Killian who was still heaping food onto his plate. "He tells me you're quite accomplished."

"I'm not so sure I meet the standards of a fae warrior, but I think I do okay."

"Now you just need to get your magic in order. Killian, I'm shocked you haven't started practising with her already."

"Veric has been doing a little, but I thought it best to strengthen Alora physically first so she wasn't so. . . squishable." He pulled a sly face at me.

I narrowed my eyes back at him.

Erela turned to me. "I don't think you've ever been that, have you?"

"No." I smiled. "Not until I came here."

There was something hiding in her expression.

"And how has your research been going? Have you found anything of interest in the books?"

"Only that your king and queen sounded wonderful," I said thoughtfully. "I know Veric speaks highly of your uncle, you must miss him."

She nodded as she delicately chewed her food.

"I was wondering if I'd be able to look in the library? If we're right about me being connected to Noteas, I think I need to look further into the history of the angels and the war."

"Of course," she said, laying her cutlery down on her plate with a clink. "I'll send word to Sylvie and she can make sure everything is in order by the time you get there."

I went to thank her, but the swish of her hand cut me short.

"I also think it's worth you looking through *this."* She passed a familiar little maroon book across the table.

I angled my head in question, trying to recall where I'd seen it, but Killian choked on his food and coughed out his alarmed words before the memory clicked. "Fucking hell, Rells. That's Eira's journal."

"It is." She straightened her spine against her dining chair.

"Erela," Killian groaned, exasperated as he rubbed his thumbs on his temples. "You know you can't take possessions from the Royal Treasury."

Erela just shrugged her thin shoulders and quirked her eyebrow at him as if to say *so what.*

"I think it could be of use," she chirped. "Besides, I didn't *just* take it," she said with wry sarcasm then gestured with her slender fingers across at me. "I've now given it, too."

"I don't give a shit myself, Rells, but I don't want your arse hauled over coals if anyone finds out."

"And how would anyone find out, hm?" She raised a pointed brow, unbothered by his annoyance. "If someone does, then they were either poking around where they shouldn't be or they won't care in the slightest. You won't squeak, and neither will Alora."

"You've broken protocol," he interjected, growing frustrated. "You've taken a personal item of the Queen's and—"

"Given it to her daughter."

My fork clattered onto my plate with a near deafening ring as it slipped from my fingers. Killian and Erela didn't even flinch at the noise.

They just stared at one another, both refusing to be the first to break eye contact.

Killian let a low growl loose as he watched her, but Erela just tipped her lip at him, unthreatened by the male display. Despite Killian's ferocity on the battlefront, Erela was made of stronger mettle in here and he broke first, scoffing his annoyance then shoving food into his mouth so he didn't have to speak.

Erela turned her knowing gaze on me, still smiling her little victory. "Hello, cousin."

"How–"

"Oh please, anyone with half a brain can see you look exactly like your parents, Alora. Which says a lot about *your* intelligence, Killian, if you thought I wouldn't figure it out while she was here." Her tone dripped with ridicule.

Killian let another growl rip at the insult, but again she remained unfazed. "I knew something was up with you before you even came here, but couldn't put my finger on it. It wasn't until you were standing in front of that portrait today that I realised. Mind you, that was only the second time I'd seen you, so I still count that as a little win." A gratifying smile plastered on her full lips as she plucked a potato off her fork and chewed. She pointed her knife at Killian. "You're a bastard for keeping it from me."

The warrior was full of arrogance as he leant back in his chair. "Telling you or not doesn't change the fact that I'm a bastard, Rells."

"No, it just makes you even more of one. She's my Gods damn family," she said coolly.

Killian just shrugged–his turn to be unfazed. "It was more important that word didn't get out who she was than to give you a happy family reunion. She needs to be protected."

"Are you implying I would announce she was here and put her at risk? She's the future of this Kingdom."

"I know she's the future of this Kingdom. Why the fuck do you think she's under my protection and training with her legion?"

"She shouldn't be with her legion, she needs to be here in her home so she can learn how to rule her Kingdom, as is her right!"

"Considering Orella gave her a personal chaperone into Endence, I'd bet she's likely here for more than a fancy fucking chair, Rells. She's—"

"Sitting right in this fucking room!" I cut in, sick of being spoken about like I wasn't right in front of them.

They both stopped and looked at me sideways. I levelled them with my annoyed glare until I was sure they wouldn't start up again.

"Sorry, Alora," Erela said and dipped her head.

"Apologies, Princess."

Erela gasped and looked at him, her temper peaking again as he used the nickname.

"It's alright, Erela." I placated her to relax. "It's usually the least annoying thing that comes out of his mouth."

Killian wiggled his eyebrows at her in a taunt, and she shot a glare back at him.

Take-no-shit hot temper comes from dad's side of the family then.

"I'm sorry Erela, I didn't want to hide it from you. Fleur and Nakir thought it best to keep it quiet until we figured out why I'm here."

She nodded. "Who else knows apart from your parents, Killian?"

"Only a few healers and Farro."

"And the Fox," I added.

Killian made a noise in recognition like he'd forgotten all about the spy.

"Not surprising," she said bluntly. "Veric?" Killian shook his head. "He's going to kill you when he finds out, Killian."

Silence fell among us again as we all took pause.

Erela laced her fingers together on the edge of the table then looked at me. "Right, start from the beginning. Tell me what happened."

We stayed in the dining room until late night moved into early morning. I told Erela everything, starting from when a strange silver horse turned up, rearing and snorting in the middle of my farm.

It wasn't until the ornate clock on the mantel chimed twice that we stopped and finally rose from the table.

Before Erela turned to leave for bed in the direction of the wing she resided in, I pulled her into a tight embrace—to my shock, she didn't hesitate to return it. It was surprising how quickly she shifted from the poised and proper delegate I'd met upon arrival to the female version of Veric. There was no hint of annoyance or animosity in her demeanour toward me now that there were no secrets making her wary.

A wash of emotion hit me as we held onto one another. Erela was the tiniest bit shorter than me, but in her heels, we stood at the exact same height, and it was impossible to tell where her hair ended and mine began. We pulled apart and I was surprised again to see her eyes lined with silver tears, just the same as mine.

"Veric and I are here for you, not only as the future leader of this Kingdom but as our cousin." She gave a bittersweet smile. "Please tell him soon, Alora."

"I will," I promised.

Killian pressed a kiss to her cheek, their spat forgotten, then together he and I walked back to the guest wing.

"How does it feel?" Killian asked as we passed through the echoing marble foyer.

I thought about it for a few steps, clutching my mother's journal to my chest. "I don't have words to describe it," I mused. "I've never had family outside of Della and Caldwell. To find out I had family out in the world somewhere was incredible. . . and now that one of them knows I'm here as well, it's. . . indescribable."

We walked slowly on, content in the dark peace that the middle of the night brings, but still, I turned over my thoughts to give Killian a more complete answer to his question.

"I always felt like I didn't belong." I saw Killian's ears perk from my peripheral as he listened. "Like I was never where I was supposed to be. But now, I think, maybe, it's because I was meant to be here instead, and that's why I always wanted to leave."

I stopped walking and looked at Killian. He stopped as well then looked down at me, running his gaze over my face as I tried to call the last of my thoughts into the open.

"You asked during our ride to Kevilla about Lito."

Killian kept his expression still, but nodded just the tiniest fraction. "You never answered."

"He was. . ." I stopped, trying to find the best words to describe him. "I was going to marry him." The words dropped like lead in the pit of my stomach.

Hurt flashed across his face, but it was gone in an instant. "Was?"

I dragged my gaze away from his and looked out an arched window letting cold moonlight flood the hallway. Gentle snowflakes drifted down and settled on the sill.

"Was."

Silent moments slipped past as I watched the world sweep and settle outside. Killian watched with me, and I sensed his attention over my shoulder.

"There was someone I was supposed to marry once."

I looked at him. Somehow, he looked smaller. His blue eyes were distant as he watched the snow fall.

I could tell he was reliving a memory. Could tell it was causing him grief.

"Was?"

"Was."

I squeezed his hand. A small gesture, but the only thing that could do anything against the hurt. Gods only knew words were useless against the anguish of a loss like the ones we were hurting from.

I couldn't stand the suffering in his expression, so I changed the topic.

"I'm worried Noteas is coming sooner than everyone thinks." I stepped closer to him and his smoky caramel scent drifted at the edge of my senses.

Killian sighed and refocused on my face. "Princess, I explained before. . . it could be—"

"Hundreds of years, I know." I let out a defeated breath. "But you can't ignore that Orella's warning is a bad sign that things are happening soon."

"I can ignore it, Alora, because that simply isn't true. Maybe it just hasn't dawned on you yet, *faeling*," he teased and took a step closer, his mood shifting now that we'd entered each other's space. "That unless that smart mouth of yours gets you killed first, you're going to live for *hundreds* of years. Not one hundred, not two. . . but several hundreds of years."

Kinda gross.

"Fae do not think in single years. You being here, and what Orella said at the temple, doesn't necessarily mean Noteas is coming any time soon."

His dark voice coated my cheeks as he took a final step in and was almost up against me as we stood in the middle of the hallway. A ghost of his knuckles stroked down my arm, like he wanted to soothe me with his touch, but pulled out of the action too late.

The silence quickly turned from the peaceful quiet that came in the dead of night, to something heated and anticipatory as we stood. I was on the precipice of a dangerous decision and my pulse thundered in my ears as I considered my next words carefully.

Everything that'd happened between us this past week, everything that had happened today, everything *I* had thought today in that bath, had built and coiled so tightly. I knew we were about to implode.

The question was simply when, and would we survive it? If we continued to go on like we were, it was likely one of us would say the wrong thing and we wouldn't.

I realised then, that Killian had been waiting for me to show the slightest hint I wanted it back. It was why he hadn't breached that gap today. He had been teetering on the edge, waiting for me to meet him in the middle if I chose to, and it was time I decided whether I wanted to or not.

Say something, Alora.

Feeling brazen, I jumped.

"So, which will be first, Killian?"

He cocked his head in a wholly fae move—the action highlighted his jawline in the moonlight.

No backing out now, Alora.

"Will it be my pretty little arse that needs saving or my smart mouth that gets me killed first?"

Killian's lip curled into a wicked smile.

Painfully slowly, he reached his hand up and cupped the underside of my jaw, his fingers curling into the hair behind my ear. He rubbed his thumb at the edge of my chin and pulled down with the slightest pressure. The action pulled my lower lip away, opening my mouth just enough for me to suck in a sharp and shaking breath. He let a deep rumble loose from his chest as they parted.

Heat radiated from him—the intensity of his scent wrapped around me. My knees were weak as I stood completely at his mercy. If my legs gave out, the only thing holding me in place would be his fist in my hair.

On second thought, that might be alright.

Killian was so tall that I had to look almost vertically to see him. His expression was dark, his burning eyes hooded and calculating. He leant down a little further so I could see him clearly—brought his face to mine and stared between my green and grey eyes before he dropped his gaze and held it at my lips. Watching.

"Definitely your mouth, Princess." His voice was thick and rough like he could barely get the words out.

His hand drifted further around the back of my head before he closed the remaining space between us and pressed a soft kiss against my lips.

Killian pulled away barely an inch, his gaze coming up from my lips to my eyes, reading for any sign that this wasn't okay.

There was none.

"I've been thinking about what happened between us in that room all day."

I could tell he was struggling to remain controlled as he spoke, so I decided to see how far I could toy with him. I pulled a look of sincere confusion. "Nothing happened in that room?"

Killian narrowed his eyes, judging whether or not I was bullshitting. I pulled on my bottom lip with my teeth and satisfaction pooled over me as his eyes dipped to my mouth again. A salacious smile stretched across his face as he realised I was being coy.

"You're right," he paused, considering his words. "Nothing happened in that room."

Killian bent at the waist, the same move he always made when he wanted to intrude on my space. His voice turned dark and dangerous against the shell of my ear. "Because if it had, Princess, I'd have left you so breathless, your smart mouth wouldn't be capable of your teasing words. Only the heavy panting I would've elicited from you when I did all I wanted."

I whimpered then swallowed the sudden knot in my throat as Killian angled his face to track the movement as it bobbed. A single breath of air left me before Killian put his hand around my throat and shoved me up against the wall with his body—rough but precise enough that I wasn't hurt on impact.

I yelped and he shushed with his husky whispers. My wings flared as they hit, and light burst from them like when they were formed by smoke. They settled immediately when Killian didn't move—his body still pressed into mine. Evidence of his *feelings* pressed even further against my belly.

Huge feelings, if I'm not mistaken.

His scent enveloped me completely, and I wanted to drown in the rich taste. His hand curled around my neck, pressing in on the side just right, while his other slammed into the wall next to my head. I could hear his fingers digging into the panelling as he tried to control himself.

"Definitely your fucking mouth," he growled an instant before he claimed me completely.

His kiss was fierce and bruising. I wanted to lean into him—into his kiss—but he kept my body pinned beneath his weight with his hand around my neck so that I had no hope. He thrust his muscled thigh between my legs, and I moaned into his mouth as it rubbed against the peak of my thighs.

At the sound that escaped me, Killian made his own frenzied growl and swept his tongue deeper into my mouth. My hips ground against his leg unabashedly, my body desperately wanting to move in some way—as an attempt to release the friction he'd spiked in my blood.

I raised my free hand and grabbed at his massive bicep, the need to have him under my fingers burned through me too strong to resist. The feel of his tight muscles under his shirt made me groan again as my thoughts flooded with another particular muscle of his that I wanted to get my hand around.

Killian shifted the hand that was at my throat and angled my head to the side, then left my mouth to graze his teeth down my neck—his wicked pointed canines dragged along my skin and made me whimper.

He bit down on the tender joint by my neck, and I gasped as the sensation made my delicate muscles clench before the slick effects of his kiss pooled between my thighs. He sucked hard on the spot, then kissed it gently to take away the sting of his bite, before coming back up to my mouth where he claimed me all over again.

The hand he had braced against the wall came to curl around my waist, grabbing hard and massaging in long strokes which matched his tongue as it swept against mine.

He broke the kiss and pulled away, leaving me breathless just like he'd promised. I dropped my hand to my side and clutched onto the wood panelling at my back to keep from reaching out to him again.

Killian let a rumble resonate before he drew in a deep breath, his blue eyes burning with heat. He planted another chaste kiss on my bruised lips and licked his own as he pulled back again—a low curse escaped him as he did.

A lock of his black hair fell forward over his temple as he lowered his forehead against mine. We were both breathless and panting as we tried to regain some composure.

There was a split second where our eyes locked, where time slowed and stretched. The heat of the moment sparked in my blood again and I knew if I jumped on it—if I closed the gap between us and kissed him again, there would be no turning back—there would be no hope of stopping ourselves.

But I dropped my eyes and let the moment slip away. That decision needed more careful consideration than what I was capable of right now, especially as I, for one, wasn't thinking with my head.

Killian was—just not with the one on top of his shoulders.

I reached up to brush the lock of hair from his face, but he intercepted my hand and held it firmly. I tilted my head in silent question and he gave a soft, breathy laugh and shook his head.

"I think that's enough touching for tonight."

"Just for tonight?" My voice was sultry and heated.

He licked his lips as he watched my own again. "Just for tonight, Princess," he promised. "But by all means. . . continue your own touching when you go inside." His wicked words made me weak all over again. He bowed and planted a kiss on the back of the hand he still held, said goodnight, then turned toward his room.

The air around me was suddenly cold and empty without his presence.

I stayed planted to the spot, and dropped my head back against the wall I still leant against, shutting my eyes tight at the renewed flood of emotions.

I opened them and watched the snowflakes once more fall slowly past the window on the opposite wall, letting their peacefulness calm me.

After a few moments of taking in the quiet scene, when I was sure Killian was out of sight and his scent had drifted away, and I could move without my knees giving out, I tiptoed to my own room.

I dropped my mother's journal onto the bedside table, all but forgotten as I eased between my sheets and did as Killian suggested—wringing the last of the heated edge the snowflakes hadn't managed to settle in my body, with Killian's name on my parted lips, hoping he was doing the same with mine.

Chapter 19
The Events

I'd been staring up at the ceiling for fifteen minutes, entirely unwilling to remove myself from the fluffy sheets. The early morning sun filtered through the window and lit my room in wintery blue light, steadily removing the shadows from around the space.

I'd fallen asleep with thoughts of Killian racing through my mind and woken with them still there. My pillow muffled the moans I made as I came around my fingers again with Killian's punishing kiss playing on repeat in my head.

I rolled over and looked at the deep-maroon journal sitting on my bedside table. I reached across and plucked it from the little glass table then propped myself up on the pillows.

I traced my fingertips along the edges of a wide gold badge inset into the centre of the journal. The elegant swirls were shaped into a diamond, and a deep-red oval garnet wobbled in its massive setting in the centre of the shining metal.

I fought the urge to consume the book for a moment longer, pausing to enjoy the feeling that after twenty-four years of not having my mother with me, I finally held something of hers—something she had treasured and held herself. I leant in and smelled the fuzzy cover. The faintest scent of camellias filled my senses—it was worn away after so many years, but still imprinted in the fabric.

I brushed away the vague memories that surfaced, unlocked by her lingering scent, and tried not to picture the clearest one I held—of her weakening on that bed and Caldwell crying at her side.

I let out a sigh along with the ache in my chest then rifled through the pages. Glimpses of her elegant script flashed as the parchment turned against my thumb.

Start at the beginning I suppose.

I cracked open the book, turning to the first page. It was dated nearly four hundred years ago—

Father took me to the legion today in Kevilla. I was meant to pay attention to his instructions, meant to listen to everything Commander Warven was explaining to me—to learn everything I needed to know when I took the throne.

But a certain male took away all my attention. The smirks he *gave me whenever he turned to check if I was keeping up sent a thrill through my body. I just hope he's not as much trouble as his name suggests.*

Knave.

I combed over the diary entries for the next hour, staying snug under the puffy quilt. So far it was little more than her love entries as she swooned over Knave, admitting to all the times she snuck out to go see him at Kevilla.

It turned out that Knave was an incredibly skilled fighter, though didn't hold a rank. I smiled a little knowing my mother—despite being over two hundred years old—was no better than the rest of us love-stricken females, ogling at the sweating, heaving bodies of males training in the broad light of day.

Like mother, like daughter.

I considered dragging myself out of bed when a knock sounded at my door. It was too gentle to be Killian, so I jumped up and padded through the sitting area to the double entrance doors, then pulled them open.

Erela stood there in a pale green gown, poised and elegant with her hair delicately wrapped in little braids with gold pins, pointed ears on show.

"Morning," we said in unison. "Do you want some tea?" I asked as I invited her in and made my way to the cream chaise in the little sitting area. "I was just going to try to figure out how to get—"

Erela waved her hand and two steaming saucers appeared on the coffee table right as we sat down. I levelled her with a look that told her I thought she was a show-off, but she smiled smugly like she already knew.

"I've got to learn how to do that. Thank you," I said appreciatively. "What brings you here?"

Erela looked over my shoulder to where the journal could be seen tossed at the edge of my bed and gestured with her chin. "Found anything?"

I followed her gaze. "Nothing yet, just the secret entries of a female in love. . . who's Knave?"

She considered for a moment. "I've never heard of him. Why?"

"My mother keeps writing about him, he's some warrior in the legion. She seems quite smitten. I thought it might have been my father, but the timing is off."

Erela made a noise of agreement as she swallowed a sip. "Legion records could tell you more about him if you wanted. Your parents met well over two-hundred years ago and were together almost from that instant onward. Besides, your father grew up and lived on the coast in Lleiscray. He never lived in Kevilla."

I contemplated as I took a long drag of the floral tea. "Killian said. . ." I paused and tried to get the words out without sounding desperate. "Even fae with moieties still love others."

"Yes, but it's different."

"Different how?"

"I can only go on what my mother told me. She was a child of a united pair—her soul was cleaved and had a moiety out there somewhere, but she never found them. My father was not her soul's other half. She explained to me she loved my father completely as anyone loves their partner. But that part of her always felt missing. That despite the full heart she had with her life and her children, it was her soul that ached and nothing else could fill the hole."

I shivered.

Sounds a whole lot like how I felt.

"That sounds. . . extreme." I felt sad for her mother—even for her father if I was honest.

"I think it's supposed to be," Erela said thoughtfully, looking into her tea. "It's why it's so treasured for moieties to find one another, why they hold such power together. There's nothing that comes close. I wish you could have seen the way your parents lit up when they were next to one another. It was like there was this tiny piece of them that dulled when they were apart, and shimmered when they were together. It was truly beautiful."

Sweet sadness settled over my shoulders as I also wished I could have seen them together—seen them holding onto one another like they were in that portrait.

But I didn't want to grieve my parents. I had already mourned my mother, and my father wasn't gone. I blew out a heavy breath to shake the emotion that had woven into my body.

"So, what brings you here? I'm sure you didn't come to ask what I was reading."

"No, I actually came to give you these."

Erela waved her hand and two worn leather books thumped onto the coffee table between us. "They are the only two tomes in our entire library with any record of Noteas or the prophecy. I thought I'd bring them to you to save yourself the trip. Sylvie said everything in there is information we already know."

My heart sank. Two.

"Do you know what they say?"

"This one," she said, picking up the first book, is a more recent history of our realm, written nearly a thousand years ago. It recounts the battle when Orias rose up in an attempt to gain power and bring Noteas back. Evander led the fae and destroyed their army with Strike and killed Orias. Orella drew the lines of their court and banished the angels to it. It mentions that after Orias' death, an angel named Nephamir began to rule them, which he still does to this day. But Noteas isn't mentioned beyond that, and nothing is written about the prophecy beyond that there is one."

I picked up the second, older book and flicked through the heavy, yellowed pages. "And this one?"

"This one is a little more interesting. It was written at the end of the first war and mostly details the events leading up to the conflict—tensions rising, Noteas and Lilla preaching a rebirth of the realm, etcetera. It says they wanted to bring forth a monster who would destroy the world and started sacrificing fae in sick ceremonies to do it."

My stomach roiled.

"Angels have no magic, you see, so they cannot create their own spells. They make sacrifices to appease their dark Gods so they may be *blessed* with what they desire."

She shuddered, and I did the same at the sick thought.

"Noteas and Lilla must have done something right by their books because they were an unmatched power. Fallen are notoriously hard to kill, but these two. . . they were *something else.*" Her tone turned uneasy.

Something else?

"But strangely, the part about the battle and what happened immediately after has been ripped out."

I flipped to the section Erela referred to. The writer recollected the towns affected first and where the final battle occurred, and then. . . nothing. Pages seeming to detail the battle, the death of Argensir, and the banishment of Noteas and Lilla had been torn out, and the story picked up in the aftermath, after Orella divided the realm some five hundred years later.

"Why would someone tear the history out?"

"Your guess is as good as mine. Everyone knows the basics though. Argensir met them on the battlefield along with the fae and sacrificed himself, and then Orella worked her magic to banish them from this realm. Five centuries later she had the prophecy that Noteas would return, so she divided the realm into three—the two Kingdoms and her own court, then chose two fae to be the beginning of the royal lines of each Kingdom."

I flipped to the end of the dusty book where the prophecy was recorded, written in a different hand, by a different scholar half a millennia later. Under the retelling of the division of the realm, written at the top of the page was the prophecy recited to me yesterday.

When Endence gathers Winter's might, Sun will shine its dawning blight.

Under the line, in the centre of the yellowed page was a shimmering gold mark that glistened as I angled it in the sunlight.

"What does this mark mean? I've seen it somewhere before," I asked as I passed the book to Erela so she could see.

"What mark?"

"Under the prophecy, in the middle there."

She squinted at the page. "There's no mark here, Alora."

I rounded the table and leant over her shoulder. "Right. . . there," I said and jabbed the page. Erela turned to look at me like I was crazy, or to check if I was joking. But as our eyes connected our expressions shifted, realisation dawning.

"You can see something here?" Shock lanced through her tone. "Draw it," she ordered and produced everything I needed with a flick of her wrist.

I ignored the items as they appeared and ran to my bed, my wings tucked in so I could move quicker. I grabbed my mother's velvet journal and tossed it to her.

"It looks like this, but. . . different," I said, referring to the diamond-shaped badge on the cover. I grabbed the quill and drew the symbol I could see in the book. Like a strange opposite twin, the swirling gold mark arced around a circular centre and formed a sort of star with four points.

Erela studied the drawing I'd done. "I've never seen this before. It's not a language or any rune symbol I know."

"We need to tell Killian."

I made for the door, not caring I wasn't properly dressed to roam a palace. I reached for the silver handle and yanked it open, but reared back in surprise as I stood face-to-face with a steely-eyed Queen Fleur, her hand poised to knock on the door I'd just burst through.

She opened her mouth to speak, but Killian came around her side and looked me over—concern in his expression, my own hiding nothing.

"What's happened?" he demanded.

"What are you doing here?" I blurted back.

"You need to sit down."

"So do you."

Killian demanded I go first, so I spent the next few minutes repeating everything Erela had said and explaining what I found in the back of the older book. Both he and Fleur lent in on that last page, trying to see the mark I told them was there—but neither of them could, nor did they recognise the sketch I'd drawn of it.

How was it familiar to me and not to them?

"But what is it?" I asked, growing impatient.

"It's a spell mark," Fleur answered. "Left for you by someone, it will reveal a message or whatever has been hidden on the page once you remove the seal."

"How do I remove the seal?"

"There are many ways spell seals can be removed, but only the correct one will work. It might require a drop of your blood so the spell knows it is you standing before the message, or it might simply be a word that needs to be spoken. It could be a number of things."

No point fucking around.

Without hesitating, I crossed the room to my dagger and pierced my thumb as I strode back. Deep-red swelled at the cut I'd made and I let a drop fall onto the gold seal.

The single bead of blood didn't even touch the aged parchment. Instead, it fizzled and disappeared into nothing—whatever spell hiding the contents underneath protected it from damage, and the page remained unchanged. I glowered at the book, giving it a mental middle finger.

Of course it couldn't be that fucking easy.

"I need to speak to Orella." Determination filled my voice.

Fleur looked to her son and they exchanged a look. "I'm inclined to agree, but you aren't ready."

I raised my voice. "Fuck being ready. This, right here. This is something." I jabbed at the book. "I'm the only one who can see this, and Orella brought me into this realm. This page is about her prophecy. This is all connected, and I need to find out what she knows."

Fleur let the outburst go, but her eyes set firmly and her brows drew together—the Summer Queen wouldn't tolerate being spoken to like that again.

"And we will, Princess, but my mother is right—you aren't ready. In many senses of the word," Killian said, trying to ease my frustration for a change.

I simmered, but he went on regardless.

"Orella sets trials to any who try to reach her, and it'd be wise for you to have an escort from someone who has survived them before. There are very few fae who have succeeded—even less who I'd trust to have you in their care."

Fleur folded her hands in her lap. "In any case, it will all have to wait."

I looked between the two as they exchanged a worried look. "Wait for what?"

"Nephamir has called his Treaty Ball in just under three weeks, and I need Killian to attend."

"Nephamir? As in the leader of the Fallen, Nephamir?"

Fleur nodded. "Every half-century, the Fallen Court hosts a ball and renews the treaty to ensure that. . . well to ensure that everyone is playing fair, to put it plainly. The angels do not tolerate the fae lightly and only invite a pair of representatives from each Kingdom. This is the first ball where there is no *official* royal member to attend on the Winter Kingdom's behalf, so Killian will go in place and represent both."

I looked to Killian who was standing behind the lounges, angled away from us, with irritation coming off him in waves. His body was stiff with tension as he stood with his arms folded over his chest, drumming his fingers against his upper arm.

Fleur continued. "He has a unique position within each Kingdom, as both a representative of Winter as Legion Commander, and as a Prince of Summer. He is primed to represent the interests of both Kingdoms."

"You're not going? Or sending anyone else? Surely it's too dangerous to just send Killian." I was shocked Fleur was sending her eldest son alone to deal with the enemies they continuously claimed were dangerous.

"I'm flattered by your concern, Princess, but I have it in hand. A truce is sworn for the entirety of the event for both the angels and the fae, I'll be fine."

"Fleur, why aren't you and Nakir going? Or sending Farro? Surely another representative should be there to support Killian."

"The more official representatives who attend, the more tense things will grow. It is far simpler if Killian goes on his own. It's purely showboating and the treaty never changes, the official side of the political procedure is simple. But also," she added, looking at us nervously, "we cannot attend because the Summer Kingdom is preparing."

"Preparing for what?"

"Farro has learned that the Fallen are sending out their warriors and whispering secrets to the vile creatures in their domain. They're planning something. It's imperative Farro is present and focused in our legion in case there is any more development. Nakir and I must ensure our Kingdom is prepared."

'Look for deception–'

Those rumours in the human realm about war and enemies looking for something washed through my mind. "So, the Fallen are playing dirty and hiding behind a treaty ball at the same time?"

"It's not surprising in the least," Erela said disapprovingly. "They're repulsive beasts."

"Isn't that more reason for Killian to have backup when he goes into their court?" I asked. "I mean there is no *official* leader of Winter, but I *am* here. Shouldn't I go and learn who these enemies are and protect the interest of *my* Kingdom?"

"You're not coming," Killian declared.

Irritation immediately flared at the dismissal–that he was once again telling me what I could and couldn't do.

"So. . . for weeks you've barely left my line of sight, you just said there's no one you'll trust me with, but now I'm staying behind?"

"Yes."

Every line of his face tightened and brooked no argument.

It's like he's never met me.

"It's far too dangerous."

"But not for you?"

"Not for me." His cocky smile spread.

"Killian will ensure everything is in hand, Alora," Fleur reassured. "At any rate, it is imperative the Fallen don't get their hands on you. Word has undoubtedly spread of your arrival, and Nephamir will be suspicious of why the Oracle has shown such an interest in you. If he discovered you were in his castle," she paused and paled, "you'd never make it out alive."

I shivered.

"But, with this news, it means we have to leave earlier than anticipated, Princess. We need to get back—"

"I'm not leaving. Not when we've just discovered *this*," I said, holding the book up. Killian let out a sigh, not in the mood to deal with my stubborn nature.

"I assure you, she's quite safe here," Erela cut in, offended.

Killian shot his glare at her, but I certainly wasn't backing down now that I had support. I stood and squared my shoulders. "This is *my Kingdom*, and I'm in *my* palace—this book is the best lead we've found in over a month, and I *will* stay here if I wish."

Killian raised a single brow at my tone, and I quickly continued before he bit back. "You have things to prepare, and considering I'm the only one who can see the symbol, it would seem I have things to prepare of my own."

Erela blew out an impressed whoosh of air.

Fleur stood. "Seems that's settled then." She made her way toward the door, and Erela and I followed with Killian stomping in tow. Fleur gave me a knowing wink as she left—a silent approval from the steely queen that I'd developed my own iron.

Erela followed her out the door and turned, waiting for the brooding commander to catch up.

Killian stepped next to the doorway without so much as looking at me. "I'll meet you in a moment. The princess and I need to have a little chat." Then he slammed the door closed.

I didn't have time to draw a breath before he shoved me up against the wall and growled low at my throat like he wanted to tear it out. One arm pressed across my chest and the other gripped my wrist, holding me in place. The move was a dangerous echo of last night's passionate encounter.

The growl sent ripples of fear and pleasure racketing through my body, straight to my core. My breaths came in panting gasps, but soothed when he dropped a kiss against the side of my neck. Then a second, slower, teasing one at my jaw.

His voice came gravelly and low. "I can't tell if I love it or hate it when you answer back."

He pulled back just enough so we could look at one another and I had to concentrate to realise he was waiting for me to speak.

Words, Alora. Say words.

"It's not my problem you haven't figured out your kinks yet, Killian. But if it's any help—it's plain to see your ego is too big to want anything other than a female who is silent and subservient."

A deep chuckle rumbled in his throat. "Well colour me disappointed. . . the Princess has me all wrong," he teased against my lips. "Let me set the record straight, Alora. . . I'd so hate for there to be any miscommunication between us," he said with an unmatched arrogance. "There's only one thing on me that's too big, Princess, and it's not my ego."

He pressed his hips against me to drive his point home.

Another gasp left me at his filthy comment and the honest truth behind it as his cock pressed against my soft pyjama bottoms.

"And as for what I want. . ." He moved to my neck again. "Subservient goes a long way, but silent would never do," he whispered against my ear. "How else could I hear you beg?"

He grabbed my earlobe between his teeth and bit down—the point of his canine pinched, drawing out a sweet, pained moan before I could stop myself. Then, suddenly, his mouth was on mine, swallowing my cry with long strokes of his tongue, pure pleasure surging through me as he ground his body against mine. The arm he had pressed across my chest dropped to palm my breast, while the one around my wrist moved up to fist into my hair.

As his scorching kiss lit me up inside, my core tightened and pooled, the peak of my thighs instantly becoming slick—all I could think was I wanted more, more, *more*.

Killian and I had been pushing each other's buttons for over a month now, and I knew just how to set him off in the finest way possible. To push at that male ego in just the right way.

I grabbed at the back of his neck, holding him steady, and pulled out of his kiss. I moved to his ear, taking a moment to regain my breath and coiled my legs in preparation. I summoned every ounce of sultry confidence I had and whispered, "I don't fucking beg."

I moved with lightning speed and strength. Taking advantage of the element of surprise, I flipped us then shoved him—his charcoal wings flaring as he thumped against the panelled wall, shock flashing across his face.

I paced back, creating distance between our bodies, then took a breath of air that was easier to get down now that Killian wasn't pressed against me.

Slowly, he stood to his full, towering height, straightening so he was no longer pressed against the wall, and his great wings twitched before he spread them further, casting a dark shadow behind him. His stare turned predatory as he looked the length of my body.

"I wonder though. . ." His voice was a rough whisper. "Did you beg for me in your dreams last night, Princess?"

Killian took a solitary step toward me. I mimicked it as I stepped back, making him come to me.

I steeled my voice. "I didn't dream of you."

I took another retreating step to match his oncoming stride. He was stalking me around the sofas, like a cat stalks a bird.

The corner of his mouth flicked up in that infuriating grin. "You lie so sweetly, Princess."

Another fluid step, another retreat.

I watched as the muscles in his thin shirt twitched, every part of his body taut and on edge, needing release—his instincts focused on his target.

I took another step away and the backs of my knees hit the plush chaise in the sitting area. I stumbled and Killian's gaze turned into one of vicious triumph. He took another step, slowly closing the gap between us, his gaze raking over my peaked nipples which betrayed my arousal through my shirt.

"Tell me true, Princess," he whispered darkly as he edged closer. He reached out and brushed my wrist with the tips of his fingers then ran them slowly up my arm. "Did you?" He leant in, dipping next to my ear, his voice a desperate whisper. "Because you begged so eagerly in mine.

Begged, and pleaded, and craved for me. Only ceasing when I slid my cock between your lips. That wicked, smart mouth felt as sweet around my skin as I imagined you tasted when I fucked you with my tongue."

My knees gave out and I dropped back onto the chaise behind me. Killian came down with me and wrapped his hand under my head before I hit the cushions. I didn't even try to contain the cry I let out as his weight crushed me and he claimed my mouth again.

This time, his hands roved as he kissed me thoroughly–his movements were controlled and precise, but scattered like he couldn't decide where he wanted to go.

He broke away and rolled to the side, then trailed his fingers down my shirt and paused at the bottom, waiting silently for permission as his fingers found the top of my pants. My answering kiss was all he needed as he dipped his hand beneath the hem and plunged down.

He let out a satisfied groan and cursed at the slickness he found waiting as he dragged his finger along my centre. I rocked my hip against his hand and raked my nails down his sides as I reached for his cock straining against his pants, palming it through the fabric.

Killian wasted no time and pushed his finger inside me, pressing his palm against my clit. I cried out and his canines flashed as he smiled.

"Answer me," he ordered.

It took a moment to understand his demand.

'Did you beg in your dreams, Princess?'

"No," I panted.

Killian cocked his head to the side, narrowing his eyes like he was trying to catch my lie.

"I was wide awake when I was moaning your name."

Killian went wild. This time, he didn't cover my cries with his consuming kiss, but watched me as he dragged more of them with every pump, as if each sound he wrought was music to his ears, edging him on to go harder, faster, deeper.

Only when Killian added a second finger and sunk it deep, hitting that sweet spot, did he kiss me through my screams as my orgasm ripped through my body and my muscles clenched around his fingers.

His cock twitched beneath my palm as my muscles turned soft and my whimpering settled.

Killian kissed me as he pulled out and rested his hand on top of my thigh. I stared up into his brilliant eyes, trying to pull consciousness back into me.

"You come so sweetly, too, Princess," he murmured against my lips and I nearly ignited again on the spot.

I hooked my fingers on the top of his pants. "Shall I see if the same can be said of you?"

But Killian dropped his forehead against mine, placating my rising desire. "Nothing is as sweet as you," he muttered, and to drive his point home he brought his fingers to his mouth and sucked, unabashed by the salacious performance. He groaned as though he'd just tasted the most decadent dessert. "Just as I imagined. Seems the only thing not sweet about you is your disposition."

I readied to give my own remark, but Killian leapt on the opportunity—leapt on me—as he rolled back between my legs and darted his tongue into my open mouth. The taste of my arousal coated my tongue and Killian growled against my body, like he was pleased with himself.

Merciful Gods, these fae are something else.

His hips matched the sweep of his tongue, grounding against my core in a deep rub. "It nearly kills me to leave without sinking myself in you."

Like a bucket of icy water had been thrown over me, all the dirty thoughts left my head, and I nudged him to move. He shifted, letting me up and perched on the edge of the low chaise, watching my reaction.

"You'll leave already?" I was annoyed at how desperate I sounded.

"Unfortunately. And there's no way in fucking hell I'm having my way with you on a Gods damn time limit." He pressed me back into the chaise and kissed me one last time, then reluctantly tore himself away.

If I was counting right, it was the third time he'd initiated a move and pulled back—clearly warring with his desires.

"I'll go back to Kevilla to prepare."

I watched him closely, not knowing what to say. *Be careful* would've sounded silly *and* unnecessary for a male as powerful as him.

But Killian filled the silence before I managed to find the right words. "Come back with me, Alora."

It sounded like a plea.

"Don't leave," I said lightly in response.

He pressed his eyes closed, as though he hated to say no to it.

"I need to figure out what that mark means, Killian. This is too important."

He sat up fully and nodded. "I know. . . but with what Farro has found about the Fallen plotting behind our backs. . . I want to make sure you're protected before this ball goes ahead."

I thought for a moment, weighing my options. "How about I spend another week here learning what I can, and I'll send word if I'm done earlier."

"Fine," he said begrudgingly, but then a devilish smile spread. "Or, I could risk sifting here each night. Check on you in person. . . see if there's anything you. . . need." He winked.

My muscles gave a tight pull, completely separate from the delicious aftershocks of the climax he'd just wrung from me. "You wouldn't."

"Oh, I don't think you know half the things I'd do," his rough voice promised.

I heard the words he didn't say.

I don't think you know half the things I'd do—to you.

"I take my duties *very* seriously, as you'll soon learn, Princess."

My belly pulled, already tight with anticipation, but I fought it and shook my head. "No, I think I'll manage without you and your *duties.*"

He made a deep noise that sounded like *sure thing* before he stood and crossed the room he'd stalked me through moments ago, then paused at the door, straightening his clothes as he waited for me. "Before I leave for Alziros, I think it would be good if we talked through. . . everything."

Everything sure was going to contain a lot, but I knew it was necessary.

I rocked on the balls of my feet awkwardly. "I agree."

"Good luck, Princess," he said in farewell then breezed through the doorway.

I clicked it shut then leant against it, staring up at the high ceiling.

I had a sinking feeling I was going to need more than luck to survive this.

More than luck to survive him, too.

Chapter 20
The Story

I didn't leave my room for the rest of the day. Instead, I poured over the two texts Erela had brought, scouring for anything that might be a clue. But with the exception of that strange mark only I could see—although I only knew the briefest version of the history—everything in the book was information I already knew.

My brain was fuzzy and my eyes were heavy from reading—and my heart had this strange ache in it that I didn't want to think about. So I admitted defeat and went to bed, leaving the increasing list of mysteries I needed to piece together for another day.

Warm sunlight shone on the glistening grounds the next morning.

I was taken aback by the warmth of the rays, deceived by the pillowed snow that covered the palace. Only after I remembered it was late spring did it make more sense.

Over breakfast, Erela asked me to tour Carault with her. I didn't want to forsake my reading list, plus, I wanted to track down the Legion records to learn more about Knave. Besides, Killian would throw a fit if he found out I'd left the palace.

Which was the exact deciding reason that made me abandon the dusty parchments and enjoy the city with my cousin.

I donned my mother's ivory cloak Veric had given me and waited for Erela at the palace doors. But the heating spell lacing the stunning material couldn't warm me the way my heart did when I saw her drift down the stairs in an identical one, the exact shade of forget-me-nots.

We walked amongst the peaked rooftops of the buildings capped with snow and bordered with creeping bluebells, though the cobbled paths remained free of the icy powder—another genius use of magic.

We looked over trinkets and treasures, paintings and creations made by those who called the city home. Everyone gave polite smiles and waves as they recognised their Steward, or called her over to talk. Erela of course kept the perfect poise her title demanded the entire time.

A lively band filled the busy main square with lyrical music—the five music-playing fae laughed and whooped as their gathered crowd tossed coins and danced along with them.

Several children ran and jumped around as they twirled to the music, their little wings stretching and flapping as they went. I was captivated by the pure joy they emanated, and I realised as I watched the happy crowd that it was the first time I'd seen a young fae.

"Children," I whispered absentmindedly.

"Faelings, yes," Erela smiled. "Though I don't know if *you* can call them children—that one there is older than you," she teased, pointing to a boy who looked no older than fifteen.

The realisation just made me smile more.

We revelled in the happy moment and I let my worries and lists of tasks fall from my mind while I took in the beauty of the picturesque city.

My city.

"Come on," Erela beckoned, linking her arm with mine. "Let's drink."

Before we knew it, it was mid-afternoon, and we were two bottles of wine down, tears of laughter streaming down our tipsy faces as we sat against the window of the high-end wine bar she'd taken us to.

There was no way I'd be able to go back and make any sense of the books waiting for me back at the palace, so we both agreed to write the rest of the evening off.

We'd grown too loud for the sophisticated bar, so we found an even louder pub that matched our mood and carried on.

It was tomorrow before we stumbled ourselves home.

I fell out of bed a while past midday. I'd gone in search of Erela once I was decent, but she was holding meetings and couldn't meet.

Gods only knew how she was capable of working.

I wished I had some of the herbs Killian mercifully gave me the last time I'd gotten rotten drunk—it was probably how Erela managed to function and show up for her duties.

My muscles stuck like glue, and my head throbbed with the remnants of last night's drinks. With no hangover cure in sight, I decided the best action to take was to clear the fogginess away with a bout of training.

Besides, I'd been idle for long enough.

I donned my battle leathers and daggers, then went into the courtyard outside my room, fighting the chill that tried to creep into my bones with sweat and exertion as I went toe to toe with the frosted juniper tree in the garden.

Being my first real training attempt since the volcac attack, and my hangover still rearing its ugly head, I couldn't help but feel the tree won. So after a measly attempt, I went straight back to bed.

The next day, I woke with a surge of revitalised energy and determination. The break in the monotony with Erela had done wonders for my productivity. I began the morning with another solo training session against the tree, then soaked the aches away in my steaming bath.

Dressed and finally ready, the only battle facing me was the list of reading I had to do, so I decided to start from the top. I returned to the study where the pile of books Erela had initially collected for me still waited.

It took two entire days to go through the remaining books, and it only succeeded in putting me in a bad mood—none of them were useful.

Annoyed at my dwindling time frame and the pile of books still ahead, I found peace at the end of each day reading my mother's journal, which continued to be her detailing her love story with Knave.

The following morning, I was determined to find out who this Knave was that my mother kept fawning over. I flung my quilt off, sending her journal, which I'd fallen asleep reading, flying off my bed and onto the floor with a *chink* as it landed on the gold badge.

I powered through my training and wing exercises in the courtyard, then after rinsing off the sweat I'd worked up, went to the library and sought out the all-knowing Sylvie.

The library ceiling was at least three floors high, and cool, clear sunlight shone in from the arched windows. Any walls not covered in towering bookshelves were panelled with decorative moulding and painted in creams and beiges and edged in gold. Long tables to sit and spread out at were placed every few shelves, and cushioned sitting areas to curl up in were dotted in between. Where sunlight from the domed ceiling couldn't reach, faelights floated above, illuminating the cavernous space.

Fae milled about in the hushed chamber, some busily searching shelves, others nestled in groups, filling the library with quiet life.

Sylvie had to be the oldest fae I'd seen so far but could still pass as being in her early forties. The stern librarian eyed me as we walked along the stacks to where legion records were kept.

I dipped my head and watched my feet as we walked, lest she make the connection of who I really was.

Sylvie left me in a shaded alcove housing the shelf I needed. I matched the dates from my mother's journal with the records I'd need, and pulled out three massive, dusty books, crossing my fingers I'd find what I needed.

Of course, I found nothing.

Knave wasn't mentioned in any enlistment records, death records, war records, or even in the housing records of Kevilla. The mystery surrounding him made me all the more suspicious of the male, despite how love-stricken my mother was.

Admitting I'd hit a dead end, I packed the books away then strolled through the library, running my fingers over embossed spines and combing over titles as I went, when a stack of books caught my attention.

Texts bound in gold and gemstones lined the shelf—tomes committed to the lives and stories of the Gods.

I was drawn in like a moth to a flame. Not just by their beauty, but from the wealth of stories of the deities that had always been an impossibility to learn about growing up as a human.

I plucked one off the shelf at random and flipped through the thick pages, skimming over the names and words within. It was about a Goddess named Zolora, who was the deity of learning and wisdom. I pulled another off the shelf about Esella, the Goddess of love and marriage, another about Nysildis, God of the hunt, and one about Loenias, the God of courage and skill.

I paid particular attention to memorising the title of the book about Meulula, the Goddess of wine and mirth, making sure I remembered to come back to her particular tales.

I bet she was good fun any night of the week.

I was about to continue on my way, but the most elaborate book still called to me. I already knew what names would be within the pages before I opened the heavy tome propped up on its own stand.

Illustrations of the Blessed Four were painted throughout the book. Each painting depicted the Gods differently, depending on who had created them—no one had seen the Gods, so no two images were the same. Though all were completed with the same meticulous detail as their carving in the city—this time, brought to life with colour and depth that the statues couldn't recreate.

They were mighty and ethereal, with bodies smooth and solid as though hewn from stone, and their eyes were lit with the well of magic they possessed.

I read a few passages telling the same information Veric had told me that first day while we stood at the foot of their statue in Kevilla. Which was that, unlike the lesser deities, the Blessed Four did not have claim over specific parts of lives—they encompassed all, and were each a divine power over everything. It was the precursor to Ryuna's tale of the loss of Hush—the Blessed Four were protectors and creators, and did not rule over others.

Mostly, I kept an eye out for the paintings within the stories, trying to learn more from the images than the words that I didn't have time to read.

I flipped to the end where images depicting the Immortal Weapons were sketched. Only Strike was drawn in detail, being the only weapon found so far. The long javelin was made of gold and gleamed with power, details of how Evander found the weapon under the ruins of a Summer temple were written in a footnote at the bottom.

On the opposite page, a depiction of Evander in Orias' uprising was painted as though it was a still frame from the actual battle, frozen on the page in front of me.

Evander hovered above the battleground, facing out at the scene below him. His black leathers were torn and his wings—which would've been the colour of caramel if they hadn't been covered in grit and gore—were spread wide. His dusty blonde braid flew out as he held the javelin above his head, poised to strike at his enemies. His broad shoulder muscles rippled as he put his strength behind the attack.

I see why everyone was so impressed by the young warrior.

I looked on and saw the sketches of Ryuna's bow Hush, made of pearl and gold. Then several drawings of Rhoston's dagger, Kiss. Different versions had been sketched into the pages depending on how storytellers depicted the changing blade to look in each—many showing a curved blade and sharp-tipped handle.

I turned the page, expecting to find drawings of the fourth Immortal Weapon—the sword, Hum, belonging to Rharuer—but instead, there was an image of a green stone.

Drawn as though I could pluck it straight off the page, the emerald green gem, the size of a river pebble, looked as though it contained the whole universe inside. I could have sworn the drawing churned and swirled with fog and tendrils as I watched it.

I looked at the footnote, curious to learn what the stone was.

Rharuer's Stone: The might of Hum's magic was contained within Rharuer's Stone. After the fall of Ryuna, to ensure the great power of His Immortal Weapon could not be wielded with conquering intent or unleashed upon the worlds, Rharuer cleaved it from his sword so that Hum might never be made complete.

Efficient.

I flipped the page, expecting to see a sketch of the weapon, but none existed.

I closed the book, setting it back to its original position, causing the gems set into the cover to shine brilliantly against the glowing lights above.

I had exhausted my lines of inquiry—now there was only one thread left to follow, and my hopes were low that the love passages of my mother's journal were going to reveal anything useful.

I tried to fight the feeling of failure that swept over me as I pushed open the doors to my room.

I wanted to curl up and enjoy my mother's journal as a way of getting to know parts of her I'd never had the chance to—not as a task I'd assigned myself.

I crossed the plush carpet to my room, rounding the bed to look for the journal I'd flung in my unceremonious exit from the sheets.

And I found it—but it wasn't the only object on the floor.

I vaguely remembered hearing a chinking sound when I'd thrown the covers back and realised the loose gem scattered beside the journal must have been the cause, but it wasn't the item that caught my attention.

Stuck on the setting once holding the garnet, was a tiny folded envelope of yellowed parchment. I plucked the envelope from the gold metal and unravelled the pages.

No fucking way.

My eyes drank up the words as they leapt across the ink. I read it twice.

Then I looked at my mother's neat script on a second, small slip of paper that had been folded along with it.

A single entry, dating hundreds of years after the first time she ogled Knave marked the page.

I closed my eyes, praying to the Gods that this was a dream. But when I opened them again, the two key pieces to this growing mystery were still etched like dark stains staring at me.

The missing section of the defeat of Noteas and Lilla, and a warning from my mother.

We are so fucked.

The shout for Erela burst out of me before I'd made it to the doors and exploded through them. An attendant down the hall startled, his short, moss-green wings jerked as he spun to look at what the commotion was.

I pointed in a random direction. "Go get Erela, now!"

He obeyed immediately.

I pressed my palm to my head in frustration as I whirled in place in the hallway. Killian was a wasted effort, he was hours away.

I went inside, pulling the doors closed behind me, and shook my hands to rid myself of the building agitation. I darted over to a cabinet where a decanter of whiskey and several crystal tumblers waited. Not my usual go-to, but I needed the comfort liquor could provide.

I wasted no time tossing the drink back in a deep swallow, but it wasn't enough. I leant over, poised to place the glass on the table, when, in the time it took to blink, magic filled the room and my senses kicked into awareness as a body sifted behind me.

"Fucking Gods!" I squealed, throwing my hands up as I flinched.

Erela yelped as she dodged the glass that blew past her head–which I'd inadvertently flung in my surprise. "What in Gods name?"

It smashed against the opposite wall and splatters of glass sprayed on the ground as it burst.

Erela turned and *tsked* in annoyance. The mess disappeared with a flick of her hand before she turned her gaze back on me.

"You scared the life out of me!"

"You scared the life out of that poor attendant," she shot back. "What's wrong?" Her eyes looked me over head to toe.

"I found something–something big. Killian needs to know, too, but it'll take ages for him to get here."

Erela rolled her eyes and shook her head in exasperation. "Wait here." She vanished–sifting before my eyes. I stared at the spot she'd just been standing in, amazed at the ability.

Gods, that's cool.

I didn't consider sifting as a way to get Killian–the ability was so rare for fae to possess and too dangerous and draining to perform frequently.

Six seconds. That's all it took before Erela reappeared right where she'd just been standing, her expression a mix of smug achievement and bated anticipation.

Two seconds later, a hulking Killian appeared, dressed once again in his battle leathers. His hand drifted by his hip where his sword hung, and his magic pooled into the air, making it thick.

His eyes darted around the room, checking for danger. "What's wrong?"

"There aren't any threats in my fucking room, you brute, now sit down." I breezed past them to collect the entries I'd just found, but halted after taking only a few steps—a sudden worry making my skin shiver. "Can anyone sift into this room?"

"No," they said in unison, tempers short.

I narrowed my eyes but would interrogate them on it later when there was more time.

I brought the journal over, telling them what the yellowed parchment was, and where I'd found it, then laid it on the coffee table so it was visible to them both, and together we read over the missing part of the history.

At the peak of the war, both sides had suffered terrible losses. The angels had dwindled in number, but such was their strength that the strongest of their kind endured, ripping and killing with sickening brutality. Fae threw out their magic to stop the angels' attacks in such completeness that they withered and died without it.

Noteas and Lilla, drunk on power and the malice they wrought, thrived on the blood-soaked battleground. Seeing their opportunity, the pair rose into the air and beseeched their terrible Gods to release their great evil. A creature of unending and ultimate power who would destroy this realm forever.

The Chimaera.

The great warrior, Argensir, knew what they were attempting to bring forth, and knowing this was the final moment, understood there was no other way. He seized his opportunity to bring down the corrupt angels as they worked their dark spell and broke through their line.

Summoning all his strength and magic, Argensir collided with Noteas and Lilla, exploding with his might—sacrificing himself to protect this realm.

Seeing their corrupt rulers stopped, and knowing they had failed, the angels surrendered their defeat. Orella, enraged by the loss of life and taint on the land, at the loss of Argensir, and in the face of his sacrifice, broke her vow, and interfered with fate.

Dissatisfied by the surrender of the wicked rulers, and claiming it was insufficient for their crimes, Orella imprisoned the leaders apart and banished them so they could not join together to bring their evil upon the realm.

Noteas was confined to the fiery torment of the sun, to burn in endless suffering in the power of the mighty star. Orella cleaved Lilla's soul from her body, imprisoned it in the frozen depths of the moon, then burned her remains to ash to ensure she could never return.

"Did either of you know this? About the Chimaera?" I asked. "Did you know they were imprisoned? What Orella did to Lilla? Killian, that story you mentioned when we travelled. . ."

He nodded as he remembered. "It was supposed to be figurative. . . an exaggeration. . . not that she *actually* cleaved Lilla's soul from her body."

My stomach roiled with the uncomfortable truth.

"We've never heard the name of the evil they tried to bring forth, either," Erela added. "There is no creature known as a Chimaera in Endence, but it could be a beast from a different realm that they prayed for their Gods to send."

"That's not everything I found though." My hands trembled as I revealed the second slip of paper underneath containing my mother's handwriting.

I thought that we knew what to do—knew what to expect. But it is so much worse than we could ever have known. The prophecy is not what we think. Noteas is not our only enemy. And they are looking for her.

A vein in Killian's temple throbbed as his face twisted in rage. His power thrummed through the room, and his dark wings shook as his whole body tensed. "FUCK!" He sent a blast of magic across the room, shattering the whiskey decanter where it sat on the side table.

There was only one other enemy who was linked with Noteas, only one *her* my mother could've been referring to.

Lilla.

Killian gave me an hour to prepare to leave. He wanted to get back to Kevilla and advise everyone who needed to know it wasn't just Noteas coming for us.

Winter needed to be ready too.

"Looks like that conversation between us is going to have to wait a little while, Princess," he muttered before leaving me to pack.

I gathered my things, including my mother's journal and the two historical texts, and was standing in the foyer within the hour. Killian left Erela and I, claiming he wanted to grab something from the study.

I was positive it was simply to give us privacy as we said goodbye.

I promised her again I'd tell Veric my secret soon—though I didn't want to take any of his focus away right now with things unravelling as they were.

Just as we'd finished speaking, I sensed Killian strutting through from the guest wing.

"Mind if I borrow this?" he called out, waving a familiar blue and gold book in the air for Erela to see. "I was just getting to the good bits before Alora complained at me for not listening to her."

I gleaned part of the title as it flashed.

Inventory.

Erela tilted her head at me. "Well, technically it's *her* book."

Killian rolled his eyes, but I didn't pay him any attention. There was something I had missed. Killian's words fell away to a muffled rumble, but I couldn't look away from the book.

"Alora."

I tried to concentrate. "Hm?"

"The book," he said expectantly. "Do you mind?"

The book. . .

I'd read that book. Itinerary was a better word. A register of the weapons stored in a dedicated vault within the palace. But I'd found nothing in it of any value to the mystery I was trying to uncover. So why did I pause on it now?

Oh, fuck.

There was nothing in it of value.

I gasped and ran. Killian cursed and called after me, but I bolted through the foyer without pause and hooked behind the grand staircase to a half-hidden door.

Two sets of footsteps hurtled behind me, but they had no hope of catching up.

Within seconds, I'd made the turns down the empty marbled hallways and slammed my hand against the intricate silver doors that led to the Royal Treasury. My hand met the warm, tingling barrier before falling away with a shimmer. The magic seal had barely faded before the doors opened and I entered to face the portrait of my parents.

Killian and Erela made it to the room right as I found what I needed to confirm my suspicions.

"What the fuck's going on, Alora?"

"Erela. . ." I said calmly—distantly. "If my parents possessed any ceremonial swords or personal weapons, where would they be?"

"They would be in here," she replied with a question in her tone.

"Not in the weapons vault?"

"No, that vault is for standard pieces. Not for anything tied to the king or queen." I sensed her eyes on the back of my head, trying to find where I was going with this.

"And how many weapons are in this room?" My voice was soft and distant, not wanting this to be right.

"Just a set of daggers on the table and your father's sword over there." She pointed to the silver blade resting against a pedestal to the side.

"What's going on, Alora?" Killian grumbled from beside me.

I closed my eyes and blew out a breath. "If this," I gestured with my head to the silver weapon, "is my father's sword. . . then whose sword is that?" I asked, pointing my shaking finger to the painting of the intricate gold sword hanging at my father's hip.

They both took a small step forward, taking notice of the giant painting hanging on the wall.

Killian looked back and forth between the gold sword in the painting and the silver one in the room, then opened the inventory still in his hands.

"It's not listed in there," I said, still facing the portrait, knowing what he'd gone to search for.

Erela looked at Killian. "I've been in the vault countless times. That sword isn't in there."

"Maybe he has it on him?"

My voice trembled. "Oh, he has it on him, alright."

"How do you know? Why are you getting worked up over a sword?" Killian took a step toward me, his wings sweeping down his back. "What is it?"

I looked at the black gem in the centre of the swirling gold handle. No, not a gem. A setting.

A hole where the actual stone was supposed to sit.

A particular green stone containing the power of the King of Gods.

"It's Hum."

Chapter 21
The Plan

Chimaera. Lilla. Hum.

The words repeated on a loop as Erela and Killian stood still as statues, staring up at the portrait.

There was no denying this–no doubts that we'd come to the wrong conclusion. The most powerful Immortal Weapon was now in play–and it wasn't some dark beast that was our biggest threat.

It was a sword that could destroy the entire Gods damned realm if united with its other half. Even without its magic, Hum was a weapon we couldn't let fall into the hands of the ones who wouldn't hesitate to use it.

Killian and Erela were talking, but their hurried whispers didn't break through the ringing in my ears. Didn't push past the words repeating in my mind.

Chimaera. Lilla. Hum.

Things were more intertwined than we ever could have foreseen, worsening with every secret we uncovered.

Our enemy had worsened from those who despised us, to those who now plotted behind our backs. Their renowned, malevolent leaders being no more than a scary bedtime story, were now a frightening reality that just doubled in number.

The worst outcome that war would break out between fae and angels was now the best possible option. The more likely reality was a story involving Gods and monsters.

Killian knew this, too, and I all but heard the cogs of his commanding brain ticking as he talked through what we needed to do to secure our Kingdoms.

Ever the protector of Endence.

But I stopped him before his out-loud musing became orders barked at warriors, and made Killian swear not to speak of any of it. Not yet.

The only thing safe to reveal was that Lilla would be coming too. That it wasn't just the Summer Legion that had to be on alert for their target, but Winter for theirs as well.

I already knew Erela wouldn't tell a soul—she was dedicated to me, to the Kingdom she so dutifully looked after. But Killian—he was dedicated to more. To his family, to Summer, to the entire realm.

Endence's mighty defender considered more than the immediate effect this revelation would have.

But my thoughts went straight to my father.

In my heart I knew—*knew*—he was with that sword. The one that could syphon magic, unleash unfathomable power capable of destroying realms. Word could not get out that Hum had been found—whether it was complete or not.

I shut down the sickening thoughts of how I'd manage to protect my family in Remberlie, as well. The hunter's rumours spreading before I was whisked away by Orella was that the fae's enemies were looking for something.

Now, it was clear that *something* was Hum, and my father had sacrificed his soul to keep it hidden.

I clenched my fists. If war did spill out into Evamere, I wasn't strong enough to protect everyone here *and* there. I needed to choose who and what to safeguard to prevent it all, and I chose Hum to do it.

If I had to keep my identity a secret, so could Killian keep this.

Moments later, Killian swept me in his arms and flew us back to Kevilla in unusual silence as we both internally processed what had just unfolded.

Gone too, was the sexual tension built from the week before.

It was nightfall by the time we arrived at Kevilla. Killian landed on the green lawn before the Hall, his boots firmly planted in the soft grass before he set me down.

He needed to organise briefs and alert those who needed to know what we'd learned about Lilla, so told me to settle down for the evening. I turned toward my little cabin on the eastern outskirts, but Killian grabbed my shirt as I retreated.

"Oh no you don't," he growled, pushing lightly between my wings in the direction of his house.

I sent a questioning glance over my shoulder, wondering what motive was driving him to keep me close, but his dark expression gave away nothing other than his male authority that demanded he be obeyed.

For once, I found myself willing.

As soon as he was satisfied I'd followed his instruction, he stomped to the Hall to inform whoever needed to know about Lilla.

I hoped Veric or Jude would've dropped by, but they were likely in the Hall with Killian.

Feeling like the energy had been sucked out from deep within my bones, I retreated to the warm guest bedroom and begged sleep to come for me.

It didn't.

The next morning, I woke late, and by the time I got my arse out of bed, dressed, and into the training ring, any of the fae I'd come to know within Kevilla had already left for the day on assignments.

Killian had gone for a few days, returning to the Summer Kingdom to personally tell his parents at the palace, and his brother at the Summer Legion in Astorla about Lilla and the chimaera they intended to end the world with.

I had to trust he kept his mouth shut about my father and Hum.

In my solitude, I busied myself with training, resuming the same regime from weeks ago, starting with running laps around the giant camp. It was a significantly harder task now that I had wings weighing me down, but I pushed, determined to be stronger.

Gods knew I needed to be to face what was coming for us.

I ran through my wing exercises to continue building their strength and wielded my daggers every spare moment I had.

Eight days passed since I'd returned, and I hadn't once seen anyone I closely recognised. Those who remained in Kevilla reassured me Killian, Veric, Jude and the others were all completely fine and were just out securing defences and running scouting missions in light of what we and the Summer Kingdom had discovered of the Fallen Court.

So I kept routine and kept to myself–trying not to let feelings of absolute uselessness tear me apart.

Another two days later, while I poured out all my frustrations on a training dummy with my dagger, light footsteps approached from behind. I whirled, knowing it was either someone from the Hall bringing serious news, or one of the males I missed so badly returning.

Thankfully, it was the latter.

Jude stood behind me, his dark eyes locked onto my movements and his deep-red wings tucked in. "Gods, Lor, remind me not to get on your bad side."

"Never." I smiled and threw my dagger down. The sharp blade pierced the grass and stuck there as I took long strides to hug him tight.

First, his arms wrapped around me, then his citrusy sandalwood scent enveloped me just as tightly. Happy to finally see my good friend and drinking buddy again, I squeezed my eyes shut, then pulled back and held him at arm's length. "You look tired, Jude."

He gave me a horrified look. "I've never looked anything other than incredible. . . even when I'm overworked." He flashed a roguish grin.

"Tell that brute of a boss of yours to give you a day off," I joked, turning to retrieve my dagger.

He barked a laugh. "Come on, I've got some time. I want to see how good you've gotten."

He led the way over to the centre of an empty training ring, his small arsenal strapped around his body as usual, glinted in the morning light.

I'd sheathed my dagger as we'd walked across, so we were both unarmed–whether or not we remained that way was yet to be determined.

Jude turned and looked me over, then stood with his hands clasped behind his back—his go-to ready stance designed to lull me into a false sense of security.

Not this time.

I matched his stance and controlled my breath, letting that air of calm wash over me. But this time, I believed it.

Jude and I stood like statues for an age—still, silent and assessing.

It was the assessing I pinned my attention on when I realised Jude wasn't still at all. As I shifted my weight to one side, Jude was there, countering it in his own body with imperceptible movements. As my fingers twitched wanting to go for my dagger, his own would flex to reach for his own. Mirroring me.

The expertise of the little warrior was impressive, to say the least.

But there was one move Jude would never expect, and it was because he'd never seen me use it. The same move he'd performed on me the first time we'd gone head-to-head that sent me flying.

It was high risk though—I'd never used my wings beyond their gentle stretching and flexing.

No risk, no reward, right?

In a burst of movement, I feigned reaching for the dagger against my thigh and watched as Jude went for his. He palmed his blade, raising his arm to strike forward in a block against my own blade—only it wasn't there.

Instead of having my blade where he expected it, I threw my arm out to give myself momentum and stepped behind him. Jude reacted too slowly, misreading what I'd planned, and whirled around, right as I jumped and threw my wings back.

They strained against my shoulders, complaining at the swift motion I demanded of them. But the gust of momentum they created did just enough as I kicked my feet out and planted them on Jude's chest, right as he looked me in the eye with glorious shock.

He didn't fly back as far as I had when he'd performed the same move, but his garnet-red wings still flared to come to his aid, and he stumbled a few steps—which I chalked up to a win.

He rubbed a palm to his chest and smirked. "I've never been so attracted to a female in my life."

"Stop trying to butter me up, Jude, it won't stop me from kicking your arse."

"I should hope not," he said seriously but winked a beat later. "Right, weapons away, we're going hand to hand. The sooner you find some depth to that power, the sooner I can watch you pull that move on Killian and lay him on his back."

I also look forward to laying Killian on his back. . .

Jude sheathed his dagger and unclasped his sword from behind his back, tossed it onto the ground, then stepped over to me.

I raised my hands in a ready stance, and his lips tipped up in an impressed smile. He turned his head in different angles, assessing my form but didn't need to change anything about it.

Feeling satisfied, he lowered into his own stance and signalled me to make the first move.

As Jude and I sparred, I fell into a rhythm as familiar and natural to me as breathing. All of Caldwell's training and instruction flashed in my mind as I blocked and struck. Soon, beads of sweat dripped down his temple, showing the strain it took him to keep pace with me.

Some small, wicked–yet growing–part of me was immensely satisfied at bettering him as we trained.

Not even all his years of experience gave him an edge as he tried to get the upper hand. Only when he used his wings did he get the better of me. Mine still protested and ached when I called on them to flare and move as I spun and leapt.

Panting and sweating with our efforts an hour later, Jude called for a stop and led the way to the drinks station. He pulled off the thick top half of his leathers as he strode across the soft grass, his bare, tanned skin rippled over his tight muscles as he moved and threw the garment on the wooden table.

My eyes instinctively dropped to his chiselled abs and widened at the lean cut of them. Slick with sweat that glistened and dripped down his smooth skin in the sunlight. It was difficult to say which was more impressive, his tight, ripped figure or Killian's massive frame.

Guess I'll need to get Killian undressed to make an accurate comparison.

"Excuse me, but my eyes are up here."

I rolled my eyes at his feigned offence.

Like he didn't know he looked good.

"Can't blame a girl, Jude," I said before downing my drink.

Jude lowered his cup and went to make another remark but stopped—the words dying on his tongue. He whirled in the direction of the mountains to the southeast. His shoulders tensed and his wings shifted.

A second later, I sensed it too. Rising pressure and the feel of brutal, pushing magic. Flocks of birds burst from the forest and into the air.

My wings tensed as I looked toward the mountain range as the feeling rose, coming from that direction. A sweep of panic raced up my spine as I spotted a dark figure in the sky. I pushed the panic down, trying to tell myself I recognised the pressure of the magic.

Killian.

Around the camp, warriors stopped to watch Killian hurtle closer. Despite not being under threat, my unease didn't settle. The power of his pulsing magic was immense.

Something was wrong.

Seconds later, Killian plunged to the ground before Kevilla Hall, landing with a tremendous blast that echoed around us. Jude sprinted over as Killian stormed into the hall, his wings spread wide, power thrumming off him as he went.

I decided I was done sitting back like a doll on a mantle. I had more use—more purpose—than what I was contributing currently. I was done missing out.

I ran to catch up with them, but before I made it up the steps leading into the room, a crash sounded from within.

I leapt up the steps and went into the Hall, immediately seeing what had caused the commotion as I went up to stand beside Jude. Plates and glasses were strewn across the floor and against the wall, food and red wine splattered everywhere.

I looked at Killian, trembling with rage—clearly the one who had assaulted the dinnerware.

He roared a curse, clenching his fists as another wall of power pushed out from him.

It pounded through my chest like an echo of a drumbeat and made my heartrate quicken.

The fae who milled about made themselves scarce, fleeing into other rooms or out of the building entirely.

A few brave souls came closer.

I noticed they were the fae higher in the pecking order who were allowed to know the details behind the decisions.

But those remaining just stood—too stunned or scared to ask what was wrong. Or perhaps they were simply waiting for Killian to speak first, I didn't know.

But Killian didn't scared me.

I took a singular step forward, closing the gap further than any of the others dared.

Killian snapped his head to me as I did, his chest heaving with anger.

His vivid blue eyes searched mine. I could tell he was hunting for the words he'd need to answer my unspoken question.

What's wrong?

We stared at each other—so focused that everything fell away. I barely noticed Veric jog up behind me to stand on my right.

Still, Killian only stared and breathed, his rage simmering throughout the giant hall.

Then, he flicked his gaze around, looking at who else stood near us. His lips tightened and annoyance flashed across his face in a snarl.

I was about to tell him to just spit it out, but his eyes landed back on me before I could speak.

"They have the other half."

I cocked my head as I tried to understand the message he'd clearly meant only for me. But then realisation ripped through, and my stomach dropped.

Hum.

They have the other half of Hum.

The Hall was as silent as a graveyard. The many sets of eyes darted between Killian and myself, but no one dared speak. They just watched as Killian struggled to retain his power from lashing out, and me who had gone preternaturally still from what Killian just said.

"Everyone out," I heard myself say as I kept my gaze locked on Killian's. I tried to sound authoritative, but the words were barely a whisper.

Several heads swung to me, silently questioning the command given by a fae who held no authority amongst them.

I expected Killian to erupt in a fury when none of them moved, but it was Veric's voice that rang out with a might I hadn't heard come from him before.

"You heard her, get out!" he roared at the crowd, his wings flaring as he turned in a circle to face them all.

All the onlookers hurried away at their general's censure—one even sifted to retreat as quickly as possible.

Jude and Veric went to go as well, leaving Killian and I by ourselves.

I turned my head to look at them both. "Stay."

They glanced at each other before stepping back to where Killian and I stood, but I turned my focus on Killian once again.

"How do you know?"

"We increased the scouts combing through the Kingdoms since we learned of Lilla, and have found more and more dark creatures creeping around. We've been tracking them, and it's clear they've been looking for something. I came across a pack of sisyns entering the Kingdom three days ago and have been watching them since. They've been lurking deep in the forests and making tracks toward the Oracle's court."

"They'd be mad to enter Orril," Veric said in disbelief.

"Why?" I asked, looking between them all.

"Orella's lands are sacred, and she would not stand to have their dark stain in her Court," Veric explained. "But what could possibly tempt them to brave entering her territory?"

A fucking world-ending magic weapon, that's what.

Killian kept his eyes trained on me, and I knew he realised I understood. "They have it, Alora. They gave it to Nephamir and are searching for the other half of it—and we are fucked if they find it."

Veric stepped between us, demanding to be answered. "Would one of you explain? First, you said they already have the other half, now they're searching for the other half? The other half of what?"

Killian gestured in Veric's direction—leaving it up to me to explain.

I squeezed my eyes shut and let out a breath before I turned to Veric. "Hum."

The only sign of life from Veric was his pulse thudding on the side of his neck. His fingers slackened at his sides and I think he forgot to breathe for a moment before shooting a look at Jude, as though questioning if he'd heard correctly.

Jude didn't look much better as he stepped closer. "What did you just say?"

Veric turned so slowly to Killian that I thought time had slowed, but that pulse on the side of his neck was still ticking at the same rate.

"Precisely what half of Hum do they have, Killian?" Veric growled.

"Rharuer's Stone."

Veric clenched and released his fist a few times before choosing his words carefully, his voice was soft, but his tone was not. "Are you telling me. . . you've known about this, all this time? We've been conducting patrols across the Kingdom because you knew they were looking for Hum?"

"No, brother. I came straight here when I learned."

"But the two of you know more than you're saying–you knew about Hum."

We nodded.

"Why didn't you tell me?" Hurt lashed through his voice.

Suddenly, it made sense–the commander hadn't trusted his general with vital information on what was happening inside their Kingdom.

"It's my fault, Veric," I interjected, and hung my head low when the pain in his eyes landed on me. "I made Killian promise not to say anything."

"Why would you keep us out, Lor?" Jude asked.

Words escaped me as I looked between the three of them. All expectantly waiting for my reply.

I grabbed Veric's hands and squeezed, looking deep into his eyes while trying to convey everything I wanted to tell him. "Because I thought I would have more time."

Veric studied me closely, his sky-blue eyes flicking between my green and grey. He cocked his head to the side. "What else did you learn at the palace?"

I froze, trying to think of the right way to say what I needed to, without blurting everything out.

"That this is all to do with me somehow. To do with why I'm here–and some of it can't be. . ." Irritation climbed up my spine and the web of secrets I found myself unintentionally weaving. "What's important right now is that Killian and I both thought we would have more time before this all became an issue. . . but ultimately, we think Valefor has Hum–"

Veric pulled back, but I gripped his hands and spoke over him as a torrent of questions spilled from his lips. "We think that's why he's been gone, that he's keeping Hum hidden. But what we need to concern ourselves with right now–in this very instant–is that the angels have the stone. Hopefully, no one else knows about the sword, and we need to pray that they don't. . . pray that your uncle really is protecting it and that it's safe. The fact that the Fallen Court has found the stone is purely shitty timing."

"Unlikely." Killian scoffed and glowered at me. I couldn't help but feel like he was implying this was all my fault.

It probably somehow was.

As Veric looked between Killian and me, his accusatory glare subsided steadily into genuine curiosity. "What else aren't you telling me?"

I chewed on my bottom lip, guilt stabbing through my chest at withholding the truth from him still. But now wasn't the right time. I needed my general focused, and I couldn't have him worried about a princess he didn't know existed–couldn't have him distracted and worrying about me and what I was about to do.

I fortified my resolve to keep the truth from him a little while longer and looked him square in his brilliant eyes. "I can't tell you now, but I promise I will soon."

Veric tilted his head. "You may not know this, but fae take promises *very* seriously."

"Good think I'm being serious then. I promise, I'll tell you everything once I get back, Veric."

His brows drew together, but I wasn't surprised when Killian's voice cut through like a sword, asking the question I expected to hear. "Back from where, exactly?"

The corner of my mouth kicked up in anticipation. The image of his incoming tantrum played out in my mind, and I couldn't wait to see it in full fruition.

I turned and made my spine go rigid–my blonde waves swished over my shoulder as they followed my turn. Killian folded his massive arms across his chest and widened his stance like he was already preparing for a fight.

"I'm going to a Ball."

"Like fuck you are."

The next several minutes were filled with a near non-stop rant from the commander—bitching about how it was too dangerous and I wasn't setting foot in there.

Blah, blah, blah.

I tuned out, focusing my attention on the decor of the Hall while he stomped around and boiled over like a kettle. It was exactly as amusing as I'd imagined, but it got boring as he went on.

Once I'd had enough, I stood from the wooden bench I'd perched on while he ranted about danger and magic and safety and preparedness. I held my palm up to him in a signal for him to shut up.

He stopped short, and his eyes flared along with his dark wings, casting a shadow across his face, which just made him look more dangerous.

But the threat was lost on me when it came to this.

"While I'm sure you think you've made excellent points, Killian, I'm afraid you're wasting your breath."

He opened his mouth to yell some more, but I cut him off again, and my voice sliced through the air with an authority I didn't know I possessed.

"Enough, Killian." Jude and Veric exchange a wide-eyed look at one another, but I ignored them as well. "I think by now we all know I'm involved in this somehow, and the events are unravelling too quickly for any of our liking."

"They will kill you as soon as they figure out you're the one Orella brought here," Killian countered. "Slowly, I might add. And if Nephamir finds out who you are. . ." he tacked on with a pointed look, "you'll need nothing short of the full force of a legion to get you out of there."

"Lucky I have one, then," I said without thinking.

Veric's eyes narrowed on me, but I refused to look at him, worried it would give me away.

Killian glowered but didn't relent. "It would have been too dangerous for you simply to come along to the treaty, let alone go there with the objective to fucking steal from them."

"Your mother said it was dangerous if other representatives went. News flash, Killian, I'm not a representative!" I threw my hands out wide.

"News flash yourself, Princess, that was before you decided it'd be a good idea to rob them," he yelled back and mocked my stance.

I rolled my eyes skyward and my shoulders back. "They won't be suspicious if you bring a date, Killian. Besides, I'm the best chance you've got."

Killian raised a singular questioning brow at this, silently judging my self-assessment.

"Don't think I haven't noticed the looks you all swap when I get the upper hand during training. I'm quick and quiet and I Gods damn know it. You've all said as much yourselves as well," I said, watching all three males.

Jude and Veric swapped that look again.

"She has a point, Killian," Jude said when no one spoke. "There are times I can barely keep up with her, or don't see her coming. She's faster than me, damn near better than me, too, and that's with only training as a human for a few odd years. She can easily kick my arse if I'm not operating at peak performance."

Killian's growl reverberated across the room.

"When she can control her magic and fly. . ." Jude trailed off and looked at me. "You'll be a reckoning, Alora."

Killian folded his arms over his chest again and rumbled in annoyance that I'd found a supporter amongst our group.

"They're right, brother," Veric added. "If the plan is to steal the stone, then Alora is your best hope. Jude would be your next best option, but his presence would draw attention, and with the stakes so high. . . I'm not sure you want second best. No offence, Jude."

"None taken. I've always been attention seeking."

I couldn't help the triumphant smile I threw at Killian, knowing he'd lost this fight.

"Nephamir won't suspect she'll be right under his nose," Veric finished.

With the reasoning leaning further in my favour, I hit home with the final justification. "They won't allow fae in their court for another fifty years. It has to be now."

Killian clenched his jaw, and a muscle ticked along with it. He looked at us one by one, his steely gaze threatening to squash us where we stood. But the three of us stood side by side, unified that we all agreed and refused to back down.

I ignored the guilt that plunged through me that they didn't know I was the heir to the throne. Because they absolutely wouldn't be okay with the plan if they did.

Killian muttered a curse again then stepped up, closing in on our space until he was toe to toe with me. "We're going to need a good fucking plan."

Chapter 22
The Enemy

It was a good plan.

As far as shitty plans go.

We worked with what information we had and came up with something that would probably—hopefully—might work.

We were playing with fire even entertaining the idea of stealing Rharuer's Stone under the guise of honouring the Treaty. Dancing with the devil. . . quite literally. But the devils were fucking around behind our backs, too, so I called it getting even.

We planned what we could, without actually knowing exactly where the stone was. Killian had a pretty good idea, but it wasn't a guarantee.

Once we were all satisfied, Killian hauled me back to our house afterwards, complaining how annoyed he was that I'd tied his hands back there. So he made a remark about tying my hands in return and gave me a real *tongue lashing*.

We had four days remaining until the Treaty Ball. A two-part event over two days, filled with politics, formality, enemies and lies—and we'd now decided to throw a dash of thievery into the mix.

Together, Kilian, Veric and Jude all took portions of my day with different forms of training. Jude greeted me as the sun rose each morning, and together we ran miles of perimeter around Kevilla before cutting through to the training ring where we would spar until the sun rose high above.

By mid-morning, sweat slicked its way down my body.

The days were growing increasingly warmer with summer approaching, so I no longer donned my battle leathers each day—instead choosing to wear thinner slate-grey pants and a pale-blue shirt.

Veric presented me with an intricate leather vest the day before, much more suited to the incoming summer weather. Thankfully, the brown armour didn't restrict my movement as I ducked and twirled around Jude, and I was thankful for the extra layer of protection it afforded my core in absence of my full leathers.

After Jude and I worked up a sweat, it was Veric's turn to instruct me during the midday heat. Sitting by the stunning lake on the western outskirts of Kevilla, Veric had one of the more difficult tasks of helping me wield my magic, which was a much more strenuous task than I initially thought.

By the end of the third day, I'd only managed to make a pebble disappear and then bring it back. I was pretty excited by it, but the achievement was rather useless in the grand scheme of things. There would be no magical defences or attacks from me if the need should arise, which was a concerning weakness if we needed a contingency plan.

I fought against the demanding feeling in my chest, telling it I was doing everything possible to be as powerful as I could be.

Finally, once the heat of the day passed, Killian would meet us on the edge of Kevilla and attempt to get me in the skies. But with all his posturing, directives and complaints of, *no, fucking hell* and *you're doing it wrong*, I'd barely managed to summon a stiff breeze with a single wing beat, let alone put together a string of them to keep me airborne. Despite not being successful, I don't think Killian minded the opportunity to berate me for hours on end.

✧ ✧ ✧

The day before the Treaty Ball, Killian flew us to Teciras, a tiny village at the base of the Asotines, and the last safe haven before the borders of the Fallen Court.

The next morning, I woke before the sun in a patch of sweat—my eyes stinging from lack of sleep, despite how hard I'd tried. I decided that running a bath was a better use of my energy than running up a sweat, so I let the steaming water soak away my rising anxiety.

Stepping out of the bathroom, I came face-to-face with a very moody Killian. The commander and prince who was about to walk into enemy territory, with a plan put together only days ago, to have a flightless, magicless princess steal an object he didn't know the location of—without the backup of his legion.

I gave him a wide berth as we silently ate breakfast.

I picked up my twin daggers from the weapons stash, ready to strap them to my thighs before we took flight. As soon as the cold metal hit my hand, Killian plucked them from my fingers and made them vanish.

"No weapons," he deadpanned without pausing and stepped past me.

"But—"

"They won't tolerate weapons, Princess. I told you this."

"Yeah, but—" I stopped short at the impatient look he levelled at me. "Fine," I groaned and stepped out along with him.

The greying dawn had given way to warm sunlight, and there was no more preparing that would help us. Killian scooped me into his arms, and with a beat of his dark wings, he flew us toward the last place we wanted to be.

Alziros.

As the Asotines gave way to rolling desert hills, a sense of unease settled in the pit of my stomach. Endence was an incredible land of magic—an unmatched beauty in all its forms. But as we crossed into enemy territory, the land turned desolate.

The Fallen Court looked as though even Endence had forsaken it.

I clung to Killian even closer, not because I thought he would drop me, but because my body simply wanted to get away. To retreat even an inch further from the dead and wicked landscape beneath us. Killian silently gained extra altitude, and I could swear his grip tightened just a fraction more.

A swift gale blew from the west, bringing a foul stench with it on the wind. I gagged as the smell settled on my tongue and at the back of my throat. Killian immediately changed our course, struggling for his own breath of clean air.

"The Olusa Moor," he rasped once we'd gotten away.

I looked over his shoulder, getting a glimpse of the rotten marsh on the horizon behind his beating wings. "What's out there?"

"Nothing but death."

I shuddered beneath his strong frame and turned to face the direction we were flying–wanting to put the awful sight behind me. But when I looked at what we were heading for, I almost preferred the Moor.

The ground beneath us steadily turned from sandy brown to dirty red, and the rolling dunes rose up in rocky cliffs that would rip us to shreds if Killian were to drop out of the sky.

But it was the towering, jagged mountains, their colour bleeding from red-brown to black, looming at the summit of the rising ground that drew my full attention. Built high amongst the stone outcroppings, and bridging gaps between mountain passes of the surging peaks, was the Fallen fortress city, Alziros.

Built with charcoal-grey stone, with rising turrets and battlements bordering the menacing fortress, the imposing structure was formidable and threatening–even on the outside.

It was at least four times the size of the Winter Palace and twice as high–built hundreds of metres up amongst the rock of the gargantuan, black mountain. The fortress would have soared above the clouds if there had been any in the sky. It was hard to imagine how any of the angels managed to breathe so high up.

Cleaving cracks split the outer walls, and the blistering desert heat made the structure wave in a mirage, making the reveal of the true size of the bastion even more frightening.

"Have we made a terrible mistake, Killian?" I asked, barely a whisper above the rushing wind.

Killian didn't answer at first, and I thought he wouldn't as my eyes watered when I couldn't take them off the fortress before us. But my blood turned cold when his answer finally cracked through the roaring wind.

"Yes."

Killian flew higher as we made our final approach to Alziros, before descending in a near vertical dive, onto a path sliced between the rocks below the fortress.

He set me down and stretched his arms and wings, wringing out the tension from carrying me. It was past noon, and the scorching sun was more brutal here in the desert amongst the dark rocks of the mountain.

I looked above us to where Alziros still loomed. "You missed."

Killian laughed. "If they see me carrying you, Princess, they'll ask why you aren't flying your own damn self."

I made a non-committal huff as we hiked up. "If I remember correctly, you didn't speak to me the last time we climbed a mountain.

"I haven't known peace since."

I punched him in the arm but I don't think he felt it.

I tried to keep the fear out of my voice. "Anything I should know before we get up there?"

"Nothing you don't already know."

I ran through what I did know, to prepare myself to survive the next twenty-four hours.

Other than reminding myself that, despite the fact these creatures possessed no magic, it didn't diminish how powerful and corrupt and hard to kill they were. Nor did it deter them from trying to bring back their evil rulers, so together they could summon their Chimaera to destroy the realm. A frightening prospect, given that their leader, Nephamir, now had Rharuer's Stone in his possession.

On top of that, we also had to concern ourselves with the fact that it was almost certain Nephamir knew that Orella had escorted a human-turned-fae into the realm, and he would most certainly be interested in *meeting* her. And if he found out *I* was the *her* in question, the death he would bring me would be slow, to say the least.

I swallowed the lump in my throat that formed at the dark thought, then squared my shoulders back, flaring my wings in faux confidence as we climbed over the last rise.

An open, circular space was paved in the same charcoal stone as the mountain, which led up to the imposing fortress wall. A black iron gate cleaved open, revealing the dark depths of the fortress beyond. Blazing lamps dotted the walls, trying to light the dim halls inside.

Movement caught my attention high above where figures stood a few feet apart behind battlements. Their eyes and attention were on us as we stepped across the pavements. I tensed but kept stride next to Killian, who didn't falter as he approached the gate.

Once we'd crossed halfway, solid, clanking footsteps came from deep within the dark halls. This time we did stop, waiting for the angels to whom the steps belonged to, to come to us.

Four males stepped into the bright sunlight, and I had to look away from the glare their armour shone into my eyes. When I could see again, I forced the noise I made from escaping my throat.

The angels stood side by side, blocking the entrance, gold spears in hand, and adorned in scuffed and tarnished gold armour.

Greaves rose to their knees and vambraces to their elbows. The style was so unlike that of the elegant Fae, but impressive in its own brutal design. Red tunics, the colour of dried blood, covered their thick frames, and I shuddered at the sickening possibility they *had* been dyed in it. A thick gold circlet ran across their brows and up the sides, flaring above their rounded ears, like wings.

But then there were their *actual* wings. Held high and tight like all the trained warriors I'd seen in Kevilla do. But instead of the smooth, leathery wings the fae possessed, the males before us had glossy feathers sweeping down theirs.

Glossy in appearance, but I noted the colouring of the male's wings standing before the gate were muted and dull. Like the lustre had been pulled from their undertones—or like they couldn't get them clean in this endless, desolate desert.

However, the most surprising feature of all was the beauty of these angels.

Erela had called them repulsive beasts. Everyone else referred to them as *Fallen* or *demons*. But the raw beauty of the thick males in front of me didn't reflect those descriptions. Though I definitely wasn't fooled by appearances—magnificent as they were—there was something *wrong* with them. Something I couldn't quite put my finger on.

Other than the fact they're evil as fuck, maybe?

The only sound in the paved entrance was the wind rushing past the fortress walls, as the four angels had a silent standoff with Killian and I. I wasn't sure if we were playing a mind game of *who moves first loses*, but I stood preternaturally still just in case.

As I waited, I wondered what would happen if it all turned to shit right here and now, between the four males and us, which side would walk away? The hard-to-kill, powerful angels—or Killian, firstborn to the moieties, King and Queen of Summer and General of their legion, Commander of Winter, with powerful magic in his veins. . . and me.

I don't think you count, you flightless chicken.

I wrung my fingers together, suddenly nervous with the surety that we'd definitely be fucked if a fight broke out. But Killian still didn't move a muscle, still kept his arms relaxed by his sides, wings curved to the edges of his shoulders, as though he wasn't bothered by the bodies blocking our path.

And it dawned on me then that he wasn't.

These males were shiny guards on protective duty, here to greet the guests. And Killian *was* all of those impressive titles.

I swooned a little at the notoriety of the male next to me, the power that he held, and pocketed the thought for later use when we were next alone.

Without warning, the guards at the gate stepped to the left and right, creating a passage through to the halls beyond, where more movement came from within the shadows.

A fifth male, taller than the others, stepped into the hot sunlight and walked toward us.

He held no weapon, but wore the same gilded armour and red-brown tunic as the others. No gold circlet adorned his head, leaving the thick, dark locks of his hair to dangle over his shoulders in their woven tendrils. His skin was a rich umber, and his feathered wings, which rustled in the high breeze, were of the same shade. Lips full and sharp, brows thick and defined, with dull hazel eyes that were cold and emotionless locked on us as he strode across the hot paved entrance.

Somehow, they pierced us as he approached, yet they were as lifeless and *wrong* as the guards at the gate.

Even still, he was a beautiful specimen. But it was as though his allegiances to those who would seek the realm harm muted his beauty.

The male's eyes locked on mine as he took his final steps, and I tilted my chin up in a silent display of tenacity. Despite everyone's warning of the danger of these denizens, whoever this male was, he would not find fear on my face. Even if I *was* bluffing.

He stopped just over the line of what constituted personal space and looked down his nose at me, right before changing his snide expression into what I'm sure he thought was a warm, welcoming smile. He turned his attention on Killian, thankfully not tall enough to look down on him.

"Prince Killian," he purred.

Killian bristled at the title, but he didn't give himself away. "Arzemas."

The angel placed his fist over his heart. "Lord Nephamir extends his welcome, and his bond of truce to you and your companions, as we renew our ties and treaty during your stay."

Killian nodded, then brought his own fist over his heart.

"On behalf of the fae Kingdoms of Endence, I thank Lord Nephamir. As the representative of both Summer and Winter Kingdoms, I accept and return the bond of truce amongst our kin, so that the ties and treaty might continue to bring peace to our lands."

After a beat, the two males dropped their hands.

Arzemas stood still a moment longer, a wicked smile spreading across his face. Too white teeth blared in the hot sunlight as his full grin widened until he opened his mouth and let out a deep laugh.

My head whipped to the side when Killian matched his laughter, and the two males clapped each other on the shoulder.

What in the fuck is this?

"Glad we got that official shit out of the way—how are you, you big bastard?" Arzemas laughed.

Killian smiled just as wide. "Stretched too thin, my friend."

Friend!

Arzemas turned his attention to me. "Nephamir was surprised to hear you had invited another guest, but we welcome all who travel with you for this important event."

"Let me introduce my Promised—"

His fucking what?

"Loraya."

"A pleasure, Lady Loraya," Arzemas purred, and reached across to clasp my hand, kissing it gently.

I realised what Killian was really doing—calling on me to show I was at ease with the Fallen—here to establish bonds of friendship, not a just political truce.

"Please, call me Lor," I said sweetly and blinked my dark lashes at him.

It made sense though. Pretend to be fast friends and they won't suspect us to turn around and rob them.

I flicked my eyes to Killian and found his burning blue ones already on me, and a knowing smile curved at my quick pick up of his strategy.

"Welcome, Lor. Come, let me show you to your room before I give you a tour." He turned on his heel and his thick, umber wings rustled in the wind as we all crossed past the guards and into the dark hallway beyond.

The clanking armour and heavy footsteps of the four guards followed behind us as we entered. Thankfully, they kept a reasonable distance, but it still set my nerves on edge.

I tried calling to my magic, to prepare in case we were ambushed from behind, but barely a flicker responded.

Not that I expected anything, but I felt better for trying.

Arzemas led us through the thick stone walls of the fortress. Up three flights of stairs, then through the twists and turns of the enormous place.

The dim hallways were wide enough for two winged males to walk abreast, but the walls seemed to press in on me. I'd never been in a prison, but I couldn't imagine it feeling any better—or worse—than this.

I envisioned being led to a cell and having the door slammed on us until the guards granted our release, but after several minutes of marching through the dark stone halls, just when I worried that I'd never see the sun again—to my utter shock—we emerged into an enormous, open courtyard.

I blinked and looked behind me, wondering if a portal clung to the open archway we'd just crossed. But there was none.

The spectacular yard was paved in light sandstone and dotted with giant palms. Black bamboo lined a wall against the jagged mountain rock, and stunning bursts of colour from the orange cannas and ginger lily fired from amongst the green foliage. A vivid pink bougainvillaea hung over the terrace roof that ran the length of the inner fortress wall. Bright, buttery yellow bells grew in thick shrubs around the archways, leading off to various parts of the fortress.

A large gazebo stretched across the far wall with vibrant pillows, and finally, in the centre, was a bronze fountain—spurting cool water into the air, which landed directly onto the surrounding pavement before it drained away between lines in the stones.

It was jarring how at odds the beautiful space was with the brutal and ominous fortress.

No, not a fortress. This is a castle.

Arzemas strode ahead, leading the way along the domed breezeway bordering the courtyard, and turned into a darkened archway that led back inside the castle proper.

The dark charcoal stones reappeared, and after another turn, we stopped at a wood-and-iron door which Arzemas pushed open.

"Your room, Lor."

I stepped inside, followed closely by Killian, and was pleasantly surprised by the warm decor. It was a little archaic and dark for my tastes, but the bed looked comfortable and the adjoining bathroom was suitable. It was a far cry from the chains and cold dungeon cellar I was expecting to be shoved into under guard.

"I'll let you both get settled and meet you in the courtyard when you're ready to meet Nephamir."

Wait.

"Both?" I whipped around, but the dark angel had already disappeared, leaving Killian and I alone in the room.

Killian's expression turned dark and full of promise.

"Not a chance in hot hell."

His face fell in mock sadness, but it didn't meet his eyes, which latched onto mine before dropping further south. "Don't play coy, *Lor.*" He snatched me by my hips. "We're *Promised* after all. The angels would never believe it if I didn't make your sweet cries ring out through these stone walls."

My lips parted with a heavy breath, unable to ward off the effects of his lust-filled words. Mouth suddenly dry and core suddenly wet, I swallowed hard, then used all my strength to summon sensible words to pause this interaction for another time.

"If you wish to take advantage of sharing a bed and *hearing my sweet cries*, then you'd better put in more effort than trying to fuck me in the heart of enemy territory," I sassed, glaring up at him.

"Soon, *Princess*," he whispered, "you'll come to learn that wringing out your sweet cries will take barely any effort on my behalf." He nipped my nose as he slapped my arse. "But I'll make sure to give you my full attention, nonetheless."

Merciful Gods.

"But even I have to admit you're right," he sighed then looked at the bed with longing as if he was already envisioning everything in his head.

"I often am. Besides, we aren't even planning on staying here long enough to require a bed."

"Depends what you plan on doing in the bed. . ." he said wickedly.

I shot him an inpatient look.

He ignored me, then flicked his wrist in that gesture I'd seen him make before, and two bags blinked into existence. One made a curiously loud clanging sound, which made my lip curl into a sly smile. The magical ingenuity of Killian's sneaky *no weapons* rule-breaking made me laugh.

"Care to explain why you're acting all chummy with Arzemas, and introducing me as your Promised? What the hell does that even mean, anyway?" I flopped onto the bed, looking up at the ceiling.

"Promised is an. . . unofficial way of telling others to keep their paws off, because they're intended for another, just without the official titles."

"Sounds like a whole lot of male peacocking."

"Oh, it is," he drawled, winking at me. "Us fae get a little. . . *possessive.*"

My belly clenched at the way he purred that last word.

"As for Arzemas—he's Nephamir's right hand, and dangerous as hell. Make no mistake, he's no tour guide. No one was lying when we told you this place was dangerous. Remember, they are Fallen—outcasts in the eyes of the Oracle and Endence itself. We are enemies, yes. . . but right now, we're here under the guise of friendship and peace. Of course we're going to be nice to one another. It's the whole point of the treaty."

"So instead of political propriety, I need to hug it out with these creatures? Be friends and play nice and share my toys?"

"Yes. Starting with Nephamir."

"Well, while we're speaking of my new best friend and his toys," I grumbled, "this place is fucking huge, Killian—there's a million places the stone could be. We're only welcome here for a little over a day, what if it's not where we think?"

"There is no one in this realm Nephamir trusts more than himself," he murmured in a low voice. "I'd bet my balls he has it locked away in his personal chambers."

"Well, depending on the size of your balls, Killian, that's either an impressive bet or you're not willing to commit to your theories."

Killian stepped between my legs then leant over my body, keeping his weight off me. His fisted hands pressed in on either side of my head, the pressure making the mattress sink.

"Oh, I fully commit, Princess," he said in a teasing whisper against my lips. My own parted immediately and he jumped at the advantage he'd gained, giving me a teasing kiss as his tongue quickly darted against mine.

He kept his burning stare on me as he took his time standing. The slow retreat gave me time to consider wrapping my legs around his waist and crashing him back into me on the bed.

But the daunting task ahead of us tonight stopped my mental walls from dropping and allowing Killian to take what he—so clearly—desperately wanted.

As soon as we have this damn stone, he'll get all the sweet cries he earns.

I pushed off the bed and strode past him with as much willpower as I could muster.

"We'd better not keep Arzemas waiting, then."

Chapter 23
The Prize

Arzemas led the way down a flight of stairs, and into a different section of the castle we'd yet to see, pointing out various rooms and giving droplets of information along the way.

We walked deeper into the castle, past hot wall sconces blaring with flame. It was strange seeing the hallways and rooms lit with them—I was so used to the bright faelights in the Kingdoms, but the angels didn't have magic, so of course they relied on fire.

Arzemas walked beside me as he went, reciting the histories behind tapestries or rusting relics mounted on the wall. I hung onto every word in case it ended up being useful later on. There was, of course, no sign of Rharuer's Stone, though that wasn't surprising.

I wasn't sure I could have kept a straight face if Arzemas had walked up to a cabinet and announced, *'Oh, and here's the stone of the King of Gods.'*

Killian believed it would be locked away with Nephamir's prized possessions in his stronghold, so that was going to be our first target.

Arzemas stopped at an iron door then pushed it open. I expected it would lead into another room, but I squinted back at the blaring sunlight that spilled through the opening.

Hot wind whipped at my braid, tearing the wispy edges free as the three of us stepped out onto a rampart. My eyes watered at the sudden heat, and my head spun at the impossible height.

It was different seeing Alziros from the air. Even though Killian had flown higher than where we currently stood, I was a distant spectator to the huge castle built amongst the jagged mountain.

Standing on the edge of one of its walls and looking down was quite a different beast.

Dizziness clawed at my edges, trying to topple me, but Killian stood like a solid barrier at my back, grounding me and keeping me upright.

The castle was a massive, lone sentinel, built into the mountain rock and hung out over crevasses.

Nausea roiled my stomach at a new terrifying thought. If this attempt to steal the stone went wrong, if *anything* happened to Killian—I was royally fucked.

No one was getting off this mountain without flying off it.

Other than the mountain pass we walked up upon arrival, the only other part of the castle that had access to the mountain directly, was well over a thousand yards away, across a massive bridge at the opposite corner of the castle, way off in the distance.

The enormous stone bridge spanned hundreds of yards from one jagged mountain to another. A chasm fell away beneath, gouging deep within the surface of the desert landscape below. I ran my eyes along the crack in the earth as it wound its way past chunks of rock and boulders and other rising spires further west.

A tall watch tower of sorts stood at the end of the bridge. The golden shine from a few dozen heads reflecting in the sun told me it was heavily guarded.

Perhaps another place the stone could be located?

But the longer I looked at the distant tower, the more apparent a strange, grotesque feeling washed over me. As though all of the corruption in the realm seeped out into the world from its dark walls.

No. . . the stone wasn't over there—and I sure as fuck didn't want to find out what was.

I hadn't taken any notice of anything Arzemas had said. He led us back inside, then down another flight of stairs, which, if I was keeping track, should've put us back on the floor we entered in on, but I didn't recognise anything.

He took us down, and through, and in, and up, and around the castle. At first, I thought he was being a thorough host, but when I considered who he was exactly, I realised he was more likely taking us on an obscure, roundabout chase through the darkening halls, purely to confuse us.

Resolve kicked its way into the forefront of my mind as I focused on keeping track of the directions we took and found he indeed was going a strange roundabout way.

Eventually, he stopped at a carved set of huge wooden doors and pushed them open.

Large, carved pillars held up the edge of the sandstone courtyard roof within, which covered more than half of the rectangular space we emerged into. Lazy afternoon light pooled in through gauzy curtains hanging across an open section, which was confusing because I could have sworn we were on the lower levels of the castle.

Two short steps led up to a platform where piles of soft pillows were arranged, and low bronze tables held bowls of fruit. Huge, grey pots, big enough for me to stand in, were placed around the open garden, bringing splashes of green and shade from the maples they held. Shallow pools of water sat in stone bowls at the edge of the open ceiling, and no less than three little blue-and-white birds flitted around between the cool water and a nearby ornate tree.

Distant soft sounds filled the air that could have come from the birds, but I couldn't make out what they were beyond everything my eyes were drinking in.

The space was even more beautiful than the sunny rooftop garden by our room. I was so thrown by the exquisite garden and architecture, that I completely overlooked the tanned figure lounging amongst the pillows.

The movement of his lean bicep on display, curling to plop a grape into his mouth caught my attention, and I couldn't believe I'd missed him sitting there.

Unmistakably, I knew this was Nephamir.

He relaxed on his side amongst the fluffy cushions, leaning back on his elbow, one leg stretched out in front of him. The hand that delivered the grape came down elegantly to rest on his bent knee. His body was lean, and thick veins corded around his forearms and down the back of his hands.

As his decorated wrist came down to perch on his knee, he turned his head slowly and snared me in his piercing gaze. It was like my legs were stuck in cloying mud, weak and wanting to give out under his stare.

Nephamir was the most alluring male I'd laid eyes on, and I couldn't deny a strange, unexpected pull toward the male.

He was devastatingly beautiful—all sharp angles and full lips. He had blue eyes, a sharp cupid's bow and short sandy blonde hair.

But I saw what lay beneath.

The evil and *wrongness* to him leaked out from his eyes and slid into the curve of his smile. Like all who lived in Endence, his face was youthful—completely at odds with his thousand-and-something year age.

He wore a vest highlighting the curve of his shoulders and lean cut of his abs—the same red shade as the other angels—and soft pants that hugged his tight physique.

He was adorned in shining gold jewellery. A thin loop of gold hung from his right earlobe and a piercing shaped like an arrow threaded across the top of his rounded ear. He had rings on most of his fingers, some topped with dazzling diamonds or rubies the size of my thumbnail. A long gold chain dipped behind his vest which plunged in a *V*—probably hiding an equally obnoxious stone.

A soft laugh breezed past Nephamir's lips before he effortlessly stood, his golden-brown wings rustling and stretching out beside him as he padded down the steps of the platform.

A wicked smile curled up his face when my eyes landed on the clear outline of his half-erect cock, hanging thick and long, beneath his silken pants, slapping gently against the top of his thigh in time with his steps.

"Your guests, Lord Nephamir," Arzemas introduced then backed away.

Killian tilted his head down in the smallest dip of an official greeting. "Lord Nephamir."

Nephamir lazily took his time before giving his reply. Looking his fill at Killian before sweeping his cruel eyes across to me. Down and slowly up, then back to Killian.

"Prince Killian," he purred, his voice like bitter honey.

Killian gestured at me. "My Promised, Loraya."

Nephamir grasped my hand and his long, soft fingers curled around my own and held me firm. He brought my hand to his lips without breaking eye contact then pressed a kiss to the back of my fingers.

"Lady Loraya," he murmured against my skin, his voice dripping with desire.

My mind scrambled, trying to remember the part I was playing.

You're not a royal, you're Killian's date and you want to be besties with the evil fucker.

I gave him a deeper bow than Killian offered. "Lord Nephamir."

He groaned, and I saw his cock twitch as his name passed my lips.

I couldn't help but feel a little violated at the response. I wanted to pull my hand free from him but knew it'd likely be viewed as disrespectful.

His gaze was yet to leave mine. "Incredible," he whispered, taking in the different shades of my eyes. "Where have you been hiding this immaculate creature, Killian? She truly is the most lovely prize."

I bit my tongue so hard I almost drew blood.

He turned, still holding onto my hand and led me over the warm stones to the cushions he'd been lying on then gracefully lowered himself amongst them, still not letting go.

I tried not to be pulled into his lap as I sat with him. He made no strong effort to do so, though I didn't doubt he'd object if I ended up there.

Killian followed but opted to lean against the pillar at the edge of the platform, plucking a soft plum from the bowl of fruit as he passed. Despite still being in the supple clutches of my enemy, I could sense Killian's full attention on me as I sat next to Nephamir. Knowing my commander was keeping such a close watch gave me a wash of calm and enough encouragement to keep up the act.

I quickly filled the quiet with conversation and curled my fingers around his. "I'm very excited for tonight." Not a lie, but he certainly didn't know I was referring to the planned heist rather than his ball.

I was walking a thin line between buttering the male up and giving him a heavy, heady message. One he was all too willing to read into.

He flashed his teeth in a smile that didn't reach his eyes. "As am I."

I gently slid my hand free from his, reaching toward the bowl of fruit to excuse myself from his grasp. He watched me like a predator as I slipped a grape between my lips. I made a point to keep his attention as I did, only to look away as I bit down on the firm flesh of the little berry.

An animalistic noise resonated low in Nephamir's throat and he swallowed.

I watched the bulge in his neck bob down then back up as he did, and knew I had him hooked.

He dropped his hand onto his thigh and I forced myself not to follow its trajectory as it rested next to his cock, still half-hard beneath his pants. The corner of his lips twitched as though he could see my internal struggle.

"Tomorrow we will secure the next steps toward our bright future," Nephamir called, raising a gold goblet filled with red wine into the air.

Killian made an air salute in response.

"But tonight, we will revel in every pleasure we desire, in celebration of what is to come between our kin. And Loraya. . . as my magnificent guest, I desire a dance with you, most."

I forced my face to not give away the disgust making my stomach squirm. "You would honour me with a dance?"

"Nothing will stop me from getting my hands on you." His eyes dipped to my lips as he raised his goblet and took a long sip.

My skin shivered.

Nephamir placed his wine back on the floor then plucked a fuzzy apricot from the bowl, biting into it. The soft slide of his teeth through the flesh grated against my heightened hearing.

All of a sudden, he was too close again, like he slipped under my barriers–that strange pull affecting me on a stronger level–so I tried focusing on the noises in the open chamber to distract myself.

The little birds splashed in the water while the wind stirred the gauzy canopy shading the gardens below it. I focused on those distant calls from earlier, but that's when I recognised them for what they were.

"As it so happens, I was about to relax for the evening before our big event." He rose and held out his hand to pull me up. "I wouldn't want to keep you from your preparations," he trailed off and gestured over my shoulder with a salacious gaze, "but you are most welcome to join me."

I turned to a second archway which I hadn't noticed until now, alone on a wall that led into the castle. Beyond, a dark wooden bed, canopied in sheer, red curtains sat in the centre of the stone room.

Peeking out from behind the curtains were three females and entirely too much flesh. Touching and moaning softly, the angels pleasured themselves and each other as they waited for Nephamir.

I tried to look away at the lustful display, but one female locked eyes with me, her heady gaze distant as she straddled the face of another, slowly rolling her hips as a moan escaped her lips.

I was no innocent female by anyone's standards, but even this display made me blush. "I don't think. . ."

Nephamir pressed against my back then leant his head over my shoulder. "I'll make sure you don't have the capacity for thoughts in there," he whispered darkly in my ear and ran a long finger down my arm.

The touch made me shiver, but it was in revulsion.

Nephamir was astonishing—cruelly beautiful and chiselled. Divine beauty, like he was a descendant of the Gods themselves—and by the size of his cock, even at half hard, I'm certain he possessed all the tools and skills necessary to live up to his claims.

But it was all moot.

He was vile, and rotten underneath all that beauty. He was the enemy who would slit my throat without remorse after torturing me if he knew who I really was.

Nephamir must have forgotten he was in the company of fae, however, capable of hearing whispers, and Killian more than easily heard his hushed words.

"Although the invitation to. . . *relax* with you, is much appreciated, unfortunately, under fae law, neither Loraya nor I can share ourselves until we are married." Killian walked up next to me then placed his hand around my waist, pulling me away from the angel and to his side. He winked at the Fallen leader. "Maybe next time."

Nephamir barked out a rich laugh and clapped Killian on his shoulder. "Well then, here's hoping the next fifty years are swift," he joked then bent to pick up his wine as we all laughed.

But the forced laugh we gave was entirely harder to fake as Nephamir straightened.

My assessment of his jewellery had been spot on.

There *was* an obnoxiously large stone set into the pendant that weighed his chain down—now freed when he stooped to pick up his wine and sitting proudly in the centre of his chest. But it wasn't a diamond or ruby like on his rings.

It was emerald green and shining with the power of a God, the smooth stone that churned and swirled with tendrils of fog, looking depthless and utterly devastating.

You've got to be fucking kidding me.

I looked to the cushions at my feet to leave the pile and lifted my hand to Killian, but he was already there, holding his arm out to lead me away from the platform—watching me.

Our eyes met and our exchanged look told me he'd seen it too. It was impossible to miss.

When I turned back to Nephamir, the stone was gone, tucked back behind his clothes. Our saving grace was that he hadn't been looking at us when it'd slipped out. He hadn't seen us notice.

I beamed a smile at him and prayed to all the Gods that he couldn't hear how furious my heart pounded.

"I look forward to our dance," I said and gave another low bow.

"I'm filled with anticipation, Loraya," he crooned, then kissed my hand in farewell.

Killian wrapped his arm around me as we walked toward the door where Arzemas waited for us. I'd quite forgotten he was still in the room.

I looked over my shoulder to see Nephamir already retreating into the bedroom and three sets of feathered wings perk up as their main event finally arrived.

I stayed silent as we followed Arzemas back to our room and let Killian hold up the conversation as we followed.

Thankfully, Arzemas took a slightly more direct route from Nephamir's chambers than the path he'd taken on the way there. Though I was paying more attention to the twists and turns and flights of stairs this time, so I recognised when we passed the same portion of hallway twice.

Sly bastard.

Arzemas left us at our door and promised that an angel named Kolva would be waiting in the courtyard to take us to the ball at sunset. Message clear. Stay in your room until the party and not a minute earlier.

I wanted to ask who Kolva was, but Killian gave a shallow dip of his head in understanding, telling me he knew the answer to that already. He shut the door behind us as we walked into the room then fell back against it.

"Hand over your balls, Killian," I groaned, rubbing my thumbs at my temples.

He let out a defeated sigh at the ceiling, not gratifying me with a response.

"How in fucks name are we going to steal it from around his neck?"

Killian stomped off to the bathroom without speaking a word. The sound of running water came from behind the closed door, so I left him to his brooding. He came out a short time later and switched places, leaving me to soak in peace as the sun began its final descent, taking all my courage and confidence away with it.

Just a little longer, Alora.

With the day's sweat successfully washed away, I re-emerged into our room, wrapped in my towel, only to find the space empty.

I called out for Killian, but there was no answer. There was, however, a garment bag hanging from the top of the wardrobe, with a little note on the hanger reading—

Wear me.

—K

I rummaged through the bags Killian had summoned into our room earlier and thankfully found everything I'd need. Truthfully, I hadn't even thought twice about dressing up—my mind was too preoccupied with the true task at hand rather than the ball.

Surely Killian hadn't been responsible for packing everything I'd needed?

When my fingers looped around a scrap of lace that was pretending to be underwear, I knew Jude was the only suspect.

I twisted the sides of my hair back and secured the pieces together with a gold pin, leaving my pointed ears on display and my champagne tresses unbound and tumbling between my wings to brush the curve of my lacy backside.

I lined my eyes with kohl and painted my lips in a glossy red the same shade as the vest Nephamir had been wearing.

That should pique his interest.

Finally, I pulled on the ties at the top of the garment bag encasing my dress, which fell with the weight of the pair of heels hidden at the bottom, revealing the stunning gown underneath.

I gaped at the exquisite masterpiece in front of me. The first thought that came to mind was that I didn't think even Jude could've been responsible for this particular item, let alone Killian.

I stepped into the backless, ruby-red dress that hugged my torso and slid my arms down the sheer sleeves. I slipped my head through the opening—a thin strip of sheer chiffon ran across the back of my neck to keep the gown secured.

Satiny, red velvet puddled from my hips down around my feet as I moved to stand at the mirror to take in the sight.

The skirt of my dress hung smooth and freely, separated by a slit at the front of my left leg that stopped at the top of my thigh.

The velvet fell away as it came to my waist, leaving my skin on display. Only a few strips of the luxurious material rose from my hips over my chest and spread down my arms like licks of flame.

Brilliant, clear stones stitched into the fabric ran up the rising tendrils of the top of my dress, with tiny red and black stones dotted around the intricate design along with them. I thought they were probably crystals, but the closer I looked in the mirror, I knew they were more than that.

Diamonds and rubies.

A dress for royalty, and nothing less.

I gave a little swish and watched the gown move—how the gemstones glittered as they caught and reflected the light.

Hopefully dazzling enough to distract from the amount of skin that was on display. Between the very high slit up my leg and the thin ribbons of flaming velvet that barely covered my nipples, I needed to be careful unless my plan was to give a whole eyeful to the angels.

If we need a distraction, I guess it could be an option.

I strapped on the sparkling gold heels that came with the gown, but something was still missing.

I rummaged through the other, heavier bag, and found a dagger tucked away on the side. I strapped it to the inside of my right leg and looked one last time at the final product in the mirror.

A soft knock sounded, and Killian's low voice reached me through the door. "Lor, are you ready?" he asked right before stepping inside.

He stopped short. Stopped breathing. "Merciful Gods. . ."

It was clear I wasn't the only one dressed for the occasion. The commander added a splash of his royal title into his dark ensemble. A deep red shirt peeked from underneath his black jacket, edged in red and gold.

"Everything okay, Commander?" I teased as his gaze raked over my body.

Killian's burning blue eyes fixed on mine, then dipped to my full red lips, and he swallowed.

I stepped up to the towering fae and pressed my weight gently against his tight stomach. I blinked my dark lashes at him and watched how his body responded. "Do you approve?"

Killian tried to clear his throat but failed, his words coming out thick and rough. "No, I don't think I do." He leant down to bring his lips against mine. "In fact, if we manage to make it out of here alive, I'm going to have to tear that fucking dress right off you."

I kept still and spoke against his skin. "Rip my dress, Killian Lòkith, and you won't make it out of here alive."

His dark chuckle rumbled through the room at my empty threat as I stepped away.

"Speaking of making it out alive," I continued, leaning against the adjacent wall. "Now that we're here, and know Nephamir has Rharuer's Stone, how exactly do we plan on pulling this off?"

Killian folded his arms over his chest and settled into the mind of the planning commander. "The plan only changes if he wears it tonight, but I don't expect him to–he doesn't want us to know he has it, and he's too mistrustful to have anyone else to guard it. The stone will be in his chambers. After we get to the ball, I'll pull Nephamir aside and distract him with treaty business–you slip out and do your thing. Get in and get out."

"And if it's guarded?"

"Then do your thing." He winked.

"If I kill any guards. . . then it won't matter that they're sneaking around, and planning uprisings—the treaty will be broken."

"Exactly, Princess, it won't matter, the treaty is broken anyway. He's going to realise eventually that we took it. The only thing that matters is we get that stone."

I still didn't feel at ease. I wanted to pull apart the other holes that I could see with more clarity now that the moment was upon us.

"You said they're hard to kill."

"You're hard to fight against."

"I'm in a dress."

"Take it off." He shrugged. "Then you'll be *really* hard to fight against."

I rolled my eyes, but he only winked.

"I can't use magic."

"Neither can they."

"What if they're stronger than me?"

"They're not."

"What if I'm outnumbered?"

"They'd have to catch you first."

"They'll have weapons."

"And you *are* a weapon, Alora. Despite how apprehensive I was at bringing you here, you were right. And you're ready. You're the only one who can do this." He stepped into my space.

Pinned between him and the wall, his dark wings shadowed us. The position immediately reminded me of the heated kiss at the Winter Palace, but I didn't succumb to the same passionate feelings.

Instead, I grew sad and deflated, fear stabbing through my chest like a blade.

I looked down at my glittering shoes. "What if I'm not strong enough? What if I'm captured?" The frightening words were barely a whisper.

Killian curled his finger beneath my chin and lifted my gaze to meet his. "I hold sway in *two* legions, Princess. They'll burn before they touch you."

I squeezed my eyes closed, refusing to let any tears fall then bit my bottom lip to stop it from quivering.

Warm hands slid up on either side of my face, and Killian's soft lips pressed against my mouth, urging me to let go.

I relented then slipped my hands up his back as I returned the slow caress.

Killian kissed me gently. Thoroughly.

Only when he was completely satisfied did he pull away. "Don't let the fear of being up close instil itself in you, Alora," he whispered above me.

I drew in a steadying breath, letting his words settle in my chest and stop the agitation rattling in my arms. I pulled my shoulders down, my wings in tight, then opened my eyes to look at Killian.

"Well, I guess if Summer has a royal spy, then Winter can have a royal thief," I said, feeling my determination build. "The only difference is the thief is also the heir to their throne."

Killian curved his lips into a wicked smile, approving of my self-appointed title.

"Okay," I said, steeling myself for the final time. "I'm ready."

Killian offered his hand as we walked to the courtyard to meet the angel escorting us to the Ball. Only, when we stepped into the dark space, no one was waiting.

Killian looked around and made a questioning rumble in his throat.

I looked around as well. "Didn't Arzemas say someone was supposed to be here?"

"Yeah, Kolva. . ."

"Who is Kolva? Arzemas said their name like you knew them already."

"She's Nephamir's daughter. I wouldn't say I know her, but we've met."

"Where is she?"

Killian made another low noise then tightened his grip on my hand. "I don't know, but I don't like this. I'm not waiting around."

Killian led the way through the twists and turns of the wide hallways, now brightly lit with torches on the walls and suspended on the high ceilings in thick chandeliers. He walked with enough purpose that I assumed he knew where he was going, but I paid attention nonetheless to make sure my mental map was accurate.

When we passed through a wide archway held up by pillars half carved from the wall, a voice split through the silence. "Oi, where are you going?"

I startled, and Killian stiffened.

I whipped around to look at a young angel who'd called to us. He was tall and skinny, his arms too long for his body like he was yet to grow into them—his brown wings like a sparrow's snapped in as he stood straight. He looked barely eighteen, but considering he was an angel I knew he was far older.

The little angel looked like he wanted to be devoured by the stone wall at his back when Killian turned his dark gaze on him. The imposing fae took a menacing step forward and towered over the soldier, his piercing gaze pinning him where he stood. Slowly, Killian lifted his hand and my fingers twitched, ready to grab my dagger should this turn ugly.

Instead, Killian merely brushed his hand across the angel's shoulder, removing some invisible speck of dust then clapped his broad hands on either side of him. "We have a party to get to," he said with mock politeness. "It seems as though you weren't invited, little fledgling."

The angel flicked his eyes to me and then back to Killian, his pulse thudding in his neck like a caught rabbit. Too scared to even respond to the insult.

"You—you're supposed to have an escort," he stammered, fear flickering across his face.

I was almost sorry for him.

"Do the angels not trust us within the walls of their castle?" Killian asked, threat rumbling in his voice. "Are Nephamir's guests—a Summer Prince and Winter Commander—who, together with his Promised, are here to renew a treaty for peace and visiting under an oath of truce, prisoners within these walls?"

The angel stood frozen, not knowing if he was actually supposed to respond.

"Is that what you're telling me, guard? Are we prisoners here?"

The little angel twitched his head no and squeaked a noise resembling the word.

"That's what I thought." Killian smiled, flashing his teeth. "Do not interrupt us again this evening, and make sure the rest of you guard dogs relegated to doing *fuck all* know to do the same—or I'll drag you to Nephamir by your feathers to explain why we're suspected of being dishonourable."

The angel swallowed hard and nodded.

I could see him shaking from where I stood. I tilted my chin up and sneered to drive the point home before Killian came back to me, his fingers brushing over my bare skin as he slid his hand over my lower back then led us away.

When we were safely out of earshot, he gave a satisfied chuckle. "That should give you a reprieve if you're seen tonight."

I crossed my fingers that he was right.

We descended the last set of stairs leading to the Hall. The massive doors were open, revealing the cavernous room beyond.

Killian and I looked at one another, trying to convey everything we couldn't speak out loud. The world fell away and became quiet in that final moment before entering the den of devils as I looked into his eyes, vivid and burning like blue flame.

I squeezed his hand and nodded just once, telling him I was ready, and together we stepped over the threshold and into hell—ironically filled with angels.

Hell looked like sex.

At least this one did.

The expansive ballroom was brightly lit with massive iron chandeliers, the orange light fighting against the draw of the dark stone walls and domed ceiling.

Females dressed in scraps of black lace and leather with delicate masks over their eyes, perched and twisted themselves in round cages dangling from the ceiling as they moved to the strange music spilling from the corner. The sultry scene made my stomach pull.

Far below, on the main floor, several hundred angels danced and laughed and drank together. While a few enjoyed other pleasures in the room, grinding and touching anything that welcomed the attention. Two angels were downright fucking behind an iron candelabra standing vigil by the buffet table.

Think I'll pass on the canapés.

Black flowers twisted across railings of little shadowed balconies that jutted from high above the dancefloor.

Arched pillars under the balconies formed a covered underpass where private areas were set in the wall, draped in black curtains that were only just opaque enough to see through.

Though I didn't think I'd wanted to peer in on anything happening behind them if they held no objection to openly partaking in what was already on display.

This is not the political event I expected.

Arzemas was standing a few feet inside the door, speaking to an angel with muted white wings. His brows creased in confusion as he looked at us, but the expression was gone in an instant. He leaned toward the male he was speaking with and whispered something I couldn't hear over the music.

The male nodded, then left, leaving Arzemas free to give us his undivided attention.

"Prince Killian," he greeted officially and bowed quickly before looking me up and down. "Lady Lor, you look immaculate." He kissed my hand and I forced myself to smile.

Arzemas plucked two glasses from the tray, passed them to us, then chinked his own against ours collectively. I only pretended to drink it.

"Right, well enjoy the ball for now, won't you? The official shit will get started when the rest of the guests arrive, and then we'll have ourselves a real party." He winked at me.

Rest of the guests? The room is already filled.

Arzemas left swiftly out the main doors, leaving Killian and I alone in a room of enemies. He placed his hand on the small of my back, leading me to the side.

I discarded the glass of wine the first chance I got, not trusting the stuff.

"Nephamir should be arriving any minute now if he isn't already in here." He kept his hand pressed on my skin and leant in close, displaying to everyone in the room nothing more than sweet whispered words of two lovers to anyone who might be watching. "First chance we get, you make your exit so we can be done with this."

I opened my mouth to respond, but a cheer erupted in the Hall as all eyes turned to the doors where Nephamir entered—a half-naked female poised on his arm.

He wore skin-tight leather pants, dark brown boots up to his knees, and a silk shirt of the same blood-red colour unbuttoned down to his navel, showing off his lean muscles—and *unadorned* chest.

Guess that leaves his chambers as option one.

Killian and I exchanged a look.

With his golden-brown wings flared, the cruel leader didn't acknowledge the crowd before he moved through them like a snake slithering through sand as it parted around him. Nephamir stopped right in front of us then flicked his wrist to be rid of the dark female clutching onto him and she disappeared amongst the crowd.

He raked his eyes down my body, lingering on my chest as though he was hoping to see past the velvet threads of flame. I kept my eyes flat as I watched him watch me, letting him look his fill, before I became his worst fucking nightmare.

Nephamir sucked his lip between his teeth and made a salacious groan as he worked his gaze back up my exposed leg. "Lady Loraya." He wasn't even trying to hide the lust in his expression and voice.

This time the shiver that worked its way up my spine was definitely one of revulsion—the enigmatic pull he'd held during that first impression was long gone. But I swallowed the bile in my throat and put on my best sweet and sultry voice. "Lord Nephamir."

"My sincerest apologies, but I must delay the dance I promised you, if only for the time being, Loraya, and steal your dashing prince."

"Anything to be concerned about, Nephamir?" Killian asked.

"Oh no," he crooned. "We have some things to get in order before the official treaty business tomorrow. Unavoidable, I'm afraid. But you have my word you'll be back with your darling Promised in no time."

Killian nodded and stepped in front of me, turning his back on the Fallen leader. I was sure it would be seen as an insult, but Killian's expression kept my attention locked.

It was clear Nephamir's request had thrown him—we hadn't expected *him* to distract *us*. I could see Killian scrambling to understand what his play was. But the way he looked at me had one clear message.

Now.

"I'll see you soon," Killian said then pressed a kiss to my cheek. He turned on his heel then left the Hall with Nephamir and his entourage, leaving me standing alone and unwatched in the room full of angels.

But despite the danger, only one emotion flooded me now.

Determination.

A slow smile spread across my face.

Perfect.

The crowd had immediately forgotten about Nephamir now that he'd left, and the self-indulgent denizens—drunk on their wine, and the lust permeating the room—certainly didn't care about the fae left behind in the corner.

I was nothing to them and they treated me as such. A speck not worth their attention.

I drifted over to the doors, watching for any eyes on me, but there were none—so I slid through the doors and into the hallway.

I rounded the corner away from the crowd hovering around the entrance doors and slipped off my heels, discarding them in the shadows behind a pillar, then retraced the route Killian and I had taken to get to the Hall.

After a few turns, I recognised a junction that Arzemas had taken during his *tour* earlier, so veered left and swept through the castle to Nephamir's chamber.

I kept my ears strained for any hint of noise ahead, but the masses were far away in the Hall. So I kept silently slinking through the quiet passages and staircases of the massive castle.

I'd been sneaking around for a few minutes already when I stepped past an archway that connected to another thoroughfare and flinched when I spotted a guard standing at the opposite end.

My movement—and most likely the vibrant shade of my dress—caught his eye, and he whipped his head toward me. But he wasn't far away enough that his own flinch didn't go unnoticed.

It was the same young guard who'd stopped Killian and I earlier, now standing in a different part of the castle. I stood tall and raised my brows, giving him a pointed look that I hoped conveyed my message loud and clear.

Surely you're not stupid enough to stop me again.

The young angel dropped his head and looked back down his hallway, letting me continue past unhindered.

Close fucking call.

I thanked all the Gods for Killian's broody disposition earlier that put the guard in his place, but I was angry at myself for the mistake.

I wouldn't be so lucky if I was seen again.

But the hallways remained empty as I went.

With my ruby-red dress sliding behind me, I silently made my way up a spiralling staircase hidden in an alcove, then darted into the last passage that led directly to Nephamir's chamber.

I pressed my ear to the carved doors, listening for any flicker of sound, but only silence came from behind. I sucked in a breath then leant against one, letting it yawn open to the dark courtyard, now bathed in night.

I ducked behind a pillar, pausing to confirm no movement came from inside the room. But even the twittering little birds were silent and still.

Confident I was alone, I dashed over to the doorway which led to Nephamir's bedroom and shuddered, hoping I wouldn't find a bed full of naked and spent females. I pushed against the door, readying myself if the room was occupied, but it wouldn't budge.

Fuck.

I looked around—a sense of urgency crept up and immediately made me nervous. I didn't expect to walk straight in, but I had hoped I wouldn't need to break anything as I went—the noise would most certainly be heard. Though with the empty hallways, I might get lucky.

No, this is too important to rely on luck.

I had one other option to try first, but it was a long shot.

Holding out my hand against the edge of the door, I concentrated on my breathing—on conjuring up the feel and the smell of the swaying grass beside the lake—on hearing Veric's words speak in my head.

C'mon Alora. You're a royal. Strong and lethal. You can unlock a Gods forsaken door.

I willed the forces of this realm to bend to my desires, scrunching my face as I concentrated—which I don't think directly helped.

My skin tingled as though someone was tipping warm water down my arm. Heat bloomed in my belly and spread across my chest, then licked further up my neck.

My eyes sprung open with the sound of the lock sliding out of place.

"Yes!" I whisper shouted, and did a giddy little celebratory bounce that Killian definitely would have teased me for. The warmth ebbed from my body as the magic rescinded, and I shook out the triumphant feeling as I reset myself for the next task.

I pushed open the door and found Nephamir's darkened room empty, which I was eternally grateful for. Both so I didn't see any naked bodies, nor anyone who'd want to kill me for breaking in.

White moonlight spilled in from the windows on the side, enough for me to go by, and I wasted no time dashing across the room to start at one end.

In my haste, I tripped on the uneven stone floor beneath a rug and stubbed my toe, then fell into an iron lamp by a chaise. I caught it as it hurtled to the cold ground, stopping the loud clatter it would've made.

"Fucking hell!" I winced as I straightened, setting the lamp and candles upright before rubbing my throbbing foot—all the while listening past my pounding heartbeat for any sign that I'd been heard.

"Right, careful now," I urged myself in a whisper after I was confident the coast was clear. I began again, searching all the obvious places—unsurprisingly to no avail. I wasn't shocked to find Nephamir didn't hide it under his pillow or at the back of the wardrobe.

Minutes ticked by as I pulled apart the room, and there was still no sign of the stone.

Think—where would you hide a stone, Alora?

Sweat coated the back of my neck as my stress levels soared. I couldn't risk staying much longer, considering it might not even be in here, but I also couldn't let this opportunity pass.

Standing in the centre of the room, my eyes drifted over the different spaces. Past his bed and furniture, wardrobe, the bathroom at the back, the sitting area I'd careened into upon arrival. I looked at each piece and feature individually—the wooden furniture, the unlit torches along the dark stone wall, the woven rug under his bed.

A strange feeling I couldn't identify—or ignore—pulled my attention back to the sitting area.

I cocked my head as I considered.

Where would you hide a stone, Alora?

I curled a wicked smile.

Answer—amongst all the rest.

I ran straight over to the spot I'd tripped on, then flipped the corner of the rug over, exposing the cold floor beneath.

I dug my nails in along the slightly raised edges of the offending slab, finding purchase against the grit. The stone scraped as it fought to be lifted from its setting, but it was clear it was already free of the binding sand.

Slower than I liked, the slab finally lifted from its space. As soon as it was free, I nearly dropped it back in place as a faint green glow emitted from the cavity beneath. It was all the reassurance I needed to know my efforts hadn't been in vain.

I set the slab down next to me with a scraping thud then leant over the hole. I had to contain the shaky whimper that escaped my throat.

With trembling fingers, I lifted Rharuer's Stone from its hiding place, almost too scared to touch the powerful gem.

But only the most silken polished stone met my touch as I wrapped my fingers around it. I leant back on my heels, lifting it from its hiding place, and taking in the allure that was Rharuer's Stone—the mighty relic that contained the power of the weapon once wielded by the King of Gods.

It was exactly as the illustration in the book showed. The swirling tendrils of fog that wrapped their way through the centre of the emerald green stone looked as though they went on forever. Dragging into a universe amongst the cosmos beneath its surface. It wasn't faceted like a gem, refracting light around and out of itself—but smooth and clear, uninterrupted and depthless. Its own source of light and power.

It was bordered in a gold mount and attached to a thick chain—clearly Nephamir's doing so he could keep it close. I had no way of wearing the stone as a pendant in this sheer dress, so there was only one option available to me.

I snapped the chain from its loop and dropped the metal into the hole I'd plucked it from. I slipped Rharuer's Stone beneath the strap of my dagger sheath against my skin, before sliding the slab of flooring back into place—resetting the room to its original state.

I stood and checked all was as it should be, then exited Nephamir's chambers with Rharuer's Stone fixed between my thighs.

✧ ✧ ✧

If I thought I was anxious sneaking through the hallways to get to Nephamir's rooms, it was nothing compared to sneaking through them now that I was successfully leaving them.

My cheeks heated with nervousness and I kept looking over my shoulder. My thumping heartbeat pounding in my ears made it almost impossible to hear if guards were patrolling up ahead.

I absolutely looked suspicious—even the scrawny little angel from earlier would find it difficult to ignore the panicked look I knew was set amongst my features. It'd been almost too easy to get the stone, and doubts that this was an elaborate trap sank their claws into my mind.

No, this stone is too valuable to use as bait.

I had to get a grip, get back to Killian, and get out of here. My mind raced, fighting against the panic to recall the mental map of the quickest way back to the Hall.

On silent, padding feet, I approached a junction in the hallway—the same one from earlier that the young angel spotted me at. I couldn't afford for him to spot me, nor stop me—so I didn't slow as I made to rush past the archway.

But, as I was about to make that final step into the open, a body came around the corner and crashed into me, sending us hurtling backwards.

A hand wrapped under my wings and circled around my waist as they grabbed me.

I reacted on pure instinct—my hand flew for my dagger as my assailant controlled the tackle, twisting us around in a spin and bursting through a door that led into a crowded storeroom.

They kicked the door closed as we fell into the space, shutting us off from the castle hallway.

I pushed at their solid chest, shoving them and their midnight wings up against the wall. But I froze in place when the sharp tip of cold steel pressed against my neck—and at who it was holding it there, looking at me with a satisfied, shit-eating grin and the same predator's look he had the first time he saw me.

But I refused to let the male see through my facade, and I prayed to all the Gods he wouldn't question anything—wouldn't wonder what I was doing on my own.

So I let confidence reign and my own gleaming, satisfied gaze shine through, as the Fox and I stood still, waiting for the other to speak.

"You might want to be careful with that, my lady," his smooth voice floated between us like smoke. "I'm quite fond of your target," he crooned then dipped his green eyes pointedly at where I held my own dagger against his groin. He flashed that wicked smile at me, his pointed canines showing. "You and I would both be quite upset if I lost it."

"I'm sure there's not much to miss," I hissed back.

He sucked an exaggerated breath between his teeth and lolled his head back against the wall behind him. He removed the hand holding his dagger at my neck, smacking it against his chest in a mocking display of being wounded.

"I just knew your words would be my undoing," he teased, repeating the same lewd remark from when we'd met then flashed that devious smile again.

I scoffed and withdrew my own dagger from the top of his thigh. The arrogant male pouted at me, as though he missed my hand being inches away from his cock.

Accusation laced my tone. "What's the queen's spy doing here?"

He gestured at me up and down. "What's the queen doing here?"

This is a spy, Alora. He won't stand being interrogated himself.

"I'm not the queen," I seethed. "Don't you know you could get Killian and I killed if you're caught here?" I folded my arms across my chest.

His green eyes watched my every move.

His grin kicked up at the corner, and I could almost see his ego inflate. "Firstly, Alora, let's get one thing straight–" he said smoothly, and adjusted his recline against the wall, tipping his hips up as he got comfortable.

Something in the way he moved made my belly coil.

The Fox rolled up the sleeves of his black shirt to his elbows as he spoke, displaying his corded forearms in the dull light. The whole act made him look even more arrogant, if that were possible.

"Those pitiful, puffed-up pigeons wouldn't have a hope in high heaven of catching me."

I rolled my eyes at the sheer vanity of this male. "A poet now, are you?"

He paused, his fingers deftly toying with his cuff halfway up his forearm. "If you want me to whisper sweet words in your ear, my lady, you need only ask." He winked while I glared at him again.

"Secondly, I was invited."

My mouth popped open as I considered his words. My eyes darted around the room, as though the answer to my faltering questions lay within the discarded jars and brooms. I must have looked like a gaping fish because the Fox slid his long finger under my chin and tapped it with enough pressure that it snapped shut.

As I looked across at the smiling son of a bitch before me, Arzemas' words from when Killian and I arrived replayed in my mind.

'Nephamir was surprised to hear you had invited another guest.'

I assumed he meant me. That Nephamir was surprised to hear Killian had invited *me.* Not a third fae. Not *him.*

"You were invited?" I repeated, disbelieving his words.

He looked offended. "I'm magnificent, why wouldn't I be?"

"Because Killian doesn't like you, for one," I retorted. "And you're a spy."

"Pfft, Killian loves me. He's just in denial," he scoffed. "Besides, he doesn't even know I'm here."

I shook my head, trying to brush off his nonchalance. "If Killian didn't tell you to come, then who did?"

"The Summer Kingdom, of course." He squinted at me as though checking I wasn't stupid. "The Summer Queen *did* tell you that Farro found out they're fucking around behind our backs, didn't she?"

"Yes, of course she did." I straightened my spine with resolve. The daunting realisation that I was alone in a tight closet with one of the most dangerous and well-connected fae in the realm suddenly hit me. "But that still doesn't explain why the angels would let a spy into their castle. What are you doing here anyway, Fox?"

His sparkling eyes flashed, and that wicked grin appeared again. "It's Kit."

"What is?"

He let out a low chuckle and shook his head. "My name. It's Kit. The Fox is just an alias. If you're going to *dress me down,* your majesty—which, you're very welcome to do in other interpretations of the phrase, by the way," he said with lustful sarcasm and another wink, "and threaten me in cupboards–you might as well know who you're talking to."

"Well, *Kit*," I drawled and his eyes dipped to my lips as I said his name. "What are you doing here?"

"Oh, just a smidge of espionage." He waved his daggered hand airily between us. "What you fail to realise, dear Alora, is perhaps these foolish pheasants don't know I'm a spy. I'm very good, you know." He smirked as his lids lowered, infatuated with his own achievements. "If they knew precisely who I was, I'm sure they would have at least *tried* to keep me out. Failed, of course–but I'm sure they'd have tried."

Fuck me, he likes the sound of his own voice.

"Besides, I simply couldn't pass up the chance to see you in this dress. I knew it would suit you." He bit his bottom lip as he looked me up and down.

No. Surely I'd heard wrong.

"*You*?" I accused. "*You* sent this dress?"

'Wear me.

–K'

"Of course me. You think Jude, or Gods forbid *Killian* should have been in charge of making sure you were dressed properly?" he scoffed. "Don't make me laugh. Besides. . . you look good with a little Summer draped over you. Like hot, glittering treasure. I'll volunteer next time you want something from my Kingdom clinging to your body if you'd like."

My eyes shuttered.

Treasure.

Of course this male was no different than the dickheads in Evamere who thought women were only nice to look at. Glittering trophies to mount in bed, and then mount on a mantle, to be seen and not heard.

Why did I think any males in this realm would think of me any differently than a sparkling, rare treasure to possess?

"Fuck you," I spat, finally able to let the words fly at him since Elden, but he completely ignored the verbal attack. I turned for the door, but Kit's next words froze me in place.

"Now, as for *my* question–what are *you* doing here?" he asked with piqued interest, letting the tip of his dagger lull in his hand to point at me as he spoke.

My lips thinned as my irritation spiked. It was silly of me to think he wouldn't question why I was alone and so far away from the ball.

But even though we were playing for the same side, Kit and I were not on the same team.

The spymaster was a collector of secrets, and mine could not be his.

I would be foolish not to think that Kit was drunk on his ego for good reason. Everyone always said the Fox was an expert at finding truths—the longer I stayed in here, the closer he would come to figuring out what I was up to, and I had to get back before anyone noticed I was missing.

I had to get out of here. Now.

"Go find your own set of secrets, Kit. I have nothing to share with you," I said evenly. I tucked my wings in and finally turned my back on him. I pulled on the wooden door, managing to open it just a fraction before Kit's palm smacked into it over my shoulder, slamming it shut.

Then I felt him.

His breath at the edge of my cheek, his scent around me—warm like pepper and nutmeg, smooth and fresh like patchouli blossoms. The fibres of his black shirt brushed against my wings as he stood over me, making me shiver.

He wasn't imposing or looming like Killian, but there was still no escaping him. No pulling away if he didn't release you first. But the spy didn't seem like the type of male to willingly let go of what he set his mind to.

"You'll share everything with me, Treasure," he said low against my ear.

Not threatening. But a promise.

As though he'd read my future. He'd seen his prize and would take it.

Bright, emerald-green eyes flashed in my peripheral, right before his long, dark lashes brushed against his cheeks as his gaze dipped to my lips—as though they'd spill their secrets right then and there.

I swallowed and fluttered my wings to shake the shiver that ran down my spine, then tugged on the door again. Kit relented, pulling his hand back and released me from the cupboard.

Released? No.

The spy didn't seem like the type of male to let go of what he set his mind to.

Chapter 25
The Fox

I dashed out of the storeroom and ran in the direction of the Hall. As I rounded a corner I looked over my shoulder, half expecting to see Kit trailing me, but mercifully the hallway behind was empty.

Too bad the hallway in front of me wasn't, and I smacked straight into a guard, built as thick and tall as Killian.

Fuck.

I went flying back and landed on my arse and wings, red dress spilling out around me, with my entire leg on show. But the angel I'd collided with didn't budge. He drew his sword and aimed it at my chest as I tried to scramble to my feet.

"Don't fucking move, fae filth," he growled down at me with hatred as I tried to prop myself up.

My mind scrambled from the impact, then faltered at the vehemence in his words. I attempted to pull the same entitled, threatening tone Killian had dealt the previous young guard, but this new male wasn't having it.

"I don't give a fuck about how important you think you are, or how important the owner of the cock who sinks into your cunt every night thinks he is. You're not where you're supposed to be, and I intend to find out what you've been up to."

There was no talking out of this one. I paled at his threat, and my body trembled with terror—worsened immediately by the five other powerful bodies that came around the corner, weapons drawn and scowls in place as they stood behind their gruff leader bearing down on me.

The fears I'd expressed to Killian about going up against angels roared in my ears—his useless solutions roared even louder.

I'm not hard to fight against when I'm splayed on the ground in my dress, I don't have magic to wield at them. They are stronger than me. I *am* outnumbered. And they have their weapons aimed.

Months of training and I still wasn't fucking good enough.

The only useful tool I had in my arsenal was my speed. But incapacitated with my legs caught in the spill of my dress, my body on top of my wings, *and* the angel's sword a foot away from me, despite how fast I could move, I wasn't willing to bet he wasn't faster.

My heart thumped, making my whole body pound with each beat, and sweat beaded at the base of my neck.

I opened my mouth in a last-ditch attempt to assuage them, but a squeak barely passed my lips before the angel cut me off again.

"Open that cunt mouth one more time, and I'll find something to fill it with to shut you up."

The assaulting meaning behind his words was plain to see as his expression darkened.

No, not his expression—the entire hallway.

The angel looked to the ceiling, his brows drawing together in confusion, checking if the fires in the chandelier had dimmed.

But they all burned just as brightly. . . and yet, not.

He kept the tip of his sword firmly aimed at my chest, but his attention pulled at the now dimmed passage as he swung his gaze over his shoulder.

I looked down the hallway and past the other five angels turning their heads in unison as well.

And then I saw *him*.

Kit rounded the corner from behind the six angels—midnight wings flared from wall to wall across the wide passage. Arms at his side, dagger in hand and auburn head tilted down, as he strode forward like death on dark wings.

I couldn't even register how he'd gotten behind the group from where we'd been in that cupboard. His green eyes were lit with burning rage and piercing focus. He held his dagger blade down, as though it was an extension of his arm, right up until he descended on them.

Kit moved so fast it was nearly impossible to track. Like curling smoke through and around them. He was untouchable. Before a guard could bring their weapon down, he'd sliced his blade through them and already moved to the next.

He didn't need to use his wings or touch his magic to get the upper hand or gain extra strength to deal a killing slash, his body and skill with the blade alone were power enough.

Blood splattered high up the walls and bodies crumpled to the floor. Kit moved and killed so efficiently that some were still falling as he stepped up to the final, enormous angel standing above me.

The angel's shoulders shook with rage as he sucked in heavy breaths, looking at the carnage the lone, dangerous fae before him had just dealt.

Almost every fae I've met has told me angels are hard to kill, yet Kit just sliced through five without breaking a sweat.

This is not just a spy—this is an assassin.

Kit stood preternaturally still, watching the last angel with a vicious sneer. Looking as though he enjoyed the wrath and rage on the angel's face, caused by the death he'd just wrought—knowing the last target before him was about to meet the same end.

The angel let out a roar as he lifted his sword arm to bear down on Kit, intending to slice him in half.

I didn't see Kit move. Couldn't track the lift of his hand or the movement of his dagger.

But one moment the angel held his sword above his head, and the next, it clattered to the ground—forgotten as he released it to grab at his other hand.

Or rather, where his other hand had just been attached to him.

As the guard had swung his right hand to attack, Kit sliced off his left, caught the thick chunk of flesh before it fell, and shoved it into its owner's mouth as he'd opened it to scream in agony.

The angel's expression changed so many times in the space of a second it was hard to note them all.

He doubled over, roaring in pain and gagging around his severed hand as the blood filled his mouth, then tried to spit his body part onto the ground.

Kit leant over just enough to bear down over him, then placed the blade of his dagger flat under the angel's chin, lifting the guard's gaze to his.

"You opened that cunt mouth one too many times," Kit purred with a depraved whisper.

The angel let out a wet sob, then a gurgled whimper as Kit slid his blade slowly forward, piercing through the angel's neck then out the back.

His legs gave out as blood spilled from the dual holes when Kit drew his blade back, falling to the stone floor with a wet smack and a clatter of muted armour.

The blood-red tunics lying in heaps before us looked almost unchanged in the aftermath of the swift devastation Kit had just dealt their wearers. But, in actuality, they were all drenched in the sticky, dark substance they were coloured to resemble.

The lighting in the corridor brightened back to its original state, though no flames grew brighter or higher. Like Kit had pulled away a black curtain blocking the flames.

He remained where he was, lashes lowered as he looked down at the enormous enemy he'd just felled without breaking a sweat. Then, he brought that green gaze slowly up to mine, pinning me beneath his stare. No longer glazed over with fury, irritation flared for the briefest second before it cleared, and then heated as he raked his eyes up my exposed leg. He kicked his lips up at me in a wicked way.

I'm beginning to think this is just his annoying face.

He crouched to wipe his dagger on the angel lying dead at his feet.

His black pants hugged his form, highlighting his strong thighs. The second my traitorous eyes dipped to his impressive physique, Kit whipped his head to me, catching me staring. Smug amusement played on his lips and a breathy laugh left him right as my face heated.

"Out with it," I ground out, finally rising to my feet, annoyance flaring in me once again as I braced for the witty remark I already knew was coming. "What brilliant taunt do you want to level at me this time?"

"I was only wondering what Killian has been doing with you these past few months. From what I know, you should have been able to easily take care of these. . . turkeys." He stood as well, looking down at the pile of twisted bodies and wings with disgust.

"Running low on bird jokes, are you?"

Kit shrugged and made a sound of impartial agreement as he sheathed his weapon. "So what is it?" he asked again when I didn't say anything. "Have the two of you been so enamoured with each other that he forgot to train you, or do I need to tell Farro to find a better general for his legion?"

I bristled at his insults and glared at the enjoyment he clearly got out of the rise he brought. But anger flooded me that I half agreed with his first statement.

I should have been able to take care of them.

"I was pinned on my wings and beneath this fucking dress, if you didn't notice."

"Oh, I noticed." His hot gaze raked down my body again.

I fisted my hand in my velvet skirts to stop the urge to slap the smirk off his face at the mention of my dress. "This is all irrelevant now, anyway. If I were you, I'd run and report to your king and queen. Tell Farro to prepare his legion."

"War was upon us anyway, Treasure, you heard Orella's ominous warning in the temple just as well as I."

'Ready for war.'

"Whether it's been declared in this attack or not, doesn't shift the precedence of what the king or queen decide to do, or what Farro and his legion does. But that's only what you'd recommend doing if you were me–but you're not. You're you. So what are you going to do now that time's up on playing happy family in your castle?"

I bit my lip, trying to hold back from entering into an argument with him and his jabbing insults. "I need to find Killian and get out of here before any of them find these bodies," I said, as I passed the fallen angels littering the passage. "I'm done with you."

"Oh yes, of course," he drawled lazily. "Run back to your *Promised,* Lor." I could feel the disdain dripping from his words aimed at my back like the point of his dagger as I dodged the pools of blood then went back to the Hall.

✧ ✧ ✧

The soles of my now blackened feet slapped against the warm stones with such speed that I had to use my hand to swing myself around the corners of the passageways as I careened around them.

I slowed my pace as the pillar I'd discarded my shoes at came into view, and gave myself all but thirty seconds to slide my glittering heels back on and comb my fingers through my tangles. I fanned my face with my hands to relieve the flush in my cheeks and sucked in a steadying breath to reassure myself.

A few more minutes to get Killian, then we can get out of here.

I flicked my hair between my shoulders, straightened my dress, and ran a hand across the sheath to check my dagger was hidden, and that—

"Motherfucker!" I roared.

The chandelier above me rattled, the candles in it flickering as they shook.

Rharuer's Stone was gone.

I just knew. *Knew!* Kit was responsible.

I hadn't even noticed him take it. He'd been so quick and skilled, that he'd lifted it from between my thighs without me realising.

A shiver prickled through my body at the thought.

I raised my fist to my forehead, squeezing so tight in frustration that my nails dug into my palm.

Okay, think clearly, Alora. At least the Fallen don't have it. It's a step in the right direction at least. We can work with this. Let's just get out of here before they find bodies and figure it out.

I rounded the corner and breezed back into the busy Hall, trying my utmost to look poised and proper, like the little lady I was pretending to be.

The dark females above were still selling their sensual acts in their cages, a few sets of angels continued to have sex in plain sight, and more groups of rowdy males packed together on the balconies above.

My eyes moved across the room looking for Killian, but any air of grace I mustered upon entering the Ball blew out of me in a single breath when I instead saw Kit, the charismatic prick, standing with a group of angels at the side of the room—amber liquid in hand, howling with laughter at something one of them had said. As though he hadn't just killed six of their kind only minutes ago.

How the fuck does he move so fast?

My eyes swept over what I could see of the room, but there was no sign of Killian. It was concerning, but on the other hand, it might mean he was still with Nephamir and Arzemas, and so my disappearance may have gone unnoticed.

I'll cross my fingers it's the latter.

But without Killian here, it meant there was only one target I needed to focus on. I stormed across the Hall, and I could have sworn the floor thrummed with each clicking footstep I took as I headed straight for Kit.

I'm the thief here. He doesn't know who he's playing with.

Halfway there, a group of snide females cut in front of me, and I lost sight of the arrogant bastard for a split second. When the females cleared, Kit was nowhere to be seen.

I turned in place, my eyes raking over every head of hair in the cavernous room, looking for the telltale tousled auburn sweeping forward up over his forehead.

There.

At the end of the covered passage underneath the balconies that passed the shadowed alcoves, Kit stood with his shoulder leaning against the wall, one ankle crossed over the other as he palmed his glass of liquor—looking straight at me.

My brows lowered in a glare, and his lips curled in a smile.

I set off toward him, this time making sure I didn't draw attention to myself. I couldn't afford a scene.

I edged around groups of angels standing and laughing together, snaking between bodies and past feathered wings. None of them gave me a drop of attention.

As I wove between the angels, I made sure to never let my gaze slip from Kit's, who never let his slip from mine.

But my concentration faltered as I passed one of those shadowed alcoves behind the black curtains. The sounds of moans and grunts and skin slapping against skin coming from within made my head whip before I could think.

Immediately, I realised my mistake. When I looked back to the spot against the wall, Kit was already gone.

I walked past the depraved acts, my stomach pulling at the thought of what was happening back there, over to where Kit had been standing, and then searched the room again.

What's the bet he'd led me past the salacious alcoves on purpose?

When I spotted him again, he was high above, standing amongst a new crowd of males on a balcony on the opposite wall, completely out of reach to me and my flightless wings.

Chicken indeed.

I folded my arms across my glittering chest, defeat rearing its head in my thoughts. Kit was playing a game of cat and mouse and made the one move he knew I couldn't counter.

He looked at me then from his lofty tower, with a smile that could only be described as dashing. He bent at the waist, lowering his exposed forearms to lean on the wide railing that looked down across the dance floor, and rolled that glass between his hands.

With singular intent, Kit raised his hand and curled his finger. Once. Twice. Beckoning me forward. He watched me like the dangerous predator he was, and his eyes glistened when I, like a fool snared in his trap, stepped out from the shadows and across the floor toward him.

Exactly like he wanted.

Perhaps he still wanted the chase. Or maybe he just wanted me within earshot so he could tell me to give up my own.

I wasn't fussed either way. At least if we were within earshot of one another, he'd hear me tell him to go fuck himself again.

But as I continued moving across the centre of the room with my eyes locked on his, Kit stood, threw the last bit of liquor back, then dipped behind the group of angels and out of sight.

Chase it is.

"Looking for me?" his smooth voice teased from my back.

I spun to face him, vitriol ready to spew from my mouth—but any and all fight flooded out of me as his deft fingers skimmed into my hands.

He moved so swift and sure, that before I'd come to realise, my hand was resting on his shoulder, feeling his strong muscles roll, and the other was cupped in his as he slowly turned us in time with the music. He slid his other hand around my waist, holding me flush against his tall form.

A different kind of satisfied, cocky smile pulled at the edges of his lips when he looked down and saw me pulled off-kilter by him *again.* His brilliant eyes left my face and watched around the room as he led me in a dance.

"Let me go," I ground out and tried to pull away.

He wasn't holding firm, but I certainly wasn't going anywhere without trying hard.

He arched his brow. "Why? Have somewhere to be, Treasure?" He gave a mocking audible gasp, and his face lit up with a devious smile. "Is it to those alcoves? You naughty thing. I must admit it, those acts even made *me* blush. . . but I'm game if you are."

"You're disgusting."

"I prefer the term *filthy.*"

"Let go of me, Kit," I hissed and tugged at his grip again.

His whispered words brushed against my ear. "Never."

He pulled back then rolled his eyes when he saw me glaring at him still. He lifted his arm and spun me out, his hands letting me go as I twirled before he stepped forward and pulled me into him again. "Happy?"

"That's not what I meant and you know it," I hissed as my hands drifted over his smooth muscles back into position.

He chuckled darkly then continued dancing. "You're very hard to please."

"You're very hard to like."

He winced with that same mock expression from before. "You wound me again with that mouth, Treasure."

'Definitely your fucking mouth. . .'

"I'll wound you in other ways if you don't quit fucking around."

"Only if you promise to kiss them better afterwards," he said with debauched intent, eyes burning into mine. "Come to think of it, I think you nicked my favourite part back in that cupboard earlier. Should we start there?"

"What are you playing at, Kit?" I growled.

He stopped our dance but didn't speak. Several sets of eyes moved over us at my tone, but none lingered. No angels cared about the two fae in the middle of the floor.

I summoned all the authority I could at the seriousness of the situation we were in and lowered my voice. "This isn't a joke. We need to fucking leave, Kit. We are surrounded. And outnumbered. And possibly seconds away from that mess in the hallway from being discovered. I need Killian. I need to find him and leave." I stepped out of his grasp.

The playfulness ebbed from his face and coldness seeped into his eyes. His lip moved into a cruel line as though deciding what cutting insult to deliver to me. But it was gone in an instant, and he slipped into that indifferent spy once again.

"Well, lucky for us he's here to save the day," he sneered then slid his eyes over my shoulder.

I turned in time to see Killian's dark form stomp through the towering doors, his power pushing further into the room. His gaze swept over the crowd and I knew who he was searching for.

His scorching blue eyes landed on me as he took another step to close the gap.

But I saw it. Saw him lift his gaze to the fae at my back, and he faltered. Just a misstep and a muscle tick in his jaw before he tucked his wings in then strode through the crowd.

My heel had barely made it into motion before Kit's warm hand snagged my wrist and pulled me back around to face him.

"I'm not playing games when it comes to what's at stake here," he said in a low hum. Then his eyes turned dark and devilish, his voice as rich and smooth as smoke. "And trust me, Treasure, when I play with you, you'll know it."

My eyes widened. I didn't know if it was a threat or a promise, but I didn't have the luxury of time to consider it. I yanked my wrist from his hold and took swift steps to Killian, closing the gap between us twice as fast. We each gripped the other when we finally breached the gap.

Panic washed over both our faces as we said the same words.

"We need to get out of here."

Killian nodded and hooked his arm around mine, steering us to the only exit. I glanced over my shoulder, but the spot I looked for was empty, as I knew it would be.

"Something's wrong," Killian muttered, speaking so softly that only my heightened ears would pick up the sounds.

He didn't elaborate, and I didn't ask. All that mattered was the exit.

"Are you okay?" he asked and peered over his shoulder to where I knew Kit was no longer standing.

I made a noise that resembled a yes, but it didn't quite make it past the lump forming in my throat.

"Did you get it?"

I shook my head the barest fraction as we passed through the Hall doors. "Later," was all I could manage. My heartbeat was suddenly a rapid throbbing against my ribs as we rounded the corner. "Can't you sift us out of here?" I pleaded.

It was Killian's turn to shake his head as we picked up our pace through the castle. "I won't risk it. I won't risk you. We just need to get outside, only another few minutes."

"Minutes?" a cold voice cut through from behind us, and we froze. "You're not supposed to leave until tomorrow."

Chapter 26

The Fall

Killian's pulsing power gathered around him. His grip tightened on my arm as we turned to see Arzemas taking long strides toward us, followed by two guards in their muted armour. That fake, toothy smile spread across his face.

"Who's leaving?" Killian countered, trying to keep the strain from his voice.

"Sounds like you were," Arzemas joked, but no humour carried into his expression.

"We were just looking for somewhere. . . private."

My wings prickled as the tension rose, setting every nerve on edge.

Arzemas gestured back behind him. "I have just the place," he winked and gestured over his shoulder, summoning us to follow him. Killian made to protest, but four more guards appeared, cutting his words off. This was not a request.

Three Fallen walked in front, and four behind, as we were escorted through another section of the castle. My breath was shaky and my mind raced, trying to think of a plan. I looked out the corner of my eye at Killian, but he'd gone pale.

I wanted to say something reassuring, or plan how we were going to get out of this, but I couldn't risk the angels overhearing.

There was nothing to do but follow.

We were led down a spiralling staircase, tight enough that our wings scratched against the dark stone wall as we descended single file. Arzemas shoved a key into a lone door at the bottom and swung it open.

Warm night air pushed in, strong enough that it blew the wisps of my hair, even as I stood on the stairs behind Killian and two guards trailing behind Arzemas. Adrenaline spiked through me.

This could be our chance.

Killian risked a glance at me, and the look he gave conveyed everything I needed to know.

Be ready.

Arzemas stepped through the door, followed by the two guards before Killian crossed the threshold outside. But devastation and fear clanged through me when I followed them into the night. My wide eyes hit Killian's, tears threatening.

Bars.

Thick iron bars caged in the long parapet. The open sky—our only hope of escape was so close, yet so far away. I looked through them and saw how impossibly high up in the mountain we still were. The wide bridge crossing to the other jagged mountain was only barely visible beyond the wispy clouds now surrounding the castle.

Killian glared at Arzemas who stopped a few steps away, standing next to a black door. "What's the fucking meaning of this?"

I wondered why Killian even bothered asking, but then again, there were a number of things we'd done, it was probably best to know which crimes they were aware of.

"We just need to have a little chat. A situation has developed. Several guards and a very significant angel are missing. That, plus there are reports that your Promised has been traipsing around the castle," he replied, undeterred by the death-promising glare Killian levelled him with.

And then I saw why—sensed the edges of the empty void.

Nulralt.

The black metal door pulsed like a gaping wound. Its sickening reach tried to claw at our magic, even from where we stood.

Killian noticed it, too. He clenched his fist, and his calculating eyes weighed our options.

If we were shoved in there, we were as good as dead.

Killian's voice was guttural. "If you think this is going to end well, Arzemas, I have some bad news for you."

A cruel smile curved on Arzemas' lips and malice flashed in his dull hazel eyes. "I'll take my chances."

Movement burst from both sides as the Fallen drew their weapons and lurched forward. Killian's magic pulsed like a shock wave in response, sending the angels several feet back.

It gave me the precious second I needed to draw my dagger and lower my stance.

But Killian grabbed my wrist, halting my advance on the still recovering forms then shot his other arm out to the side. The iron cage blasted under the pressure of his magic, and he shoved me toward the hole he'd created. My arms flung out to catch myself on the bent and wrecked edges.

"Run!" he roared, and turned back to the ensuing carnage. An angel rose and charged at us, but Killian kicked his boot out, slamming his heel to their chest with a sickening crack.

I launched myself through the hole. My spine screamed against the strain as I spread my wings wide to slow as I fell the two-storey drop onto a lower, open parapet with a heavy smack.

Wincing, I looked up to Killian, waiting for him to follow.

But he didn't.

His dark shadow blocked the opening he'd created, and the pressure of his magic grew more intense. The sounds of fists cracking against skin and armour clanking against stone rang out from above.

Then a roar rent through the air amongst the sound of steel slicing and hacking. "RUN!"

The commanding and urgent order to save myself ripped into me.

I reluctantly obeyed, my chest panging with guilt at leaving him behind. But we couldn't take to the skies together, and if he wasn't capable of escaping himself, I needed to get out of here and get help if I had any hope of saving him.

I sprinted. Kicking off my heels, I threw every ounce of strength I had into my legs and tore down the high wall, wings pressed in tight against my back, with the velvet puddle of my red dress trailing behind me.

I had one option available if I had any hope of making it off this fucking mountain alive, and a castle full of Fallen to run past to get to it. The only hint of luck on my side was that all the guards on patrol had been pulled from their duty to the inner confines of the fortress—the path ahead was clear.

A crescent moon hung in the sky, appearing closer and larger as it drifted in and out behind thin clouds, as though it were trying to look down on the perilous scene playing beneath it.

Seconds after I took off, the pulse of Killian's magic severed—cut off entirely—and the air felt empty.

No.

Only two explanations existed, and I prayed it had everything to do with Nulralt and nothing to do with his heart not beating.

I ran as fast as a lightning strike under the stars, streaking across the stones at the edge of the castle. I couldn't let them catch me, couldn't let them near me. Fear tried to drag me down, drown me in the wash of emotions and risks of the situation I was in—but I needed to make it out of here, and couldn't let doubt take root in my mind.

I didn't dare look over my shoulder. Instead, I strained my ears to listen over the ripping wind, listening if any wing beats rode the gusts to snatch me as I fled like the thief in the night I was.

But none came.

Every look of surprise on Killian's or Jude's face, every comment from our training that confirmed my speed, every skill I'd honed—I used it all to fuel my escape.

My chest burned like fire, my legs stung as if venom ran through my veins instead of blood, and my bare feet ached as they pounded against the harsh stone then leapt down to a lower floor.

Now I was on the same level as the bridge and I could see the beginning of it up ahead. My throat was dry and scratching as I dragged in gulping breaths.

I was on the wrong side of the castle to use the path Killian and I had hiked up to get here, I was still hundreds of metres in the air and the castle fell away from the rock with no chance of climbing down the sides.

My only hope of salvation was making it across the bridge to the other mountain, surviving long enough to get to either Kingdom on foot, or hiding long enough until someone came looking.

I pulled to a halt at the bridge's entrance then checked my surroundings. It at least gave me a short reprieve from the exertion.

Braziers burned every few yards across the bridge, so there had to be guards around somewhere tending to the fires, but I wasn't going to stick around to find out where they were. I either encountered them, or I'd be gone before I did.

There was no time to prepare or think anything through. Barrelling onward was the only option now.

The bridge was a straight shot across the massive expanse to the other jagged peak. Low walls bordered the sides, and the pillars supporting the structure disappeared down into the inky, black void beneath—down to the chasm that gouged through the mountain pass.

I ran again, this time slower so I wouldn't be heard, in case I needed to gain the element of surprise if I had no option but to fight.

Without my thudding footsteps and pounding heartbeat thundering in my ears, the noises of the night filtered in—so I listened for anything that didn't belong, cataloguing everything within range.

Thin fog drifted in the dying wind—I had run so far across the bridge, that neither end of it could be seen. Only the flaming orange fires hazing behind the low clouds showed me there was still further to go.

But then—beyond the fog, a sound echoed that didn't belong.

Again.

Again.

I skidded to a halt and froze. I had nowhere to run or hide—no hope of escaping.

All the while, the scuff of a single set of boots, lazily walking up the path kept sounding.

Then a slow, striking clap split the air.

Once. Twice. Three times.

"I congratulate you, my lady. You got further than I expected."

The blood drained from my face.

Nephamir.

He emerged from the fog like sheer curtains pulled back around him. His tall, golden form strolled to me, wings held just beyond his shoulders, his cruel eyes raking over me from top to bottom, lingering again on the exposed skin at my breasts.

"I wasn't expecting to get anywhere until your lackeys tried to shove me in a cell," I retorted, not quite masking the shake of fear in my voice.

"I don't know why you're surprised. You and Killian were always going to wind up in my dungeon."

"Except I'm not in your dungeon," I levelled back at him, my smart mouth deciding this was the perfect time to take charge. I refused to go down without a fight.

Believe in your strength, and none are stronger than you.

"A situation I'm about to rectify," he crooned, as right on cue, ten more angels stepped out from behind the veil of fog and into view, with their weapons drawn and focus locked on their only target.

Me.

I backed up a step, my fingers twitching to grasp my dagger—but they were too far away and would intercept my attack. I had to get closer to take advantage of my speed if I wanted any chance of taking down one or two.

Believe in your strength, and none are stronger than you.

But they all stayed in formation behind Nephamir, who continued to take slow, stalking steps toward me.

"But first. . . let me tell you a story."

"Sorry Nephamir, it's not my bedtime yet," I cut back, and he chuckled.

"No, but I'll have you in *my* bed soon enough," he said calmly.

I clenched my jaw.

"Did you know that there were once two great powers in this realm?" He wandered from side to side as he spoke. "Together, they were a well of unfathomable power—revered for their strength. They planned on remaking this world into a realm even the Gods themselves had never seen the likes of before." He raised his hands, praising Noteas and Lilla's memory, but then his gaze and words turned dark and low, vehemence spitting from his mouth. "Then one day, a third power, who had no right sticking her nose where it didn't belong, decided to make it very, *very* difficult for those two beings to finish their plans."

"Sounds like they weren't as powerful as you think they were," I chided, trying to sound unaffected and distanced. I pretended to look at my nails, hoping that not giving a shit about his story would get under his skin.

It worked.

Nephamir glared at me. "Now, stop me if you've heard this part, my lady, but fast forward a few thousand years, and imagine my surprise when I hear a gripping tale that the very same meddling bitch brought her very own little lost fae into the realm."

Fuck.

"What would I know of Orella's motives?"

"Oh, nothing I'm sure, she's always kept her secrets close—but I can't help but find it too much of a coincidence, considering everything else happening with the prophecy."

What the fuck does that mean?

Nephamir read the question in my expression and his lips raised in a cold sneer. His words turned even darker. "You foolish faeling. . . your kind really know nothing. Just you wait, *Alora*, it's going to make the reveal so much more. . . *thrilling*."

Panic bled from my neck down my spine, and my eyes widened in fear. Nephamir barked out a cruel and mocking laugh as I shrunk small, then he doubled over as the excitement of his game filled him with wicked delight.

He knew. Since the very start, he knew who I was, and just bided his time. Toyed with me.

'Nothing will stop me from getting my hands on you.'

"Your attempt was admirable. Truly, I would never have believed you were stupid enough to think coming here was a risk that would pay off. But here you are," he said gesturing at me up and down, his evil smile curling across his face. His voice turned gravelly and harsh when he next spoke. "And I intend to find out why."

My eyes widened, and my heart hammered.

"Oh, Alora. . . don't look so scared," he purred. "We're just going to chat, you and I. And then after, you and I are going to. . . *relax*. For a good long while, while you tell me all your secrets."

My stomach roiled at the heinous underlying threat.

"Squeal what you know quick enough, faeling, and I'll let you enjoy it. Resist. . ." He chuffed and smiled. "Well, you'll only be hurting yourself. It makes no difference to me, in fact, I rather prefer it."

I wanted to throw up, and every hair on my body raised as fear and adrenaline spiked my blood

"I'm going to have such fun with you, Alora."

At that, all ten guards stepped out from around him and slowly stepped forward.

Fury roared and the creature in my chest scratched, demanding to be let out and lay waste to everything in my path.

Fuck the element of surprise.

Time was up—and I would not go willingly.

I slipped my dagger from its sheath and twirled it.

Nephamir's obnoxious laugh cracked through the night again. "Haha, the little faeling has *teeth!"*

I levelled my gaze at the approaching angels, watching for any sign that would give away their attack. But instead, I glimpsed movement from my peripheral—a form that flashed across the night sky and blocked out stars as it flew.

My heart leapt in my chest that Killian had escaped, and we'd stand a chance of getting out of this alive. But the magic that pulled in the air like an unstoppable force wasn't the heavy pressure of Killian's power.

It was piercing and deadly, inescapable and ultimate.

I risked darting my eyes to the shadow rocketing toward the bridge and immediately saw the intent flaring in his green eyes. Practically heard his voice as though he was screaming at me.

Jump.

At the same split second the guards pushed their weight into their feet and wings to launch at me, I flung my dagger at Nephamir's head then bolted to the low wall of the bridge on the far side of Kit's approach.

As I planted my foot on the ledge of the bridge wall, the air pulled and hissed behind me. I imagined it's what a star sounds like in the milliseconds before it implodes, or like a banshee drawing in a breath before its reckoning scream.

I turned my body to fall backwards as I leapt over the edge and saw Nephamir cupping his cheek, blood dripping between his fingers and a venomous glare aimed at me. At the precipice of when gravity claimed my body, time slowed as the heads of all eleven angels turned to see the arrow in the dark, come to rip them apart.

Night detonated and the bridge exploded with deafening force. Chunks of rock and stone became projectiles that would end me quicker than the angels could have ever hoped to achieve.

But it was the fae projectile who'd caused the explosion that collided into me, his chest smacking into my body as he snatched me mid-air and shot through the dark, weaving and dodging the shooting debris like he already knew where it would fall.

I threw my head against Kit's chest, clinging to his shirtfront, and shut my eyes against the rip and roar of the wind. The breakneck speed at which he flew was terrifying, but the spy didn't falter. Didn't hesitate.

He tilted down and took a straight shot for solid ground, easing off as the bottom of the deep gorge came into view. With more gentleness than I expected, Kit landed, then set me on a boulder in front of him, secluded amongst the rubble.

High above us, the explosion Kit had caused still rolled in a fireball of flame and dust where the bridge once was. I kept clutching onto Kit's shirt and my muscles shook from panic.

A sob burst from my throat, and tears spilled from my eyes.

Kit dropped his forehead to mine and shushed me gently. I knew my emotions were shot because I didn't even consider pushing the male away.

"He knew. The whole time he knew it was me," I sobbed, unable to stop my panicked thoughts. "He would have killed me, Kit–he said he would. . ."

Kit pressed his hands on my shoulders and swept them down in long, slow strokes along my arms, speaking hushed words to me. I wanted to tune him out, go numb and fall into the hysteria that wanted to claim me–but Kit's words cut through it all, just the same as he cut through the air to get to me.

"I have you," he reassured, and a single breath blew past his lips. He repeated it over and over. "I have you. I have you."

I listened to the tenor of his voice, believing the words as they kept me grounded and present. He spoke them as though he needed to believe it, too.

Slowly, I blinked then pulled my head back just far enough so I could look up at him, my hands still clutching into his shirt, not wanting to let him go.

His expression held none of his usual confident swagger or bored indifference. He went wholly still under my scrutinising eyes as I tried to read the emotions on his face.

The answer was right at the tip of my tongue when a second explosion ruptured the silence of the night, and a fireball burst out from the castle wall high above.

I whipped my head up at the carnage. "What–"

"That would be Farro," he murmured as if knowing any loud noises would set me off. "His personal unit."

I brought my gaze back to Kit, disbelief halting my thoughts. "You–you went and got help for us?"

A pitying smile touched his lips as he regarded me. "They were always here, Alora," he said as though he couldn't believe I didn't already know that. "You really think your allies would have let you walk in there without a contingency plan?"

I dashed the tears from my eyes, embarrassed that I hadn't made the same decision to bring backup.

"Queen Fleur said it was safer if–"

He bristled. "Yes, well the Summer Queen doesn't always have all the information to make the right calls."

"Isn't that your job?" I levelled, and his shit-eating grin washed over him immediately.

Of course he can find the strength to ride his ego after such a terrifying ordeal.

"Yes. Which is exactly why Farro decided it best to provide backup when he heard you were attending the Ball."

"Farro gets to call shots, just like that?"

"Considering the two fools who went in there were his brother, and the female who will one day be leading her Kingdom alongside him, I think that would grant him some sway in the matter."

"Fleur doesn't seem like the type of female to tolerate not being listened to."

"You haven't met Farro." He grinned again. "Let's just say it runs in the family."

Another explosion boomed, and smoke billowed through the air. "Doesn't seem like he's very happy," I surmised, looking up at the castle. It was almost a world away from this far below.

"He's not," Kit said as he still watched me. "They had his family, after all."

"Killian's already out?" Relief washed over me.

"If he's not already, he will be soon. I'd better get up there," he sighed. "They're good, but almost useless without me."

I scoffed, amazed that his ego was never far away. He tugged on his rolled-up sleeves, and I noticed that he still looked completely put together—not a single deep-red strand of arrogant, arching hair was out of place.

"Wait here. I'll tell Killian where you are, and you'll be in the arms of your beloved soon," he purred, then flashed his teeth at me in that cocky smile.

"You're a wanker."

"Only when I think of you in that dress, Treasure." He winked, then shot into the sky and away before I could slap him.

The silence of the land pressed around me now that I was alone, and a wave of rising anger quickly simmered beneath my skin.

Not at Kit's taunts, or that he had now saved my life—twice—meaning I now owed the egotistical prick no less than two life debts.

But at my own failing.

Here I was thinking my skill with a dagger, and a few weeks of fae agility put me on an even standing with these creatures.

With *any* of them.

All this effort and training and I still wasn't strong enough.

I pulled my dagger out and twirled it in my hands as I paced—the glittering gems on my dress were dull in the moonlight, as if they weren't capable of shining anymore after all they'd been through.

As I turned in place, fear crept up with my anger. Nephamir had mentioned the prophecy and said that we knew nothing.

What didn't we know?

I startled when a massive explosion cracked high above. The sky lit up with a ball of flames detonating within Alziros again, this time shaking the mountain it perched upon. Chunks of rock and stone broke from the castle and jagged peaks around Alziros in the wake of the blast, kicking up clouds of dust as they cracked and tumbled down the mountainside.

Killian held a lot of animosity for his younger brother and his power—the title and privileges it granted him. But I wondered if he was grateful for it, now that Farro was up there using it to save his life? Or whether his power would draw a deeper rift between the brothers, having it put on show because Killian was unable to save his own?

But the thoughts left my head with dizzying speed when his magic pressed around me. Like an unstoppable force, Killian slammed to the ground a few steps from me, the immense force so great I didn't know how he hadn't snapped his legs upon impact.

Before I'd managed to take a step, Killian breached the gap and pulled me to him, squeezing me tight against his chest. His sweet and smoky scent was hidden beneath the smell of blood and dirt and ash. When he finally released me, I could see why.

Half of his face was swollen and already bruised, he had a split lip, a cut above his eye and blood dripping from somewhere on his scalp. A white strip of cloth was tied around his arm, already stained with too much blood, and another around his thigh. The fact he was still standing was a miracle.

"Gods," my voice cracked. "Killian, I'm sorry. I'm so fucking sorry—"

"Shhh. Don't. Don't apologise," he murmured, his voice hoarse and broken. "I should be the one atoning for this fucking mess." He kissed the bridge of my nose.

I shook my head, the guilt dripping from both of us was enough to drown in. "You saved me tonight, Killian. You sacrificed yourself to get me out. . ." My voice fractured under the pressure of tears that spilled onto my cheeks.

"You're the one who had to make it out, Alora." He placed his heavy hands on either side of my face.

We could have sat there for hours thanking and apologising, but we'd already overcome enough tonight.

"Then let's really get out of here, Killian," I whispered. "Take me home."

Chapter 27
The Reveal

The flight back to Kevilla was slow.

Bruised and bleeding from holding off the Fallen, Killian was zapped of energy and it showed. His wing beats stuttered and his eyes glazed over while he flew.

"Hey big guy, don't fall asleep on me," I said as we passed the southern edge of the lake, tugging his torn and dirty jacket to focus him.

Killian blinked back the haze sliding over his eyes and hugged me tighter as though he caught himself loosening his grip.

My eyes immediately looked down at the terrain below, judging if I'd survive the fall. We were flying considerably lower than we had on the way there, but I still didn't feel like plummeting to the earth from above the treetops.

"I won't drop you," he slurred when he caught me assessing.

"Yet for some reason, I don't believe you," I teased.

He only grunted in response.

I tried almost everything to help him over the hours we flew. First, I suggested we find somewhere to sleep then fly later, but he wouldn't risk being out in the open in our state. Nor was he interested in having someone else come help, insisting *he* was carrying me home and doing it *now*. He continued to refuse each and every suggestion I made that we stop and rest.

I used all the sarcastic remarks in my arsenal to rouse even a modicum of bite back into his tired state, but they fell on deaf ears. So I tried going all serious along with him, asking him to tell me what had happened, but he ignored that too—which was fair.

His head drooped with exhaustion as he pushed past his limits, all because I couldn't fly myself. So I offered to remove my dress to make his load lighter—pun intended—but he ignored me and continued the rhythmic beating of his wings to carry us home. I was considerably thankful he didn't actually take me up on the offer, because I'm not sure I had the strength to fully commit.

The sun radiated its strength across everything its early light touched when Kevilla came into view. The sight was so welcoming that I nearly wept. It felt like a lifetime since we'd been home, but in truth, it had only been just over a single day. More than twenty-four straight hours awake—no wonder Killian was about to collapse.

Which was exactly what he did when he flew to the grassy patch before the steps of his house.

There was no graceful landing or powerful slam into the earth below—but a struggle to maintain his level, a stumble, then an unceremonious drop to the ground. I caught myself, my bare feet padding into the soft grass as I fell from Killian's hold, then turned to see Killian buckle and drop to his knee. His fists planted heavily on the ground to keep him from going down head first.

Veric was there a moment later, Jude a second behind him. Worry pulled at their expressions as they ran up to us. I didn't miss the sweep over my own condition they each completed before focusing on their Commander.

"He needs a healer. He's lost a lot of blood, and he's exhausted."

The two males stooped to grab Killian under his arms and support his massive frame as they carried him into his house.

Behind us, a flurry of movement told me other warriors sought to complete the task of tracking down the healer.

"What happened?" Veric asked, straining against Killian's weight.

"They knew who I was all along," I told them as they lifted Killian up the stairs and onto his bed. "They set a trap. Killian got me out but he was caught in the struggle. Nephamir cornered me on the bridge, but the Fox came for me before Farro blew Alziros apart to get Killian from the cells."

"Fucking Gods," Veric whispered.

I rubbed my temples and pressed my eyes closed. They were so hard to pry back open.

Veric said something about holding a meeting, but I didn't quite register the words. Then, his blue eyes were right in front of me, his vanilla scent coaxing warmth around my tired frame and his hand rested on my shoulder.

My resolve cracked and tears stung my eyes as I slumped to the floor.

Veric knelt before me. "Hey, you're home now. It's okay."

I squeezed my eyes shut and shook my head. "No, Veric. It's not. Nothing is okay."

His eyes were soft and tender when I looked at him again, which just made me feel worse, and I could tell he wanted to keep trying to make me feel better.

"This is all my fault. It all turned to shit because I was there. They tried to put us in a cell because I was there. Nephamir leapt on the opportunity to take me because I was there."

Jude stood on the other side of the bed beside Killian's limp form, his skin trembling with enough force I could see it from where I sat.

I looked up into Veric's kind face, concern etched into every facet as his gaze flicked between my green and grey irises. I watched his eyes widen as the terrible truth of our reality spilled from my lips.

"I just started a war."

I barely spoke to anyone after I left Killian's room when the healer arrived yesterday. Veric had immediately disappeared to his meetings and I only emerged from my hideaway to check Killian was still alive, but after the fifth time I'd tiptoed into his room within an hour, the healer ordered me to stop worrying and then gave me a tea steeped with herbs that would help me get some rest.

I blinked back the claws of sleep still trying to drag me under its hold the next morning. Jude was stretched out on the bed beside me, fingers linked behind his head as he watched me gulp down the steaming bowl of soup he'd brought.

"Feel better?" he asked when I finished.

"Sort of," I sighed, then placed the bowl on the side table. "Is Killian awake yet? Is he okay?"

"He's okay—just woke up. He's bathing right now. The healer said it was a bloody miracle he even made it back with the injuries he had."

"I tried to stop him, but he wouldn't listen."

"Of course he didn't," he scoffed half-heartedly, but when I didn't laugh at the little jab, Jude bumped me with his shoulder. "Don't blame yourself, Lor."

"How can I not, Jude?" A tear slipped past my defences. "This is all my doing. I was so underprepared. If I hadn't suggested I go in there to get that stone, then—"

"Then Killian still would've been amongst the enemies who always planned on betraying us, except he would've been on his own."

The weight of that thought was heavier than the guilt already on my shoulders.

"Killian wasn't alone though. Farro made sure his brother had others in there with him—others waiting on the outskirts in case it went sideways, too. Farro had the foresight to pre-empt the attack, and we didn't. Killian just had *me*. Useless me."

Pained silence tore at my skin, and Jude's gaze turned sympathetic for just a moment. "Hindsight is the biggest adversary of a warrior, Lor. An impossible beast to defeat unless you can learn from it," he said. "Sure, we could have had a unit ready and waiting on the outskirts, but if the treaty was being honoured properly, and we were found, the Fallen would've seen it as an act of war. We could have sent someone else in with Killian, but the list of possibilities for *who* is small, especially when the intention was to keep things calm. No one else was better equipped than you to go in there with him—to do what needed to be done. Remember that, Alora. Despite the fuckup it turned into, it was still the best-case scenario."

I mulled over his words and tried to let them sink in. They were logical but my sense of regret wouldn't let them settle.

"The Fox was pretty well equipped to be in there with him," I retorted, my mood souring at the memory of Kit and his antics within Alziros.

"That spy is somehow always the exception to any situation." Jude pulled on his lip. "Though, I'm not sure he could have passed off as Killian's date." He laughed, and this time I did join in. Seeing me smile, Jude started bubbling away keeping me in fits of giggles. "Me on the other hand? I'd gladly volunteer for an evening with him if he weren't so terrifying. But, Gods! Have you seen him? I mean you have eyes, right? Could you just imagine—"

It was then that the bedroom door swung open and Veric stepped in, relief washing over his face the instant he saw me.

Relief washed over me, too, that I didn't need to imagine anything about Kit.

I shoved my blankets off and jumped out of bed at the same time he rounded the edge and swung me up into a consuming hug. I'd forgotten how tall he was.

"I'm sorry, I wanted to be here when you woke up, but I couldn't get away from the Hall," Veric said, his words muffled through my hair as he spoke them against my neck.

"I only recently came to," I said against his powder blue shirt. Veric finally released me, setting me gently on my feet, and I paused to look up at his kind face.

He looked so handsome. His summer-blue eyes glittered in the bright sunshine streaming in from outside, highlighted further by the colour of his shirt. I just hoped they didn't turn sad and betrayed when I told him the secret I'd been keeping all these weeks.

But time was well and truly up on that—I had a promise to keep.

"How are you feeling?"

"Shitty, but not for the reason you might think."

"I've been in meetings all morning and heard Killian was awake, so I came as soon as I could."

"I'm glad you're here now." I grabbed his hand. "I need to fill you in on everything."

"We've already received word from someone in Astorla detailing how they breached Alziros at the end, what happened with you on the bridge, Killian in the cell, and how everyone got you out. It's mostly all in hand. Though it'd be good to know what happened before things turned to shit, but we can wait for Killian."

"Wait no longer," the deep voice murmured from the door. Veric's face lit up with a smile at seeing Killian safe and well then crossed the room to pull him into a crushing hug. The brothers-in-arms slapped each other on their backs in a male display of affection. Killian turned his vivid eyes on me and we passed a silent exchange.

You're okay, I'm okay, thank you, we made it.

He was still sporting a fat lip, a bruised cheek, and the top of his left arm and leg were wrapped in fresh bandages, but it was a huge improvement from how he looked when he'd gotten us back.

"Alora was about to give us the inside scoop on what happened in Alziros," Jude chirped from his spot on the bed.

"Actually, there's something I need to tell you before we get into all that," I said, looking at Veric, and the mood stilled.

"About what you learned in Carault. . ." he surmised.

Veric took a step closer to me but stopped when the next shaking words left my mouth. "I did learn a lot of truths up there, Veric. About how I'm tied to all this, and a deep well of other secrets—but what I need to tell you. . . I learned before I went to the Winter Palace." My voice cracked. "And it's time you learned the truth."

Tears spilled down my cheeks, and I didn't know if my body could take being stabbed with any more guilt than it had already taken. "Part of it I learned the day I arrived in Endence, when Orella brought me here, and the other part, the day I arrived in Kevilla. And I've had to keep what I learned secret until I figured out why I've been brought here."

Jude sat up and placed his feet on the floor as if he was bracing himself. Veric still hadn't moved.

I cleared my voice. "You both know that my father was the one who trained me to fight." They both nodded, though I never stopped looking at Veric. "What I didn't tell you, was when I awoke from transitioning, I found out that Caldwell is not my biological father."

No one in the room moved or spoke, or so much as breathed as the truth finally poured out.

"I know this because I was told my mother was devoted to her moiety."

"Moiety," Jude gasped then looked at Veric and Killian as if to check they were hearing the same words.

"And I only found out my father's name when Queen Fleur told me about him the day I arrived in Endence."

"What *is* his name?" Veric asked, his words barely more than a whisper.

A single, unbidden tear rolled down my cheek. "Valefor."

The breath that Veric inhaled was shaky and silent. He remained as still as stone, but as soon as the truth passed my lips, his eyes flicked over my features. As if he could see my face clearly for the first time—all the similarities between us that finally made sense to him.

Jude slapped a hand across his open mouth as he stood from the bed. "Alora, you're—"

"I'm Eira and Valefor's daughter."

"—the heir."

"My cousin," Veric said, his eyes still searching my face while he made sense of it all.

I let out a sigh of relief that there was no hurt in his eyes like there had been the week before when he found out we'd kept secrets from him.

But as soon as the breath was out, and I was hopeful the moment between us would lighten, Veric's expression turned venomous.

I blanched at his expression and the hatred that boiled beneath his skin.

His brows lowered, his eyes lost their summer shine, and his lips curled into a snarl. "You fucking bastard," he rumbled in a low threat.

Not at me—but at Killian—who didn't have time to react before Veric sifted in front of him and slammed his fist into his left cheek.

Jude moved with lightning efficiency around the bed to get between the two males, but Veric threw his hand out, and a wave of power blew through the room strong enough that it was a clear warning not to intervene.

But Killian just rubbed his turned cheek, then let out a rough laugh, as though, above all else, he was impressed with the hit Veric had managed to land on him.

"You get that one free shot, Veric. For the truth about your princess we've held onto," Killian said, a statement that told everyone in the room the fight wouldn't go any further as he straightened to look at his general. "But it was necessary—"

Smack. Veric's fist collided with the right side of Killian's face in another punishing blow that Killian didn't anticipate.

My hand flew to my mouth in shock while Jude grabbed my other. I couldn't tell if the little squeeze he gave me was one of comfort that it would all be okay, or of warning that we'd need to duck and cover any second.

"I don't give a fuck about the title you prick," Veric roared to the now hunched Killian. "You let my fucking cousin go into Alziros without me."

Surprise hit me at what Veric was really saying. He wasn't angry about being lied to—he was angry he hadn't been there to help me.

A strange feeling flooded my veins at the sight of him standing over his commander and friend, ready to beat the shit out of him.

"She's my fucking cousin, Killian." But the fight had left him. He looked at me and his voice broke. "She's my fucking cousin. . ."

In the same instant, we moved and crossed the floorboards to get at one another. This time, the way he held onto me was more.

The way I held him back was more.

More fierce. More consuming. More important.

Tears flooded down both our faces and emotion washed over us as we cried and laughed at finally having found the other.

He pulled back and brushed his hands across my cheeks, smoothing back the strands of hair that had stuck against my skin under my tears.

"Gods, it's so damn obvious. Look at you. I can't believe I never saw it." His expression was nothing but amazement and fondness—and love.

"Erela was far more observant." I laughed. "I'm sorry I didn't tell you sooner."

He shook his head, silently telling me the apology was unnecessary. "I understand why, your majesty," he said with slow reverence as he lowered onto his knee with his head bowed and fist over his heart.

Jude followed his lead. Killian shot me a bemused look from the doorway now that he'd recovered, but he also dipped his head in a shallow bow.

I was taken aback by all three males bowing to me in the confines of the bedroom, which now felt increasingly cramped.

My hands gripped Veric's shoulders and I gently beckoned him to stand. "You don't bow," I said to him. "Or you," I repeated, turning to Jude, and only continued when they were both on their feet. "You don't bow. I'm just Alora to you. Promise me, knowing I'm supposed to be your heir doesn't change anything between us."

A gentle smile curled Veric's lips. "Knowing you're my princess doesn't change anything," he promised then paused to grab my hands. "Knowing you're my family changes everything."

Veric and I spent the middle of the day by the lake. Together, we laid in the sun, our matching champagne hair resting in the grass with lightly freckled faces tipped to the sky as he recalled everything he could think of about my parents. Our cream and pearl wings brushed against the other's as I listened to the warm tenor of his voice relive his happiest moments.

I told him more about Della, and he promised to sneak us to the human realm so we could visit her. By mid-afternoon, my eyes were tired from all our laughing and crying.

Jude stopped by to check on us, but only long enough for me to explain the importance of keeping my identity secret. I would reveal my title when the time was right—and at the brink of war, when their chain of commands were established, now wasn't it.

Not that they needed to be told. I knew the two males before me could be trusted not only with my secrets, but with my life.

In the late afternoon, Veric and I walked together into Kevilla from the lake. The entire legion had been called in from the Kingdom to make preparations, and already warriors were arriving.

I marked every face I laid eyes on.

Despite still standing beneath the wings of those who so diligently ran my Kingdom in my stead, these fae were *my* subjects. My responsibility. And I would make every effort to ensure they were prepared for this war. Starting with making sure I was ready to fight alongside them through every hurdle.

I still wasn't skilled enough to go up against the angels, and I still couldn't control my magic fully. I was a fae from the royal line, one of the cleaved, and had been trained for years by Caldwell before being instructed by some of the most powerful fae in Endence. Yet despite all this, I still wasn't close enough to be of worth in this upcoming war.

And that needed to change.

Veric led the way into the hall where crowds of fae were already gathering to eat and drink the night away.

I was worried that the Winter Legion wasn't moving quick enough to get organised before the angels retaliated and a full-blown battle broke out, but Veric reassured me that Farro and his unit had blown a hole so deep—not only into Alziros, but into their attempts at sneaking around—that they posed no imminent threat.

He was amused by my *human way of thinking,* as he put it and explained that wars moved much slower when you have the benefit of a thousand-year lifespan on your side to plot your attacks.

With my anxiety of being stabbed during dinner placated, I was able to settle and decided to enjoy the evening with fewer burdens weighing me down.

Luckily, my favourite drinking buddy was already set and waiting with his unit when Veric and I walked up. Killian sat amongst the group too, his standard brooding expression plastered on his face.

His body perked as Veric and I walked over. He and I were yet to talk about everything that happened in Alziros—hell, we hadn't even talked about everything that happened in Carault, so I was itching to get him alone for a few different reasons.

After casting his gaze over me, he looked at Veric warily, like he was gauging whether he'd be on the receiving end of one of his punches again—but pulled a look of superiority as though silently telling Veric he wouldn't let another hit go unanswered.

But Veric stepped straight up to Killian and they reached out together, grasping their hands on the other's forearms then nodded in that purely male way that conveyed they'd just had an entire conversation without speaking a single word.

I marvelled at the simplicity of males, and their lack of need to rattle off their every thought as I rolled my eyes and snatched the proffered glass of wine Jude held out for me.

I was about to throw my head back and gulp down at least a third of the smooth nectar when Lyra peeked out from behind Killian and joked loudly with the other members of Jude's unit, drawing my attention.

She leant over to pluck a buttered roll from the centre of the food-laden table, her cleavage on full display as she bent.

I dropped my glass with a crowd-silencing shatter.

Everyone at the table froze and looked at me—though Jude's eyes went to the wasted wine splattered over my boots first.

A few of the surrounding tables stopped to take in the drama. A crowd of loud fae in the distance just let out a raucous cheer at whoever was already drunk enough to be breaking glasses.

But Lyra was the one who had my eyes locked on her cleavage, and so was the one who snapped me out of my plummeting thoughts first. "You okay there, Alora?" she asked. Not unkindly, but she certainly wanted an explanation why I couldn't stop staring at her tits.

"Your tattoo," I said, and every set of eyes at the table swung to Lyra's chest along with mine.

Whoops.

"What of it?" she asked with a bemused smile and stood so she wasn't displaying herself anymore, smoothly backhanding one of her legionnaires who murmured a disgusting joke under his breath.

The memory of the first time I'd met Lyra resurfaced.

The tale she'd told of Evander who wielded Strike, the legendary star-shaped javelin, and how she had a mark tattooed above her heart in recognition of the weapon he had used.

A four-pointed star.

"Killian, that mark. . ."

It took him only another moment to understand.

It was the spell mark in the back of the book. Evander's mark. The mark of Strike, the Immortal Weapon of Ruasis.

I turned and threw myself between bodies to the exit as Killian scraped his chair back and rumbled an instruction to *stay here*, no doubt aimed at Veric and Jude.

I ran out of the hall—clawing my way out of the crowded space.

I blew through the front door of Killian's house, took the stairs two at a time, rounded the door into my room then pulled out my stowed bag from under the bed containing the books from the Winter Palace.

Killian lunged through the door right as I pulled out the ancient tome, then flicked to the back of it where the prophecy was etched, right above a swirling gold symbol that only I could see.

"It's the same mark. I knew I'd seen it before, I just didn't think it was from looking at Lyra's chest."

Killian sat at the edge of the bed next to where I knelt.

"He had one of the Immortal Weapons. . . but what does Evander have to do with Noteas and Lilla returning?"

"It's not about Evander though," Killian interjected. "It's about you. Someone left that mark for you to uncover. So the question is, what do *you* have to do with Evander?"

I didn't have an answer for that.

"Well, your mother said either blood or a word would do the trick. Blood didn't do anything, so here goes nothing." I closed my eyes then drew in a breath as I lifted the book closer to my face. "Evander," I said softly against its golden swirls.

Nothing.

I pulled my lips into a thin line as I thought.

"Untouchable Warrior."

Also nothing.

"Ruasis. Strike."

Still no change.

"Maybe it's for my eyes only," I thought aloud, then pointed my finger at the door. "Get out."

But the dark fae just laughed as he pulled me off the floor. "Or maybe you chased the wrong thread, Princess."

I dropped the book onto the bed next to him, then dropped my head onto his shoulder and pouted. "I thought I was onto something."

"Everything will reveal itself in time, Alora. We will figure this out. At any rate, I'm glad I got you alone," he said after a pause, and I lifted my head to look at him.

I smiled. "Me too. . . how's your face?"

"Not as bruised as my ego is that I didn't pre-empt the second hit," he said laughing.

No sympathy then.

"When Erela found out who you were at the Winter Palace, I asked you something."

"I remember."

"Same question."

'How does it feel?'

"Incredible." I smiled. "Having my own set of *people*. . . it's. . ." I searched for the right words. "Beyond important. Finding out I have family here has been more significant to me than finding out I have a crown. Now, there's just one more to find."

"Everything will reveal itself in time," he repeated, then captured my lips against his with a tender kiss.

I pulled back from him and looked into his fiery-blue eyes and saw so much burning back at me. We had so much to tell the other.

"Killian, about Alziros–"

"I don't want to go around and around apologising and wishing we'd done things differently, Princess. We just need to make sure we never find ourselves in that predicament again."

"I know. Jude said that much to me this morning as well," I said, then stood, grabbed the book from the bed and walked it over to the dresser against the wall. "But I wanted to thank you for risking your life to save me. I guess that's two life debts I owe you now."

I cringed at how big my tally already was.

"You're no damsel, Princess. You weren't in need of saving–you were in need of escape. Jude was right with his assessment. . . when you have magic and can fly, you'll be a reckoning."

"Yes, well those are the next jobs on the list." I crossed my ankles as I leant back against the dresser.

"Not getting the stone? It was all for nothing if we don't have it."

"We do have it."

Killian angled his head in question. "You said–"

"It was in Nephamir's chambers, just like you thought, but Kit stole it off me right after I made my way back."

Killian twitched. "He told you his name?"

"He said I might as well know it if I was going to yell at him."

He huffed a laugh. "He usually tells others to say a final prayer to the Gods, not his name, but tell me why I'm not surprised you yelled at him?" He let a long exhale loose then ran his hand down his face with frustration. "Okay. Well, in the grand scheme of things, it's significantly better than the Fallen having it. . . but if Kit has the stone, it's as good as gone."

But my shit-eating grin, haughty enough to rival even that of the spy himself, was plastered to my face. It grew even further when Killian narrowed his eyes at me.

"Did Veric tell you the only magic I'd managed to pull off before leaving for Alziros was making a pebble disappear?"

Killian dropped his hand as realisation dawned.

I flicked my wrist, and a familiar, smooth weight filled the palm of my hand. I lowered my slender fingers to reveal the churning, emerald-green gem radiating its gentle glow into the room.

"Kit might be the spy, but I'm the thief," I said with smug indifference.

"You—" he whispered as he got to his feet, "brilliant, fucking, female," he let out in time with the three strides he took to cross the floorboards. He lifted me beneath my thighs and I wrapped them around him as he pressed a punishing kiss to my lips.

A rewarding kiss.

His tongue swept against mine as he held me, kissing me thoroughly. He broke away laughing as he looked down at Rharuer's Stone, still wrapped in my hand.

Killian pushed his weight into me, keeping me pinned against the dresser by his body, and I dropped the stone into his waiting palm. He lifted it between us and we surveyed it, marvelling at its beauty.

Rharuer's Stone truly was the most remarkable thing to watch. A galaxy of a God's power, held within the smooth, glistening surface.

Killian wrapped his fingers around it, clinging tightly as though it might vanish without being locked in a vice grip. Then he turned his attention back on me.

Still wrapped around his centre, Killian rubbed his thumbs along the tops of my thighs and ground his hips into me, pushing me harder into the dresser at my back. I let out a gasp at the indecent move, the pool of warmth it immediately brought out at my core.

"I vaguely remember you making some sort of offer to remove your clothes for my benefit," he growled, then captured my bottom lip between his teeth, canines pinching.

I snickered and decided to play along. "I'm sure we could think of a way to both benefit from having my clothes removed." My voice was low and husky, lust blatantly coating my words, but I didn't care.

Killian and I had danced this tune before, and I wanted to complete the steps this time.

His free hand came up and held onto my jaw, angling me just right, so he could take me however he wanted—but he didn't kiss me. He positioned his mouth so that the slightest movement would have us pressed against each other, then spoke with calm authority. "What did I tell you about saying *please*?"

A whimper escaped my lips before I could stop myself, but Killian swallowed it as he claimed my mouth. We captured each other's breaths and groans as our hands and tongues swept across the other's.

He pushed his hips against mine again, and this time, his hardened length stroked against my centre. The desire to have it driving into me instead, nearly sent me climaxing right then and there as Killian continued to grind against me.

I grabbed at his shirt, trying to get my hands between us so I could rip it off. I pushed my back against the dresser to suggest he should step back and head toward the bed, but Killian planted his weight, seeming intent on remaining where he stood so he could control the exchange right where we were—where he was able to kiss and touch all that he wanted.

On second thought, here works fine.

Killian released my jaw then dropped his hand to cup my breast over my shirt and released a curse.

I threw my head back as he toyed with my body, and a wicked sensation pulled in my belly, making me grow hotter by the second—as though the room had caught fire from the heat of our steamy exchange.

But a smooth voice from the doorway cut through every exhaled breath and pant echoing in the room with lethal rage.

"I hate to interrupt, Killian," the male voice sliced like a blade, "but you seem to be holding something of mine."

Killian startled and dropped me as if I were a sack of stolen goods. He drew his blade and aimed it at the intruder, his power rising to build around us like a thick wall.

But the pressure of his magic faltered when he saw who it was.

I landed with a grunt, barely getting my legs underneath me in time to catch my fall. My recovery was almost as unceremonious as the drop.

"Get the fuck out of my house," Killian threatened while he moved his other hand behind his leg, as though he hadn't already been caught with the stone.

Kit leant against the doorframe a moment longer, contemplating whether he wanted to enact on the violence that gleamed in his emerald-green eyes. But he blinked, and it was gone, smooth and refined poise washing over him as he straightened then stepped into the room. His midnight wings relaxed as he lazily strolled up to Killian.

"Gladly, General." He held out his hand. "As soon as I have what I came for."

I stepped around Killian's wing to slap Kit's hand away, insults ready to fly, but fast as a whip, Kit snatched my hand before it made contact, and held it in his tight grip. Slowly, those green eyes slid to mine and he clicked his tongue with superior disapproval, each *tsk* a telling-off.

"It would appear you're also capable of undoing me with your *hands* as well as your mouth, Treasure," he purred and let go of me when I yanked away.

I bared my teeth at him and the act sent him smirking.

He tipped his palm back out, waiting for the stone to be deposited.

Killian let a brutal growl resonate across the room, and I thought he was going to tear Kit's throat out. He certainly looked like he wanted to.

Kit just kept that shit-eating grin plastered like he welcomed the challenge. As though he'd relish it if Killian made that first move.

To my horror, Killian didn't unleash his rage, but instead placed Rharuer's Stone in the centre of Kit's waiting palm, letting out another feral growl.

"That's a good boy," Kit crooned like he was rewarding a loyal dog, then turned to walk away before Killian could beat the shit out of him.

"You have what you want, now get the fuck out," I threatened. I couldn't stand the sight of the smug bastard any longer.

"Ah," he paused me with the lift of his finger. "See, that's where you're wrong."

Instead of leaving like I thought he was going to do, Kit sauntered over to the armchair in the corner, flopped down in it like he owned the place, rested one leg on his knee then conjured himself a glass of liquor.

He swirled it as he spoke. "I told you, I'd leave when I had what I came for, and I only have half of the things on my list."

A terrible feeling washed over me that I didn't want to know what the other item was.

"It was a neat little trick you managed to pull off, Treasure. It's been an age since a fae has managed to get the upper hand on me," he said around a sip, ignoring the vehemence dripping from Killian and I.

I bared my teeth at the nickname.

"So colour me surprised, when I checked my pockets after saving your life, only to find my Treasure had stolen my little treasure." He pouted. "More disappointed than surprised, if I'm honest. When I fantasised about your hands sliding all over my body, I was aware of it happening at the time."

This time *I* let a growl rip through the room, but he snapped his teeth at me playfully, as though my reactions fuelled him.

"I'm not your anything," I seethed.

He took another casual sip of his drink, smacking his lips together before he lifted his eyes back on me. "Wrong again, Treasure."

My wings twitched as I waited for him to explain—as Killian's temper pushed toward boiling point.

"From this moment, you're now my responsibility."

Cold dread seeped down my spine. "How do you figure that?"

"Because before you two lovebirds flew off into the sunrise the other night, I found the real hidden treasure hiding away in Alziros."

Killian stilled and even I couldn't help myself from hanging on the edge of his words.

"Coalescing from his nice, warm, ten-thousand-year holiday in solitary confinement—resting and healing with every resource those degenerate ducks can get their hands on, is none other than the big baddie himself."

No.

"You lie," I breathed, looking him up and down as he lounged back in the armchair, unfazed by the terrible information.

"You're sure?" Killian whispered like he was too afraid to speak any louder.

I was shocked that Killian believed the male immediately.

"Saw with my own eyes," Kit replied, with no humour in his voice. "Noteas has been freed from the sun."

Silence fell between us all, and I realised then. "The eclipse. . ."

Killian shot Kit a look but I ignored them—my thoughts were too consuming.

"How he got here doesn't matter—what is important is that I get exactly what I came for, so we can all get ready for one hell of a fight."

I glared at him. "What else have you come to claim as yours?"

A gleam flashed across his eyes—lit from within as he smiled. "What an interesting choice of words, Treasure."

I glared. "I have no time for your shit-stirring, spy. What do you want?"

"You."

I scoffed. "You're more deranged than I thought if you think I'm going anywhere with you, especially with Noteas freed. I need to be here. In my Kingdom. Helping my legion." I folded my arms over my chest with determination.

"And here I thought you wanted nothing more than to see Orella," he sighed with fake exasperation.

I tried to school my reaction, but my traitorous ears perked and he saw it. The wink he gave made my lip curl in a snarl.

"To find all the explanations to your unanswered questions. To wield your magic. Learn to fly. *Lead* your legion—not just help it."

I needed all of those things, and he knew it—knew the exact words to say.

"You won't get to Orella with the brooding bat you're keeping around, Treasure," he said, gesturing at Killian, who took a single step forward with his fist clenched. He halted with a single arched brow from Kit. "You won't get any of it if you stay here."

Veins in Killian's neck bulged, and I was afraid they'd burst as he growled. "What the fuck are you insinuating?"

"Apologies, I thought I was being clear. . . You are not enough, Killian."

Killian roared then sifted across the room to stand over the still-sitting spy.

Kit didn't even flinch—just took another slow sip of the amber liquid, then stood. Killian didn't give an inch, so Kit slowly rose as though he was crawling up the enormous male.

Despite not being taller or wider than Killian, somehow the spy still managed to look down at him as he spoke. "You were chosen by your queen for your skills to train Alora. But it was clear from Alziros, that the only thing you've managed to teach the princess in all her time here is how to get herself caught."

I bristled along with Killian, but neither of us spoke.

"You've been released from your duties in this regard, General. I'll take it from here." He moved toward the door.

A nasty telling-off and unpleasant dismissal if ever I heard one.

"On whose orders?" Killian barked at his back.

"You already know the answer to that," the spy said over his shoulder as he paused on the threshold. I recognised the repeated phrase Killian gave to Kit back in Elden.

"Tell Farro to go fuck himself," Killian seethed, then his harsh power rose and pressed in around the room in preparation to attack.

But as soon as the heavy weight of magic crushed against my chest, it was gone. Replaced by a wash of dark, threatening power that rolled and ebbed against my skin.

I sprung my eyes open, not having realised I'd shut them in the first place, only to find Killian straining against an invisible force like he was struggling for breath. His power snuffed out within the time it took to blink.

I knew who the power belonged to. Had sensed it in its ultimate form on that bridge. But Kit didn't even look like he was doing anything other than standing in the doorway—though in reality he was pressing in on and restraining one of the most powerful fae in the realm.

Kit's face was a cool wash of calm, but something lethal shone behind those green irises. "I'm sure he already frequently does fuck himself, General. Just as I'm sure it will now be your new reality without your pretty pet to warm you."

Killian slammed to his knees, and I screamed out his name. Screamed for Kit to stop, but he ignored me.

The disrespectful message Killian had barked for his brother was not only offensive to his family but insubordinate to his own commander.

Kit took two casual strides over to Killian then bent at his waist to loom over the struggling general and whispered at him. "Now, if you'd like to sort it out with Farro himself, that can be arranged, Killian. I'll fetch him for you right now. But either way—I won't be leaving without Alora."

Killian's whole body shook.

I didn't know if it was from pain at whatever Kit's magic was doing to him, or if Killian was fighting Kit's hold. Either way, I hated the way he looked small. Hated the way his veins throbbed and his skin turned purple.

A strange, strained whimper sounded from his throat that sounded like he was reaching his limit.

"Stop it," I demanded. But the two males continued their stare off as their hatred bled into the room.

"Kit, please," I pleaded.

He looked at me. His eyes landed on my green and in an instant, he let Killian go.

Killian fell forward, catching himself as he threw out his palm, coughing and heaving in gulping breaths.

I wanted to rage at the spy, but seeing Killian reduced to a simpering puppet made me pause. Kit was too powerful. Too consuming. And if this was how he treated the general from his own Kingdom, who he'd known for hundreds of years, then how was I going to fare if I tried anything?

Then a different kind of rage hit me. Once again, the realisation of how useless and unable to help I was resurfaced. And just like that, the roaring, fiery violence churning within me was snuffed out. Consuming responsibility, and a sense of failure washed away the flames.

I'd been failing this entire time. Barely scraping past the trials that had been placed in front of me, and hadn't once been able to complete them on my own merit. I'd not once been as strong as I needed to be. Not once able to wield my power the way I desired.

Like it or not, Kit was right. Not about all of it. Killian hadn't let me down.

I had.

I had failed myself. And all the things I wanted—needed—to have in my arsenal—the strength and abilities I needed to gain, the answers only

Orella could provide. . . I wouldn't get any of them here. And if I wasn't powerful enough, then I would be useless in this war. Useless to lead and protect my Kingdom—to protect my family in Evamere if this war spread to them.

The fight left me in a released breath. "I'll go with you," I whispered, but the words rang like a knell through the room.

Kit stood tall and slid his hands into his pockets, surprise sweeping across his features. "I expected more of a fight from you, Treasure."

"Well, we can't all get what we want now, can we, Kit?"

He smirked, and his eyes dipped to my lips. "I think *I* just did."

But I didn't have the energy to rise to his taunt. Now that the failure had washed away my anger, all I was left with was crushing emptiness.

I think Kit could see the damage beneath my eyes because he didn't provoke any further. "I'll meet you out the front," he murmured, then left the room as silently as he'd entered.

Tears welled in my eyes as I dropped to my knees in front of Killian, but he wouldn't meet my gaze. I clasped the sides of his face, forcing him to look at me.

His broken expression nearly tore me in half.

"I don't blame you, Killian. Don't hold yourself responsible," I urged, wanting to make sure he heard the truth in the words. "But that doesn't mean he isn't right about the rest of it."

Killian winced.

"I nearly jeopardised the future of this entire realm with my naivety. I won't be responsible for the deaths of my subjects without ensuring I did everything I could to protect them in the first place. Caldwell trained me my entire life so I'd never be outmatched by an adversary. And since coming to Endence, I haven't come across a single one I *could* defeat." Killian hung his head lower as I spoke, but I pulled his head up again. "I need to change that truth—and I need to know Orella's."

I leant forward and pressed a slow kiss against his damp forehead. The sweat from the invisible attack of Kit's magic dripped from his temples.

On silent feet, I picked up the bag stashed under my bed, stuffed an outfit in, along with the book still sitting on the dresser, then strapped my daggers to my thighs. Thighs that still burned with the struggle to keep hooked around Killian as he kissed and grabbed at me only minutes ago.

Killian still hadn't moved. He'd been crushed in a way that ran deeper than I fully understood—I could see that. And no stalling or reassurances from me were going to help him out of it.

I paced down the stairs and straight out the door, finding Kit standing with his back to me, his hands still in his pockets and his face tipped up at the night sky.

Sensing my approach, he stepped back in a half-turn to look at me. His face held no sign of his usual predatory look—but instead, was more cautionary. As though he knew he'd stepped over a line. But because it'd been necessary, it was the most remorseful look I was going to get.

Yet even still, that shine in his eyes held a flicker of accomplishment.

'Well, we can't all get what we want now, can we, Kit?'

'I think I just did.'

He curled his wing around me as I stepped against his side. I tucked mine in so they didn't brush then shoved my bag against his chest with a satisfying thump.

Kit tilted his head like he was silently asking if that had been completely necessary. He tossed the bag into the air at head height and flicked his wrist as it ascended, making it vanish to that far-off hidden space where all things went and all things waited to be called upon.

Then a wry smile spread across that devilish face as he pulled Rharuer's Stone from his pocket between us. The soft green glow lit the space between our chests, casting light on the three eyes of the exact same shade that looked down at it. Then he turned his hand over and waved it through the air like a magician performing a trick for children, and the glow was gone—tucked away in that same secret space.

"Lest you get any ideas, thief," he purred down at me in a tease.

"Stop toying, Kit," I murmured at the ground, my sense of crushing defeat weighing on my voice.

He slid his warm hand under my jaw, then curled his finger, urging me to look up at him. I let him tilt my face up, but I didn't meet his eyes. Even so, I could see a shadow pass over his expression as he looked at me.

"I was harsh in there, but I don't apologise for it, Alora. I meant what I said in Alziros—you should have been more than capable of going up against them, and you weren't." His dark voice slid over my skin. "News that Noteas has been freed moves up our timeline. Now. . . he's not stupid enough to show his face anytime soon, but we don't have time to fuck around and find out if ten-thousand years has done anything to curb his ambition. We have the advantage that we know exactly what they're after, so we need to stop this fucking mess before they figure out how to get Lilla back."

I kept my eyes trained on the ground.

Fuck him for making sense.

"You know what you need to do to prepare for this—to survive this. And there is only one other fae in this realm more capable of giving you what you need than I am, Alora."

My control snapped and I glared at him. "And when will the mighty Farro deem me important enough to come down from his pedestal to give me a helping hand?"

Kit's smile turned gentle. "Not Farro, Alora. You," he said, and the weight of that realisation hit me harder than the weight of failure I was already being crushed by.

A tear fell from my eye, hitting my shoe with a splash like it, too, was heavier than the single drop.

But the silence was broken by another voice across the darkness coming to tear me further apart.

"Alora?"

"Veric," I sighed with relief when I saw my cousin jog toward me, followed by Jude.

His face went from curious to concerned when he saw my pained expression. Saw who I stood next to.

"What's going on? What are you doing here, Fox?"

The voice that crooned across to them was the unflappable mask of the spy they all knew and feared. "Your queen and I have some business to take care of together."

How he already knew that Veric and Jude were in on the secret was frightening, but the two males weren't thrown by it.

In unison, their expression darkened and their wings flared. "Like fuck you do," Veric growled and his magic pulsed.

Kit giggled.

"It's okay, Veric," I said, but my voice shook and he stepped up to me. "I have to go."

For the third time today, Veric and I held onto one another. Jude squeezed my hand from where it was curled against his neck.

After whispering my reassurance in him to lead our legion, I let go then stepped back to Kit, who wasted no time snaking his arm around my waist.

Veric snarled again, this time braving the gap, and smacked his vice grip down on Kit's wrist.

My eyes flared at the move, and fear ripped through me at what Kit might do against him. But he didn't move. He dipped his gaze to the offending hand then lifted it back to Veric, a questioning arch to his brows.

"If my cousin comes to any harm—"

"Yes, yes. You're very scary, General. Threat received," Kit said in a bored monotone. "Now remove your hand, before *I* remove *it*." The implication that the removal would be of the permanent variety wasn't lost on any of us.

A tremor made my skin prickle at the gruesome memory of the severed hand he shoved into the hulking angel's mouth and made me queasy.

Veric snatched his hand away. There was nothing he could do to stop this.

Kit hitched me flush against his lean body. Every aspect of his melded into the darkness that clung around him. All except those green eyes and his ruffled red hair. "Shall we, Treasure?" he purred against my skin.

Jude stepped forward like he wanted to reach out and stop us, but Kit's glare turned dark and lethal. "Follow us, and you lose the wings that carried you into the air," he promised.

His midnight wings stretched wide, and he curled his other hand under my knees, holding me tightly against his chest.

The first thing on my list is to learn to fucking fly, so I can stop being hauled around like a saddlebag.

I shut my eyes against the incoming wind that was about to cut at us. Remembering the lightning speed he could reach made me tuck my head in further against his chest and draw in a shaking breath. His smooth and spicy scent slid down my throat and swept itself around my body as I clung to him.

With a giant sweep of his wings, we rose into the air with more gentleness than I anticipated. But as we came level with the rooftops another sound boomed above the steady beat coming from Kit's wings.

And then the owner of the sound burst through the door of his house.

"Alora!" Killian roared, his voice reaching up to me along with his heavy power pulsing into the air. His burning, blue eyes locked onto me as I rose higher.

"Killian," I called out, but the sound was barely past my lips when Kit threw his wings out and shot us into the night.

I kept my eyes trained over Kit's shoulders as the lights of Kevilla grew smaller by the second, waiting to see Killian's dark shadow in the distance.

"He won't be coming after you, Treasure," Kit murmured in my ear.

"You don't know that."

"Oh, but I do." His voice was sinful and smooth like smoke. I pulled back to look at him, and his green eyes burned into mine. "No one gets in the way of what I want."

I blanched at the darkness that shone behind his eyes.

"You're all mine now."

Epilogue
The Moiety

Pain, like I've never known, pierces my body constantly.

At first, it was gentle awareness that thrummed in my chest.

There was no question who she was when I laid eyes on her—no denying the desire to have her close.

But I am too selfish to not consume her body and soul while she rises to the trials that face her. Too weak to be vulnerable and not fall at her feet.

So I stayed distant. Put up the facade. Didn't let her see.

But now I've paid the toll, and the pull to her has changed.

There is nothing gentle in the way I need.

Now—I crave her.

That fucking mess in Alziros has sent me over the edge. I'm amongst the list of guilty who failed her that night, and my soul screams at me to unite itself and protect her.

But *he* thinks he has some fucking claim on her.

His posturing sets my possessive nature so fucking wild, that I might just damn the consequences and kill him.

That is, as long as she doesn't kill me first.

Alora's going to fucking lose it when she finds out it's me.

Acknowledgements

It feels surreal that after years and years of having this story bubble away in my head, then months and months of writing, followed by months and months of editing, that I now have a book in need of an acknowledgements page. Not a notion that only exists in my mind, not mindless scribblings written in a journal, not countless Google docs leading nowhere, but an actual, real-life, completed book.

First and foremost, I'd like to thank the beta readers who offered their time and dedication to reading this. Whether it was a portion, or a chapter, the whole thing or just the blurb, I went into this project a complete novice and have come out of it the other hand with a wealth of knowledge thanks to those fantastic people, so thank you.

In particular, my thanks goes out to Margaret, my grammar guru. The countless hours you spent as well as the learning you imparted upon me is priceless, and I cannot thank you enough.

To my editor, Emily Marquart–thank you for your keen eye and the critical feedback you provided that transformed this book into something I am so incredibly proud of. You have given such brilliant insights into this little world I've created and I'm so grateful to have found you.

To the team at MiblArt for creating the most incredible cover art and making this story look as captivating as I dreamed it would be. You're the best!

The biggest thanks of all goes to my big sister, Bec. You've always been the person I looked to in many areas of life, and it was your love of reading that inspired my own. And without my love of reading, I wouldn't have developed a passion for writing. Thank you for introducing me to books–for reading me stories like the Magic Faraway Tree, The Adventures of the Wishing-Chair, Harry Potter and so many others when I was little. And for more recently, always willing to chat about the smuttiest, dirtiest books we can get our hands on! Specifically, thank you for your help with this book. Giving me your honest opinion of, "it wasn't shit," was really touching, and gave me the confidence I needed to keep going! Haha!

My three brilliant kids, Alexander, April and Oliver, who are truly some of the most impressive humans I've met, my heart belongs to you. No matter what I accomplish in life, you three will forever be my greatest achievement. I love you all endlessly.

And finally, to my husband, Brendan—my biggest supporter in life. Thank you for being an incredible dad to our three magnificent kids and for encouraging me to grab hold of this dream, especially when I was feeling silly for it. You are my moiety in this world, I felt it as soon as we met, and I couldn't do life without you. I love you, Bear

About The Author

Krichelle Parke is an emerging Australian author with a passion for fantasy stories. Her love of fae, magic, incredible lands of unending possibility and steamy, slow-burn tales with fated mates, morally grey love interests and enemies to lovers' tropes has guided her reading journey—and has had a direct hand in taking her down this new adventure of writing.

Follow Krichelle on social media for all updates on her upcoming work.

@KrichelleParke on Twitter

@K.M.Parke on TikTok and Instagram

Alora's journey continues in the next gripping instalment

There are several things Alora knows–
The prophecy is fulfilling
Noteas is back
Lilla is coming
Orella is waiting
Hum is hidden
War is looming
And Kit is driving her fucking mental.

But what she doesn't know, is that her moiety is ready to claim her.

Designed by Destiny
Book Two

Coming soon

It took less than an hour to reach Orril's Gate—a great, open archway several storeys tall that looked like it was made of pearl and gleaming with gold filigree. We were met by three sentinels, impeccably dressed and crowned with gold circlets, armed with spears and serious expressions. They were each a force unto themselves, with matching, impressive, white wings.

One stepped forward and held his palm out, signalling to stop.

He spoke with the authority of a king. "Only those deemed of worth may enter Orril. Who be you to consider yourselves of true honour and deserving enough to tread within Orella's sacred haven?"

"I protect Orella's chosen," Kit replied with equal command.

All three guards flicked their gaze to me and widened it at what they saw.

I guess I shouldn't be surprised Orella's sentinels know who I am.

"Alora seeks Orella's trials in judgement for an audience. Who be deemed of worth to enter, if not her?"

"Very well, Alora, she who was chosen. You may enter Orril and face trial."

Fucking ominous. . .

The guard's gaze locked on Kit. "Who be you, to be deemed of worth to protect such a fae and be blessed to enter with her?"

Kit didn't falter. "I am a shadow, who can destroy in the night, and vowed to this fae with unbreakable magic. He who has passed Orella's trial and given word of his fate from her lips. I enter because I am already deemed worthy."

Holy shit.

The guard assessed Kit and looked impressed by his answer. "Then enter, Alora who was chosen, and her shadow bound by magic.

www.ingramcontent.com/pod-product-compliance
Lightning Source LLC
Chambersburg PA
CBHW070612310726
48982CB00001B/61

9780645634761